Also by Sherry Thomas

The Burning Sky

THE
PERILOUS
SEA

SHERRY THOMAS

BALZER + BRAY
An Imprint of HarperCollinsPublishers

Balzer + Bray is an imprint of HarperCollins Publishers.

The Perilous Sea

Copyright © 2014 by Sherry Thomas

Library of Congress Cataloging-in-Publication Data
Thomas, Sherry (Sherry M.)
  The perilous sea / Sherry Thomas. — First edition.
        pages   cm. — (The elemental trilogy ; #2)
  Summary: "After returning to Eton College, Titus makes a shocking discovery in his
mother's diary that causes him to question everything he believed about his and Iolanthe's mis-
sion"— Provided by publisher.
  ISBN 978-0-06-220732-6 (hardback)
  [1. Fantasy.]   I. Title.
PZ7.T3694533Pe 2014   2014002115
[Fic]—dc23   CIP
                                                                                    AC

Typography by Erin Fitzsimmons
14 15 16 17 18 LP/RRDH 10 9 8 7 6 5 4 3 2 1
❖
First Edition

To Donna Bray, who is simply the best

CHAPTER ✦ 1

THE GIRL CAME TO WITH a start.

She was being pelted with sand. Sand was everywhere. Beneath, her fingers dug into it, hot and gritty. Above, wind-whipped sand blocked the sky, turning the air as red as the surface of Mars.

A sandstorm.

She sat up. Sand swirled all about her, millions of sepia particles. By reflex she pushed at them, willing them to stay away from her eyes.

The sand stayed away.

She blinked—and made another pushing motion with her hand. The flying particles receded farther from her person. The sandstorm itself showed no signs of abating. In fact, it was worsening, the sky becoming ominously dark.

She had power over sand.

In a sandstorm, it was much better to be an elemental mage than otherwise. Yet there was something disconcerting about the discovery:

the fact that it *was* a discovery; that she'd had no idea of this ability that should have defined her from the moment of her birth.

She also didn't know where she was. Or why. Or where she had been before she awakened in a desert.

Nothing. No memory of a mother's embrace, a father's smile, or a best friend's secrets. No recollection of the color of her front door, the weight of her favorite drinking glass, or the titles of books that littered her desk.

She was a stranger to herself, a stranger with a past as barren as the desert, every defining feature buried deep, inaccessible.

A hundred thoughts flapped about in her head, like a flock of birds startled into flight. How long had she been in this state? Had she always been like this? Shouldn't there be someone to look after her if she didn't know anything about herself? Why was she alone? Why was she alone in the middle of nowhere?

What had happened?

She set two fingers against her breastbone. The pressure inside made it difficult to breathe. She opened her mouth, trying to draw in air faster, trying to fill her lungs so that they wouldn't feel as empty as the rest of her.

It was a minute before she gathered enough composure to examine her person, praying for clues—or outright answers— that would tell her everything she needed. Her hands were not forthcoming: a few calluses on her right palm and little else of note. Pulling up her sleeves revealed blank forearms. A look at the skin of her abdomen likewise yielded nothing.

"*Revela omnia,*" she said, surprised to hear a deep, almost gravelly voice.

"*Revela omnia,*" she said again, hoping that the sound of her own speech might trigger a sudden cascade of memories.

It didn't. Nor did the spell bring to light any secret writing on her skin.

Surely her isolation was only an illusion. Nearby there must be someone who could help her—a parent, a sibling, a friend. Perhaps that person was even now stumbling about, calling for her, anxious to locate her and make sure that she was all right.

But she could hear no voices carried upon the howling wind, only the turbulence of sand particles hurtled about by forces beyond their control. And when she expanded the sphere of clear air around her, she uncovered nothing but sand and more sand.

She buried her face in her hands for a moment, then took a deep breath and stood up. She meant to start on her clothes, but as she came to her feet, it became obvious that she had something in her right boot.

Her heart somersaulted when she realized it was a wand. Ever since mages realized that wands were but conduits of a mage's power, amplifiers that were not strictly necessary to the execution of spells, wands had turned from revered tools to beloved accessories, always personalized, and sometimes to a silly degree. Names were woven into the design, favorite spells, insignia of one's city or school. Some wands even had their owners' entire genealogy engraved in microscopic letters.

She would dearly love to see her family history laid out before her, but it would be more than good enough if the wand had an *In case of loss, return to* _____ inscribed somewhere.

The wand, however, was as plain as a floor plank, without any carvings, inlays, or decorative motifs. And it remained just as bare when examined under a magnifying spell. She had no idea such wands were even made.

An oppressive weight settled over her chest. Loving parents would no more give a child such a wand than they would send her to school in garments made of paper. Was she an orphan then? Someone who had been discarded at birth and brought up in an institution? Elemental magelings did suffer from a higher rate of abandonment, since they were so much trouble in their infancy.

Yet the clothes she wore, a knee-length blue tunic and a white undertunic, were of exceptionally fine fabric: weightless yet strong, with an understated gleam. And though her face and hands felt the heat of the desert, wherever she was covered by the tunics she was perfectly comfortable.

The tunics did not have pockets. The trousers underneath, however, did. And one of those pockets yielded a small, rectangular, and somewhat crumpled card.

A. G. Fairfax

Low Creek Ranch
Wyoming Territory

She had to blink twice to make sure she was reading correctly. Wyoming Territory? As in the American West? The *nonmage* portion of the American West?

She tried several different unmasking spells, but the card provided no hidden messages. Expelling a slow breath, she put the card back in her trouser pocket.

She had thought all she needed was a name, the tiniest of clues. But now she had a name and a clue, and it was worse than if she'd had no insight at all. Instead of staring at a blank wall, she was looking at a single square inch of tantalizing color and texture, with the rest of the mural—the people, places, and choices that had made her who she was—remaining firmly out of view.

Without meaning to, she slashed her wand through the air, all but growling. The swirling sand retreated farther. She sucked in a breath: eight feet from where she stood, a canvas tote lay half-buried in the sand.

She launched herself at the bag, yanking it out of the sand. The strap was broken, but the bag itself was undamaged. It was not terribly big—about twenty inches wide, twelve inches high, and eight inches deep—nor was it terribly heavy—fifteen pounds or thereabouts. But it was quite remarkable in the number of pockets it had: at least twelve on the outside, and scores upon scores inside. She unbuckled a large outside pocket: it held a change of clothes. Another of a similar size stored a rectangle of tightly packed cloth that she guessed would expand into a small tent.

Pockets on the inside were carefully and clearly labeled: *Nutrition, each pack one day's worth. Vaulting aid: five granules at a time, no more than three times a day. Heat sheet—in case you require warmth but need to remain unseen.*

In case you *require warmth.*

Would she have addressed herself in the second person—or was this evidence that someone else had been intimately involved in her life, someone who knew that such an emergency bag might come in handy someday?

Thirty-six pockets of one entire interior compartment were stuffed with remedies. Not remedies for illnesses, but for injuries: everything from broken limbs to the burn of dragon fire. Her pulse quickened. This was not a camping bag, but an emergency tote prepared in expectation of significant, perhaps overwhelming danger.

A map. The person who had meticulously stocked the bag must have included a map.

And there it was, in one of the smaller exterior pockets, woven of silken threads so slender they could barely be discerned with the naked eye, with mage realms in green and nonmage realms in gray. At the top was written, *Place the map on the ground—or in the body of water, if need be.*

She lay the map flat against the sand, which, with the heat of the sun blocked by the turbulent sky, was rapidly losing its warmth. Almost immediately a red dot appeared on the map, in the Sahara Desert, a hundred miles or so southwest of the border of one of the United Bedouin Realms.

The middle of nowhere.

Her fingers clutched at the map's edges. Where should she go? Low Creek Ranch, the only place she could name from her former life, was at least eight thousand miles away. Desert realms typically didn't have borders as tightly secured as those of island realms. But without official papers, she would not be able to use any of the translocators inside the United Bedouin Realms to leapfrog oceans and continents. She might even be detained for being somewhere she shouldn't be—Atlantis didn't like mages wandering abroad without properly sanctioned reasons.

And if she were to try nonmage routes, she was about a thousand miles from both Tripoli and Cairo. Once she'd staggered to the coast of the Mediterranean, assuming she could, she would still be at least three weeks from the American West.

More words appeared on the map, this time above the very desert in which she was stranded.

If you are reading this, beloved, then the worst has happened and I can safeguard you no more. Know that you have been the best part of my life and I have no regrets.

Long may Fortune shield you.
Live forever.

She passed her hand over the words, barely noticing that her fingers were trembling. A dull pain burned in the back of her throat, for the loss of the protector she could not recall. For the loss of an entire life now beyond her grasp.

You have been the best part of my life.

The person who had written this could have been a sibling, or a friend. But she was almost entirely certain that he had been her sweetheart. She closed her eyes and reached for something. Anything. A name, a smile, a voice—she remembered nothing.

The wind shrieked.

No, it was her, screaming with all the frustration she could no longer contain.

The sandstorm shrank away, as if afraid of what she might do.

She panted, like a runner after a hard sprint. About her, the radius of clear, undisturbed air had increased tenfold, expanding a hundred feet in each direction.

Numbly she spun around, searching for what she dared not hope to find.

Nothing. Nothing. Absolutely nothing.

Then, the silhouette of a body in the sand.

CHAPTER · 2

The Domain ✦ *Seven Weeks Earlier*

"HIS SERENE HIGHNESS PRINCE TITUS the Seventh," announced the stone phoenixes that guarded the four corners of the grand terrace, their voices bell-like and resonant.

Titus stopped at the edge of the terrace, the celebrated garden of the Citadel before him. Elsewhere in the garden, there were informal, even intimate areas, but not here. Here acres of evergreen shrubs had been meticulously trimmed into hundreds of parterres, which when viewed from above formed a stylized phoenix, the symbol of the House of Elberon.

The evergreens, bred by the Citadel's master botanists, bloomed late in summer. And every year the color of the flowers changed. This year the blossoms were a deep, vibrant orange, the color of sunrise. Dalbert, Titus's valet and personal spymaster, reported that he had seen the phoenix emblems on Delamer's public buildings painted a similar hue of fire, often accompanied by a hasty scrawled *The phoenix is aflame!*

The last time the phoenix was aflame, the January Uprising had soon followed.

In the space between the landscape phoenix's two upraised wings, a large white canopy had been erected, brilliant in the light of the afternoon sun. Under the canopy, a diplomatic reception was in full swing. Attendants in the Citadel's gray livery wove between guests in jewel-toned overrobes, offering hors d'oeuvres and glasses of chilled summer wine. A fine, ethereal music drifted on the breeze from the sea, and with it, the sounds of soft laughter and involved chitchat.

Titus inhaled. He was jittery. It was possible he was responding to the strain beneath the party's apparent gaiety, but in truth it was, as always, all about Fairfax, his powerful and incandescent elemental mage.

He descended a flight of wide, shallow steps, and walked the length of a statue-lined avenue, a retinue of twelve in tow. As he approached the canopy, the entire gathering bowed and curtsied. He might be without any real powers, but he was still, ceremonially speaking, lord and master of the Domain.[1]

An exceptionally beautiful woman came forward, a smile on her face: Lady Callista, the palace's official hostess, the most renowned beauty witch of her generation, and one of Titus's least favorite persons on the face of the earth.

For he aimed to destroy the Bane, Lord High Commander of the Great Realm of New Atlantis and the greatest tyrant the world had ever known, and Lady Callista was very much a servant of the Bane. Not to mention, though he had no concrete evidence to support his suspicion, he had always believed deep down that Lady Callista had been the one responsible for the death of his mother.

"My lady," he acknowledged her.

"Your Highness," Lady Callista cooed, "we are delighted you could join us. Please, allow me to present the new ambassador from the Kalahari Realm."

Titus was quite happy to see visible bags beneath her eyes. Life had not been easy for her since the evening of the Fourth of June, when Atlantis's most prized prisoner had disappeared from the Citadel's library. In the same library, on the same night, the Inquisitor, one of the Bane's most loyal and capable lieutenants, had met a sudden and unexpected end.

Lady Callista had the bad luck to be the last person to walk into the library before Haywood's disappearance. She had also been the one to order a pool of blood in the library cleaned up, when Atlantis would have very much liked to have a few drops of that blood, in order to find out who had been responsible for the death of the Inquisitor.

As a result, despite her years of service as an agent of Atlantis, she was watched as heavily as Titus, her movements confined to within the boundaries of the Citadel. Moreover, every week she had to meet with Atlantean investigators, each interview lasting hours, sometimes an entire day.

A distracted and distressed Lady Callista was one less threat to Titus.

Introductions done, Lady Callista left Titus to chat with the new Kalahari ambassador and those family members who had accompanied him to the Domain. Titus was never completely comfortable in such social situations—he suspected he appeared both stiff and ungracious. If only he could have Fairfax by his side. . . . She knew instinctively how to put people at ease and he was always much more relaxed in her company.

It should have been an idyllic summer in the Labyrinthine Mountains for them—watching the shifting of the peaks, exploring hidden waterfalls, perhaps even sneaking up to the phoenix aeries in the highest ridges, in the hope of seeing a fiery rebirth. Not that they were not going to work hard: their plans had included hundreds of hours of grueling training, just as many devoted to the mastery of new spells, not to mention a covert undertaking to find out where her guardian had ended up after disappearing from the Citadel's library. But the most important thing was that they were going to be together, as much as possible, every step of the way.

From the moment he stepped out of the rail coach that served as his private translocator, however, it became apparent that he would be watched every second of his holidays. A terrifying thing to realize, when he had her concealed on his person, in the shape of a tiny turtle, under the effect of a potion that lasted no more than twelve hours.

He managed to smuggle her out of the castle in a nerve-racking dash, leaving her, still in turtle form, inside an abandoned shepherd's hut. He meant to go back later to escort her to the safe house he had prepared, but ten minutes after he returned to the castle he found himself whisked off to the Citadel, the Master of the Domain's official residence in the capital city, from which he could not escape to the mountains with either ease or secrecy.

He and Fairfax had discussed dozens of contingency plans, but nothing close to this scenario, in which she would be stranded in the Labyrinthine Mountains by herself. For days he could scarcely eat or sleep, until he saw a three-line advertisement at the back of *The Delamer Observer*, announcing the availability of various bulbs for autumn planting: It was her, informing him that she would meet him back at Eton, at the start of Michaelmas Half.

He had nearly burst with relief—and pride: trust Fairfax to always find a way, no matter how dire the situation. From then it was one long, excruciating wait for the end of summer, for the moment when they would meet again.

The end of summer had come at last. He had permission to leave for England immediately following the reception. He did not know how he held himself together, speaking to group after group of guests. One minute he would be short of breath at the thought of holding her tight, the next minute dizzy with dread—what if she did *not* walk into Mrs. Dawlish's house?

". . . before you will rule in your own right. I must admit I had hoped to see you at some of my briefings this summer."

Two seconds passed before Titus realized he was expected to respond to Commander Rainstone, the regent's chief security adviser.

"According to court tradition, I should be seventeen before I take part in council meetings and security briefings," he said.

And he was not due to turn seventeen for several weeks.

"What difference does a few days make?" asked Commander Rainstone, sounding vexed. "Your Highness will come to age at a most unstable time and will need all the experience you can muster. Were I His Excellency, I would have insisted that Your Highness be made familiar with the running of the state much sooner. "

His Excellency was Prince Alectus, the regent who ruled in Titus's stead. Alectus also happened to be Lady Callista's protector.

"What would you have me know?" Titus asked Commander Rainstone.

She had been a member of his mother's personal staff, long ago, before he was old enough to remember anything. He knew Commander Rainstone primarily from her occasional trips to the castle in the Labyrinthine Mountains, to brief him on matters having to do with the realm's security, or at least those matters she thought he was old enough to understand.

Commander Rainstone glanced at the crowd and lowered her voice. "We have intelligence, sire, that the Lord High Commander of New Atlantis has left his fortress in the uplands."

This was news to Titus—news that sent a frisson of chill down his spine. "I understand he dined here at the Citadel not long ago. So it cannot be all that unusual for him to leave the Commander's Palace."

"But that event in and of itself was extraordinary: it was the first time he had stepped out of the Commander's Palace since the end of the January Uprising."

"Does this mean Lady Callista should expect him for dinner again?"

Commander Rainstone frowned. "Your Highness, this is no joking matter. The Lord High Commander does not lightly depart his lair and—"

She stopped. Aramia, Lady Callista's daughter, was approaching.

"Your Highness, Commander," said Aramia amiably, "I apologize for the intrusion, but I do believe the prime minister would like a word with you, Commander."

"Of course." Commander Rainstone bowed. "If you will excuse me, Your Highness."

Aramia turned to Titus. "And you probably have not seen the new addition to the Defeat of the Usurper fountain, Your Highness, have you?"

Nearly five months ago, at a party not unlike this one, Lady Callista had administered truth serum to Titus on behalf of Atlantis—and she had done so via Aramia, whom Titus had considered a friend. If Aramia had any regrets concerning her action, Titus had not been able to sense it.

"I have seen the new addition," he said coolly. "It was completed two years ago."

Aramia reddened, but her smile was persistent. "Allow me to point out some features you may not have noticed. Won't you come with me, sire?"

He considered refusing outright. But a stroll away from the canopy did have some merits—at least he would not have to speak to anyone. "Lead the way."

Defeat of the Usurper, the largest and most elaborate of the ninety-nine fountains of the Citadel, was the size of a small hill, featuring scores of wyverns being felled by Hesperia the Great's elemental powers. The long reflecting pool before it extended almost to the edge of the manmade headland on which the Citadel sat. Cliffs dropped three hundred feet straight down to the pounding surf of the Atlantic. In the distance, a pleasure craft, all its sails furled, bobbed upon the sunlit sea.

Aramia glanced back. Titus's retinue, eight guards and four attendants, had followed them. But now, with a wave of his hand, they slowed and stayed out of earshot.

"Mother will be angry with me if she knew what I am about to do." Aramia reached inside the fountain and flicked the rippling surface. "And she won't admit it but she is quite frightened by all the meetings with investigators from Atlantis. They make her take truth serum and they are . . . they are not nice at all."

"That is what it is like to run afoul of Atlantis."

"But isn't there something you can do for her, after what she has done for you?"

Titus raised a brow. After what Lady Callista had done for *him*? "You overestimate my influence."

"But all the same—"

"There you are!" came a clear, musical voice. "I have been looking for you all over."

The young woman who approached from the far side of the fountain was eye-wateringly beautiful—skin the color of brown sugar, a face of almost exaggerated perfection, and a cascade of black hair that reached to the backs of her knees.

Aramia stared, agape, as if unable to believe that there existed one who rivaled her mother in sheer loveliness.

Titus, who had always been wary of beauty of such magnitude, thanks to his proximity to Lady Callista growing up, had moved past the woman's features to examine her overrobe. One sometimes heard overrobes ridiculed as resembling upholstery, but this one looked to be actually *made from* upholstery—from an elaborate lampshade, he corrected himself, with all the tassels and fringes still attached.

"Would you mind giving me a moment with His Highness?" She spoke to Aramia, her tone courteous but unmistakably firm.

Aramia hesitated, glancing at Titus.

"You may leave us," said Titus. He had nothing more to say to her.

Aramia walked away, looking back all the while.

"Your Highness," said the young woman.

She had addressed him without first being addressed by him. Titus did not hold to such nonsense when he was at school, but here he was in his own palace, at a diplomatic reception, no less, where the guests loved such etiquette almost as much as they loved their own mothers, possibly more.

It occurred to him that while she could pass for a member of the Kalahari ambassador's entourage, he had not seen her earlier, among the crowd under the canopy—and a woman who looked as she did would not have gone unnoticed.

Not that it had never happened before, a mage crashing a palace party without proper credentials. But the Citadel was on high alert, was it not, after the events of early June?

"How did you get in?"

The woman smiled. She was not much older than Titus, twenty or twenty-one. "A man immune to my charms—I like that, Your Highness. Let me get to the point then. I am interested in the whereabouts of your elemental mage."

He had to fight against his shock, to not point his wand at her and do something rash. So he rolled his eyes instead. "Your masters have already asked me all the questions. They have even put me under Inquisition. Must we go through more of the same?"

Her hair streamed in the breeze coming off the sea, like a pirate banner. She extended an arm and rolled up her sleeve. On her forearm was a mark in stark white lines, a four-tusked elephant crushing a whirlpool underfoot—a symbol of resistance in many realms near the equator. "I am not an agent of Atlantis."

"And why should that change my answer? I have no knowledge of the whereabouts of that girl."

"We know she is the prophesied one—an elemental mage more powerful than has been seen in centuries. We also know it would be disastrous for those of us who yearn for freedom if she fell into the Bane's hands. Let us help her. We can make sure the Bane never comes near her."

What would you do if the Bane did come near her? Would you kill her so that he never gains her? And what would stop you from killing her from the very beginning, if your sole aim is to keep her away from him?

"Good luck finding her, then."

She leaned closer to him, obviously not about to give up. "Your Highness—"

Shouts erupted. Titus turned around. Guards were running down the steps. His own retinue came sprinting toward him.

"Oh dear," said the young woman. "It appears I must take leave of Your Highness."

With one pull, her ridiculous overrobe came off entirely. A swift shake and it smoothed and flattened into—of course—a flying carpet, much bigger and finer than the one Titus possessed.[2]

The young woman, now clad in a close-fitting tunic and trousers the color of storm clouds, leaped onto the flying carpet, and with a mock salute at Titus, sped off toward the waiting boat in the distance.

CHAPTER 3

The Sahara Desert

THE GIRL SHOVED THE MAP into her pocket, grabbed the bag, and sprinted toward the body. But instincts she didn't even know she possessed halted her halfway. Her loss of memory, the trauma remedies in the emergency bag, the note on the map—*the worst has happened and I can safeguard you no more*—everything about her situation shouted serious and, perhaps, relentless danger. The person in the sand was just as likely to be an enemy as an ally.

She pulled out her wand, applied a protective shield to herself, and advanced more cautiously. The prone body wore a black jacket and black trousers, a band of white shirt cuff peeking out from underneath a jacket sleeve—nonmage clothes for a man. Nonmage clothes for a man from a different part of the world.

He was lanky in build, his hair dark despite a coating of dust, his head turned away from her. Her stomach tightened. Was he the one? If she saw his face, if he called her name and clasped her hand in his, would everything come rushing back, like the happiness and good fortune that one always regained at the end of a heroic tale?

Despite his nonmage attire, he had a wand in hand. The back of his jacket had been ripped, exposing a somber-colored waistcoat underneath—had he tried to protect her? As she drew nearer, his fingers flexed and then tightened on the wand. A wave of relief washed over her: he was still alive and she was not entirely alone in the vastness of the Sahara.

It was with a good deal of difficulty that she restrained herself from going right up to him. Instead she stopped ten feet away. "Hullo?"

He didn't even look in her direction.

"Hullo?"

Again, no response.

Had he lost consciousness? Was the movement of his fingers she'd spied earlier but the involuntary motions of someone suffering from a concussion? She picked up a few grains of sand and tossed them gently in his direction—a tentative knock, so to speak. Five feet from him, the sand hit an invisible barrier in the air.

He turned his head toward her and raised his wand. "Come no closer."

He was young and good-looking. But his face failed to trigger a flood of memories. It did not even bring about any vague twinge of recollection, except to make her wonder whether she was as young as he.

"I mean you no harm," she said.

"Then let us part as friendly strangers."

Her heart pinched at the word "strangers." Then her eyes widened: what she had thought to be his waistcoat, beneath his torn jacket, was actually flesh that had been—what? Burned? Infected? Whatever had happened, it looked horrifying. "You are hurt."

"I can look after myself."

He was still civil, but his meaning was quite unmistakable: *Go. You are not welcome here.*

She did not want to force her company on him, even if he were the only person in a hundred-mile radius. But that wound of his—he could die of it. "I have remedies that might help you."

He exhaled, as if the effort required to speak exhausted him. "Then leave them behind."

What she would have liked was for him to tell her things in exchange for the remedies—how had he come to be in the desert, who or what had injured him, and did he, by any chance, know a way for them to reach safety again. Perhaps his lack of reciprocity indicated that he wasn't as desperately injured as he appeared to be; if she were so badly hurt, she wouldn't be so fastidious about accepting help.

Or so she supposed. In truth she had no idea how she would have acted, since she had no memory to guide her choices.

She shook her head a little and dug into her satchel. "It would help me decide which remedies to give you if you can tell me what kind of injury you have."

"I need remedies that relieve pain, disinfect, expel toxin, and regenerate skin and tissue," he answered, his tone clipped and aloof.

She was beginning to regret her offer to help. How did she know she herself wouldn't need those remedies in the very near future? But she extracted the remedies he'd asked for, along with a quantity of food cubes, and sent them to the edge of his shield with a levitation spell.

"Are you an elemental mage with power over water?" she asked.

His reply was a half grimace followed by silence.

"Are you or are you not?" she persisted. All the remedies in the world wouldn't do him any good when thirst killed him in a few days.

"How long are you going to draw out this good-bye?"

She almost took a step back. He snarled as if he had been born for it, the disdain in his voice sharper than wyvern teeth.

She yanked out a pair of waterskins from the satchel and willed water from underground rivers and oasis lakes to flow to her, while suppressing the urge to utter a wildly mean-spirited retort. He might be surly, but she couldn't simply abandon him without any water—and no point calling him names when he was already at a disadvantage.

Water, however, did not materialize on command. She told herself that water, an actual substance, would take its time arriving, and in uncertain quantities, depending on the distance and abundance of the nearest source.

But what if she had no power over water? Then she was as doomed as the boy.

A minute passed before the first drop materialized, suspended in midair—she briefly closed her eyes in relief. The boy watched as the water globule grew, remaining utterly unimpressed.

She filled the waterskins and threw them in his direction. One landed directly on the sand with a gurgle and a plop. The other, which she had hurled a little harder, made his shield shimmer slightly before falling to the ground.

That caught her attention. The waterskin would have bounced off a normal shield. But here, if her eyes did not deceive her, the shield, which was in the shape of a dome, had absorbed the impact.

A tensile dome. If the boy had made it himself, he must be quite the mage.

"Now that you have displayed your prodigious kindness, will you just go?" the boy all but growled.

"Yes, I will," she shot back, "now that you have shown your immense gratitude."

He had the decency not to respond.

She muttered under her breath as she secured all the flaps inside and outside the satchel and strapped the satchel shut. So much for the hope that this sweet-faced boy might be her protector—the only one who would ever matter to him was himself.

Her heart ached with grief for the stalwart ally she could no longer remember. Her fingers spread over the satchel, the physical manifestation of the meticulous care he had taken with her. But how she wished she could recall just one detail about him. His laughter, she thought, if nothing else, that was the memory she would like to carry with her for—

Her ears pricked. The sandstorm howled as it ever did. But now it sounded as if it was striking large objects in the air—large objects approaching at tremendous speed.

Was rescue on the way? Or further danger? In either case, she had better see who was coming before deciding whether to let them see her. Earlier she had cleared the air for almost a hundred feet around her; now she allowed the sandstorm to take over, except for the space between her and the boy.

He, too, listened carefully, his brow furrowed with concentration.

There were no vibrations in the ground so the approaching objects had to be aerial vehicles, which implied the presence of mages, as the nonmages' hot-air balloons and flimsy airships would not be able to advance against a sandstorm of such magnitude.

The boy hissed. For the first time, his expression betrayed fear. "Armored chariots."

Her heart dropped. He was right, the sounds were metallic. Only Atlantis had such vehicles. And at all costs, she must stay away from Atlantis's grasp.

She didn't know why, she only knew that it was imperative. Otherwise, all would be lost.

The din of sand striking metal diminished, then disappeared altogether. The sandstorm had not abated; the Atlanteans were clearing the air as she had done earlier.

"Let me in under your dome," she demanded.

She would be quite defenseless out here, if the armored chariots decided to dispense death rain—she could whip air into motion, but she could not purify it.

"No."

It would be a waste of time to appeal to his better nature, so she didn't bother. "Would you like me to signal to them where you are?" she asked, as she picked up the nutrition cubes, the remedies, and the waterskins from the sand. "It's my understanding you can't move much."

The boy bared his teeth. "Your kindness is truly remarkable."

"And your gratitude humbling to behold. Now let me in or get ready for Atlantis."

Her ruthlessness surprised her. Had she always been such a hard bargainer, or was she but responding to the boy's cold-bloodedness?

"Fine," he said through clenched teeth. "But I am not letting you in without a nonharming agreement. Put a drop of your blood on the dome."

A boy who practiced blood magic—she shivered.[3] A nonharming agreement wasn't as fearsome as a blood oath, but still, all blood magic was powerful and dangerous, to be entered into only with extreme caution. "Only if you reciprocate."

"You first," he said.

She took out a set of compact tools she had seen in her satchel earlier, jabbed a slender pick into her finger, and touched the dome.

It was like touching the top of a giant jellyfish: cool, soft, yet resilient.

The boy grimaced. From reluctance, she thought, until she realized that it was from the pain of movement to take a pocketknife out of his jacket. He extracted a drop of blood and sent it outward to the dome, which absorbed it as thirsty soil would soak in water.

Next thing she knew she was in it to the elbow. She drew back, startled.

"Hurry," said the boy.

The dome was slightly sticky on her skin as she pushed through. Sitting down next to the boy, she willed sand to rise and cover the dome, not stopping until it was pitch-dark inside.

Thirty seconds later came the soft thuds of armored chariots landing nearby.

Atlantis, it would seem, knew exactly where to find them.

CHAPTER · 4

England

TWO HOURS AFTER THE INTRUDER had escaped the Citadel, Titus walked through the front door of his residence house at Eton College. Mrs. Dawlish's parlor, brimming with printed chintz and needlework flowers, was as neat and proper as always. But the walls reverberated with the noise of thirty-five pupils stomping up and down, greeting friends they had not seen since the end of Summer Half.

A bittersweet sensation expanded inside Titus's chest: in this house he had spent some of the happiest hours of his life. He could almost hear Fairfax's boastful words and see the gleefully cocky expression on her face.

He broke into a run, pushing past a gaggle of junior boys clogging up the parlor, and taking the steps three at a time. At the stair landing of the next floor stood a cluster of senior boys—but she was not among them.

In the split second he took, trying to decide whether to shove those boys aside too, Leander Wintervale turned around and saw him.

"Did you hear the news, prince?" Wintervale greeted Titus with a hearty slap to the back. "Fairfax made the twenty-two, alongside myself, of course."

A long moment passed before Wintervale's sentence made sense: he was talking about cricket. At the beginning of Michaelmas Half, twenty-two boys were selected as candidates for the next year's school cricket team. They would split into two teams and play each other all year long. Then the best eleven would be named to the school team come Summer Half, for the pride and glory of facing off against teams from Harrow and Winchester.

"Does—does Fairfax know?"

Wintervale grinned. "Fairfax hasn't stopped boasting about it since he heard the news."

Relief tore through Titus, making him lightheaded. She was here. She had made her way back. "Where is he?"

"Gone to High Street with Cooper."

Titus swallowed his disappointment. "What for?"

"Tomorrow's tea stuff, of course, or we'd have nothing to eat," said Wintervale, not noticing any of the emotions that buffeted Titus. "By the way, Kashkari will not be joining us for a few days. Mrs. Dawlish had a cable from him. His steamer ran into some rough weather in the Indian Ocean and he reached Port Said only today."

For four years, Titus had paid no particular attention to Kashkari, the Indian pupil with whom he and Wintervale took their afternoon tea—Kashkari was mainly Wintervale's friend. But a few months ago Kashkari, unbeknownst to him, had played a crucial role in keeping Titus out of Atlantis's grasp.

"Port Said," said Titus. "So he has to put in at Trieste, cross over the Alps, and pass through Paris before he can get here."

The whole of the summer holiday was barely enough time for the round trip from England to India and back. Kashkari would be lucky if he got to spend a week with his family in Hyderabad.

"You forgot to mention the English Channel. It's the worst." Wintervale shuddered. "In the first year of our Exile, my father wanted the family to have an authentic nonmage experience. So we crossed the English Channel on a steamer and I puked my guts out something proper. I had a great deal more respect for the nonmages afterward—I mean, the hardship these people endure."

Leave it to Wintervale to talk like this within easy hearing of at least half a dozen boys. Words such as "discretion" and "caution" held no meaning for him. He knew enough to not announce outright that he was a mage, but otherwise his inclination was to continually blurt out the first thing that came into his head.

It was part of his charm, that he was so frank and unguarded.

"In any case," Wintervale went on, "Kashkari doesn't—"

A chorus of "Fairfax!" and "We heard you made the twenty-two, Fairfax!" drowned out the rest of Wintervale's sentence.

Titus gripped the banister and slowly, slowly turned around. But through the space between the balusters, he could only see a huddle of junior boys in their waist-length short jackets.

He took a step down, then another, then two more. All at once there she was, in a senior boy's uniform of a crisp white shirt and a black tailed jacket, playfully scolding a boy who barely came up to her shoulder. "What kind of question is that, Phillpott? Of course I will be one of the eleven. In fact, West is going to take one look at me and quake in his brogues, because I am going to wrench the captaincy from his grasp."

The jauntiness in her eyes, the certainty of her tone, and the innate gentleness as she fluffed the boy's hair—a fierce gladness swept over Titus. "Are you ever going to acquire any humility, Fairfax?"

She lifted her head and gazed at him for a full two seconds. "I will, the moment you come into some social graces, Your Highness."

Her retort was accompanied by a smile, not the wide grin she flashed for the junior boys, only a slight lift of the corners of her lips. All at once he felt her relief—and behind that relief, a trace of exhaustion.

His chest constricted. But the next moment, she was beaming again, and poking the arm of the senior boy next to her. "Don't just stand there, Cooper, say something to His Magnificence."

Cooper bowed with a flourish. "Welcome back, Your Highness. Our humble abode is honored by your august presence."

Of all the boys in the house, Cooper was probably Fairfax's

favorite, because he was as silly and enthusiastic as a puppy, and because she enjoyed Cooper's wide-eyed awe at Titus's princely aloofness.

Titus upheld that princely aloofness. "One could say my august presence is diminished by your humble abode, but I will not think too closely upon the matter."

Fairfax laughed, the sound deep and rich. "*Your* humility, prince, shines like a beacon in the darkest night," she said as she ascended the stairs. "We can only aspire to be so great yet so humble."

Sutherland, behind Wintervale, cackled so hard he almost choked on the apple he was eating.

She drew up even with Titus. The pleasure of her nearness was almost painful. And when she set her hand on his shoulder, the sensation was all electricity.

"Glad you made it, Fairfax," he said, as quietly as he could.

Now he could breathe again. Now he was whole again.

When Iolanthe Seabourne came to in utter darkness, naked and in agony, she had not been remotely alarmed: the pain was par for the course for resuming human form after the effect of a transmogrification spell wore off. Her lack of recollection of the hours she had spent as a tiny turtle also did not bother her—without a blood oath binding her to the prince, there was nothing to preserve continuity of consciousness while metamorphosing from one form to another.

Titus's absence, however, brought a sensation of cold completely unrelated to the temperatures of the night. Where was he? It was unlike him to leave her without a blanket for warmth, or a note to explain his movements.

Had he been taken by Atlantis? Was that why he had to get her away from him, so that she wouldn't lose her freedom at the same time? The roar of her blood was such that her ears rang as she grimly dug around the hut for something to cover herself.

Her anxiety subsided somewhat after she unearthed changes of clothes, nutrition cubes, and coins in the seemingly abandoned hut. Even better, a student pass issued by a small conservatory somewhere in the northeast of the Domain. She had not been chucked away at a random location in desperation. Something had come up and he needed her out of the castle; without enough time to get her to a proper safe house, he had instead deposited her at a way station.

Dressed and with half a nutrition cube in her stomach, she stepped outside the hut to investigate her new whereabouts. The castle was no more than three miles away to the north. A far-seeing spell revealed the flag of the Domain, a silver phoenix on a background of sapphire, streaming atop the highest parapet.

She frowned. If the Master of the Domain was in residence, his personal standard, that of a phoenix and a wyvern guarding a shield with seven crowns, should be the banner flying over the castle.

Where was he? Her misgivings returned with a vengeance. She must get out of the mountains and find out what was going on.

The castle was situated near the eastern front of the Labyrinthine

Mountains. Theoretically, it should be no more than twenty or twenty-five miles, as the crow flies, from the plains. But when the mountains moved without rhythm or pattern, twenty or twenty-five miles as the crow flies might very well take a week on foot.

Provided that she didn't become hopelessly lost.[4]

It took her four days, two and half of which were spent thinking she had become hopelessly lost. Fortunately, the closest villages and towns were accustomed to seeing lost hikers stumbling out of the mountains, dirty and disoriented, in desperate need of a wash and a meal.

The first thing Iolanthe asked for, before a wash and a meal, was a newspaper. It was almost the anniversary of Titus's coronation and every year, to mark the occasion, a parade was held in Delamer. If the parade was canceled, then he was in trouble.

But no, the parade would take place the next day, and the Master of the Domain would attend several ceremonies and give out prizes to exemplary students.

A kindly farmer offered her a lift in his ancient chariot, pulled by an even more ancient pegasus, to the nearest town that had expedited services. From there she was able to catch a translocator to a larger town, which happened to be a hub of expedited highways.

Being at the hub made her heart palpitate: there could be agents of Atlantis, lying in wait for her. But she had to move quickly—and she *was* protected by an Irreproducible Charm that made it impossible for her image to be reproduced and transmitted.

She reached Delamer that evening. The next afternoon, from quite some distance away, she watched Titus pass over Palace Avenue on a floating balcony, flanked by the regent and Lady Callista. He did not wear his grandfather's sunburst medal, to signal that he was under house arrest or any other type of captivity. But he was encircled by guards and attendants, with barely enough room to breathe.

She could not go near him while he was thus surrounded. Her only choice was to leave him a coded message in *The Delamer Observer*, head to Eton, and hope that he, too, would be given permission to go back to that nonmage school.

Departing so soon—and by herself—was not how she had envisioned her summer. She debated whether to remain in Delamer for some more time, so that she could arrange for a meeting with Titus or find out on her own something of Master Haywood's whereabouts. But in the end, she decided it was far too risky to stay longer: there was a subtle tension in the mood of the capital; even just standing in line to buy a bit of something to eat, she overheard whispers about agents of Atlantis being particularly active.

To get out of the Domain by instantaneous means required documents she could not provide. But traveling within the Domain was easy enough with the student pass. By expedited highways and ferries she arrived on the Melusine Archipelago, one of the Domain's outlying island chains.

She had learned in the teaching cantos of the Crucible about a secret store of sailboats on the southernmost isle of the archipelago. The travel restrictions Atlantis had implemented did not prevent nonmage means of locomotion, and a good, fast sloop was sometimes just the way to make an escape.

Her command of air and water came in handy for the one hundred and twenty miles of open ocean to Flores, one of the northwestern islands of the Azores. From there she bargained a passage on a whaling ship to Ponta Delgada, and at Ponta Delgada she hopped on a steamer to the Madeira Islands.

She could have remained on Madeira. But when she learned, moments after disembarking, that a French cargo freighter in the harbor would be pulling anchor and setting out for South Africa in two hours, she hesitated only a minute before running to the harbor agent's office to inquire as to whether the French freighter also took passengers.

Titus had created a good background for Archer Fairfax, the identity she assumed when she was at Eton, by setting Fairfax's family in Bechuanaland, a place where other Eton students were unlikely to visit. But that otherwise spell, as effective as it was at school, would disintegrate if agents of Atlantis took it into their heads to discover the exact location of the Fairfax family farm.

She did not stay long in Cape Town, but she spent her entire time there conducting a fervent campaign of disinformation via a battery of new otherwise spells. Now, should inquisitive agents of Atlantis come through, they would be told that the Fairfaxes had just departed: a distant relative had died and left Mrs. Fairfax a decent sum of money, and the family decided to enjoy their good fortune by getting rid of the farm and taking a trip around the world—without the son, of course, who had to go back to Eton for Michaelmas Half.

Rather pat, as a story, but then Iolanthe had always imagined these fictional parents of Fairfax's to be the sort who were lured to Africa by romantic notions, only to become disillusioned that the agricultural life yielded little romance—or profit, for that matter. With an unexpected windfall, they would gladly take off for parts unknown, for the adventure and thrill Africa had long ago ceased providing.

With her "family" out of the way for the foreseeable future, Iolanthe booked herself a berth on the next Liverpool-bound steamer out of Cape Town. For the next three weeks hope and fear battled for supremacy in her heart. One moment she would be ecstatic at the thought of seeing Titus again, the next minute, overcome by uneasiness. What if he did not come back to Eton? It made more sense, didn't it, for him to be kept in the Domain and on a much shorter leash?

The closer she was to Eton, the worse the pins and needles became. Reaching Mrs. Dawlish's and finding no trace of him flooded her with dread. She escaped the commotion of the house by latching on to Cooper, who was leaving to put in orders for tea stuff on High Street.

Cooper chattered happily about the other pupils who had made the twenty-two, especially West, the boy who everyone believed would be the next captain of the school team. Iolanthe heard very little of what he said. She hadn't traveled nine thousand miles on her own for the game of cricket, no matter how enjoyable.

"Can you believe there are only four months left in 1883?" said Cooper as they neared Mrs. Dawlish's door again.

"Is it 1883?" Iolanthe swallowed. "I keep forgetting."

"How can you forget what year it is?" Cooper exclaimed. "I sometimes forget the day of the week, but never the month or the year."

She gathered up the courage to push open Mrs. Dawlish's door. In the midst of the parlor, surrounded by junior boys, Titus's voice carried to her. And suddenly she was ready to win a hundred cricket matches, write a thousand Latin papers, and live among dozens of noisy and sometimes smelly boys for the remainder of her life.

He was back. He was safe. She scarcely knew what she said or did for the next few minutes, until they extricated themselves from the other boys, with the excuse that the prince needed to unpack his things.

The moment the door closed behind them, he kissed her. And went on kissing her until they were both breathless.

"I am so glad you are safe," he said, his forehead against hers.

She spread her fingers over his shoulders, over the warm, slightly scratchy wool of his daycoat. Beneath her hands, his frame was spare but strong. "I was afraid they wouldn't let you out of the Domain."

"How did you get out?"

She touched the top of his collar. His clothes had been laundered with some kind of evergreen essence; the faint fragrance reminded her of the spruce-covered ridges of the Labyrinthine Mountains. "I'll tell you after you make me a cup of tea."

The Master of the Domain started to pull away. "I will do it now."

But she wasn't ready for him to leave her embrace yet. She caught his face between her hands. When she'd passed through Delamer, she had bought a pendant with his portrait on it. The whole of summer, she'd only had that tiny image for company. But now she could drink him in—the dark hair, slightly longer than she remembered, the straight brows, the deep-set eyes.

She rubbed a finger across his lower lip. His eyes grew dark. He pushed her against the wall and kissed her again.

"So . . . cream or sugar in your tea?" he asked after a few minutes, his breaths uneven.

She smiled and rested her cheek against his shoulder, her breaths as ungoverned as his. "I have missed you."

"It was a mistake for us to go back to the Domain together. I should have realized that when agents of Atlantis could not locate you here at school, they would come to believe that you must still be in the Domain. I should have known they would watch me relentlessly."

She laid a hand on the front of his jacket. "It wasn't your fault. We were both lulled into a false sense of security."

He took her hand in his. "Of course it was my fault. My task is to keep you safe."

"But I am not meant to be kept safe," she said, rubbing the pad of her thumb along the outside of his palm. "I am meant for fearsome risks and epic clashes. Remember? It's my destiny."

He leaned back, surprise written over his face. "So you believe it now?"

After all the harrowing and marvelous events of the previous Half, how could she not? "Yes, I do. So don't apologize for not guarding me every second of the day. I am but walking the path I am meant to—and a little danger here and there serves to keep my reflexes sharp."

Wonder came into his eyes—wonder and gratitude. He touched his forehead to hers again, his hands warm on her cheeks. "I am so glad it is you. I cannot possibly face this task with anyone else."

At the catch in his voice, unexpected tears stung the back of her eyes. They would be at each other's side until the very end—she cherished that certainty even as she feared it. "I'll keep you safe," she said softly. "Nothing and no one will take you away from me."

Because it was far too early in the Half for actual crying, she added, "Now make me some tea and tell me all about how terrible it was to spend your summer in the same opulent palace as the most beautiful woman in the world."

"Huh," he said.

And delayed the tea-making some more.

CHAPTER ✦ 5

The Sahara Desert

PAIN BURNED THROUGH THE BOY'S flesh. He clamped his teeth over his lower lip, not sure whether he was trying to keep quiet or remain conscious. It did not help that the dark beneath the makeshift sand dune was thick and impenetrable—it made him think that all he had to do was close his eyes and sweet oblivion would be his.

"I've set a one-way sound circle so no one can overhear us," came the low, slightly scratchy voice of the elemental mage he could not get rid of. "Now I'm going to amplify outside voices."

Instantly a gruff voice boomed in the boy's ear. "—sibility, Brigadier?"

"We will have our elemental mages clear as much of the area as possible, to improve visibility," answered a woman. "A one-mile radius has been set. Man the stations and start the dragnet. One regiment from the center out, two from the periphery in."

Part of him wanted to turn himself in—Atlantis would give him something to dull the marrow-rotting pain. But the desire to remain free was so great, it was almost primal.

It was the only thing he knew.

Not his name, not his past, not a single event that might shed light on how he came to be in the middle of a desert, badly wounded, only this: he could not allow himself to be captured by Atlantis or its allies, or all would be lost.

The calls and shouts were now only those of soldiers obeying orders. The elemental mage countermanded the earlier spell for voice amplification. An abrupt silence descended, still and suffocating.

The boy weighed his scant options. Without any memories, he could not vault away, even if he had the vaulting range to put himself beyond this radius Atlantis was establishing. Were he able to see to any distance, then he could blind vault. But with the sandstorm obscuring everything, that too was out of the question.

If only he had had the presence of mind earlier to ask the elemental mage to punch a tunnel of clear air in the sandstorm, then he would have been able to distance himself from that torrent of suspicious solicitude.

He had been almost entirely convinced that the elemental mage had been responsible for his injury. Who else would be so close at hand, if not an enemy? Who else would continue to prowl at the periphery of his dome, despite his express wish to be left alone?

The elemental mage's fear of Atlantis could have been an act. The blackmail to get under his dome certainly could have been a feint for finishing him off. The elemental mage's willingness to give the first drop of blood, however, had taken him aback.

One could wreak much mischief with voluntarily offered blood. Only a fool—or someone with absolutely no ulterior motive—would have dared as the elemental mage had. Now, from an almost certain enemy, he had become an unknown in the equation.

"Did you hear their plan of action?" said the elemental mage.

He grunted an answer.

"I'm going below the surface—it's what I should have done in the first place, instead of getting involved in any kind of blood magic."

"Then why did you not?"

"I'm sure you always think lucidly and from every angle when there are armored chariots bearing down on you," the elemental mage said, with an arch tone. "In any case, my earlier failure to consider this particular alternative is your good luck. I can take you below with me."

The offer stoked his suspicions anew. Was the elemental mage a bounty hunter of some sort, concerned that a cash prize might be spoiled by Atlantis's arrival on scene? "Why do you insist on clinging to me?"

"What?"

"You push your company on me."

"Push my—have you been raised to walk on by when there is a severely wounded mage lying on the ground?"

"So asks the one who engages in blackmail."

The elemental mage muttered something that verged on obscenity. "I guess you'd prefer to stay here then. Good-bye and long may Fortune shield your most charming self."

He could not see in the dark but he could feel the sand to his right shift—the elemental mage was sinking down. "Wait."

"What do you want?"

He wavered for a moment. "I will come with you."

A nonharming covenant was not as airtight a bond as a blood oath: nothing prevented the elemental mage from turning him over to a third party that wished him ill. But under the surface, where there were no third parties, he should be safe enough.

"Are you sure? I might take it as permission to further push my company on you."

The elemental mage's voice dripped with sarcasm. Reassuring, that: he vastly preferred someone who wanted nothing to do with him. "I will have to endure it for your remedies."

The elemental mage burrowed beneath him, the movement causing a wave of agony. He ground his teeth and concentrated on modifying the tensile dome into a normal, mobile shield, which should keep a bubble of air around them and prevent sand from falling onto his back.

The elemental mage wrapped one arm around his neck and hooked a leg behind his knees. They began to sink, sand excavated from underneath flowing up either side of the shield to the top.

"And how do you know my remedies aren't poisoned?" said the elemental mage as they descended.

"I assume they are."

"I look forward to applying them to you then."

They sank more rapidly. Something was not quite right. The elemental mage had seemed rangy of build, but with their torsos pressed tightly together, he did not feel nearly as much skeleton as he had anticipated. In fact . . . in fact . . .

He sucked in a breath—and hissed at the pain that shot through him. But there could be no doubt about it. "You are a girl."

She was unmoved by his discovery. "And?"

"You are dressed as a man."

"You are dressed as a nonmage."

He did not know that. When he had come to, he had been lying on his back, hot sand digging into the open wound on his back. It had been all he could do to turn onto his stomach and build the tensile dome—he had paid no attention to what he wore. And later, when he needed a sharp implement, he had simply tried a pocket, without thinking about whether mage attire would have a pocket at that particular place.

The whole thing was becoming more incomprehensible by the minute. Waking up in the middle of a desert, injured, with no idea how he had come to the place was bad enough. Now nonmage clothes too?

They stopped.

"Bedrock in three feet." She slipped out from underneath him.

His nails dug into the center of his palm, fighting against the fresh, searing pain brought on by her movement.

A clear, blue mage light grew and spread. "I am going to look at your wound. You'll be a burden to me if you can't move on your own."

With the nonharming covenant in place, she could not do anything to worsen his condition. Still, unease seized him at the thought of being more or less at her mercy. But he had no choice. "Go ahead."

She cut away his clothes and sprinkled a cool, fragrant liquid onto his wound, a rain that doused a raging wildfire. He heard himself pant—from the blessed reduction of pain.

"Now I need to clean the wound," she warned him.

Innumerable particles of sand had dug into his flesh. It might be a literal bloodbath to take them all out. Dread roared in his head; he clenched his teeth and said nothing.

The pain returned, sharp and tearing. He swallowed a scream and braced himself for more. But she only sprinkled more of what must be tears of the Angels on his back.

"It's done," she said. "I removed all the grains of sand at once, since we don't have much time."

He would have expressed gratitude, if he were not shaking too much to speak.

She applied layers and layers of various ointments, dressed his wound, and offered him a handful of granules. "Gray ones for strength. Red ones for pain—otherwise you'll still hurt too much to move."

He swallowed them whole.

"Stay where you are for a minute, for everything to take effect. Then we must get going."

"Thank you," he managed.

"My, words I thought I'd never hear from you," she said.

She checked and double-checked all the labels as she put the remedies back into her bag, with the care of a librarian reshelving books according to a particularly rigid reference code.

Now that he knew she was a girl, he was astonished that he had thought her a boy until they had been pressed together from shoulders to knees. Yes, there had been the man's clothes, the short hair, and the somewhat gravelly voice, but surely . . . He could only shake his head inwardly at the potency of assumption.

She glanced up, caught him staring, and frowned—she had a rather fearsome frown. "What's that cold thing inside your clothes?"

He was only just beginning to become aware of a chill against his heart, which he had hardly noticed earlier, when the pain from his back had crowded out all other sensations. Gingerly, he put one hand under his jacket. His fingers came into contact with something icy.

An attempt to move it chafed the back of his neck. That something was a pendant. He yanked the cord from around his neck.

The pendant was the shape of half an oval. The other half was clearly missing. Where was it? Who had it? And did the temperature of his half of the pendant indicate that the other half was far, far away, perhaps on a different continent altogether?

He sat up and examined his ruined clothes—jacket, waistcoat, and shirt. According to the labels sewn into the seams, they had been made by a tailor of Savile Row, London.

He found the pocketknife he had used earlier, engraved with a coat of arms that had a dragon, a phoenix, a griffin, and a unicorn in the quadrants. The waistcoat yielded a watch, made of a cool, silver-gray metal, engraved with the same coat of arms. The jacket's inside pocket contained a wallet—and again the same coat of arms.

Inside the wallet was a negligible amount of nonmage currency, British, by the looks of the coins. But more important, there were several cards, all with the same coat of arms yet once more, and on the other side, the words *H. S. H. Prince Titus of Saxe-Limburg.*

Was he this Prince Titus? What kind of place was Saxe-Limburg? There was no mage realm by that name. And as far as he knew, not a nonmage one either.

She handed him a tunic from her satchel. He destroyed the ruined clothes, stowed the pendant inside the wallet, and shoved the wallet and the watch into his trouser pockets. A hot, unpleasant sensation tore across his back as he lifted his arms overhead to pull on the tunic, but it was ignorable.

She tossed a waterskin his way. He drank nearly half of the contents of the waterskin, gave it back to her, and pointed at the broken strap of her satchel. "I can repair that for you."

"Go ahead, if it will make your conscience feel better."

He rejoined the two halves of the strap. "Why do you assume I have a conscience?"

"Indeed. When will I stop being such a bumpkin?"

She enlarged the space in which they found themselves and stood up. "*Linea orientalis.*"

A faint line appeared underfoot, running due east.

"Where are you headed?" he asked, a better question than *Where are we?* He did not want to betray the fact that he had no idea of their location.

"The Nile."

So they were in the Sahara. "How far are we from the Nile?"

"What do you think?"

A cool challenge was in her eyes. He realized that he enjoyed looking at her—the arrangement of her features was aesthetically pleasing. But more than that, he liked the assured way she carried herself, now that she no longer bothered to be nice to him. "I do not know enough to tell."

At his admission, she cast him a speculative look. "We are seven hundred miles west of the Nile."

"And how far south of the Mediterranean?"

"About the same."

That would put them approximately a hundred, a hundred twenty miles southwest of the nearest Bedouin realm, one allied with Atlantis, no less. The armored chariot must have taken off from an Atlantean installation in that realm, which would explain how they managed to arrive on the scene so fast.

But why? Why would Atlantis come racing? Was it for the same reason that he would rather endure any amount of pain than be caught?

He rose to his feet—and would have wobbled if he had not braced himself with a hand against the sand wall, which felt almost damp against his skin.

"Can you walk?" she asked, her tone bordering on severe.

"I can walk."

He expected her to say something cutting, along the lines of how she would gladly leave him behind if he could not keep up. But she only handed him a nutrition cube. "Let me know when you need to rest."

An odd sensation overcame him: after a moment or two he recognized it as embarrassment. Mortification, almost. There was still a chance, of course, that everything about her was a pretense. But it seemed more and more likely that she was simply a very decent, even compassionate, person.

He took a bite of the nutrition cube, which tasted like lightly flavored air. "I guess this is also poisoned, like your remedies."

The corner of her lips lifted slightly. "Of course."

She excavated along the line she had made, maintaining a moving space just large enough for them to walk abreast. The air he breathed was cool and slightly moist. The sand that crunched beneath his feet had a barely perceptible sheen of wetness. Overhead and to either side of them, sand flowed backward, making him feel a little dizzy. Making him feel as if he were in a submarine vessel, navigating in the dark depths of a strange ocean.

A quick test told him that they were ninety-three feet below the surface. A mobile dome—even an adamantine dome—could not hold up under the weight of so much sand. Only the girl's elemental powers kept them from being buried alive.

Her face was almost blank with concentration, her eyes downcast and half closed. Her hair was blue-black in the mage light and the cut of it made him notice her bone structure and her full lips.

She glanced at him—he had been staring. He turned his attention to his wand instead, which he recognized as a replica of Validus, Titus the Great's wand. Upon entering adulthood mages typically chose to commission original designs for their wands; before that, they were often given wands that were copies of those once wielded by legendary archmages.

So nothing there, other than that he was probably still underage and that someone in his family admired Titus the Great.

"Does that tell you who you are?" she asked, her chin pointing toward his wand.

The significance of her question did not escape him. *Does that tell you who you are?* She assumed that he did not otherwise know his own identity. Which was quite true but hardly the conclusion someone would come to, from knowing him for all of a few minutes, unless . . .

Unless she also did not know that about herself.

He handed over one of the cards from his wallet. She examined it carefully, front and back, murmuring spells to reveal hidden writing. But it was what it was, an ordinary nonmage calling card.

"Do you have anything that tells you who you are?" He asked the same question in return.

She looked up for a second, as if debating whether she wished to give any answers, reached into her trousers pocket—and went completely still. He heard it too. Something was coming up from behind them, something big and metallic, scraping the bedrock as it approached.

CHAPTER ·6

England

"TAKE A LOOK AT THIS," said Iolanthe. She opened a drawer, took out a framed photograph, and handed it to Wintervale.

Wintervale, Cooper, and Titus were in her room. They had just come back from their last class on a short day. It was hours from tea-time, but she had offered to share a cake from High Street and Mrs. Dawlish's boys were not known to turn down opportunities to eat.

Wintervale whistled at the photograph. "Nice."

Cooper took the framed photograph from him. "Pretty."

"I kissed her," said Iolanthe.

Titus, who had been examining a tin of biscuits from her cupboard, did not look up. "I have killed more dragons than you have kissed girls, Fairfax."

"And how many dragons have you killed, Your Highness?" asked Cooper eagerly.

"None."

Wintervale nudged Iolanthe. "Fairfax, I do believe the prince has insulted your manhood."

"My dear Wintervale," said Iolanthe, "the prince has just admitted to having never brought down a single firedrake in his entire life. How could *he* possibly insult *my* manhood?"

Titus glanced at her then, a slight, knowing smile on his face. The effect of that smile was a streak of heat across her skin.

Cooper thrust the photograph toward Titus. "Do you want to see the girl Fairfax kissed, prince?"

The prince barely scanned the picture. "Ordinary."

"His Highness is jealous because he wishes he could have kissed her," Iolanthe said to Cooper and Wintervale.

"I do not kiss commoners," said Titus, looking her full in the eyes.

She was most certainly a commoner, without a drop of aristocratic blood. And he had most certainly kissed her at every opportunity.

"No wonder you are so ill-tempered all the time," she replied.

Wintervale and Cooper laughed.

The door swung open and Sutherland poked in his head. "Gentlemen, I have excellent news: we could be looking at twenty-four hours of debauchery."

"Every day of my life is twenty-four hours of debauchery," Titus said, his attention again on the biscuit tin. "You will have to do better than that, Sutherland."

This took Sutherland aback. He was one of those boys who had thought Titus an insignificant Continental princeling who ruled over a dilapidated castle and ten acres of land. But after the events of the Fourth of June, Sutherland had become rather more respectful. He stood at the door, blinking a little, not quite sure how to respond.

"Don't listen to him, Sutherland. His Highness knows as much about debauchery as he does about killing dragons," said Iolanthe. "Now tell me your news."

Sutherland cleared his throat rather sheepishly. "My uncle has a house in Norfolk, on the coast. He has agreed to let me have the use of it to entertain a few of my friends. We can make a trip of it Saturday and Sunday—play a bit of cricket, shoot some grouse, and lay waste to a very fine collection of cognac."

Wintervale was on his feet. "I am all for it."

"And everyone else?" Sutherland gestured at the rest of the room.

"They too, of course," Wintervale answered for them.

"Excellent. I will have my uncle issue a letter to Mrs. Dawlish, stating that he will ensure adequate supervision and allow only activities that strengthen both body and soul."

"Which encompasses laying waste to his very fine collection of cognac, I take it," said Iolanthe.

"Precisely!" Sutherland winked. "And if Kashkari returns in time, let him know he is also invited."

Sutherland sauntered off. Wintervale and Cooper, too,

departed, after they had ransacked Iolanthe's supply of cake. Titus remained, consuming a scone at a leisurely pace, studying her from across the room.

It was possible that over summer he had become broader across the shoulders. And perhaps half an inch taller. But his eyes were still the same, young and ancient at once. And his gaze, focused entirely on her . . . heat again swept through her.

They had kissed at every chance, but those chances were far less often than she liked. She only locked her door when she changed or bathed, so the boys were used to walking into her room after a perfunctory knock, often without even waiting for a reply—and boys came and went all the time. To change that abruptly might make someone like Cooper ask her why, in front of other boys.

His room was the safer place, but he had not been in his room very much of late: he was constructing another entrance to his laboratory, a folded space that was currently only accessible via a lighthouse more than five hundred miles away, too strenuous a distance for her to vault to day in and day out.

But when he was done, she would be able to reach the laboratory from a former brewery a few miles away. In the laboratory, they would have safety and privacy. Not to mention, in the laboratory was the Crucible.

And she had an inkling that in the Crucible, they might do far more than just kiss.

"What are you up to?" He tilted his chin at the photograph, left by Cooper on her desk. "Who is the chit?"

"That's the chit who will save your hide."

His expression changed—he understood now that the girl in the photograph was her. But since she was protected by an Irreproducible Spell, her image could not be accurately captured. She had wanted to see what would happen if she were photographed, and the answer was that a different face altogether had appeared.

He picked up the photograph and looked again. He would see a young woman of good bone structure and wide-set eyes in a fashion turban. "Where was this?"

"Tenerife, the Canary Islands. On my way to Cape Town."

The steamer had been in port for supplies for half a day. She had gone ashore, walked around, saw a photographer's studio, and decided to have a bit of fun.

"Perhaps I need to rethink my policy on not kissing commoners," he said.

"I'm glad you can see past your prejudices," she murmured.

He gazed at her another moment. "I should go."

She gathered up her resolve. "Have you chosen a place? A place in the Crucible?"

For when they wanted to do more than just kiss.

He rubbed a finger along the back of a chair. "Have you been to 'The Queen of Seasons'?"

"No." There were so many stories in the Crucible.

He didn't quite look at her. "She has a summer villa."

She approached him slowly and laid her hand against the black cashmere waistcoat that peeked out from underneath his uniform tailed jacket. "Are you making the summer villa extra nice for me?"

Their eyes met. "What if I am?"

She smiled. "Just remember, no flower petals on anything, anywhere."

His expression changed briefly. "Do I look like someone who would strew petals on anything, anywhere?"

"Yes." Her smile widened. "You look like someone who thinks a few bushels of rose petals is the epitome of romance."

He yanked her to him for a kiss that lasted all of half a second. "I make no promises."

And then he was gone, leaving her alone with her still tingling lips.

The next afternoon was the first cricket practice.

Iolanthe changed into her kit and knocked on Wintervale's door. No one answered. Odd—she was under the impression that they were to walk to practice together. And Wintervale took such things seriously.

She knocked again. "Wintervale! You there?"

There came a thump, as if someone had leaped off a chair and landed heavily.

She was just about to knock again when the door opened.

"Where's the prince?" Wintervale asked urgently, without preamble.

"Out for a walk. Anything I can help you with?"

As the words left her lips she saw the still-open wardrobe behind Wintervale. Understanding dawned. Wintervale was probably needed by his mother at home. His usual mode of transport was the wardrobe, which acted as a portal, but Lady Wintervale had sealed the portal last June, after Iolanthe had made unauthorized use of it.

The irony was, Iolanthe could vault far enough to take Wintervale to his home in London. But she dared not reveal her secret to him.

Wintervale thrust a hand into his hair. "No, it has to be Titus."

"Ah, Wintervale, there you are," said Mrs. Dawlish, huffing a little from having climbed the stairs. "I've a telegram from your mother. You are needed home urgently. I've already sent for the carriage to be brought around, to take you to the railway station. You should be home in an hour and half."

Wintervale groaned. "An hour and half? That is an eternity. If only I were a stronger vaulter."

"What?" asked Mrs. Dawlish.

"What?" Iolanthe echoed, since she also wasn't supposed to understand what Wintervale had said.

Wintervale shook his head, as if he were admonishing himself. "It's nothing. Thank you, Mrs. Dawlish. I'll be down right away. And can you make my excuses to West, Fairfax? I probably won't be back before supper."

"Of course."

Iolanthe saw Wintervale to the waiting carriage below, then

walked to practice by herself. As she approached the playing fields, someone called her name.

She turned around. It was a boy of about nineteen, also in his kit, tall, long-limbed, and straight of bearing. His dark blond hair was cropped short and he sported a rather impressive mustache. His features, slightly too irregular to be labeled classically handsome, were nevertheless quite attractive to look at.

It took her a moment to recognize him—the last time she'd seen him, he'd had longer hair and no mustache. "West! Just the person I was looking for. Wintervale had to leave for a family emergency and he wanted you to know."

West, like Wintervale, had been a member of the school cricket team last Summer Half. Wintervale's selection had thrilled everyone at Mrs. Dawlish's house. But West was that much higher than Wintervale on the ladder, since he was widely expected to be captain of the eleven come next summer.

Iolanthe had briefly met him when her house team had played his house team. Her team had lost, but it had been an excellent match, the outcome uncertain until near the end.

West offered her his hand to shake. "I hope nothing is terribly wrong in the Wintervale household."

"I should think not, but his mother likes to have him on hand whenever she is feeling unwell."

They walked a minute or so in silence before West asked, "You are a friend of Titus of Saxe-Limburg, aren't you?"

Until the past Fourth of June, she would have said that most of the boys in Mrs. Dawlish's house probably couldn't remember the name of Titus's made-up Prussian principality of origin. But since then, she had fielded quite a few questions from boys who had seen the grand family entourage that had descended on the school and were consequently made curious about the prince. "Yes, I live next door to His Highness."

"He seems an interesting character," said West.

Iolanthe did not need to answer, as they had arrived and the cricket master wanted a word with West.

But yes, an endlessly interesting character, her prince.

Baycrest House, Sutherland's uncle's property in Norfolk, sat upon a high promontory jutting into the North Sea, with many gables, a cloistered garden at its back, and a small crescent of sheltered beach to the side, accessed by a hundred feet of rickety ladders that had been bolted to the cliffs.

The boys were quite ecstatic. Cooper, in particular, hollered as he ran up and down, as if he had never seen the sea—or a house, for that matter—in his entire life.

The other boys and Iolanthe were just about to have a bite to eat when Cooper called down from an upstairs balcony, "Gentlemen, our friend from the subcontinent has arrived!"

Iolanthe and the prince exchanged a look. She liked Kashkari. She was, in addition, quite grateful to him for the help he had given

Titus and herself. Still, she was more than a little nervous at the prospect of meeting Kashkari again: Kashkari listened, and his intelligent eyes missed nothing.

But this Half she was better prepared. During her summer of steamer journeys, she had made her way through a number of books from the ships' libraries, especially those dealing with the political geography of the British Empire. Since she came ashore in England, she had read *The Times* every day. When she had time, she took a look at *The Daily Telegraph*, *The Illustrated London News*, and *The Manchester Guardian*—sometimes it felt as if she studied for Kashkari's return more diligently than she'd ever reviewed for any examination in her life.

Kashkari looked the same, doe-eyed, striking, and stylish. But after a quarter hour or so, Iolanthe actually began to relax. The boy who walked into Baycrest House did not seem to possess the same razor-sharp powers of observation Iolanthe had been half dreading.

When he asked after her holidays and her family, and she told him about the Fairfaxes coming into some money and selling the farm, he only nodded and said it was a good time to get out of Bechuanaland, before the hostility between the English and the Boer tilted into open war.

And then he moved on to Wintervale's absence. "Does anyone know about the emergency chez Wintervale? Mrs. Hancock told me he went home near the beginning of the week and hasn't come back yet."

"That's right," said Cooper. "He went in such a huge hurry he left half a Chelsea bun behind—and you know Wintervale, he never leaves food unfinished."

"Did anyone see him go?"

"I was there," said Iolanthe.

This time, Kashkari's attention was more focused on her. "How did he seem?"

"Vexed, but hardly in a state of devastation."

Iolanthe had expected Wintervale to return the next day. When two days had passed with no sign of Wintervale, she had become worried. But Titus had told her that it wasn't unusual for Wintervale to be gone as long as a week, if his mother needed him.

"He should come back soon, shouldn't he?" asked Kashkari with a slight frown.

"I wouldn't be surprised if he turned up here tomorrow. You know Wintervale, he wouldn't miss this if he could help it," said Sutherland. "But back to us, gentlemen. What say you we go down to the beach, build a fire, and tell ghost stories when it's dark?"

Cooper all but squealed. "I love ghost stories!"

Titus glanced at him. He always looked at Cooper as if the latter were a cocker spaniel that somehow managed to speak in a human tongue. But these days Iolanthe rather fancied that Titus was beginning to betray a slight fondness for the boy.

But when he spoke, he was again the grand prince who could

not be bothered with lesser mortals. "Commoners and their enthusiasm," he said. "Where is the cognac I have been promised?"

The day was growing late when they started for the beach. The breeze from the sea had become loud and stiff. Gulls wheeled overhead, seeking one last bite of supper while light still lingered.

Iolanthe shook her head as she helped gather driftwood: the great elemental mage of their time, not allowed to snap her fingers and summon a roaring fire out of thin air. By the time they had a fire going and sausages dripping fat into the flames, it had become quite dark, the stars tiny pinpricks against the inky sky.

The ghost stories started with Cooper's visit to a haunted house, followed by Sutherland's uncle's experience at a particularly hair-raising séance, and Kashkari's tale of a spirit who kept visiting his great-grandfather, until the latter rebuilt a house that had been burned down by Diwali fireworks. Iolanthe contributed a story she had read in the papers. Titus, surprising her—and probably everyone else around the fire—narrated a chilling tale of a necromancer who raised an army of the dead.

When all the ghost stories had been told and all the sausages they'd carried down roasted and eaten, Sutherland produced another bottle of cognac to share. Iolanthe and the prince touched the bottle to their lips without actually imbibing—anything that had a strong taste of its own could disguise the addition of truth serum or other dangerous potions. Everyone else drank with varying degrees of purpose and dedication. Kashkari, in particular, astounded Iolanthe by taking liberal swallows—she would have thought that he drank sparingly, if at all.

A small silence fell—and stayed. The boys stared into the fire. Iolanthe studied the interplay of light and shadows upon their features, especially Kashkari's. Titus, too, watched Kashkari.

Something was not quite right with him.

"I don't know what I'm going to do," said Cooper out of the blue. "My father is counting the days until I can join his firm of solicitors. And I don't think I can ever tell him that I haven't the slightest interest in the law."

Iolanthe was taken aback by the sudden turn in the conversation. "So what do you want to do?"

"That's just the thing. I haven't the slightest idea. Can hardly go up to the old man and say, 'Sorry, Pater, don't know what I like, but I do know I hate what you do.' " He grabbed the bottle from Sutherland. "At least you don't have to undertake a profession, Sutherland. You have an earldom waiting for you."

Sutherland snorted. "Have you seen the earldom? The manor is falling down on itself. I'll have to marry the first heiress who will have me and we'll probably hate each other for the next fifty years."

Now everyone looked expectantly at Iolanthe. She was beginning to understand: spirits were the truth serum of the nonmages— except they partook it willingly and shared under its influence what they could not bring themselves to say completely sober.

"I might not be at school much longer. My parents have decided that after their world tour, they will buy a ranch in the American West—Wyoming Territory, to be specific. And I have a sinking feeling they will want me to go out and help them with it."

It was the story she and Titus had decided upon, to explain her likely hasty departure from school one of those days.

"Not much longer for me, either," said Titus. "I have enemies at home and they have their eyes on my throne."

This caused a collective intake of breath, the loudest from Cooper, naturally.

"There won't be a coup, will there?" he asked, his voice unsteady.

"Who knows?" Titus shrugged. "There is all kinds of intrigue going on behind my back. But you do not need to worry, Cooper. What is mine, I keep."

Cooper swayed a little. For a moment Iolanthe thought he might tip over from the combined effect of cognac and excitement—this must be one of the few times Titus had addressed him without ordering him to vacate the premises.

But Cooper righted himself and the boys turned to Kashkari, who signaled for the bottle. "If we'd had this conversation before I went home for the holiday, I'd have turned up my hands and said, Sorry, boys, there isn't much in my life I can honestly complain about."

He took a swig of the cognac. "But then I went home and arrived just in time to celebrate my brother's engagement. And as it turned out, my brother is going to marry the girl of my dreams."

Iolanthe was shocked, not so much by the specifics of Kashkari's revelation as by the fact that he chose to divulge something so intensely private. Granted she had met him only months ago, but nothing she knew of him had indicated in the least that he was the sort to be open about his heartache.

"My God," murmured Cooper. "I'm so sorry."

"My sentiments exactly." Kashkari smiled grimly and raised the bottle. "Here's to life, which will kick you in the teeth, sooner or later."

The Queen of Seasons' summer villa sat on a narrow peninsula that sliced into a deep, glacier-fed lake. The sun had just climbed over the peaks that ringed the lake; the water was almost the exact same shade as the luxuriant ivy that climbed over the creamy walls of the villa.

Titus stood on the terrace that overlooked the lake. Overhead, from the trelliswork of the pergola, trailed tendrils of green vine and clusters of honey-colored florets.

A beautiful venue, whether bathed in sunrise or moonlight. No place could ever be perfect enough for Fairfax, but this one came close.

"And they lived happily ever after."

He came out of the Crucible to the much more mundane

surroundings of the laboratory. After he and Fairfax had pushed and shoved the heavily inebriated boys back up the cliff to the house, he had come to the laboratory to work. The boys anyway were not going to get up before noon, and he wanted to finish making the new entrance as soon as possible.

Life was uncertain, his particularly.

He yawned. It was now almost nine in the morning. He exited the laboratory to an abandoned barn in Kent. From there it was a quick vault back to his room at Baycrest House.

Fairfax was there, waiting for him, flipping the pages of a book she had pulled from the bookshelf—in deference to his rank, Titus had been given the best room in the house, with a private bath, a wide balcony that looked out to the sea, and two shelves full of leather-bound volumes.

"Is it ready yet?" she asked. She meant the new entrance into the laboratory.

"Almost. I have to wait about twenty-four hours, and then I can complete the final step."

"I miss the Crucible," she said. "It must have been at least three months since I was last inside."

After the Fourth of June, he had moved his copy of the Crucible to the laboratory to avoid confiscation by Atlantis. There was another copy in the monastery in the Labyrinthine Mountains, but they had neither of them been able to visit the monastery over the summer.

"It will not be long now."

"Did you have to shovel out bushels of flower petals?" she teased.

Barrels. "No comment."

"Well, I am not going for the decor, in any case."

"Now you tell me."

She grinned. "Go to sleep. You look tired."

He fell backward onto the bed. "I am getting old. I used to stay up all night and look better for it."

"Your mirror lied," she said, drawing a blanket over him.

He took her hand and kissed the pads of her fingers. "Thank you," he said. "For everything."

"What can I say?" she said, her voice growing fainter. "This damsel loves rescuing princes in distress."

He smiled as he fell asleep.

And when he woke up, he was still smiling.

He had dreamed of the two of them on the terrace of the Queen of Seasons' summer villa. But instead of kissing, they had been sitting on the ornamental parapet, and she had been telling him a long and involved joke.

He had laughed himself awake—though now that he had his eyes open, he could not remember what she had said.

The next moment her voice came through the window he had left slightly open. She was outside, talking to Cooper. Her exact words were blurred by the wind and the surf, but it was enough to know that she was nearby, not only safe but in high spirits.

He sat up, and his hand pressed into something hard on the bed—the book she had left behind. A small, ornate clock on the windowsill caught his attention: fourteen minutes after two o'clock.

Interesting. It was the exact time mentioned in his mother's vision that saw him witnessing the feat of elemental magic that would change the lives of everyone involved. Because of that vision, whenever he was at the castle, he used to lie down after lunch and have Dalbert call him at precisely fourteen past two, so everything would be, to the letter, what had already been ordained.

He stepped onto the balcony, to a bracing breeze from the sea. On the horizon, a storm gathered, but here everything was still sunny and mild—or as mild as it could be for the beginning of autumn on the North Sea. Below, Cooper and Fairfax played a game of croquet on a patch of lawn. They both waved as they saw him. He nodded very regally.

"Will you join us, Your Highness?" called Cooper.

Titus was about to answer when his wand suddenly warmed. The warming was rhythmical, one moment hot, one moment normal—the wand was relaying a distress signal. And not just any distress signal, a nautical one, specific to seafaring vessels.

There was a mage ship nearby?

"Give me a few minutes," he told Cooper.

He scanned the sea, but there were no vessels out and about. Fairfax, too, was searching. She would have felt the distress signal in his spare wand that she now carried in her boot.

He set a far-seeing spell—and reeled. Five miles out, in the middle of the North Sea, sailed an Atlantean vessel. It was not a warship by any means, but looked much bigger than a patrol boat. A skimmer—meant for pursuit at sea.

What was it chasing?

Several seconds passed before he located the dinghy fleeing from the skimmer.

He reeled again as he recognized the only passenger in the dinghy: Wintervale.

CHAPTER · 7

The Sahara Desert

WHATEVER THE CONTRAPTION COMING UP behind, it was big and moving fast.

Titus turned to the girl. "Can you break through stone?"

Doubt crossed her face, but she only said, as she extinguished the mage light that lit their way, "Let's see. Hold on to me."

He wrapped his arms about her. They descended through several feet of sand, and then, more slowly, into solid bedrock, which fractured underfoot, the debris flowing up and out to allow them passage.

Just in time for the contraption to sweep overhead, scraping the bedrock like a giant metal comb. The teeth of the comb were only an inch and a half apart—no way for them to slip through.

"How fast do you think it is moving?" asked the girl.

She brought back the mage light. Belatedly he realized that he still had his arms around her. He let go. "Ten miles an hour, or thereabouts."

But the well she had made was so narrow they still stood nearly nose to nose. Her skin was blue-tinged in the mage light; a smear of rock dust across the ridge of her nose looked like tiny specks of lapis lazuli.

"The search area is one mile in radius," she said. "The dragnet would need six minutes to go from center to periphery, and six minutes to return to center. Depending on how far we are from the center, we can go for five or six minutes before we meet it again."

He shook his head. "The brigadier said there is an outbound dragnet as well as an inbound one. They will likely meet at the halfway point and switch directions. So it will be only two to three minutes, if that, before the sweeper comes back."

She frowned. It would be inefficient, not to mention dangerous, for them to stop every couple of minutes to drill a hole.

"In that case, I'd better tunnel beneath the surface of the bedrock. Can you crawl for nearly a mile?"

"I can, but we do not need to. We can levitate each other."[5]

She looked almost impressed at his idea. "Let's do that."

She excavated a horizontal passage four feet from the top of the bedrock and crawled in on her stomach. He, behind her, entered feet first and face up, until the soles of their boots touched. They levitated each other a few inches off the floor of the passage. A small river of rock debris began to flow underneath them, toward the back. Every fifteen seconds or so, he pushed against the walls of the tunnel and propelled them forward.

They made steady progress as the sweeper scraped back and forth overhead. When half an hour had passed, she enlarged the tunnel somewhat for them to sit and rest. He drank greedily from the waterskin she handed him, surprised by how thirsty he was, even though the tunnel was as cool as a cellar.

His watch measured distance as well as time. He showed her that they had moved about a half mile from where they first sank down below the surface of the desert.

She nodded. "You all right?"

His wound hurt, insistently and noticeably. But compared to the agony earlier, the pain was nothing. "I am fine. You?"

She appeared surprised by the question. "Fine, of course."

Next to her, a tiny sphere of water appeared, spinning lazily mid-air as it grew fatter. These days elemental mages were more likely to be the entertainers at birthday parties than anything else. Her powers, on the other hand . . .

"You were going to show me something, before the dragnet caught up with us," he said.

"Oh, that." She pulled a card out of her pocket and held it toward him.

He examined the card. *A. G. Fairfax.* "Do you mind if I call you that?"

She shrugged. "Go ahead." The cool challenge came back into

her eyes. "Should I address you as Your Serene Highness?"

"You may announce a prince as such, but you address him as only 'Your Highness,' " he said. "For example, 'Your Highness, it has been a privilege to crawl through a cramped, airless tunnel with you.' "

She scoffed, but without rancor. The water sphere had grown large. She took the waterskin from him, refilled it, and put it back into her bag. He realized only when she glanced up and their eyes met that he had not looked away from her this entire time.

"Your Highness," she said, her tone half-mocking, "may I have the honor of excavating another half mile of passage for you?"

"But certainly," he answered, handing back her calling card. "When we are on the throne again, we shall remember and reward your loyalty and devotion."

She shook her head at his pomposity, but he could see by the tilt of her lips that she was amused. And it startled him that in the midst of all the danger and uncertainty, he felt a leap of pure delight at having made her smile.

They found out the next minute that they could not levitate each other again.

"The levitation spells we used earlier were probably close to wearing off when we stopped—we would not have noticed since we were only three inches off the ground," said the boy who might or might not be a prince. "If that were the case, a quarter-hour wait would be required. Which means we can try again in about"—he glanced at his watch—"seven minutes."

He was still in pain—he held himself carefully to avoid unnecessary movement. People reacted differently to pain: some wanted sympathy and help; others preferred to suffer alone, to not have witnesses in their hour of affliction. He was probably the latter kind, the kind who became bad-tempered when faced with an insistent do-gooder.

Or . . . "Did you think I was the one who injured you?"

He seemed amused. "That is only occurring to you right now?"

"Why should it have occurred to me sooner? I didn't do it."

He raised a brow. "You are sure about that?"

The question stumped her—she had no way of knowing for certain, did she? If he had harmed her protector, then she could see herself exacting vengeance. But on the other hand, his was not a wound caused by elemental powers.

She pointed that out.

He moved his lips in an eloquent representation of a shrug. "Are you telling me you do not know how to make a potion?"

Did she? At the question, she began to recall all kinds of recipes—clarifying potion, bel canto draught, light elixir. She rubbed her temples. "Do you know why you are in the guise of a nonmage?"

"I could be an Exile. The clothes I was wearing came from a place in London, England, and I recognized it as a street known for tailor shops."

"Savile Row?" The named rolled easily off her tongue, surprising her.

Surprising him as well. He shifted—and winced in pain. "How do you know?"

"When you said a street known for tailors in London, it just came to mind." And yet she could not recall her own name.

"So we retain knowledge and skills we have acquired," he said, "but we have no personal memories."

This implied the use of precision memory spells. Blunt-force memory spells required only the will to do damage, but precision memory spells were contact requisite: the mage who had so neatly cut away her memories must have accumulated many hours of direct physical contact with her, in order to be able to wield such spells over her.

Most contact-requisite spells required thirty-six hours of contact; the more powerful ones needed seventy-two hours. Except infants being held by parents or siblings, or lovers who could not leave each other's embrace, mages simply did not touch one another enough to be able to deploy contact-requisite spells. Of course there were ways around it, but in general the contact-requisite threshold ensured that a great many potentially dangerous spells were not used willy-nilly by anyone with a grudge.

In this case, however, that contact-requisite threshold raised thorny questions: it meant her memory had not been taken by an enemy, but quite possibly someone she knew very, very well.

That someone had made sure that she retained her fear of

Atlantis. And whoever had applied the memory spells to the boy had done the same.

"Do you—do you think we knew each other?"

He looked at her a long moment. "What do you think are the odds that two completely unconnected strangers ended up in the middle of the Sahara Desert, within a stone's throw of each other, both missing their memories?"

The idea was an uncomfortable one, that she might be linked to this boy in some significant manner.

"But it remains to be seen whether we were allies or enemies," the boy added. He checked his watch. "Shall we get going?"

It would be ridiculous to describe rock as soft, yet the next section of bedrock she tunneled through most certainly felt softer to her, easier to manipulate.

They advanced more rapidly, which should have pleased her, yet the closer they drew to the one-mile boundary, the more uneasy she grew.

"We must be almost there," said Titus. "Ten, fifteen yards left at most."

She stopped.

"You all right?" he asked.

"Our progress has been too easy, don't you think?"

"What do you suspect?"

She shook her head. "I can't be sure. But the armored chariots knew exactly where to find us, so it stands to reason that the soldiers looking for us know that I am an elemental mage. They should realize that I can make my way through rock, and yet they have been content to just comb the sand."

"I can vault to the surface and check."

"No, that would be too dangerous."

"Do you want to stay here for some time, and see if anything develops?"

She stared at the end of the tunnel, twelve inches from her face. It looked as if it had been gouged by a beast with steel claws.

"Never mind. Let's just keep going."

"You should not ignore your instinct."

"Well, there is no other way out, and it can't be a good idea to stay here waiting for something to happen."

Chunks of rocks broke off. The end of the tunnel receded by a few inches, and then a few more inches—her elemental powers at work.

"Move us forward," she told him.

After a second or so, he did as she requested.

"The memory spells that have been used on us—quite sophisticated, wouldn't you say?" she asked, after they had advanced several more feet.

They had been largely silent during the excavation, so she could concentrate on the task at hand. But now she needed something to distract her.

"And quite illegal," he answered.

"I don't understand the point of it all. The memory spells were tailored specifically so that we do our best to stay out of Atlantis's grasp, but wouldn't that be easier if we knew why?"

"You are assuming the one who applied the spells wanted to help." He pushed her forward again. "But if—"

Pain struck deep inside her head, pain like a burning stake being driven through her skull.

She barely recognized the deafening scream as her own.

CHAPTER · 8

England

WINTERVALE'S ENTIRE PERSON SHOOK. HIS lips moved—whether with curses or prayers, Titus could not tell. And he kept looking back, at the enemy ship closing in on him.

Titus swore. Five minutes ago, if anyone had asked him, he would have said that Fairfax was the only one for whom he would risk anything. But he could not simply let Wintervale fall into Atlantis's grasp, not when the whole thing was unfolding before his eyes.

He took a deep breath. Before he could vault, however, Wintervale spun around and pointed his wand at the skimmer.

The surface of the sea seemed to shudder. Then it turned eerily calm, like a sheet that been stretched perfectly flat across a mattress. The next moment, Titus had the strangest sensation that the sea was caving. It was: a whirlpool formed, enormous currents of water churning around a central eye.

The skimmer, caught by the edge of this maelstrom, attempted to navigate its way out. But the maelstrom expanded with terrifying speed, its eye ever deepening and widening, exposing the actual seafloor hundreds of feet below.

The skimmer fell into this colossal crater. Immediately, the maelstrom ceased its rotation. All the water that had been spun outward rushed back in, crushing the skimmer under its volume and weight.

Titus clutched the railing, agape.

"Fairfax, what are you looking at?" came Cooper's voice. "It's your turn."

Fairfax, had she caused the maelstrom? But she was gazing up at him, her expression as stunned as he felt.

"Play your turn, Fairfax," he said, a reminder to her that she must keep playing her part.

He retreated into his room and reapplied the far-seeing spell. The displacement of that much water had caused violent waves, tossing Wintervale's dinghy about. Wintervale seemed not to notice at all. His arms were wrapped about the small mast, his face wet with seawater—or was it tears? And his expression was one not of confusion, but of wonder and incredulity, as if he knew exactly how the whirlpool that swallowed his pursuers had come about, but simply could not believe it had in truth happened.

A particularly large wave buffeted the dinghy. The next one capsized it entirely. Titus gritted his teeth and vaulted. As expected, he landed in the frigid waters of the North Sea, the cold like shards of glass.

Blind vaulting—paradoxically named, as one blind vaulted with one's eyes wide open, using only visual clues as a guide, rather than personal memory—was notoriously inaccurate. He could have rematerialized a mile away. But fortunately, in this instance, he was only a hundred feet or so from the upside-down dinghy.

Wintervale surfaced, gasping and flailing.

"*Eleveris*," Titus shouted, swimming toward Wintervale, not daring to vault again for fear of finding himself farther away.

Wintervale screamed at being suddenly airborne. He thrashed, turning over and over a few feet above the waves, as if he were rotating on a spit.

The waves battered Titus. But at least Wintervale, held above water, could not drown. Titus's muscles protested as he fought toward Wintervale. Fifty feet. Twenty-five feet. Ten feet.

"Titus!" Wintervale shouted. "Thank goodness. Fortune is no longer spitting in my face."

Titus closed the last few feet of distance between them, grabbed Wintervale's arm, and vaulted them both to the beach beneath Sutherland's uncle's house.

Wintervale promptly vomited.

Titus waited until he was done, kicked sand and pebbles over the mess, and led him ten feet away. Wintervale crumpled to the ground. Titus crouched beside him, cleaned him with a few spells, and checked his pulse and pupils.

"What were you trying to do?" Wintervale rasped. "You know I can't vault more than half a mile."

"Unless you could swim five miles to land, vaulting was our only choice."

Wintervale was already shivering.

"Wait here." Titus vaulted to his room, grabbed a towel and a change of clothes, and vaulted back down. "You need to change out of those clothes."

Wintervale's fingers shook as he tried to undo the buttons of his jacket.

"*Exue*," said Titus.

Wintervale's jacket flew off. As Titus repeated the spell, Wintervale's waistcoat and shirt also made themselves scarce.

"S-smashing spell, that," stuttered Wintervale, his teeth chattering.

"The ladies agree with you," said Titus.

He turned around before doing away with Wintervale's trousers. Then he vaulted back to Baycrest House to change out of his own dripping clothes, scanning the sea for signs of other Atlantean forces as he did so. A familiar knock came at his door as he was buttoning his new shirt.

Fairfax.

"Come in," he said, shrugging into another waistcoat.

Her face was pale as she closed the door behind her. "What's going on? Where's Wintervale?"

He thrust his arms into a jacket. "On the beach, changing his clothes. I will find out what is going on."

She came nearer. "Are *you* all right?"

He thought it a strange question until she took his hand: he was shaking without being aware of it.

"Must have been the cold—the water was freezing," he said, extracting a vial from the emergency remedy pack in his luggage.

But as he spoke, he was thinking not of the frigidness of the sea, but of those moments just before the nautical distress signal came: rising from his bed, glancing at the clock, noting the time—fourteen minutes after two—then stepping out onto the balcony.

There was a terrifying familiarity to the chain of actions. And *that*, as much as his sodden clothes, had made him tremble.

He pulled her in and pressed his lips to her cheek. "Keep the boys on the side of the house away from the beach. Keep an eye on the sea. And do nothing that would reveal yourself to anyone—do not even think about using your powers to dry those clothes of mine, for instance. If Wintervale is not safe, then neither are we."

Wintervale had put on dry clothes but he was still shivering. Titus gave him the warming remedy he had brought.

"I need to get you somewhere you can rest. Think carefully: Did the Atlanteans know where you were headed?"

"No," said Wintervale, his voice hoarse. "They didn't even know who I am."

"Are you absolutely sure?"

"Yes."

Titus was far from assured, but he did not have many choices. "In that case, I will take you up to Sutherland's uncle's house."

Wintervale blanched. "Please don't vault me again."

Wintervale was in no shape to be vaulted again just now. In fact, he could scarcely stand. Titus glanced at the steep cliff and the rickety ladders, and sighed. "We can do without vaulting."

Wintervale was about the same height as Titus, but at least a stone heavier. As Titus started his ascent, Wintervale on his back, he felt like Atlas, carrying the weight of the whole world. "Why was Atlantis chasing you? We thought you were home with your mother."

"They weren't chasing *me*. And we weren't at home. My mother and I were in France. In Grenoble."

Titus clambered over a protrusion of rocks to reach the next ladder, straining not to tilt backward. "Grenoble?"

As far as he knew, the town did not host an Exile community of any appreciable size.

"Do you know who Madame Pierredure is?" asked Wintervale.

"Old lady who fought Atlantis?" Madame Pierredure had indeed been an old lady, but she had also been the chief strategist for the rebellion in the Juras ten years ago, and had been responsible for a series of brilliant victories. No one had heard of her since the end of that spate of rebellions and insurrections. If she was still alive, she must be quite ancient. "I thought she was dead."

"That's what we all thought," said Wintervale. "Then Mother

heard news that Madame was in Grenoble. She was keen to see for
herself that Madame was still alive—they had known each other
back in the day. And she wanted me to come along to meet Madame
in person, if the rumors turned out to be true.

"We traveled under assumed names and stayed at nonmage
hotels. Everything was fine until last night, when we had news
Madame had arrived at a hotel in *centre-ville*. We went to a café in
the square outside the hotel. Left and right there were mages—we
could hear them whisper about Madame Pierredure. That was when
Mother stood up and told me we were leaving. She said something
felt wrong, that if it was all hush-hush and secret, with news traveling only along trusted channels, then there shouldn't be nearly as
many mages gathered in a place that has very little Exile presence,
waiting for a glimpse of Madame.

"I should have listened to her. But instead—" Wintervale took
a deep breath. Titus could almost see him grimacing. "Instead I
said we should stay, for the chance to witness something historic.
We were arguing back and forth when she stopped talking and just
grabbed me. That was when I realized that mages at the far end of
the square were dropping unconscious. And then I looked up and
saw the armored chariots."

Titus tensed. A narrative almost always took a fateful turn with
the entrance of armored chariots.

"We couldn't vault, so we ran," Wintervale went on, his voice
strained. "Had we gone back to our lodging, we probably would have

been all right. But one man in our corner of the square shouted that he had access to a dry dock and could get us to England fast."[6]

"About twenty of us followed him to a house on the outskirts of town. We crowded onto a vessel in the cellar. The next moment it dropped into the sea and we all thought we were safe. But not two minutes later, we had an Atlantean frigate behind us.

"It was all chaos on board. Mother asked where Sutherland's uncle's house was—I had told her earlier I was missing the party to be with her. I said it was somewhere within a few miles of Cromer. That was the last thing I knew. When I came to, it was morning. I was on the dinghy and it was sailing itself. I had no idea where I was and Mother . . ."

Wintervale gulped. "She's lived through rough times," he said fervently. "She must be all right."

Lady Wintervale was the only other person who knew that one of the "boys" at Mrs. Dawlish's was the great elemental mage sought by Atlantis. If she were arrested and interrogated . . . Titus could only hope that Atlantis would not think to ask her questions on that particular subject.

They were almost halfway up the cliff. Titus inched along the narrow footpath that would take him to the next ladder, adjusting Wintervale's arms so the latter did not inadvertently strangle him.

With Wintervale's tale finished, Titus had no choice but to ask the question that disturbed him far more than it should. "Did you make the maelstrom?"

Wintervale had largely stopped shivering, but now he trembled. "I'm not sure how that happened. The Atlantean skimmer came out of nowhere. One minute I was dozing off and the next minute it was there." He exhaled slowly—as if trying to push away the memory. "I panicked completely. All I could think was, if only I were a more powerful elemental mage, I would open up a huge whirlpool right before the skimmer and then I'd be safe from it."

The fact that Wintervale was an elemental mage was never the first, second, third, or even fourth thing Titus recalled about him. *If I want to make a fire, I use a match,* Wintervale had once confessed to Titus. And that had not been false modesty. Spent coals could produce bigger sparks than the glimmers of fire Wintervale summoned. And one would probably die of thirst waiting for him to fill a glass with water.

Then again, great elemental mages tended to be unexceptional as children, until their powers manifested in adolescence. Titus had thought it was too late for Wintervale to undergo such a transformation. But obviously he was wrong.

"So you wanted to make a huge whirlpool?"

"I did. And the next moment, all this power I'd never felt before poured out of me and the sea did exactly what I wanted it to do. I guess . . . I guess I'm a better elemental mage than I thought I was."

Titus's arms burned as he pulled up to the next rung. "You might get into *Lives and Deeds of the Great Elemental Mages* if you are not careful."

The sound Wintervale made was halfway between a laugh and a sob. "I wish Mother could have seen it. When we still lived in the Domain, she was so unimpressed with my powers she didn't bother to have me declared. She would—she would have liked to see what I was able to do today."

"Yes, this changes things," Titus said slowly.

Everything, possibly.

By the time he reached the top of the cliff, every muscle in Titus's body screamed.

Fairfax had done as he asked: no one threw open windows to yell in surprise at Wintervale's sudden appearance. Titus half carried, half dragged Wintervale the rest of the distance to the front door.

"I am going to vault inside. Wait a few seconds before you ring the doorbell," Titus told Wintervale. "And if anyone asks why you look like death, tell them it was something you ate on the train."

Back in his room Titus pointed his wand at his soles and got rid of any debris that clung to them. The doorbell clanged distantly. He stepped onto the balcony. Fairfax and Cooper were still at their game of croquet, with Kashkari added as an observer.

"So you managed to get out of bed by three," Titus said to Kashkari.

"I was out of bed by noon," said Kashkari. He looked as if he had not been allowed to sleep in three days. "Spent the next two hours on the floor, writhing in agony."

"At least you are upright," said Cooper with rather obscene cheer, considering he drank as much as anyone did. "Sutherland is still moaning under his blanket, as far as I know."

Fairfax swung her mallet. The doorbell rang again. She tensed, but she did not say anything.

Kashkari rubbed his temples. "Is someone ringing the bell?"

The butler appeared. "There is a caller by the name of Wintervale. Should I say Mr. Sutherland is at home to him?"

"Yes!" Kashkari and Cooper answered at the same time. Kashkari, swaying slightly, started immediately for the house. Cooper hurried to catch up. Fairfax, after a glance at Titus, followed suit.

Titus was the last to reach the front of the house, where Wintervale was being warmly welcomed back into the fold.

"What's the matter?" Kashkari peered at him. "Have you been drinking too? You don't look good."

"Something I ate on the trip." Wintervale turned to the butler. "I'd like to lie down for a bit, if you have a bed to spare."

"It will take us only a minute to make up a room for you, sir."

"You can use my room until then," Kashkari offered, bracing his arm around Wintervale's middle.

Wintervale looked toward Titus, seemingly reluctant to go with Kashkari. But the latter was already moving him along. "Watch your step."

"You should take all the rest you can," Titus reminded Wintervale. Kashkari's bed was as good a place as any.

"I'll go tell Sutherland you are here," said Cooper as he passed by Kashkari and Wintervale on the stairs.

Fairfax did not follow them, but came closer to Titus. "I'll ask for a tray of tea for you, Wintervale." She spoke loud enough for everyone to hear. Then, in a whisper to him alone, "You want to tell me what happened?"

She was worried about him, and concerned for the situation. But though she was on edge, she remained very much in charge of herself.

Whereas he felt like the Atlantean skimmer, caught in an inescapable maelstrom. "There is something I need to check first. Will you keep an eye on Wintervale until I get back?"

"Of course. What do you need to check?"

It was a betrayal to speak those words. But he did, because he did not lie to her. "My mother's diary."

Princess Ariadne's diary sat at the center of the worktable in Titus's laboratory. He stared at it. Had he made the mistake of a lifetime? Her vision, the one of him standing upon a balcony and witnessing an act of stupendous elemental power—had she meant Wintervale, rather than Fairfax?

I need to see them again, those entries.

Everything in him yearned toward Fairfax. In a world of utter uncertainties, she had proved to be the strength he could rely on, when his own strength failed.

But what if she was not the One?

Please, let it be Fairfax.

The diary responded—at least to the first part of his request.

28 September, YD 1014

The day of his birth.

*A man stands somewhere. He could be anywhere, a mountaintop,
a field, or before an open window. All I see is the back of his head and
the blue sky beyond. Yet even in so limited a vision, I see—or rather, I
feel—his shock.*

He is reeling.

And that was that.

13 November, YD 1014

Joy pierced him. The day before Fairfax was born. This had to be
a good sign.

*The same vision, slightly expanded. Now I know it takes place at
about quarter after two o'clock. Though the time could be deceptive, just
as the date had been at Eugenides Constantinos's bookshop.*

When I used to read all the books about seers I could lay my hands on, almost every one of them had mentioned rubbish visions, those visions that had no significance whatsoever. The mage who always saw what he ate a week into the future, for example.

I wonder if this is a rubbish vision. Though, of course, even rubbish visions eventually predict something. The mage who saw what he ate stopped having those visions—and one week later he was dead.

And it is odd that I seem to have this particular vision only when someone is in confinement for childbirth.

Whose confinement? Who gave birth on the night of the meteor storm?

He turned the page.

I caught Eirene reading from my diary.

It shocked me to no end.

I had always believed Eirene one of the most honorable mages I had ever met. But she refused to even give me a reason for her snooping.

My confidence is shattered. Am I so terrible at judging character? Am I surrounded by mages seeking to betray my trust?

He had checked the roster of his mother's staff at the time of the diary entry, but had found no one by the name of Eirene.

27 March, YD 1016

This vision again.

Nothing new, except now I am convinced the man in the vision is a very young man, perhaps a boy still. I cannot say why I think so, but I do.

9 July, YD 1018

A wider view of the young man. As the phenomenon that staggers him unfolds, his hands grip the railing of the balcony, his knuckles stark white.

Titus remembered this, gripping the railing in stupefaction at Wintervale's maelstrom.

And the term, "railing." Could the marble balustrade that encircled the grand balcony outside his bedchamber in the castle be called a railing? And had his hands been anywhere near the balustrade when Fairfax's lightning had come down?

He could not recall at all.

His heart pounded with dread.

13 April, YD 1021

The day after his mother learned that he, and not she, would be the next sovereign of the Domain, when she realized that her own death was imminent and that this particular vision, long thought of as insignificant, was actually anything but.

I have been waiting for this vision to return. Thankfully I did not have to wait too long.

Finally I see the young man's face. I had suspected that it would be Titus, but now I know it is. He appears to be asleep at first, his hand over an old book—my copy of the Crucible, or something else? Now he rises, checks the time, fourteen minutes after two, and walks out to the balcony.

But what does this all mean? I feel as if I should know but I do not.

17 April, YD 1021

The very last entry. It would fill two entire pages, front and back, then snake around all the margins. Only the first few paragraphs would deal with the actual vision. The rest consisted of instructions to Titus, what he should do, what he must learn, and how he was to accomplish this impossible task that she had realized would be his.

He had come hoping to vindicate Fairfax's place in his life. Now all he wanted was for there to be no more details that would tilt the balance in Wintervale's favor. As long as nothing forced him to conclude that it must be Wintervale, he would go on believing that his destiny lay with Fairfax.

I wish so much of this vision was not from the back, for I love looking upon my son's face in the moments before the elemental phenomenon shakes him. Yes, I know now that it will be an elemental phenomenon and I know now what a dreadful turning point it will be.

Has already been.

But until then, he smiles, my son, his face bright with joy and anticipation.

It was all Titus could do not to scream.

He had not smiled before Fairfax's lightning had come down—had emerged from the Crucible aching and grim. But before Wintervale's arrival, he had been dreaming of Fairfax.

And fool that he was, he had grinned from ear to ear in utter happiness, when everything was about *Wintervale*. And had always been.

He closed the diary and buried his face in his hands.

So quiet, almost unnoticeable, the sound of dreams splintering.

CHAPTER ✦ 9

The Sahara Desert

TITUS FELL ONTO THE JAGGED chunks of rock that littered the bottom of the tunnel. The contact drove flares of bone-scraping pain into his back. He clenched his teeth, hooked his boots with Fairfax's, and yanked her back a few inches. "What is wrong?"

She panted as if she had been very nearly strangled. "I don't know. When I moved forward a moment ago, it was as if . . . as if spikes were being pounded into my ears."

The kind of levitation spell they used was not one that required constant attention. For it to suddenly fail usually implied that the mage who wielded the spell had lost consciousness. But she had not. He could only imagine what kind of actual agony had caused her mind to recoil like that.

"Are you better now?"

Her voice was unsteady, bewildered. "Much, much better, after you pulled me back. I feel—I feel almost fine."

Not a timed curse, then, or a reaction to toxic substances in the air.

"Can you widen this tunnel enough for me to get past you? I want to see whether I come across the same thing."

When she had done as he asked, he maneuvered himself to the spot where she began screaming, then *past* the spot. Nothing at all happened to him.

Thinking perhaps it was because he was feet-forward, he turned around and went head first. Still nothing.

"No?" she asked.

"No."

Her breaths echoed in the cramped space. "Let me try again."

"It may not be a good idea." Though he would have probably chosen to do the same.

Her jaw was set. "I know. And sorry about dropping you on your back earlier."

"I was fine."

He made sure he had a hand around her ankle as she crawled forward. The moment she screamed again, he yanked her back. She trembled, her face ashen.

Now he knew why Atlantis was in no hurry. "The one-mile radius is a blood circle."

"What is that?" For the first time there was fear in her voice.

"Advanced blood magic. It will kill you to venture out of the circle."

She swallowed. "Then you had better go. Take the water, take—"

He interrupted her. "You forget that I could be the one who constructed the blood circle."

She blinked. Not cynical enough, this girl. They knew nothing about each other, except that they had ended up in the same place at the same time, with one of them hurt—of course they could be mortal enemies.

"If that is the case," he went on, "I can break it."

Mortal enemies or not, she had provided crucial help for him. And he was not about to abandon her in her hour of need.

Perhaps he was not cynical enough either.

Hope flared in her eyes, but extinguished quickly. "Atlantis would have tried much harder if they knew that the blood circle wouldn't be able to pen me in."

"Maybe they do not know that I am here."

He clambered back to where the blood circle must be and took out his pocketknife. With a bead of fresh blood in his palm, he thrust his hand at the unseen boundary. "*Sanguis dicet. Sanguis docebit.*"

Blood will tell. Blood will show.

No tingling or sensation of heat on his skin, which he would have expected to feel if he were the one responsible for the blood circle.

"Wait," she said.

She extinguished the mage light. In the ensuing darkness, something glimmered faintly before his eyes, an almost transparent wall.

"Does that count as a reaction?" she asked.

He drew his hand back; the darkness became complete. He

thrust his hand forward; again the wall appeared, a phosphorescent latticework. "I did not construct the blood circle, but it would seem I am related to the person who did."

Blood magic had first developed to ascertain kinship. Any voluntarily given drop, no matter to what other purpose it had been put, could still attest to consanguinity.

"Does that mean you can still break the circle?" Her voice betrayed a vibration of excitement.

"No, I will not be able to. I might be able to weaken the circle, but that could simply mean you are killed a bit more slowly if you try to breach it."

In the darkness there was only the sound of her rapid breaths. He called for light. A blue luminescence suffused the length of the tunnel. She sat with her wrists on her knees, her face shadowed.

"It is too early for despair," he said. "We have hardly exhausted all the options."

Her teeth sank into her lower lip. "You know more about blood magic than I do. What do you suggest?"

"First I want to see whether you are related to the person who set the blood circle. It would help if that person has no claim of kinship on you."[7]

She extracted a drop of blood and sent it floating toward the blood circle. Whereas his blood had been immediately absorbed by blood circle, the tiny floating sphere of her blood bounced off like a pebble striking a tree trunk.

That he was related to the one who had set up the blood circle and she not at all raised uncomfortable questions. But he did not bother to ponder those questions—it was not as if he was unaware of the possibility that they had wished each other harm before the memory spells had taken away their pasts.

"By the privilege of kinship," he said in Latin, and offered another drop of his own blood. "I ask that the blood circle harm not one who matters to me."

It was standard language, yet it felt strangely true: the girl mattered to him.

"That should have reduced the potency of the blood circle somewhat. I can put you under a time freeze, which should further protect you. Is there anything you can do to boost your chances of survival? Any remedies that can counteract traumatic injuries brought on by the mage arts?"

She ran her fingers over the top of satchel, then her expression brightened. "I have panacea in here."

His eyes widened—panacea was extraordinarily difficult to come by. "Take a triple dose."

She extracted a vial, counted out three small granules, and swallowed them. "So now that you have weakened the blood circle, you put me under a time freeze, and shove me past?"

"I wish it were that simple. Should you survive, you would still be in critical condition. And I cannot bore through rock, so—"

A loud crack, like a boulder splitting in two. They looked up: the ceiling of the tunnel was fracturing. When she had unknowingly tried to cross the blood circle, she must have signaled her precise position.

And now Atlantis had found her.

"Grab everything," he shouted, lunging toward her.

He took her by the arm and vaulted just as the top of the tunnel pulverized.

CHAPTER · 10

England

SOMETHING WAS WRONG, IOLANTHE WAS certain of it, the sense of foreboding a hard weight upon her chest.

But *what* was wrong?

On the solid, four-poster bed in Kashkari's room, Wintervale snored softly. Kashkari sat in a chair by the bed, a finger sandwich from the tea tray Iolanthe had asked for in hand, reading a novel titled *Frankenstein; or, The Modern Prometheus*. He had given a book called *Twenty Thousand Leagues Under the Sea* to Iolanthe, but she had set it down after the first few lines about a "mysterious and puzzling" phenomenon at sea.

She moved about the room, examining the densely patterned pewter-on-blue wallpaper, straightening the knickknacks on the mantel, and tucking the duvet more securely around Wintervale's feet. His forehead was damp but cool. His eyelids fluttered at her touch, but he slept on.

It always surprised her that Wintervale was not taller than the prince—he seemed to take up so much more room: he never stood in a doorway but with both arms over his head, his hands on the lintel; his speech was always accompanied by a great deal of animated gesticulating; and no matter how much Mrs. Dawlish complained, he continued to slide down banisters and land with huge thumps that reverberated through the entire house.

In a way, he was one of the most rugged, manly-looking boys in the entire school. But at the same time he was also far more childish than the prince, Kashkari, or even someone like Sutherland. Hardly surprising: as long as he remained a child, he wouldn't have to deal with the heavy expectations of being Baron Wintervale's only son.

It had always been there in Wintervale, the fear of being all too ordinary, of being nothing and no one compared to his father. But now he no longer needed to worry. Now he had revealed himself to be a wielder of the kind of elemental powers she could only marvel at.

If only his accomplishment hadn't made Titus, probably the most self-possessed person she knew, act so strange and jittery.

She walked to the window and used a far-seeing spell to scan the gray waters of the North Sea. At the approximate location where Wintervale had created the maelstrom, wreckage bobbed on the choppy waves, but thankfully no bodies—or body parts. And no armored chariots circled overhead, ready to turn their gaze upon the Norfolk coast.

Sea Wolf. That had been the name of the Atlantean skimmer, painted in Greek—ΛΑΒΡΑΞ—white letters against the steel gray of the hull.[8] The ship had gone down so fast; the crew probably hadn't even had time to transmit a distress signal.

A quiet knock came at the door. She turned to see Titus slipping into the room.

"How is he?" he asked.

"I'm not sure," answered Kashkari, setting aside his book. "He said it was something he ate, didn't he? But his stomach doesn't seem to bother him, as far as I can tell. On the other hand he is clammy and his pulse is erratic."

Titus glanced at Iolanthe and her unease surged. Kashkari might not see it but Titus was shaken. No, stricken. She was reminded of the time the Inquisitor suggested that his mother was but using him to fulfill her own megalomaniacal needs.

Titus took Wintervale's pulse. "You two want some fresh air? We can have a maid come sit with him for a bit."

"I'm all right," Kashkari answered. "I can always open the window if I need some air."

"I'll come with you," said Iolanthe.

Titus led the way out. They took a path that skirted the promontory to a ledge underneath an overhang, which could not be seen from the house. The sea swelled below—the storm clouds were encroaching upon the coast, the salt-scented wind cold and insistent. Titus drew a double-impassible circle.

Without waiting for her to prompt him, he recounted what had happened to Wintervale in Grenoble: the trap that had been set by Atlantis, the flight from the square, the dry dock that launched a vessel directly into the North Sea, the Atlantean frigate that appeared almost immediately thereafter.

Throughout the recital, his voice remained completely flat. This was not how one told a triumphant story. Wintervale was a sworn enemy of Atlantis, and a boy whose enthusiasm and amiability belied a deep fear of failure. Today, facing the most perilous moment of his life, pursued by the very enemy that had driven his family into Exile, he had risen to the occasion as few could.

Titus should rejoice, to have such a powerful new ally at hand, and yet he looked like a man condemned.

A nameless fear twisted inside Iolanthe.

"Lady Wintervale must have stunned Wintervale in order to send him away for safety," said Titus. "But Atlantis found him—and the rest you saw."

"Had I been Lady Wintervale, I would have disabled the distress signal on the lifeboat," she said, trying to sound normal. "That was probably what allowed Atlantis to track Wintervale down."

Titus's throat moved. "Would that she had remembered to do so."

He spoke quietly, but the vehemence in his words was a punch to her gut. She could hold herself back no more. "There is something you are not telling me. What is it?"

All at once he looked haggard, as if he had been traveling on foot for months and months, and could scarcely remain upright. She lifted a hand to brace him before she realized what she was doing.

"Just tell me. It can't be worse than leaving me in the dark."

He gazed at her a long moment, the way one would at the dearly departed. Dread strangled her.

"When we read my mother's diary after my Inquisition, do you remember the entry that mentioned my standing on a balcony, witnessing something that would shake me profoundly?"

His words seem to reach her from a great distance, each syllable faint and tinny. She nodded, her neck stiff.

His eyes were on the storm clouds that turned everything in their path gray and dreary. "I had always assumed that she meant the balcony outside my bedchamber at the castle. Whenever I was at the castle, after lunch, I would lie down and use the Crucible—because that was what she had seen in the vision, me waking up with my hand on an old book that might be the Crucible. And I always had Dalbert call me at fourteen minutes past two, the time she had specified in her vision.

"And so it was on the day we met. I was awakened at fourteen minutes past two. I walked out onto my balcony. And barely a minute later, your lightning."

For some reason, the fact that he had it timed to the minute filled her with horror. Or perhaps it was the way he spoke, like an automaton, as if he could only get the words out by pretending they had nothing to do with him.

With *them*.

"This afternoon," he went on, "I woke up at exactly fourteen minutes after two, and walked onto a balcony."

She stared at him. Had she somehow drunk as much cognac the night before as Kashkari? She was unsteady on her feet, and all ash and grit inside her mouth. "Do you mean to tell me that your mother's prophecy actually referred to Wintervale, and not me?"

Her voice, tentative and thread-thin, barely sounded like her own.

He nodded slowly, still not looking at her.

Her voice shook. "You are sure?"

He stood still, his expression completely blank. The next moment he was on his knees, his hands over his face. Shock burned through her. This was a boy who had held himself together even in the midst of an Inquisition. But now he was falling apart in front of her.

Numbness spread in her, gray and wooden. She did not understand anything at all. How could Wintervale be the Chosen One when it was up to her to brave the dangers, defeat the Bane, and keep Titus alive throughout it all?

"I am sorry," came Titus's barely audible words. "I am so sorry."

She only shook her head—and kept shaking her head. This was her destiny, her *destiny*, not an old jacket that could be handed down to someone else.

He was wrong. He had to have made a mistake.

"Show me your mother's diary," she said. "I want to read those visions for myself."

A minute later, the diary was in her hand. The words that appeared swam a little, but she pored over them with a resolve that felt almost frivolously optimistic next to his bleak hopelessness.

When she came across the beginning of the last entry, he said, "This was when I knew. I smiled today, when I woke up, because I had been dreaming of you."

Pressure built behind her eyes, a pain that was not going away. She kept reading.

Suddenly everything makes sense. This is not some random sighting, this is the moment Titus first comes into his destiny. Everything I had learned so far about elemental magic and elemental mages points to a revelatory feat that announces the arrival on the scene of an extraordinary elemental mage.

The boy who should have been the great elemental mage of my generation was said to have brought a dead volcano back to life, the eruption visible for hundreds of miles. (He is also said to have died young of illness, but Callista had informed me in strict confidence that the then-Inquisitor Hyas had told her that no, the boy's own family had killed him, rather than let him be taken into the local Inquisitory's custody.)

This, then, is most likely what Titus is witnessing, the manifestation of the great elemental mage who would be, as he would say in a different vision, his partner for the task.

She was utterly confused. "That's it? As *you* would say in a different vision? Is she talking about that conversation we had the day I came to Eton, when you first told me what you planned to do?"

The irony might kill her outright.

"I have never come across the vision she mentioned."

Iolanthe had always regarded Princess Ariadne's visions with something approaching awe. Their accuracy and almost eerie relevance had opened her mind to the possibility that she might be meant for something greater than a professorship, and might have a responsibility to look out for not just herself and Master Haywood, but the world at large.

So it was with a sense of disorientation that she saw for the first time how much Princess Ariadne's visions depended on Titus's action in order to become fulfilled. Years ago, she had read something that dealt with this paradox of a prophecy coming to pass because—and only because—those who had seen the prophecy worked tirelessly to make it happen.

What was the term for it?

"Created reality," she said.

"What?"

"You follow her prophecies to the letter, for them to come true."

He looked uncomfortably defensive. "One can never change what has already been preordained."

Growing up, she had heard that a hundred times. Everyone had. "Not standing in a prophecy's way is not the same as giving up your entire life to make every last detail of reality match what she had set down decades ago."

"I do not know of any other way to make this work."

He looked so defeated, the back of her throat stung.

The rest of the entry did not help her cause, as it kept referring to the One. "There is no reason that Wintervale must replace me. We can work together, all three of us."

"But my mother always specified one partner and only one partner."

"Did she forbid you from having more than one?"

"We cannot approach her visions with that kind of glibness. A seer of her caliber comes once every five hundred years and we would have accomplished nothing if it were not for her guidance."

He could be so cynical, her prince, and yet his faith in his mother was heartbreakingly pure.

"But that means you will be headed to Atlantis with Wintervale." The thought made her blood run cold. "Then you will be as good as dead."

"I *am* as good as dead—it is all written in the stars. I had thought . . . I had thought I would have you." His eyes dimmed. "But I cannot argue with the force of destiny."

She gripped his arm. "Do I not also have the force of destiny on my side? It was your mother who wrote the very words that led me to summon my first thunderbolt. You might be dead today if I hadn't killed the Bane in the Crucible. Not to mention that I was born on the night of the meteor storm—you can't mean to tell me that Wintervale's birth date had been falsified too."

"But my mother was never one of those who predicted the birth of a great elemental mage on that night."

"Fine, so birth dates don't matter. But remember, Helgira in the Crucible looks exactly like me. That has to mean something, right?"

"Of course it does. But you read what my mother wrote—"

"You are hinging everything on the merest, merest of details. Your mother mentioned no names. You saw me bring down a bolt of lightning at fourteen minutes past two o'clock, on a balcony. Isn't that enough? Is our partnership not something worth preserving?"

"If only the choice was mine, you know I would choose you a thousand times every day. But this is not my choice. None of it is my choice. I can only walk the path that has been laid out."

She let go of him, understanding dawning: the diary was not just his mother's words. To him, it *was* his mother, the voice of destiny itself. And he would never disobey Princess Ariadne, in this world or the next. "So this is my dismissal?"

"No!" He cupped her face. "I can never dismiss you from my life. I—"

Don't say it, she shouted in her head. Don't *say it.*

"I love you," he said.

All at once, the wretchedness inside her turned into anger. She shoved the diary back at him. "You don't love me. You loved a convenience—you loved that I happened to fit into your plans."

His eyes were full of hurt bewilderment. "How can you say that?"

"How can I say that? How can *you* say what *you* just said? Who was it that swore up and down that I had a destiny, that I always had destiny even if I didn't know it? Has it even been a fortnight since you told me that you were so glad it was me, that you could not do this with anyone else? But now you could. Now you say 'thank you, but no thank you,' as if I were a kitchen maid to be replaced at will!"

"Iolanthe—"

He rarely called her by her real name. The vast majority of the time, even when they were alone, he addressed her as Fairfax, so as to never get out of the habit.

"No," she said reflexively. "Unless you are about to tell me that you are wrong, there is nothing you can say that I want to hear."

He clutched the diary to his chest, his face ashen. "I am sorry. Forgive me."

After everything they had gone through together, everything they had been to each other, was that all he had to say?

She turned and walked away.

"There you are," cried Cooper, as Iolanthe stalked into the house. "Wintervale is unwell, Kashkari is nursemaiding, and Sutherland is paying a call at a neighbor's house. I was getting bored of my own company. What say you to a game of billiards?"

Iolanthe did not want to take part in such a peaceful pastime. If only Cooper had suggested a few rounds of boxing—as an elemental mage brought up to channel her anger via violence, she was in desperate need to smash her fist into someone's face.

"I don't know how to play," she told Cooper.

"I'll teach you."

He looked so hopeful she hadn't the heart to turn him down. Titus could thrill Cooper by saying no, but that was because Cooper viewed Titus as a demigod, powerful and capricious, not to be reasoned with. Iolanthe Cooper considered a friend, and he was much more sensitive to how his friends treated him.

"Lead the way, then," she said. Wallowing in misery on her own or playing a strange nonmage game—what was the difference?

The first drops of rain struck the windows as they reached the billiard room, which reeked of cigar smoke, the scent embedded in the crimson curtains and the slate-blue wallpaper.

On Iolanthe's turns, Cooper acted as her adviser, explaining angles and shot selections. When Iolanthe sank her first ball, he clapped. "Well done, Fairfax. Soon you'll be as good at the table as you are on a cricket pitch."

And a fat lot of good that would do her. But she said nothing.

On Cooper's next turn, as he circled the table, strategizing, he asked, "Did you really say last night that you might be leaving us for the American West?"

Her hand tightened on the cue stick. She hadn't thought at all of what to do with herself, now that she was no longer required for the Great Endeavor. "My parents are not good planners. Tomorrow it could be quite a different scheme."

"If you don't want to go out to the Wyoming Territory, you could come and work at my father's firm," said Cooper, with wholehearted hope. "Maybe lawyering wouldn't be so terrible, if I had a friend nearby. And you'd make a good solicitor—I'd stake money on it."

She didn't know why her eyes prickled all of a sudden—perhaps it just felt good to be needed.

This was something she had not appreciated enough: as petrifying as it was to be informed that she was the key to the Bane's downfall, it had been, at the same time, an enormous compliment. To be singled out like that meant she was special, that her existence mattered.

Now, the opposite: that she did not matter and was not special, and any illusions of grandeur were but that, illusions.

And to hear that from the boy for whom she had risked her life more than once, traveled half of the circumference of the Earth, and with whom she was going to . . . She could not bear to think of the Queen of Seasons' summer villa, now swept clean of flower petals.

"Thank you for that offer," she told Cooper, and briefly gripped his shoulder. "It's very much appreciated."

Cooper looked both pleased and embarrassed. "Well, think about it."

She could not. Any attempt to responsibly and realistically consider the future was like breathing water, a sharp, indescribable pain that radiated deep into every cavity of her skull.

It was all she could do to hold herself together, so that she did not involuntarily burn down Sutherland's uncle's house.

Every breath was despair.

Part of Titus was convinced he was being punished for having been too happy, for forgetting that life's cruelties were never far away. The other part was a crazed prisoner, screaming in the dungeons, unheard by the outside world.

When the rain started in earnest, he vaulted back to the laboratory, to safely stow away his mother's diary. Then he left in an unholy hurry, so that he would not be tempted to pick up the diary and throw it across the room.

Why must he give up Fairfax? Why, if he was a prisoner of his destiny, could he not have his little window, his small square of the blue sky above?

Back at Baycrest House, he stood a long time outside the door of the billiard room, listening to the crisp sounds of cue stick striking ivory, and to Cooper's involved explanation on how she ought to place her next shot.

How could he make her understand that he needed her as much as ever? More, probably: the mere thought of ushering Wintervale to the Commander's Palace in the uplands of Atlantis made him want to crawl into a deep, dark place and never come out again.

Cooper started talking about plans for the Half, another tennis tournament before it became too damp to play on the lawn, a chess competition for those dark, rainy nights, and what did Fairfax think of him getting a guinea pig to keep in his room?

Titus could almost feel her grief as Cooper chattered on. She would have enjoyed all these things, the guinea pig included, in a different time, when Eton was her refuge and her link to normalcy. Without her destiny, the school was just a place with lavatories she could not use.

He left then, because he could not stand the pain in his own heart. He did not want to go see Wintervale, but he made himself head in the direction of Kashkari's room: none of this could be blamed on Wintervale, who was as much Fortune's fool as the rest of them.

A worried-looking Kashkari was in the passage outside the room.

"What is the matter?" asked Titus.

"I went to the water closet. When I came back, Wintervale was on the floor, unconscious. He said he couldn't remember what happened and he wouldn't let me send for a physician. I got him back into bed and I was just about to go down and ask you whether I should disregard his wishes and send for one anyway."

"Better not. His mother is distrustful of physicians who are strangers to her. Wintervale takes after her in that respect."

"But what if he has a concussion?"

"And what can a physician do if he does have a concussion?" Titus had only the most rudimentary knowledge of nonmage medicine; he hoped he was correct here.

"True," Kashkari conceded. "But what about the possibility of cranial bleeding?"

"Let me see him."

Wintervale was awake.

"I hear you got out of bed and fell down," said Titus.

Wintervale looked sheepish. "I woke up and nobody was here, so I thought I'd get up and join everyone. Maybe I was just weak from hunger."

Titus doubted it. Wintervale had mentioned mages falling unconscious in Grenoble. He had been in the vicinity; he could very well have inhaled something.

"Fairfax asked for a tea tray for you earlier," Kashkari said. "There's still half a smoked salmon sandwich and two pieces of Madeira cake."

Titus shook his head. "No, nothing more taxing than plain toast."

Kashkari was already headed for the door. "I can go get some from the kitchen."

"Would you?" Wintervale said gratefully.

When Kashkari had left, Wintervale asked for Titus's help to walk him to the water closet.

"Do I remember you telling me last Half that Atlantis was hunting for a mage who brought down a bolt of lightning?" asked Wintervale as he shuffled along with the gait of an arthritic old man.

"Last I heard, they are still searching."

He maneuvered Wintervale into the water closet and waited outside. When Wintervale was done, he leaned on Titus to walk back. "Why exactly does Atlantis want a powerful elemental mage?"

"They never told me and I hope you will not have to find out."

"So . . . what do I do?" Wintervale sounded fearful.

You go back in time. You leave that square when your mother tells you to. You never encounter the armored chariots. You never sink Atlantean ships. And you never destroy anything that is priceless to me.

"What do you want to do?" Titus said carefully. He was almost sure he did not sound bitter.

"I don't know. I don't want to sit at home and cower. I don't dare ask any Exiles for help finding Mother—she always said that there were informants among the Exiles. I don't know where our money is kept and I don't know anyone who isn't either an Exile or an Etonian."

"Atlantis watches me at school," said Titus, helping Wintervale back onto the bed. "So if you are trying to hide from them, school is not the best place for you. I can loan you the funds for you to lie low somewhere."

Fortune shield him, he was deliberately trying to push Wintervale away.

"Let me think about it," Wintervale said, biting his lips. "For a moment I was really happy. We were going to join the rebellion and finally I would have a purpose. But now . . . I don't know what to do anymore."

Titus's chest constricted: Fairfax could have said those exact words.

Kashkari came through the door, bearing a tray with a cup of tea and a few slices of toasted bread.

"You all right?" he asked Wintervale. "Haven't taken a turn for the worse, have you?"

"No," answered Wintervale. "Not yet."

Food turned out to be a disastrous idea. Wintervale began to retch almost as soon as he had swallowed the last of his tea and toast. Then he emptied the entire contents of his stomach into the chamber pot.

And just when they thought he was finished, the retching would begin all over again, until Titus was sure he must be heaving up his spleen, and perhaps his appendix too.

During a lull between Wintervale's abdominal episodes, Kashkari pulled Titus aside. "He must see a doctor. If it continues like this, he could become dangerously dehydrated."

"I might have something that could help him," Titus said. "Let me look in my luggage."

He left the room and vaulted to his laboratory, where there were thousands of remedies. The problem was that he was not a trained physician. He could not tell what ailed Wintervale and the antiemetics he had on hand each had rather specific applications. He eliminated those having to do with pregnancy, food poisoning, motion sickness, and an overconsumption of alcohol, but that still left him with dozens of choices.

He took a handful of those most likely to be useful and returned to Wintervale's bedside.

"You carry all these medications with you for stomach troubles?" asked Kashkari, sounding both impressed and baffled.

"Delicate constitution, what can I say?"

Titus measured out a spoonful of an antidote—he was beginning to suspect that perhaps the Atlantean frigate that had caught up to the ship launched from the dry dock had put something in the water, so that those who jumped ship would find themselves disabled. And perhaps some of the waves had washed over Wintervale as his dinghy sped away.

Wintervale swallowed the antidote and lay quiet for a few minutes. Titus sighed in relief.

Wintervale jerked up and vomited again.

Titus swore and gave him a remedy intended for magical ailments—perhaps a curse had been directed specifically at Wintervale. Wintervale vomited blood.

"What are you giving him?" cried Kashkari. "Does it contain bee venom, by any chance? He's allergic to bee venom."

"I am giving him the most advanced German medicine," Titus retorted, as he grabbed a handkerchief and wiped the blood from Wintervale's chin. "And it contains no bee venom whatsoever."

"For God's sake, don't give him any more."

"Surely you have *something* that'll work," rasped Wintervale.

Titus looked through the rest of the tubes. *Vertigo. Appendicitis. Bilious complaint. Infection-related emesis. Inflammation of the stomach lining. Foreign expulsion.*

He picked the last one, an elixir that should cause any harmful substance in the body to precipitate and be expelled.

"Try this and pray hard."

They must not have prayed hard enough, for Wintervale immediately went into a seizure.

CHAPTER ◆ 11

The Sahara Desert

WIND SHRIEKED, AS FIERCE AS that of a hurricane. Sand obscured the sky and pelted Titus's person. He and Fairfax were back in the same spot where they had been before she took them below the surface, and thankfully they had not materialized right on top of an Atlantean.

But Titus was disoriented: he thought Atlantis's own elemental mages had cleared the airspace inside the blood circle, in order to facilitate their search.

"It's my doing," said Fairfax into his ear. "I didn't want us to be seen."

Except now they also could barely see beyond their outstretched hands.

"*Deprehende metallum,*" she murmured.

Her wand turned some thirty degrees in her hand. He goggled at her—her spell aimed to detect the presence of metal and the only big, metallic items nearby were the armored chariots. But the idea was just mad enough to make sense. And if he remembered correctly, an armored chariot had landed only a short distance away.

He drew a sound circle and outlined a plan of action to Fairfax. She listened, her expression grave.

"You can pilot an armored chariot?"

"It is my understanding that it operates on the exact same principle as a beast-drawn chariot. But that is the easy part."

Or at least, easy compared to the problem of her survival.

She slowly exhaled. "Let's carry it out, then. May Fortune walk with you."

"No need to be so noble and stoic." He squeezed her hand. "Save that for when you are actually dying."

Which could be in a few short minutes, if everything they had done proved inadequate to preserve her life.

"I am going to be as noble and stoic as I like," she rebutted, "so that years down the road, you will still grow misty-eyed when you remember that impossibly valiant girl from the Sahara, before you fall face-first into your drink."

Her words were arch, but her hand trembled in his. Suddenly, the idea of losing her became unthinkable.

"And you, by then a toothless crone, will smack me on the back of the head and shout at me not to fall asleep at ten o'clock in the morning." He pulled her to him and kissed her on her cheek. "You will die, but not today, not if I have anything to say about it."

They crawled underneath the nearest armored chariot. On the ground, the vehicle resembled a heavy-bellied bird, squat and ungainly. But armored chariots had never been about elegance, only deadliness.

Titus's shoulders almost touched the boots of a pair of soldiers. The soldiers, despite their protective gear, had their arms raised to their faces to shield against the sandstorm, as Fairfax whipped the desert inside the blood circle into an even greater frenzy.

He did his best to breathe slowly, with control—once he made his first move, there was no stopping until he had carried it through.

Or failed altogether.

She laid a hand on his shoulder, signaling that the sandstorm was as violent as she could make it. He took another deep breath and mouthed, *Tempus congelet. Tempus congelet.*

The chaos of the scene provided a rare opportunity to apply a time-freeze spell to each Atlantean soldier. This gave Titus approximately three minutes.

He and Fairfax ducked out from underneath the armored chariot, took the soldier's wands, which were in the shape of an octagonal prism, and hurried toward the armored chariot's starboard hatch. The seam of the hatch was barely visible, but when they flipped open two small round covers and pushed the Atlantean wands into the protected openings underneath, the hatched opened quietly.

The interior of the armored chariot was suitably austere for a military transport vehicle, all steel sides and titanium ribs. Titus applied the time-freeze spell to the pilot before the latter could turn around.

He and Fairfax climbed into the armored chariot and shut the hatch. Immediately he applied the time freeze to her. A mage under a time freeze was immune to most spells and curses; he hoped it would offer her extra protection against the blood circle. If not, at least it should delay her reaction for a few minutes.

He strapped her into one of the harnesses attached to the fuselage and sprinted to the pilot, dodging handhold straps that hung from the ceiling. The pilot's wand was already wedged in an octagonal opening next to the seat.

In front of the pilot, rising up from slots on the floor, were a set of reins. Titus wrapped his hands around the pilot's, picked up the reins, and shook them. The armored chariot rose, silent except for the relentless assault of the sandstorm.

He banked and turned the armored chariot's nose around. The place where Fairfax had signaled her location was at the eastern rim of the blood circle. He pointed the armored chariot southwest.

A glance backward showed Fairfax motionless, looking perfectly normal for someone under a time-freeze spell.

Now it was all a matter of luck.

He pushed the armored chariot to its maximum speed, using the clock by the pilot's seat to gauge the amount of time he had remaining. At one minute fifteen seconds into his flight, he yanked hard on the reins. The chariot came to a sudden halt and would have thrown him against the viewports if he had not held on to the strapped-in pilot.

He ran back, opened the hatch, unstrapped Fairfax, and dropped her to the ground. Then he closed the hatch, turned the vehicle around, and raced back toward the blood circle, using the gauges on the dashboard to retrace his path exactly. Upon arrival, he parked the vehicle in the same orientation as earlier, leaped out, closed the hatch behind him, returned the wands to the soldiers, and vaulted.

But when he reached the spot in the desert where he had left Fairfax, she had disappeared without a trace.

CHAPTER · 12

England

TITUS CRASHED INTO THE LABORATORY and extracted a vial of granules, each one worth his weight in gold.

Panacea.

When he returned to Baycrest House, Kashkari was struggling to keep Wintervale from choking on his own tongue. Titus took hold of Wintervale's head and somehow managed to force a double dose of panacea down the latter's gullet.

Almost immediately, Wintervale's convulsion subsided into mere quivers. Beads of sweat appeared on his brow and his upper lip. He panted, even as a bit of color returned to his face. Within ten minutes, he had dropped off into an exhausted slumber.

Kashkari wiped the perspiration from his own brow. "Now that's German medicine I wouldn't mind keeping around."

Titus looked at his watch—they needed to be back at Mrs. Dawlish's before lights-out. "We had better get him to the railway station," he said, still panting with afterfright, "or we will miss our train."

Kashkari gripped the back of a chair, likewise breathing heavily. "We have all these strong backs—getting him there is the least of our concerns. I just hope the movement of the train won't disagree with him."

"He will be all right," said Titus.

Wintervale had enough panacea in him to survive an execution curse, let alone a little rattling from a railway car.

"I hope to God you are right," said Kashkari. "I hope to God."

Iolanthe shared a rail compartment with Cooper and Sutherland, where they played a game of vingt-et-un, betting halfpennies on the outcome of each hand. In the next compartment, the other three boys maintained an unbroken silence. Before they boarded the train, the prince had pulled her aside and let her know that Wintervale was under the effect of panacea. She had nodded and walked back to Cooper.

Vingt-et-un was the easiest nonmage card game she had played yet, since she had only to worry about the numbers on her cards adding up as close to twenty-one as possible without going over. But even so, she begged off from further rounds after they changed trains in London. Leaving the compartment, she stood in the corridor, staring out of the window as the city's outskirts rushed by, street lamps and illuminated windows growing more and more sparse as they headed into the countryside.

The door of the next compartment opened and closed. Her heart twisted. But the person who came to stand next to her was not Titus, but Kashkari.

"I was sorry to hear that you might leave us," he said.

He was talking about the Fairfaxes and cattle ranching in Wyoming Territory.

"All I wanted was for everything to continue as before. But changes come and I can't stop them." She glanced at him. "You know how it is."

Kashkari smiled faintly. "In my case it was more like, 'Be careful what you wish for.' I have always wanted to meet the girl of my dreams."

"Love at first sight, eh?"

"More like astonishment at first sight."

"She is that beautiful?"

Kashkari had a faraway look in his eyes. "Yes, she is, but I have always known what she looks like. I was shocked to see her in the flesh, when and where I least expected it."

They must have passed a church; the sound of bells tolling was just audible above the rumble of the train. Iolanthe wondered, half in despair, whether there was anything more for her to say than "I'm sorry." She truly felt terrible for him—and she wished she had better comfort to offer than tired phrases that had no meaning anymore.

Then she was staring at Kashkari. *I have always known what she looks like. The girl of my dreams.* "Do you mean to tell me, you have *literally* seen her at night, as you lie asleep?"

Kashkari sighed. "Except my dreams failed to let me know that she would be engaged to my brother."

Was Kashkari talking about *prophetic* dreams? "Remember last Half, when you told me that an astrologer advised you to attend Eton? My knowledge of astrology is very shallow, but enough to know that the stars rarely give such specifics. Was the astrologer interpreting a dream for you instead?"

"Good deduction. Yes, he was."

"What did you see?"

"The first dream had me walking around Eton. I didn't know where I was, but after I'd seen the same dream a few times, I asked my father about this school in an English river town, with the ramparts of a castle visible in the distance. I drew for him the outline of the castle. He didn't recognize it, but when he showed it to a friend who'd been to England several times, the friend did, and said it looked like Windsor Castle.

"I didn't go to the astrologer with that dream—I thought it simply meant I would someday visit the area. But then I started seeing a different dream, of dressing myself in these strange, non-Indian clothes and looking in the mirror. We found out that the clothes were the Eton uniform. That was when we consulted the astrologer, who said my stars proclaimed that I would spend most of my youth away from home. After the consultation, my mother turned to me and said, 'I guess now we know where you are headed.'"

"That's . . . rather amazing," said Iolanthe, rather amazed.

She didn't know nonmages dreamed like this about the future, but it was narrow-minded of her to assume that only mages could tap into the flow of time, since visions had nothing to do with either subtle or elemental magic.

"It sounds occult, so I don't go around telling everyone. I mean, people here are very fond of their séances, but still."

"I understand," said Iolanthe.

They were nearing Slough when she remembered to ask, "So . . . does this mean you weren't in love with the girl of your dreams, only that you kept seeing her?"

She hoped so for Kashkari's sake.

"I wish." Kashkari sighed. "I have been in love with her all my life."

Titus knocked on Fairfax's door. "You there, Fairfax?"

A long silence elapsed before her response came. "Yes."

A high wall of an answer. *Yes, I am here, but you are not welcome.*

It was almost lights-out at Mrs. Dawlish's. One last batch of boys was coming out of the lavatory. Hanson asked whether anyone had seen his Greek lexicon, which prompted Rogers to run to his room and get it. Sutherland, whose room was across from Cooper's, called for Cooper to open his door; when Cooper did, a pair of socks flew across the width of the corridor, along with a "You took off your socks in my room again!"

She had loved this: the normalcy and silliness of so many boys squeezed into tight quarters. Titus set his hand against her door and wished that he could force time to flow backward. "Good night," he said, hating the futility of it all.

She said nothing.

Down the hall, Kashkari emerged from Wintervale's room—despite Titus's reassurance that Wintervale's condition would not worsen while he slept, Kashkari had elected to remain by Wintervale's side.

Titus walked over to Kashkari. "How is he?"

"Same. Sleeping soundly, vitals strong—as far as I can tell." Kashkari hesitated a moment. "Are you absolutely sure you did not give him anything with bee venom as an ingredient?"

"Yes, I am sure," said Titus, not particularly caring whether Kashkari believed him. "Good night."

His head throbbed as he walked once more into his laboratory after lights-out. He had a three-hundred-mile one-time vaulting range and had never yet vaulted enough to establish the upper limit for a personal daily range. But with all these trips to the laboratory in the past twenty-four hours, he might be approaching that boundary.

He had brought with him all the remedies that he had taken out of the laboratory: the panacea and the miscellany of remedies that had given Wintervale so much trouble. Titus preferred to be neat—he had very little time to lose to disorganization—but this night he could not handle the otherwise simple task of reshelving the remedies, beyond collecting the vials into a pouch and shoving the pouch into an empty drawer.

The panacea, however, could not be so cavalierly treated. That particular vial he put back into its proper place in the emergency bag he had prepared for Fairfax.

He traced his fingers along the strap of the bag, one of the places where he had left hidden messages for her. He had better erase the messages, which dealt not with their task but with sentiments that were easier to set down in writing than to speak out loud. But he did not want to; it would be almost like erasing her wholesale from his life.

Exhaustion washed over him—not just fatigue, but the loss of hope.

He took a dose of vaulting aid to help with his headache, sat down at the long worktable at the center of the laboratory, and opened his mother's diary. It was the cruelest master he had ever known, but it remained his only trusted guide in an ever-shifting landscape.

February 25, YD 1021

I hate death visions. I especially hate death visions of those I love.

Titus almost closed the diary. He did not want to be reminded of the details of his death, details that made it real and inescapable.

But he could not help reading on.

Or, for that matter, a death that would distress someone I love. But I suppose there is no way around it. Death comes when it pleases and the survivors must always grieve.

He exhaled. It was not his death. Whose was it then?

Fog, a thick yellowness, like butter that had been dropped in dirt. A few seconds pass before I can distinguish a face in the fog. I recognize it immediately as belonging to Lee, dear Pleione's son.

Wintervale.

He is still a young boy, but several years older than he is now, staring out from behind a closed window at the dense, shifting fog that seemed to be pushing against the glass, looking for a way in.

He is in a bedroom. His, perhaps. I cannot tell, as it is furnished with a great deal of somberness, in a style foreign to my eyes.

No sounds inside or outside the house. I begin to think this might be a silent vision when he sighs audibly, a sound too wistful, too heavy with loss and yearning for a child so young, a child who should want for nothing.

A shriek shatters the quiet. Lee recoils, but runs to the door of his room and shouts, "Are you all right, Mama?"

He is answered by another blood-curdling shriek.

He runs into a corridor—it is a fine house, I am sure, but feels too shabby and cramped for someone of Baron Wintervale's fabulous wealth.

Now he is in a larger, more ornate bedroom. Pleione has thrown herself over the body of her husband. She is sobbing uncontrollably.

"Mama? Papa?" Lee stands by the door, as if afraid to move. "Mama? Is Papa . . ."

Pleione trembles—Pleione, who has always been so composed, so in control of herself. "Go downstairs and tell Mrs. Nightwood to take you to Rosemary Alhambra's house. And when you get there, ask Miss Alhambra to come and to bring the best physician she can find among the Exiles."

Lee remains where he is.

"Go!" Pleione shouts.

He runs, his footsteps echoing through the corridor.

Pleione returns to her inert husband. Tenderly she cups his face and kisses him on his lips. Her hand trails up and lifts the hair at his temple. I gasped as I saw the faint red dot at his temple, the telltale sign of the execution curse.

So it was true, then. The cause of Baron Wintervale's death had been given as a catastrophic failure of the heart, but rumor had circulated for years that he had died of an execution curse ordered by Atlantis.

He must have been dead for hours, given how muted the red dot had become. By the time Lee returns with Rosemary Alhambra and a competent physician, the dot—and its twin on the other temple—would have disappeared altogether.

Pleione's gaze turns hard. She grips his lifeless hand. "Perhaps the Angels will have mercy. But I will not. I will not forget and I will not forgive."

And then she collapses again upon him and weeps.

My vision ended there. I came out to see Titus playing by himself, tracing a small twig on the surface of the fishpond.

I rushed over and hugged him tight. This surprised him, but he let me go on hugging him for a long time.

I had wondered why, in my vision of Baroness Sorren's funeral, it had been so sparsely attended. Granted she is more admired than beloved, but she commands such extraordinary respect that I had always found the emptiness of her funeral both upsetting and ominous.

Now I understood.

This uprising of ours is going to fail. Few will dare to come and pay their last respects to Baroness Sorren because she will have been executed by Atlantis. And Baron Wintervale, while he might escape in the meanwhile, before long he too will succumb to Atlantis's vengeance.

And me, what about me? Should our effort collapse, would the secret of my involvement be revealed? If so, what would be the consequences?

"Want to come feed the fishies with me, Mama?" Titus asked.

I kissed the top of his head, my sweet, wonderful child. "Yes, darling.

Let us do something together."

While we still could.

Titus remembered that afternoon. They had not only fed the fish, but played several games of siege and gone for a long walk in the mountains. He had felt quite giddy—it was not often that he was the recipient of his mother's undivided attention. But beneath his pleasure, there had been a sense of unease. That somehow it could all be taken away from him.

It had been, only weeks later.

And now again, everything that mattered to him had been wrenched away.

Nothing and no one will take you away from me, Fairfax had said.

Nothing and no one, except the heavy hand of destiny itself.

It seemed to Iolanthe that she did not sleep a wink, yet in the morning she suddenly jerked awake. It was pitch-dark outside. She called for a bit of fire so she could see the time. Ten minutes to five.

The irony. This was the time she had woken up daily in the last Half. Bleary-eyed, she would throw on some clothes and go to Titus's room, where he would already have a cup of tea waiting for her. A few sips and it was into the Crucible, to train her to the limits of her endurance.

As they waited for the completion of the new entrance to the laboratory—he no longer dared to keep the Crucible at school—training had not yet started for this Half. But she had known it would be even more arduous. Because they had won a battle and not the war. Because the road was long yet.

And now their paths had diverged and hers had run smack into a wall.

She swung her legs over the side of her cot and dropped her face into her hands. How to stop being the Chosen One? How to return to an ordinary life when she had come wholeheartedly to believe that she was the very fulcrum upon which the levers of destiny pivoted?

She washed, dressed, made herself a cup of tea, and sat down at her table to memorize the Latin verses that had been assigned in class, all the while feeling like an actor onstage, performing a choreographed sequence of actions.

I live for you, and you alone.

I am so glad it is you. I cannot possibly face this task with anyone else.

How easily did such fervent declarations lose all their meaning, like the green leaves of summer turning brittle and lifeless with the onset of winter. He had loved her because she was the most integral part of his mission. Now that she was no longer, out she went like yesterday's newspaper.

She could not breathe for the agony in her chest.

And the terrible thing was, her heart—and her mind—understood that she had been discarded, but her body didn't. Her sinews and bones longed to be inside the Crucible, battling dragons, monsters, and dark mages. She couldn't stop her fingers from tapping restlessly against the edge of her table. And every other minute she sprang up from her chair to pace in the room that had become a prison.

It seemed dawn would never come and none of the boys would ever stir from sleep. She leaped in pure relief as she heard footsteps and a knock somewhere down the hall. But hesitation came over her as she gripped the door handle. What if it was Titus?

She yanked open the door all the same.

It was Mrs. Dawlish and her second in command, Mrs. Hancock, who also happened to be a special envoy of Atlantis's Department of Overseas Administration.

Kashkari's door opened at the same moment.

"Morning, Kashkari. Morning, Fairfax," said Mrs. Dawlish, smiling. "You two are up early."

"Those lines don't memorize themselves," Iolanthe replied, injecting into her voice a brightness she did not feel. "And good morning to you, too, ma'am. Morning, Mrs. Hancock."

"I heard from the night watchman that Wintervale had to be carried into the house when you came back last night." Mrs. Dawlish shook her head. "Exactly what wholesome activities were you boys up to at Sutherland's uncle's place?"

"Swimming in frigid waters all day and singing hymns around the hearth all evening, ma'am," said Iolanthe.

"Really?" Mrs. Hancock countered with a raised brow. "Is that so, Kashkari?"

"Close enough." Kashkari came out into the corridor, in his

white tunic and pajama trousers. "But Wintervale didn't come to us until yesterday afternoon. Something he ate on the journey disagreed with him."

Mrs. Hancock opened Wintervale's door, entered, and turned on the gas lamp on the wall. Mrs. Dawlish went in after her. Kashkari and Iolanthe exchanged a glance and followed suit.

Wintervale slept, deeply and peacefully. Mrs. Hancock had to shake him several times before he opened one eye. "You."

Then he was back asleep.

Mrs. Hancock shook him again. "Wintervale, are you all right?"

Wintervale grunted.

Mrs. Hancock turned to Iolanthe and Kashkari. "That's an odd kind of abdominal ailment, isn't it?"

"He was in a bad way last night, puking his guts out," Kashkari answered. "The prince gave him some medicine prepared by the court physician of the . . . the . . ."

"The principality of Saxe-Limburg," Mrs. Dawlish said helpfully.

"Right, thank you, ma'am. I imagine the medicine was probably mostly opium and Wintervale is just sleeping it off."

"And I imagine Herr Doktor von Schnurbin would not be pleased that you are openly discussing the secret ingredients in his most excellent remedies," came the prince's voice from the door.

Iolanthe felt asphyxiated. For as long as she remained at Eton, she would have to play the part of Titus's friend. But now there was no foundation left for their friendship: their shared destiny had been their great bond; without it, she was but a mistake he had made somewhere along the way.

"Good morning, Your Highness," said Mrs. Dawlish. "I don't doubt your remedies have done Wintervale a world of good, but he needs to be seen by a physician."

Iolanthe glanced at Mrs. Hancock. Mrs. Hancock knew who Wintervale was. She probably also knew that Lady Wintervale would never consent to such a thing as his being seen by a nonmage physician. But Mrs. Hancock seemed quite content to let Mrs. Dawlish take charge.

"Better send a cable to his mother, then," said the prince. "She will dispatch their private physician—the Wintervales are very selective in their choice of doctors. And have one of the charwomen sit with him, in case he needs something."

Mrs. Dawlish did not take exception to his imperious tone, but she was quite firm in her own response. "That private physician had better come by tomorrow, at the latest. We are responsible for Wintervale's welfare while he is under our roof and such things cannot wait. Now you boys get ready for early school."

Mrs. Dawlish and Mrs. Hancock left. Kashkari yawned and returned to his own room.

"Fairfax," said the prince.

She ignored him, walked past him to her own door, and closed it.

A faint light was beginning to come through the curtain. She grabbed a tin of biscuits and walked to the window. Another day was dawning. A vapor-like fog undulated close to the ground, but the sky was clear, and soon a rising sun would shed a reddish-gold tint upon the tops of the trees.

The same copse of trees from which she had gazed wistfully at the window of this room, just before she had left the prince, because she had wanted nothing to do with his mad ambitions.

She squinted. Were there people in those trees or were her eyes playing a trick on her? She opened the window and leaned out, but now she could see only trunks, branches, and leaves that largely still clung to the memories of summer, with only a few turning yellow and crimson here and there.

When she was small, every October Master Haywood would take her to see the autumn colors in Upper Marin March, where September and October tended to be clear and sunny. They would stay at a lodge on a lake and wake up each day to the splendor of an entire slope of flame and copper foliage reflected in mirror-bright waters.

Master Haywood.

Master Haywood.

She thought of him all the time, of course, but in a wistful way, as astronomers longed for the stars they could not reach. But Master Haywood was not separated from her by the vastness of time and space; he was only hidden away.

Guilt charged through her. If she had wanted it badly enough, she would have unearthed *some* useful information by now. Except she, convinced of her greater purpose, had not taken a single step toward locating him.

She marched out of her room and knocked on the prince's door.

"Fairfax!" The glimmer of cautious hope in his eyes made her lungs hurt. He reached forward as if to touch her, but stopped himself. "Please, come in."

She stepped into what had been one of her favorite places.

"Some tea?" He was already moving toward the grate.

She steeled herself. "No, thank you. I only want to ask you if the new entrance to the laboratory is ready."

He stilled. "It will be by this afternoon."

"Is it all right if I make use of it? I need to look up some things in the reading room."

"Yes, of course. You are more than welcome to it. Anytime."

That undertow of despair, was it hers, or his? She clutched her hands together behind her back. "That's very kind of you, Your Highness. Thank you."

"Is there anything else I can do for you?"

"No, thank you."

He looked back at her. "Are you sure?"

"Yes, I am sure," she made herself say.

She returned to her room and leaned for a minute against the door.

So this was what it had come to, this stilted courtesy, like that of a divorced couple who must still deal with each other.

With she being the one who hadn't found anyone else, of course.

CHAPTER · 13

The Sahara Desert

TITUS SPUN AROUND, FEAR LIKE a dagger in his lungs. He was about four miles out from the blood circle. Here the true sandstorm raged and visibility was less than three feet. A blessing, as they could have no better protection from pursuers. But he could not possibly find her, if she had moved as little as—

A hand gripped him around the ankle. His wand was pointed and a savage assault spell about to leave his lips when he realized it was her. She had hidden herself under a layer of sand.

He crouched down, took her by the arm, and pulled her out.

She was barely conscious and he could see smears of blood around her lips, but she managed to open her eyes. "You all right?"

Before he could answer, she vomited a stream of blood into the sand.

He could hardly breathe for the panic that erupted inside him. If the panacea could not keep her alive, then no power he possessed would help.

He cupped her face. "Go to sleep. Go to sleep and you will be fine."

Her eyes closed and she dropped off.

There was no point doing anything except taking shelter. From one of the larger pockets on the outside of Fairfax's satchel Titus unearthed a tent that had been folded down to a tight square. As flying sand struck it, the material of the tent changed from a nondescript green to the exact same color and opacity as the sand—a camouflage tent. Even better, it could be pitched in a number of shapes, some of them quite passable imitations of natural formations. He settled on one that looked like a gentle undulation of the land, maneuvered Fairfax inside, crawled in after her, and sealed the tent from within.

His back again felt as if it were on fire. He took more pain remedies and allowed himself to nap for a bit, jerking awake every time there came the noise of sand against metal—an armored chariot in the vicinity—then dozing off again as the danger receded.

When he woke up for good, he ate half a nutrition cube, and made a thorough study of the contents of her bag. Besides the well-stocked pharmacy, she had just about everything a fugitive could conceivably need, including a raft, heat sheets, hunting ropes, and reins that could be made to fit wyverns, perytons, and assorted other winged steeds.

Each item came with an explanation on its use written on paper as thin as onion skin yet as strong as canvas. Overly detailed explanations, as if the writer had expected the satchel to end up in the hands of someone much less capable than Fairfax.

It was when he progressed to the smallest compartment of the satchel that his brows rose sky high.

> *Atlantean civilian wands, 2.*
>
> *Angel keys, 6.*
>
> *Destination disruptor for Delamer East Interrealm Hub,*
> *Translocator 4.*

Atlantean civilian wands were state issued, each one numbered and registered, used as a means of personal identification. Penalties for reporting theft, loss, or accidental destruction were high, to discourage any Atlantean from owning duplicates.

But duplicates still cropped up periodically on the black market. On the other hand, angel keys, so called because there were no doors they could not open, were far rarer and almost prohibitively expensive. And a destination disruptor tailored to a specific translocator—that could not have been obtained from the black market even if one had a fortune to spend.

Had Fairfax intended to travel to Atlantis by illegal means and, once there, pass herself off as an Atlantean and . . . open doors she had no business opening?

He took her hand. Her pulse throbbed, slow and steady.

The cessation of the sandstorm was as abrupt as that of a summer storm: inundation one moment, clear skies the next. He let go of her hand and listened for a good minute at the opening of the tent before venturing outside to investigate.

Stars were out, bright and innumerable. He squinted, looking for dark moving spots in the sky—without flying sands hitting them and giving away their locations, armored chariots could be descending right above him and he might not know. But for now, no danger loomed overhead.

Their options were remarkably few. She was in no shape to be vaulted—in her current condition, vaulting ten feet could kill her. They had no vehicles and no beasts of burden. Staying in place was out of the question: they were still too close to the blood circle. The farther away they were, the less likely Atlantis would be to find them.

He made ready to walk.

The wind was sharp as icicles. Temperatures had plunged; Titus's nose and cheeks were numb with cold.

His lightweight tunic, however, kept him warm. The hood of the tunic protected the back of his neck and the top of his head; his hands he kept inside the sleeves, only reaching out occasionally to check Fairfax's pulse.

She floated in the air alongside him, her hands tucked in to her own sleeves, most of her head covered by a scarf he had found, and a heat sheet wrapped over her trousers and boots, which were not made of mage material. Around her middle was a hunting rope, mooring her to him.

She slept peacefully.

Every minute or so he pointed his wand behind himself to delete his footprints from the sand. Every thirty seconds he scanned the sky with a far-seeing spell. He was headed southwest. The first squadron of armored chariots he spied flew at top speed toward the northeast, away from them. The next squadron was more inconveniently placed several miles to the south. While not exactly in his path, there was a chance that they might circle around and pass overhead.

He had been walking for about three hours when he spied tors erupting from the ground, like pillars of a ruined palace. He veered toward them. Fairfax was beginning to sink, the levitation spell wearing off. The night was moonless, but the mass of stars overhead gave the air a faint luminosity; in the pitch-black shadows of the rock pillars, it would be safe for him to put her down and rest for a few minutes.

Soon his boots no longer sank inches with every step. But his calves protested with a different sort of strain—the land was rising, slowly but unmistakably. And the rock pillars, which from a distance had seemed remarkably straight and uniform, up close resolved into zigzagging, windblown shapes, some with boulder-like tops that balanced precariously on their sand-worn stems.

Fairfax now floated no higher than his knees, the hem of her tunic occasionally brushing against the ground. He wanted her to stay airborne until they were inside the rock formation. But she was sinking too fast to last the rest of the distance. He untied the hunting rope that connected them and set her down.

Her temperature was fine—no hypothermia setting in. Her pulse was also fine, slow but steady. When he coaxed her awake to drink some water, she smiled at him before returning to sleep.

Did she dream? Her breathing was deep and regular. No frowns or fluttering of the eyelids marred the tranquility of her features, almost invisible except for a slight sheen on her cheek and the ridge of her nose. She did not remotely look like a rebel who wanted to topple empires. He would have guessed her to be an upper academy student, the sort whose competence and dedication would annoy her classmates, were it not for her willingness to help them prepare for their examinations.

He turned her hand in his, staring through the dark at her palm, as if lines he could not even see delineated the events that had led her to this time and place. He raised her hand to his lips. The next moment he realized what he was about to do and dropped her hand in a hurry, embarrassed.

Another far-seeing spell revealed that what he had earlier thought to be a single squadron of three armored chariots to the south were actually three different squadrons. Now that he was standing at a much higher vantage point, he could see the light flooding from their bellies, illuminating every square foot of desert in their path as they circled, searching.

They were drawing nearer. He needed to move Fairfax and himself inside the rock formation, or they would be all too visible to that cold, sharp light.

Most likely, there were other creatures that lived inside the shelter offered by the rock formation. Morning dew that gathered on the underside of stones might provide enough moisture to last a well-adapted creature for days. And when there were lizards and tortoises, there would also be scorpions and snakes. Better that he investigate the terrain, to make sure that he would not put her down on top of a nest of vipers.

Leaving Fairfax under a tensile dome, he headed toward the rock formation. His breath steamed. The ground beneath his feet was slippery, a layer of sand on top of hard stone. And above, a spectacular nightscape, the Milky Way slanting across the arc of the sky, a luminous, silver-blue river of stars.

Against this backdrop reared the nearest of the rock columns. At the top of the column rested a bulbous, impossibly balanced boulder. He stopped and squinted. Something seemed to be swaying on the boulder. A snake? A dozen snakes?

His blood ran cold. Hunting ropes. Of course Atlantis would have placed hunting ropes in such a place, in probably all such places in a fifty-mile radius, shelters that he would gravitate toward when he realized how difficult it would be to remain hidden in the open.

He had stopped in the nick of time. The hunting ropes had just begun to stir, sensing his movement. Now he and they were at an impasse. If he moved, they would come after him—and hunting ropes enjoyed speeds far superior to that of a mage on foot. But if he did not move, he and she would both be caught in the glare of the armored chariots' search lights.

He ran. Behind him, dozens of hunting ropes dropped down, one solid plop after another. His feet pounded; his heavy breaths filled his ears. Yet still he could hear them slithering, far lighter and faster than any real snakes.

He slid into the tensile dome just as they reached him. But his safety was temporary. Already they were digging. The ground beneath the dome was hard and compact, but still, it would only be a matter of time before they came up from under him.

He reached for the emergency bag. As he did so, the edge of his hand brushed against something long and flexible. He jumped, a scream rising to his throat, before he realized that it was the hunting rope fastened to Fairfax's person, *their* hunting rope, and not one about to attack him.

A quick untying spell and the hunting rope loosened from Fairfax, separating into three lengths. He took one length and rubbed it end to end three times. "Bring back a scorpion."

The hunting rope shot out of the tensile dome in the direction of the rock formation. All the other hunting ropes that had been climbing over the tensile dome, or trying to dig underneath, sprinted after it.

What ensued sounded like the ground being whipped with a dozen riding crops.

His hunting rope, while in pursuit, would not stop trying to reach its objective, even if it had been tackled by two dozen other hunting ropes trying to pin it down and tie it up. The hullabaloo should attract all the other hunting ropes in the area, if there were more of them lying in wait, and keep their attention off him.

He gripped Fairfax's hand in relief.

Only to recoil in alarm as a beam of light came around the rock formation, followed by another, and yet another. Above them, silent and dark, armored chariots cut through the night, like beasts of the deep.

CHAPTER · 14

England

IOLANTHE WAS STANDING BY THE window, peeking out from a gap in the curtain, when the prince came into her room.

"What is it?" he asked.

"It's possible I saw someone watching the house from behind the trees in the morning. I couldn't be sure."

"I would not be surprised. As far as Atlantis is concerned, I am still their sole lead to your whereabouts. If I were them, I too would have me under watch."

It made sense. She stepped back from the window. "Shall we go then?"

He offered her his arm so she could hitch a vault with him. She bit the inside of her lower lip: she had not touched him since he had broken the news of his mistake in selecting her as his partner.

But this was life: no matter how dramatic the rift, at some point, the daily mundanities took over again, and they must go on living next door to each other, dining at the same table nightly, and even, occasionally, coming into physical contact.

She set her hand on his forearm and he vaulted them to the interior of a small, empty building, a locked brewery on the grounds of a country house. Apparently it wasn't unusual for the butler of an English estate to brew his own ale, especially as the beverage often figured as part of the servants' compensation. But the current master of the house was a leader of the temperance movement. As a result, the brewing equipment had been scrapped and the facility shuttered.

Titus gave her the password and the countersign. She turned the handle of a broom cupboard door, and walked back into the laboratory for the first time in months. It looked more or less the same: books, equipment, and ingredients neatly arranged on shelves, with many cupboards and drawers the contents of which she had yet to explore, since she had visited so infrequently.

Three times in total, in fact: the first time on the day they met; the next time, when he turned her into a canary; the third time, at the end of Summer Half, just before they traveled back to the Domain together.

She had been incandescent with happiness that last time. They had both been—they had overcome so much and grown so close. She remembered running hand-in-hand with him toward the laboratory, giddy with hope and fearlessness.

It had been a different age of the world altogether.

"Fairfax," he said softly.

She turned around. Their gaze held for a moment. He looked drained; she, probably worse.

He set down the Crucible on the worktable. "Here you go. It is yours for as long as you need."

He spoke with such care, as if she were infinitely fragile and one wrong syllable could shatter her. But she was not fragile—she was a wielder of lightning and flames. *Someday your strength will overturn the world as we know it,* he had once said.

What was she to do now with all that strength, all that power? Pack it away like an overrobe that had gone out of fashion?

"And feel free to make use the laboratory anytime," he added, "now that you can get here easily."

In time she might become less bitter, but now all she heard was the offering of lesser gifts, as if that might make up for his taking away the one thing she truly wanted. "Thank you," she said woodenly, "most kind of you."

An uncomfortable silence followed.

She bit the inside of her cheek, sat down at the worktable, and put her hand on the Crucible. "I'll be off, then."

"If you do not mind me asking, what are you hoping to find in the reading room?"

"The identity of the memory keeper." The one who had defrauded Master Haywood. Iolanthe had no doubt the woman was involved in his disappearance.

Titus looked alarmed. "You will not do anything rash, will you? You are still the one Atlantis wants."

Just no longer the one he needed. All the nuisance of the fugitive life and none of the satisfaction of actually mattering.

"I can't do anything rash until I have the information," she told him.

But she did not go directly to the reading room. Instead, she visited the "The Dragon Princess," one of the most apocalyptic tales in the entire Crucible. Ruins smoldered under a flame-roiled sky; the air was all smoke and ash. High upon the rampart of the last fortress standing, half deafened by dragon screeches, she called down one thunderbolt after another, littering the scorched earth with dead wyverns and unconscious cockatrices.

An elemental mage was always more powerful in a state of emotional turmoil.

The effort depleted her—she had never called down so many bolts of lightning in such a short time. Her fatigue wrapped about her, like a cocoon, and made her feel safe, because she was too tired to feel.

And that was how she made the decision to go to the Queen of Seasons' summer villa.

It was a stunning place, ocher roofs and terraced gardens against the backdrop of a steep, rugged massif. Bright red flowers bloomed in stone urns that must be centuries old; fountains splashed and burbled, feeding into a pond from which rose dozens of pale lavender water lilies, their petals held together like hands at prayer.

The air was fragrant with the scent of honeysuckle, mingled with the sun-warmed, resinous note of the cedar forest that sprawled in the surrounding hills. The temperature was that of a perfect summer day, with enough of a breeze that one was never hot, but also enough heat for a cold beverage to be enjoyable.

On a terrace shaded by climbing vines, such beverages had already been laid out, along with an assortment of ices. She tried one that looked like a pinemelon ice, and was shocked to realize, as the tart, fresh flavors burst upon her tongue, that it was indeed pinemelon ice, which she hadn't tasted in years, since it was a specialty of Mrs. Hinderstone's sweets shop, on University Avenue, just minutes from the campus of the Conservatory of Magical Arts and Sciences, where she and Master Haywood had lived.

Footsteps echoed. She turned around to see Titus coming out from the open doors of the villa, about to start down the steps that led to the terrace. He froze as he saw her. Her cheeks scalded; he looked as mortified as she felt.

After an interminable silence, he braced his hand on the balustrade of the steps and cleared his throat. "How do you find the ice?"

"Very palatable." She managed to find her voice. "I've only ever had the pinemelon-flavored one at Mrs. Hinderstone's in Delamer."

"When I was in Delamer this summer, I had Dalbert bring me some of Mrs. Hinderstone's ices to try—since you mentioned the place."

She had mentioned it only once, in passing, when they were discussing something else altogether. "Did you like them?"

"I did, especially the lumenberry flavor. But the pinemelon is nice too."

"Master Haywood always had the lumenberry. I preferred the pinemelon."

"I was hoping one of them would be your favorite," he said quietly.

From what he had told her, it was not difficult to modify details in a story inside the Crucible: one only had to write the changes in the margins of the pages. So it was not as if he had sneaked back into the Domain and smuggled out the ices against all odds. But still something fluttered in her stomach, followed by a feeling of constriction in her chest.

He had wanted everything to be perfect.

And it would have been.

It would have been.

At her silence, he cleared his throat again. "I was just about to leave. Enjoy your ice."

He disappeared on the tail end of those words, leaving her alone in a place where they were supposed to be together.

She had come because she had not been able to help her curiosity. However difficult the experience might prove, she had wanted to see the place he had prepared for her—for them. Why had he come back? He already knew exactly what he had done with the place.

Because she wasn't the only one who wished that the maelstrom had never happened. Who was drawn to the summer villa, despite the pain it would cause, to imagine what it would have been like, had things been different.

She wiped at her eyes with the heel of her hand.

How did one fall out of love without falling apart at the same time?

The reading room, the main library in the teaching cantos of the Crucible, was vast. It might very well be infinite, for all Iolanthe knew: shelves went on until they converged into a single point in the distance.

She approached the help desk—an empty station near the door—and said, "I would like everything available on Horatio Haywood from the last forty years."

Books populated the shelf behind the desk: compilations of student-run newspapers on which he had served as reporter and editor; journals that published his scholarly articles; the dissertation he had written for his Master of the Art and Science of Magic degree from the Conservatory.

She picked up his dissertation. There had been a copy of it in their home, which she had tried to read as a little girl and had understood nothing of. But now, as she flipped through the pages, her eyes grew wider and wider. She knew Master Haywood's research specialty had been archival magic, which dealt with the preservation of spells and practices no longer in popular usage. But she'd had no idea that his dissertation revolved around memory magic.

In the dissertation, Master Haywood traced the development of memory magic and chronicled the remarkable precision of the spells at the height of its popularity.[9] One could erase memories by the hour—by the minute if one really wanted to. And by the outlines of precise, concrete events. Enjoyed oneself enormously at a party, with the exception of a drunken kiss? With one quick wave of the wand, it would be as if the kiss had never happened—the party was now a long, unmarred stretch of outstanding memories.

She left the reading room reluctantly—there were set times in the day, called Absences, when Mrs. Dawlish and Mrs. Hancock counted their boys, to make sure the latter hadn't gone missing. The prince was still in the laboratory, seated opposite her, flipping the pages of his mother's diary.

It was as if a fist had closed around her heart, seeing him spending time with his one true love.

He looked up. "Did you find anything useful?"

She was determined to speak normally. "Master Haywood did his dissertation on memory magic, the kind that the memory keeper eventually applied on him."

"So he supplied the expertise that was used against him?"

"Probably."

He was silent for a moment. "Do you want to find out whether *you* have memory lapses?"

The question astonished her. "Me?"

He pointed his wand at himself. *"Quid non memini?"*

What do I not remember?

A line appeared in the air, straight and marked at regular intervals, like a tape measure. With a wave of his wand, the line moved closer to Iolanthe, so she could see that it was a timeline, divided into years, months, weeks, and days. About three-fifths of the timeline was white, the rest red.

She had never seen anything like it. Even Master Haywood's dissertation had mentioned nothing of the kind. "This represents the state of your memories?"

"Yes."

"What happened when you were eleven?" Three days short of eleven, actually. That was when the line abruptly turned red.

"I learned that I would die young. And I decided to rid myself of the memories of the details of the prophecy, so I would not be constantly preoccupied with them."

You would not die young, not if I—she barely stopped herself from speaking those words aloud. Wintervale would have to keep him alive now, Wintervale who was not known for his ability to remain cool under pressure.

She said instead, "It's harmful, isn't it, to suppress memories for so long?"

"Depends on how you do it. See those dots?" The dots were black in color and floated above the timeline. The first one coincided with the color change of the timeline, the rest were distributed at three-month intervals. "They show how often that particular memory is allowed to surface in my mind. The color and shape of the dots assure me that the exact same memory is excised again each time, and that nothing else has been tampered with."

"You worry about people tampering with your memories?"

"It is almost impossible for that to happen without my full consent—the heirs of the House of Elberon are protected by many hereditary spells to make sure they do not become unwitting puppets in the hands of others. But I can do it to myself. This tool reassures me that I have not been persuaded to tamper with my own memories and then forget about it." He waved away the memory line. "Would you like to see the state of your memories?"

"You believe my memories have been tampered with?"

Her question seemed to surprise him. "You do *not* think so? Your guardian is an expert. The memory keeper is another expert. They had a huge secret to protect in you. Between the two of them, it would be almost impossible for you to come through unscathed."

For the longest time she had not known that she could control air, but she had thought her ignorance the result of an otherwise spell. Could it have been caused by memory magic instead?

"Show me, then."

He pointed his wand at her. She gasped: the representation of the state of his memories had been a simple line, but hers was an entire mural. There was almost no part of the nearly seventeen-year-long timeline that had not been tampered with. It showed white for only the first few months of her life. Then all colors of the rainbow appeared, some in several gradations. Above the timeline were not only dots, but triangles, squares, and pentagons—all the way to dodecagons. And whereas on the prince's memory line, the dot that represented his suppressed memory stayed the same size, on her line, the shapes kept increasing in size at every iteration.

Her mind is not quite her own. Master Haywood had said that a long time ago, about the elderly mother of one of his colleagues. Iolanthe never thought that could apply to her, but it did. Her memory was riddled with holes.

The prince peered at the timeline. "They are all compound events."

"What is a compound event?"

"When my suppressed memory is allowed to surface, and then resuppressed, I remember the surfacing, I just do not remember what surfaced. But for you, every time your memories are allowed to surface, all the memories around the surfacing are also suppressed. So that you do not realize that there are things about yourself you cannot recall."

She examined the pattern of the resurfacing. "Every two years."

"Two years is at the very edge of the margin of safety."

So the memory keeper didn't want to corrupt the health of her mind, but she also didn't want Iolanthe to remember more often than she absolutely must. "The next time I will remember is in the middle of November, if the pattern holds."

"Your birthday."

Her birthday, during the meteor shower, which in the end had portended no greatness. The trickery by the memory keeper, the sacrifices on the part of Master Haywood—they were all ultimately meaningless.

"They could have saved themselves a great deal of trouble," she said, her tone harsh. "Master Haywood threw away his entire life."

The prince looked down, closed his mother's diary, and said, "Let us go. The physician for Wintervale should arrive any moment now."

CHAPTER ⋆ 15

The Sahara Desert

THE ARMORED CHARIOTS WERE ADVANCING all too quickly.

Despite the frigid night air, Titus perspired. Fairfax could not be vaulted. He would not manage to levitate her again so soon. Hiding inside the rock formation was not an option: at least half of the hunting ropes he had just diverted would come after them en masse. And there was not even enough sand underfoot in which to bury themselves, just a scant half inch that was no help whatsoever.

He murmured a prayer, slipped out of the tensile dome, and blind vaulted toward the western horizon, materializing halfway up a massive dune. Pointing his wand skyward, he sent up a silver-white flare that burst midair into an intricate pattern he could not recognize from where he stood.

He blind vaulted again, northward this time, and sent up another flare, hoping it would appear to be an answering signal to the first one, which not only still hung in the air, but had expanded to remarkable dimensions, bright and huge against the starscape—a phoenix, its wings lifted high.

A deep breath and it was back to the rock formation, to Fairfax's defense, should the armored chariots prove unwilling to be diverted. The armored chariots, however, were gone, speeding toward the beacons, the second of which was also an enormous phoenix, flame-colored and warlike.

They were no ordinary beacons, yet he had produced them without even thinking.

He pushed back inside the tensile dome and fell to his knees. "I am beginning to think I do not want to know who I am, or who you are, if this is the sort of danger that keeps chasing us."

She slept on, unconscious of their peril. He rested his palm against her hair for a minute, glad for her safety.

But there was never any rest for the weary. "Time to go on the run again, Sleeping Beauty."

She seemed to be moving. Lightly and easily, like a raft carried downstream by a wide, calm river. Or she could be floating on clouds, as one sometimes did in dreams.

Every time she stopped, she was given water. At some of those occasions, she tried to wake up; other times she did not even possess the will for the attempt, drinking while she slept on.

When she finally broke through again to consciousness, they

seemed to be in a cave of some sort, dark, warm, and stuffy. She could not see him, but she could hear him beside her, his breaths deep and slow.

She said a silent prayer for his well-being before heavy slumber towed her under again.

The next time she woke up, she was in the same space, and it was bright enough for her to see that she was alone. The two waterskins were both there. The one next to her had a mouthful of water; the other, not even a drop. Her eyes half-closed, she willed water from underground rivers and oasis lakes—or even moisture that clung to the underside of rocks—to flow to her. Several minutes passed before the first drop materialized. She filled his waterskin three-quarters full before she became too exhausted, barely managing to cap the waterskin before it fell from her hand.

The same dream came to her again, of floating sweetly down a tranquil river. She traveled the length of the Nile, or so it seemed, before she realized that she actually was floating, but on air, thanks to a levitating spell.

It was dawn. Half of the sky had turned a fish-belly shade of translucence. To her left, at the very top of a mountainous dune, the sand was already the color of molten gold. Had they been on the move all night?

When she'd first treated him, she had applied a liberal amount of topical analgesic. But its effect would have worn off quite a while ago, he would not have been able to reach every part of the wound by himself, and the granules would only be halfway effective without the topical remedy calming the wound at the source.

So he had to be in quite a bit of pain—from time to time he sucked in a breath, as if through clenched teeth. But he walked silently and steadily, pulling her along.

She looked behind. Not a boot print to be seen anywhere—he had taken care to erase all traces of his trek.

"You are awake," he said, turning toward her.

Dirt smudged his face. His eyes were sunken, his voice raspy, his lips badly cracked. She felt a shock of something that was not gratitude alone—something that almost approached tenderness.

"Give me the waterskins now—I don't know how long I can stay awake."

He pressed the waterskins into her hand.

"How long have I been sleeping?"

"This is the second morning since we met."

So not yet forty-eight hours since they found themselves in the Sahara.

"Is the coast clear?" They were not in Atlantean custody—that was always something worth celebrating.

"No," he said. "They are looking for us."

"Is that why we are abroad only at night?"

"They search at night too. Last night there were riders on pegasi."

"Did they get close?"

"Not too close. I found some incendiaries in your bag before we started and set them to go off at various times. The riders were mostly circling about those spots."

"I can't believe I slept through it all."

"The panacea will keep you asleep as long as you are on the verge of dying."

Given that she was already feeling sleepy again, that was a sobering thought. The water globule had grown big enough, and she directed a stream to fill the waterskins.

He stopped. "I had better put us down for the day. We will be too visible in daylight."

She capped the waterskins. "Did you find a cave yesterday?"

"No, I used your tent. Pitched it in the shadow of a sand dune, but it still got hot in the afternoon, when the sun came around. Today I plan to move it at noon."

He formed the tent into the shape of a half tube and maneuvered her inside.

"I can cover the tent with sand," she said as he sealed the opening of the tent.

"No, you should not exert yourself any more than necessary. Remember that you were dealt a near-fatal blow less than forty-eight hours ago."

"I'll just see what I can do before I fall asleep again."

The flow of sand was rather sluggish, but she could hear it rising against the side of the tent. Titus applied a stream of anti-intrusion spells, all of which were aggressive, some to the level of viciousness.

"You don't actually expect us to be found under sand, do you?" she asked, alarmed.

"I worry about sand wyverns."

"But the Sahara doesn't have dragons."

"The deserts of central Asia do. If I were Atlantis, I would send for sand wyverns the moment I realized I needed to be looking for fugitives in a desert. They specialize in sniffing out prey that are hidden under layers of sand—or even rock. And they can burrow at terrifying speeds—so even if you were at full capacity, your ability to get us underground would be useless against them."

"That is assuming Atlantis would go through that sort of trouble for us."

He sighed. "I have a feeling they would. I have a very unpleasant feeling that we—or at least you—might actually be important."

This unnerved her. "I don't want to be important."

"I have kept track of the armored chariots in pursuit, since each has a unique identification number. That first night itself, I counted twenty-three different ones. Now if we assume that the blood circle forms the center of a coordinate plane, and all the armored chariots I saw were searching one quadrant, that means almost a hundred armored chariots were out looking for us, very possibly more." He looked at her. "Now you tell me whether we are important or not."

"Fortune shield me," she murmured.

"Exactly."

Sand had covered the entire tent. It was now still and dark inside.

He called for mage light and handed her a waterskin. "Drink. You are out in the elements as much as I am."

It was as she took her first swallow that she realized she was almost asleep again. She closed her eyes. "So what are we going to do?"

"You sleep," he said, his voice seeming to reach her from far away. "I will take care of everything."

CHAPTER 16

England

THE PHYSICIAN WAS A QUACK, of course, but he was a distin-guished-looking quack who spouted enough likely sounding balderdash to convince Mrs. Dawlish that Wintervale would wake up rejuvenated—and soon.

Mrs. Hancock, on the other hand, was not fooled. After the physician left, she cornered Titus in his room. "Your Highness, with all due respect, that man was a charlatan if I ever saw one."

"But the nurse who came with him is an Exile, and very much qualified in the medical arts," Titus lied fluently.

Mrs. Hancock frowned, possibly in an attempt to recall the nondescript nurse. "And what was her opinion?"

"Same as what the quack told you, that Wintervale's life is not in danger and that when he wakes up, within a few days, he should be fine."

Mrs. Hancock adjusted the perfectly starched cuffs of her blouse.

"That is what panacea does, repairing the body while it sleeps. But what I am interested in, Your Highness, is the root cause of Wintervale's condition."

"That the nurse was not able to determine."

"And you?" Her gaze was penetrating. "You do not know of it either?"

Titus propped his feet up on his desk, knowing well such disrespect to furniture annoyed Mrs. Hancock. "This is what happened on Sunday. Wintervale arrived at Sutherland's uncle's house somewhere between half past two and quarter to three. He looked clammy and said he would not mind a nap. He napped for a while, then took some plain toast, which caused him to vomit. Naturally, I suspected poisoning by Atlantis, so I gave him two antidotes."

Mrs. Hancock raised a brow. "*Naturally* you suspected poisoning by Atlantis, Your Highness?"

"Given the suspicious manner of Baron Wintervale's death, of course."

"Atlantis had nothing to do with Baron Wintervale's death."

"No, no, of course Atlantis would not seek to strike at a leader of the January Uprising who was still young enough and ambitious enough to have a second go at rebellion someday."

Mrs. Hancock was silent for a moment. "I see Your Highness's mind is made up. Please continue with your account."

"The antidotes made Wintervale's vomiting worse, so I gave him a different remedy, which unfortunately contains bee venom as an ingredient, and Wintervale, unbeknownst to me, is highly allergic to bee venom. At that point he went into a seizure and I had no choice but to administer panacea."

Titus had deliberately painted a picture of incompetence. Much better to give the impression that his physicking had made Wintervale devastatingly ill than to let Mrs. Hancock suspect that something was truly the matter with Wintervale.

And if she were to question Kashkari, the latter would probably tell her that Titus denied giving Wintervale anything with bee venom, but then it was not as if the Master of the Domain would admit such a stupid mistake on his part to a nonmage nobody.

"I would advise that Your Highness not practice medicine on the boys of this house in the future," Mrs. Hancock said wryly.

Titus scowled. "Wintervale only received help because he is a second cousin. The other boys of this house are not worth the excellence of my remedies."

"Then Mrs. Dawlish and I must consider ourselves fortunate. We will keep a close eye on Wintervale."

Titus glared at her. "And why are you so interested in Wintervale all of a sudden? Are you not here just to report on me?"

Mrs. Hancock was already at the door. She turned around a few degrees. "Oh, is that why I am here, Your Highness?"

And then she was gone, leaving Titus to frown at that unexpected question.

❖ ❖

"You don't suppose he has the African sleeping sickness, do you?" Cooper asked Kashkari.

They were in Wintervale's room, which had been too full earlier for Cooper and Iolanthe to get in. But now, only Kashkari remained, doing his schoolwork on Wintervale's crowded desk.

"Mrs. Dawlish asked. The physician said no," answered Kashkari.

"Well, either way, it's a magnificent feat of dozing," said Cooper, leaning over Wintervale.

Awake, Wintervale was on the fidgety side, a boy of tremendous energy who didn't always know how to get rid of it. Asleep, he seemed calmer and more mature. Iolanthe gazed at him, willing him to be a different person when he woke up, a person to whom she dared entrust the life of the one she loved.

Don't you dare listen to what he says about his early death. Don't you dare believe it and leave him behind.

Cooper nudged her. "Shall we to our Greek homework?"

She started. "Right-o. After you."

They went to her room and opened their books.

"I envy the Greeks," said Cooper. "They didn't have to learn Greek—they already knew it."

"You are right—lucky them," said Iolanthe. "God, how I hate Greek."

"But you are good at it."

"Only because you are terrible at it, so my mediocrity looks good by comparison."

Cooper tittered. "I know what you mean—you make me look like a decent card player."

Iolanthe laughed in spite of herself. She *was* hopeless at nonmage card games.

The prince opened her door and walked in. Her laughter fled. He looked at Cooper, who was predictably awestruck.

She wondered whether Titus was making an extra effort for Cooper these days: he was always more aloof, more majestic whenever Cooper was around.

The thought hurt, as if someone had stuck a needle into her heart.

Without Titus having to say a thing, Cooper had gathered up his books and notes, bid him a rather breathless good-bye, and closed the door after himself.

"Can I help you?" she asked, keeping any inflection out of her voice.

"I need to speak to you." He set a sound circle. "Mrs. Hancock was asking about Wintervale's condition, and that made me remember I actually had a diagnostic tool in the laboratory."

From his pocket he took out something that looked like a mercury thermometer used by nonmages.

A Kno-it-all gauge. "I thought nobody used these anymore."

"Because they do not offer an instant diagnosis, not because they are inaccurate." He handed the gauge to Iolanthe. "I checked Wintervale just now."

Iolanthe held it up to the light. Instead of the tiny lines that marked degrees of Fahrenheit, the gauge had tiny dots with equally tiny words written next to them. As she rotated the triangular glass rod, lenses built into the rod magnified the letters and the readings.

Heart function. Liver function. Bone density. Muscle strength. So on and so forth, dozens and dozens of vital signs and metrics evaluated.

She must have gone past fifty acceptable readings when she came to one that showed red. *Gross motor skills.* Not surprising, as Wintervale currently could not even get out of bed on his own.

Almost to the end of the long list, another unacceptable reading. *Mental stability.*

Iolanthe squinted. But no, she had not misread. "Are you sure the gauge is properly calibrated?"

"I tested on myself first. It was fine."

"But there is nothing wrong with Wintervale's mental stability." Wintervale might not possess an extraordinary mind, but he certainly had a *sound* one.

"That is what I always thought."

"Maybe he was shocked by what he managed to do." She certainly couldn't get it out of her mind. All those powerful currents of water, spinning around that monstrous, ever-deepening eye. The *Sea Wolf*, so small in comparison, so helpless.

Titus looked away. "His mother is not quite right. Not outright insane, at least not all the time. But you have had dealings with her. You know she can be unreliable."

Iolanthe had indeed dealt with Lady Wintervale, who had once almost killed her. But then it was also Lady Wintervale who had later saved her—and the prince by extension. "If she is sometimes unbalanced, it is because of her Exile and the death of her husband, not because of anything inborn for Wntervale to inherit."

He was silent. Suddenly she wondered whether he had hoped the Kno-it-all gauge's reading could be his way out of a partnership with Wintervale.

If push came to shove, she would accept that reason—she trusted herself to keep him alive far better than Wintervale—but she would not be happy with it. She wanted him to choose her because he dared to defy his mother's dictates from beyond the grave, not because an out-of-date diagnostic tool didn't know how to assess the mental state of someone under a panacea-induced sleep.

"You already know I think Wintervale is the last person who should accompany you to Atlantis. But he is *temperamentally* unsuited for the task, not non compos mentis."

He walked to her window and peeked out from the gap of the curtain, as she had done earlier, when he'd arrived to take her to the laboratory. After a minute or so, he looked back at her. "Remember the memory spells we discovered on you this afternoon?"

"How can I forget?" The shock of it, having her memory shown to be riddled with more holes than a sieve.

"May I have a look at your memory line again?"

She shrugged. "Go ahead."

He recast the spell and the memory line appeared between them, filling almost the entire width of her room, all the colors and patterns making her feel as if she were looking at him through a pane of stained glass.

"Is there something specific you want to check?"

"See the subsidiary lines that connect the shapes representing the suppressed memories to the main line?"

The subsidiary lines were as fine as spider silk. "Yes?"

"They are green for most of the timeline. But look here"—he pointed at the last set of subsidiary lines that branched out, from the most recent instance of the resurfacing of her memories. "These latest lines are black, which means that the memory keeper has made it so that your memories would no longer resurface."

The implication of it was a hard thud in the back of her head. "Am I going to end up like Master Haywood?"

Master Haywood had become a husk of his former self: because his buried memories had not been allowed to resurface, his subconscious mind had pushed for more and more self-destructive means to attract the memory keeper's attention.

Titus dissipated the memory line. "Do you ever feel your mind in a state of ungovernable restlessness?"

"No. At least, not yet."

"Then you still have time. And we will find a way."

She laughed, more than a little bitterly. "We?"

He met her eyes. "Of course. You are still the one I love. You are the one I will love until the day I die."

She meant to dispute it, to tell him that his avowals were only words without the force of action behind it. But she did not say anything.

He kissed her on her forehead, gazed at her another moment, and left.

The next afternoon Iolanthe was in the reading room again, poring over Master Haywood's dissertation. This time, the section on how one could protect oneself from memory spells.

At the height of memory magic's popularity, mages tried to achieve a certain amount of immunity against possible attacks. The dissertation listed pages upon pages of different safeguards to prevent or minimize the erasure and rearrangement of memories.

Iolanthe pinched the bridge of her nose. Master Haywood had known all this, but had not thought to defend himself—or her—with a few of these safeguards.

He must have trusted the memory keeper as she had trusted the prince, never for a moment believing that a bond such as theirs could be anything but invincible.

Come to think of it, even if he never thought to be wary of the memory keeper, he should still have sought to give Iolanthe more information, knowing that should the memory keeper be unable to reach Iolanthe, she could be left without vital knowledge.

What if he had?

She sat up straighter. In the emergency pack that he had thrust into her hands, just before she left the Domain, there had been a letter. She had checked the letter for hidden writing. There had been none—or at least none that was within her power to reveal.

But what about the envelope?

She could not say the password to exit the Crucible fast enough.

Back in the laboratory, someone held her hand.

The prince. He was watching her, the longing in his eyes palpable.

You are still the one I love. You are the one I will love until the day I die.

Almost without thinking, she reached out and lifted a strand of his hair—only to suddenly come to her senses, an electric pain in her heart.

She got off the stool on which she had been sitting and walked to the cabinet that held those things she had brought with her from the Domain. She found Master Haywood's letter, and set both letter and envelope on the worktable. *"Revela omnia."*

"I already tried the envelope," said the prince.

Of course he would have tried it, he who approached his mission with a no-stone-unturned thoroughness.

"There has to be more. My suppressed memories only resurfaced every two years. If anything happened to the memory keeper before she could reach me, I would be without facts important to my survival for a long, long time—and I refuse to believe that Master Haywood wouldn't have prepared for that possibility." She tapped her finger on the envelope. "Can you make it so that secret writing is only made visible if a revealing charm has a countersign attached?"

"You could. But then it requires you to know the countersign."

She scanned the letter. She did not know the countersign. If Master Haywood used one, he must have included it in the letter. And if he had done so, he would have called attention to it by setting it slightly apart in some manner.

Her eyes fell on the second postscript. *Do not worry about me.*

Could it be? She tried the revealing charm on the envelope again, while silently reciting *Do not worry about me* as a countersign.

Immediately new writing appeared on the envelope.

But only if you are armed with a knife and willing to use it.

"Try it on the letter, too," said the prince, his voice full of barely leashed excitement.

She did, and was rewarded with *Oysters give pearls.*

"'Oysters give pearls, but only if you are armed with a knife and willing to use it,'" she read the sentence aloud. "Should this mean something to me?"

"Give me a moment." The prince went inside the Crucible and came back a minute later. "It is a line from an Argonin play called *The Fisherman's Pilgrimage.*"

Argonin was considered the greatest playwright the Domain ever produced. Iolanthe had studied some of Argonin's plays at school, but not *The Fisherman's Pilgrimage.*

The line had been given in two parts, as password and countersign. But to what?

All at once she knew: for something that Master Haywood had reason to trust would always be on her person.

Her wand.

Her wand too was stored in the laboratory—it would be difficult to pass herself off as nonmage if she were caught with it. She retrieved it from the cabinet and turned it about in the light.

It had once been her pride and joy, her wand, a piece of extraordinary craftsmanship. Emerald vines and amethyst flowers had been set onto the surface; the veins of the leaves were composed of hair-thin filaments of malachite, the pistils and stamens of the flowers tiny yellow diamonds.

A wand especially commissioned for her birth, Master Haywood had told her, to be an heirloom piece. And she had not wondered too much how her parents, both still students, both from terribly modest backgrounds, had managed to afford it.

But now she knew it was not the Seabournes who had ordered such a spectacularly costly wand, but the memory keeper, the most untrustworthy person she had ever known.

Her mother, if the prince was right about it.

"Oysters give pearls," she said aloud, and recited the rest silently.

The wand slid apart. The inlays had been done on a shell, which now detached from the base of the wand to reveal a separate core. Four small objects had been embedded in the core; they were identical looking, pea-size lumps as black as coal.

The prince leaped to his feet. "These are the vertices of a quasi-vaulter."[10]

The only device known to circumvent a fully established no-vaulting zone—and most likely what had enabled Master Haywood's disappearance from the Citadel last June.

"I have been trying to buy a quasi-vaulter on the black market for five years," the prince went on. "Not a single one came up for sale in all that time."

But now she had one at her disposal and would be able to escape from anywhere. Once.

He picked up the lumps and handed them to her. "The vertices are contact requisite and need to be on your person for at least seventy-two hours before they will transport you. It is quite likely that was already done when you were an infant, but you want to make sure."

She dropped them into the inside pocket of her jacket and carefully sealed the pocket shut. "But where is the target?"

A full quasi-vaulter set came with five pieces, four vertices and a target to be placed ahead of time. She was fairly confident the target wouldn't be inside an active volcano, but she would have preferred to know where she was going.

"Somewhere Atlantis cannot find, I hope," said the prince. "You are making impressive progress, by the way. What do you plan to do should you locate your guardian?"

Questions of the future hurt—all possible courses of action invariably involved her leaving Titus for parts unknown. "Set him free and go into hiding."

"Have you thought of a place?"

She shook her head. "Time enough to think about that once I manage to actually free him."

"Please let me know if I can help in any way," he said solemnly. "It is still as dangerous as ever for you out there."

She wanted to hold his face in her hands and tell him that it was not danger that she feared. No anymore. But she only nodded. "Thank you. I had better go now—cricket practice in twenty minutes."

When Iolanthe arrived at practice, to her surprise, Kashkari was already there, dressed in his kit, no less.

She shook hands with him. "Are you joining us, sir?"

"According to West, when they drew up the list for the twenty-two, I was number twenty-three. Therefore I will be playing in Wintervale's stead until he is no longer incapacitated."

"I'm surprised you were willing to leave his side. How is he today?"

"I was with him for some time just now. He woke up for a whopping thirty seconds."

"That's something."

"That is something indeed. And he seemed to be in good spirits, though he was disappointed not to see the prince."

A few other cricketers arrived, followed by a man hauling a heavy-looking black case. The man opened the case and began assembling a contraption—a camera.

"What's going on over there?" she asked Kashkari. "Is that Roberts?"

"That's Roberts. This is his last year and the third time he's been chosen for the twenty-two, but he hasn't made the eleven yet. Rumor has it he's been talking about having a photograph taken so that whether he is selected for the eleven or not, it would appear as if he had."

Iolanthe snorted. "You have to applaud that kind of initiative. Although—" She turned to Kashkari. "Don't you know whether he makes the eleven?"

Kashkari could have dreamed about that, for all she knew.

"I haven't the slightest idea. Never dreamed about the Eton and Harrow games."

"What do you dream about then, other than coming to Eton? And have those other dreams come true?"

"There was one time when I was little, when I dreamed of a birthday cake for my seventh birthday. Mind you, birthday cakes are not the norm. In our family we always made Indian sweets for birthdays. But on my seventh birthday, I was indeed served a Western cake with candles blazing on top, just as I'd dreamed."

Her younger self would have found his gift fascinating. But

now her view of seers and visions had been colored with a sharp prejudice. The entire point of life was the ability to make one's own choices. Foreknowledge of anything—especially the circular kind, such as Kashkari's presence at Eton because he'd dreamed of it—was terribly limiting and ran counter to the concept of free will.

"But did you *want* a birthday cake?"

"I didn't think so much of whether I wanted a birthday cake. At that point, only one other of my dreams had come true—that my grandmother's old classmate would come to stay with us. So I was far more interested in whether this dream too was prophetic."

"Have you ever thought about a different life for yourself? One that doesn't involve leaving your family to come to Eton?"

"Of course I've thought about it."

"Do you regret the path not taken? The dreams, they don't allow you any choice, do they?"

"It's a very Western point of view to see visions of the future as eternal truths chiseled in marble, which must not be tampered with or otherwise disturbed. We view a vision more as a suggestion, one among many different possibilities. After I had a slice of that birthday cake, I asked if I could also have some *ladhoos*—this dense, round confection that I adored—and lo and behold I was given a plate of *ladhoos* too. And when it came to Eton, I never viewed those dreams as binding. The question was always, did I want to have this adventure, and in the end I decided, yes, I did."

"So there were dreams you ignored?"

"Well, there was one I had more or less decided to ignore, as an experiment, because it had seemed both stupid and utterly insignificant. I'd seen it a few times in the past two years. I would be in the prince's room at night, with a number of other boys. And then, I would roll up the sleeves of my kurta and climb out of the window and down the drainpipes."

Iolanthe started.

"I wear my kurta only to bed—meaning it was past lights-out. It just didn't seem like something I would do, climbing out of a window for mischief in the middle of the night. But when the scene unfolded in reality, it had to do with Trumper and Hogg and their rock throwing. Suddenly it seemed like a very worthwhile thing to do, going after them."

And by doing so, he had revealed himself to be the "scorpion" the Oracle of Still Waters had spoken about, someone from whom she could seek aid.

"Was I there in your dream?"

"You were speaking just before I climbed out the window. I was never able to recall what you said, but yes, you were there."

"Gentlemen, I hate to interrupt this engrossing conversation, but practice is about to start," said West.

It had been an engrossing conversation indeed. Iolanthe hadn't even noticed West's approach. She shook hands with him. "We are drawing a crowd today."

West glanced at the dozens and dozens of boys gathered at the edge of the playing field. "That's nothing. Wait until the Summer Half."

"Cooper and Rogers, over there," said Iolanthe to Kashkari.

Cooper waved. Iolanthe blew him an exaggerated kiss. Both Cooper and Rogers bent over laughing, as if it were the funniest thing they had ever seen.

"Does the prince not come and watch you play?" asked West.

"He has about as much interest in cricket as he has in medieval French grammar," Iolanthe answered.

"Is that so?"

West's tone seemed casual, but Iolanthe could sense his disappointment—a subtle movement in the set of his jaw, the way he carried his bat closer to his person.

Why should West care whether Titus came to the practice?

Was he an agent of Atlantis, by some chance?

This possibility distracted her so much that it was not until they were twenty minutes into the practice that the significance of what *Kashkari* had said fully made itself understood.

Kashkari had seen her—or Fairfax, rather—several times in dreams in the past two years, while Fairfax was only supposed to have been absent from school for three months, according to the stipulations of the prince's otherwise spell that had created and maintained Fairfax's fictitious identity.

When Iolanthe had finally turned up, under the name Fairfax, Kashkari would have known that Fairfax hadn't been absent for a mere three months, but had never been seen in Mrs. Dawlish's house until that moment.

No wonder at the beginning of their acquaintance he'd asked Iolanthe so many questions and made her so nervous. He had suspected from the first second that some pieces about Fairfax did not fit together.

That Fairfax, who was supposed to have lived under Mrs. Dawlish's roof for the past four years, did not exist until the start of Summer Half.

Iolanthe kept glancing at Kashkari as they walked back together to Mrs. Dawlish's. He was possibly even more difficult to read than the prince—and he accomplished it without the haughtiness the latter wore like a suit of spiked armor.

It amazed her now, behind that gentlemanly amiability, how much Kashkari had kept to himself. Not only his own secrets, but hers too, never revealing anything of his inner thoughts, except perhaps an occasional question that left her flailing for an answer.

But why was he divulging all these closely held secrets to her? And why now? Was he trying to tell her something?

Or was it a warning?

The prince came out of his room as she and Kashkari reached the stair landing of their corridor at Mrs. Dawlish's. "Our lackeys have our tea almost prepared."

They usually had their tea in Wintervale's room. Now that

Wintervale was indisposed, the location had temporarily moved to Kashkari's room. Iolanthe didn't want tea, but she also didn't want to drag the prince back into his room to unburden herself, not with Kashkari already saying, "A pleasure to host my friends."

Kashkari's room was almost as spare as the prince's. A rather ancient-looking rug covered the floor. On the bookshelf gleamed brass plates that bore oil lamps and small heaps of vermilion and turmeric. Above this diminutive altar, the painted image of the god Krishna, sitting with one foot upon the opposite knee, a flute at his lips.

"Nice curtain." She pointed her chin toward the sky-blue brocade drapery, which provided a splash of color in the otherwise plain room.

"Thank you. Something more substantial on the window for the English winter—otherwise cold air just seeps in."

Junior boys came, bearing plates of hot beans on toast and eggs. Kashkari poured tea. They talked about Wintervale's condition, the latest news from India, Prussia, and Bechuanaland—this last forcing Iolanthe to participate. The chair might as well have grown thorns. How much longer must they keep this up? And why had the prince come at all? Yesterday he had begged off tea altogether.

She glanced at the clock. Twenty-five minutes had passed. Five more minutes, and she was leaving.

A light knock came at the door.

It was Mrs. Hancock, with a letter for Kashkari. "This just came in the post for you, dear."

Kashkari rose, took the letter from Mrs. Hancock, thanked her, and returned to the table. The envelope was a brown, square one, with large black letters written across both the front and the back. *PHOTOGRAPH INSIDE. PRAY DO NOT BEND.*

Kashkari put the letter aside, sat down, and then, with what for him passed as great agitation, rose again. "It's no use."

"What?" asked the prince.

"I know what it is: a portrait from my brother's engagement party. I can't avoid it forever so I might as well open it now."

"If you would like us to give you some privacy—" began Iolanthe.

"I've already unburdened myself to the two of you earlier. It would be silly to pretend otherwise." He opened the envelope and handed the photograph to Iolanthe. "That's her."

Three people were in the frame—Kashkari, a young woman in a sari, and a handsome young man who must be Kashkari's brother. The woman's hair was covered by the sari. An enormous nose ring—with a chain attached somewhere in her hair—obscured a good bit of her face. But still it was easy to see that she was extraordinarily lovely.

"She is beautiful enough to be the girl of anyone's dreams."

Kashkari sighed. "That she is."

Iolanthe passed the photograph to the prince, who took a sip of tea as he accepted the photograph from her.

Almost immediately he began coughing—and kept on coughing.

Iolanthe was bewildered—the Master of the Domain was not the kind of boy to choke on his tea. Kashkari stood up and struck the prince forcibly between the shoulder blades.

The prince, panting, returned the photograph to him. "My tea—went down the wrong way. She is—handsome indeed."

"She seems to have a strong effect on not just you," Iolanthe said to Kashkari.

The prince gave her a strange look. "How did she and your brother meet, Kashkari?"

"It's an arranged marriage, of course."

"Of course. What I meant was, is she from the same city as you?"

"No. We belong to the same community, but her family settled years ago in Punjab." Kashkari smiled weakly. "They could have found any girl to be my brother's bride, and it had to be her."

The prince rose to leave shortly thereafter. Iolanthe stayed a minute longer. Then she was knocking on his door—she must speak to him about the implications of Kashkari's prophetic dreams—and found herself dragged inside.

"Kashkari—" she began.

He cut her off. "That woman in the photograph—she was the one who crashed the garden party at the Citadel. The one who escaped on a flying carpet. The one who asked for *you*."

CHAPTER · 17

The Sahara Desert

HE WAS STILL SLEEPING, HIS shoulder touching hers, when she woke, perspiring.

Inside the buried tent, it was dim and prodigiously hot. She called for water, drank her fill, and topped the waterskins. Then she sat up, called for some mage light, and turned her attention to the prince. He was sleeping on his stomach, without his tunic. She sucked in a breath at the sight of the bandage on his back: if it were bright red, it would be one thing, but it was blood mixed with an inky dark substance—an appalling sight.

"Just my body expelling the poison." His words were slow and sleepy. "I took every antidote in your bag."

She took off the old bandage and destroyed it. "What in the world was it?"

"It has to be venom of some sort, but I cannot feel any puncture marks."

"I don't see any either." She handed him a few granules for pain. "It just looks as if your skin has been eaten away by acid, or something."

"But this substance is organic, because the antidotes did work."

She shook her head. "Such a large area. Almost as if someone had a bucket of venom and just threw it at you."

And yet he had walked goodness knew how many miles in this desert, dragging her along.

She cleaned his wound, applied more topical analgesic, and then spread a regenerative remedy. "Do you know what I am reminded of? Have you ever read the story of Briga's Chasm?"

"Yes."

"Do you remember the pulpwyrms that guard the entrance to the chasm? Those nasty creatures that are big as roads? They are said to spew an endless stream of a black substance that can dissolve a mage down to just teeth and hair."

"But pulpwyrms are not real."

"Now why must you upset a perfectly good hypothesis with such bothersome things as facts?"

The corner of his lips lifted—and disrupted her train of thought. She stared at his profile, longer than she ought to, before she remembered that she had a task at hand.

"How long have you been up?" he asked.

She pull out two other vials. "Five minutes or so. I filled the waterskins."

"You actually sound awake, for once."

"I'm slightly groggy, but I don't feel as if I'll start snoring in the next minute."

He hissed as she sprinkled the contents of one vial onto his back. "Good. I was about to go deaf from your snoring."

"Ha!" She decanted another remedy onto his wound, counting the drops carefully. "Speaking of being important, isn't the Master of the Domain named Titus? It isn't a very common name."[11]

He thought for a moment. "It is quite common among the Sihar."[12]

She was taken aback, but it almost made sense—the Sihar were known for their enthusiasm for and mastery of blood magic. "You think you are Sihar?"[13]

"I have not the slightest idea. I just did not want to be one of those people who lose their memories and decide they must be the Master of the Domain." His brows knitted together. "On the other hand, night before last I set off two beacons. Two huge phoenix beacons. And the phoenix does stand for the House of Elberon."

She put away all the remedies and rebandaged his back. "Maybe you were a lowly stable boy in one of the prince's households, where you acquired a love of phoenixes. Having had enough of shoveling muck day in and day out, you set out on an adventure that took you across oceans. You slew dragons, met beautiful girls, and won accolades for your courage and chivalry—"

"And ended up half-crippled in the middle of a desert?"

"Every story must have such a terrible moment, or it wouldn't be interesting."

He blew out a breath of air. "I think I have had quite enough of adventures. In the last thirty-six hours, at least three times I thought I would expire of fright. I am ready to beg His Highness to take me back into his employment, so I can shovel muck out of his stables in peace and quiet for the remainder of my natural life."

She grinned. "I love a man of ambition."

He smiled again. And again she was quite, quite distracted.

"I have to admit," he said, "the desert night sky is stunning. I would not mind an opportunity to enjoy it without Atlantis on my tail—a campfire, a cup of something hot, and the entire cosmos for my viewing pleasure."

"A man of ambition—and simple tastes."

"What would *you* do, if Atlantis were not chasing us from one end of the Sahara to the other?"

She thought about it. "You might laugh, but if Atlantis weren't in the picture, I'd wonder whether I am falling behind in my classes by being in the Sahara in the middle of an academic term."

He did laugh.

"Laugh all you want. I am not going to apologize for my burning desire to succeed in my studies."

"Please do not. Besides, I will wager that is what your beau loves most about you."

She sat back on her haunches. "How do you know about him?"

"The hidden writing on the strap of your bag."

She grabbed the satchel. *"Revela omnia."*

Words appeared. *The night you were born, stars fell. The day we met, lightning struck. You are my past, my present, my future. My hope, my prayer, my destiny.*

Her protector.

"The man is mad about you," said Titus.

She looked back at him, the grime, the exhaustion, his lips cracked from the sheer desiccation of the desert. Her own lips were in nowhere near as terrible shape—he had taken better care of her than he had of himself.

"You could be him, for all we know," she said, securing a new piece of bandaging to his person.

He shifted. "I could not possibly write anything like that. I am sorry, but there ought to be a law against such sentences as 'The day we met, lightning struck.'"

With a wave of her hand, she got rid of the grit that had become stuck in his hair. A few other cleaning spells and he was almost spotless. "Maybe you were too busy packing for every eventuality to polish your words."

"We former muck-shoveling stable boys can pack and produce deathless prose at the same time."

The mage light caught a few specks of discoloration on his shoulders: a smattering of freckles, which she had not noticed before. Quite an appealing detail on an otherwise strong, tight frame, like a constellation for the fingertip to explore, to move from point to point and—

The texture of his skin—and the fact that he started—made her realize that she *was* touching him.

"You skin is a bit sticky," she said quickly, though it wasn't at all. "All that perspiration doesn't come off just with spells. Let me wash you with some water. You'll feel more refreshed."

"That might be too much trouble. You should take more rest."

"Fortune shield me, I have literally been sleeping for days."

The globule of water she summoned spun furiously in the air, reflecting her agitation. What was the matter with her? She should take the excuse he offered her and leave him alone. But she couldn't seem to stop.

She wetted his hair and used the washing bar from the satchel, which produced a soft, fat lather. Her fingertips pressed into his scalp, working the lather into every strand. She summoned more water to pour over his hair. The water that sluiced down she sent back out of the tent, toward the center of the nearby dune.

When she was done, she drew out the water that still clung to his hair and waved it away. With her fingertips, she patted his hair, making sure that it had dried properly.

And now, she would lift her hand and tell him, *All done*.

Instead, her palm slid down to his nape. Then, as she watched, half horrified, her fingers spread out where his shoulder joined his neck.

He sucked in a breath.

She opened her mouth to tell him that none of it was happening, that it had to be a hallucination on his part—and hers. But the warmth of his skin beneath her hand was no illusion. And curiously, that skin grew cooler as her hand traveled to the edge of his shoulder and down his arm.

All of a sudden he was on his knees, facing her. They stared at each other. His eyes were blue-gray, she noticed for the first time, the color of oceans of unfathomable depths.

She loved her abstract protector, but she knew only this boy, who gave her more water than he gave himself. She traced a finger down his cheek. He caught her hand. She held her breath, not knowing whether he would push her hand away or press his lips into her palm.

A ground-shaking roar shattered the moment.

CHAPTER · 18

England

"THAT MAKES SENSE."

Whatever reaction Titus had expected from Fairfax, upon being told that Kashkari's beloved was a mage who wanted her handed over, this was not it.

"What do you mean?"

She told him about her two separate conversations with Kashkari concerning his prophetic dreams, culminating with the dream about her, long before she had ever stepped into Mrs. Dawlish's house. "It's fairly safe to assume that Kashkari is from a mage family, probably one in Exile."

"You should have told me much sooner. Anything that affects you I must know right away."

Everything had changed, yet nothing had changed. He still lay awake at night, worrying about her safety. And when he woke up each morning, she was still the one he thought of first and foremost.

She tapped her fingers on the top of a chair—the one in which she used to sit, when they trained in the Crucible together in the Summer Half. "Kashkari has not betrayed me, so for now we can assume he means neither of us harm. What we need to know is why, after keeping his own identity a secret for so long, he now chooses to reveal himself to us."

The inside of Titus's skull throbbed. He could not believe that he had lived in the same house as Kashkari for so long without ever guessing the truth. What else had he missed? "I need to consult my mother's diary first."

That was the wrong thing to say to her, but she gave no reaction other than turning down one corner of her lips.

"I would prefer to make my decision after I have gathered all the available intelligence. It would be criminal to ignore what she might have foreseen." He hated that he felt compelled to defend how he chose to proceed.

She smiled slightly—or was it a grimace? "You must do as you see fit, of course."

"I am not looking forward to it, you know. I am—"

She gripped him by the front of his shirt. "Don't. You have made your choice. Now commit to it! If you are going to ask Wintervale to face the Bane, then he deserves at least that much from you."

Her voice, halfway between anger and anguish. Her eyes, dark and ferocious. Her lips, full and red, parted with her agitated breaths.

He should not, but he cupped her face and kissed her. Because they were past the point when words were any use. Because he was once again afraid to die. Because he loved her as much as he loved life itself.

A loud knock had them hurriedly pulling apart.

"Are you there, prince?" Kashkari called. "Wintervale is awake and he wants to see you."

Wintervale was sitting up in bed, a big smile on his face.

"Titus, good to see you. You too, Fairfax. How did the cricket practices go? Did they miss me?"

"Desperately," said Fairfax, smiling convincingly. "Boys threw themselves down, howling and beating the earth, when your absence was made clear."

Wintervale placed a hand over his chest. "Now that warms the cockles of my heart."

Flinging aside his blanket, he set his feet on the floor. Both Titus and Fairfax sprang forward to help him. But Wintervale raised one palm to indicate that he wanted to stand up himself.

Fairfax, strong as she was, barely caught him when he tipped over. "God almighty, Wintervale. There must be full-grown steer in Wyoming less heavy than you are."

Surprise was written all over Wintervale's face. "What is this? I felt perfectly fine just now."

"You have been bedridden two entire days," said Titus. "Hardly surprising that your legs are wobbly."

"Guess one of you will have to help me to the lavatory then."

"That is a task for a real man," said Titus. "I am afraid you will have to step aside, Fairfax."

"I knew it. You are still bitter from the time we compared our bollocks."

Wintervale tittered as he shuffled out, his arm over Titus's shoulders.

He was warmly greeted up and down the corridor. On the way back, they stopped several times to talk to boys who wanted to know how he was getting along.

"Gentlemen, let Wintervale go back to bed," came Mrs. Hancock's firm voice. "If you wish to visit him and chitchat, do it in a way that will not tax him."

"Mrs. Hancock wanted to see you as soon as you woke up," said Kashkari, who must have gone to fetch her.

Wintervale grinned at the woman. "Of course you would, dear Mrs. Hancock."

Fairfax was still there in Wintervale's room when they returned. She helped Wintervale settle back into bed. But as more and more boys trickled in, she slipped away, largely unnoticed.

Iolanthe opened the door to the laboratory to the sound of a type-writer clacking.

The prince had a typing ball, which transmitted messages from Dalbert, his personal spymaster. The typing ball had once been stored in a cabinet in his room at Mrs. Dawlish's, but he had moved it to the laboratory for safekeeping.

The brass keys, looking like chunky quills on a very nonthreatening porcupine, stopped pistoning up and down as she reached it. She rolled out the piece of paper that had been set on the tray underneath.

The message would appear to be gibberish, but he had taught her to decipher the code. She had asked him to, she remembered with a pang, the day she first decided that she would actually help him with his impossible goal.

A strange thought burbled up from the depths of her mind. She had condemned his love as weak, because he would not choose her over his mother's words, but what of *her* love? Was it of any greater strength or constancy? He was, as ever, headed toward ruinous peril, and she would let him go to it with nothing more than a *Fortune shield you*.

She stood for a minute with her fingers on her nape, trying to relieve a tension in her neck that simply would not go away. Then she sighed and started Dalbert's report.

Your Most Serene Highness,

Per your instruction, I have looked into the events in Grenoble, France. According to my sources in Lyon and Marseille, the Exile communities in those cities had been warned against going to Grenoble, because of intelligence suggesting that it might be a trap.

Exiles from those communities did make the trip to Grenoble, but with the express purpose of warning mages who had come from as far as the Caucasus, drawn by rumors of Madame Pierredure's return. They report that they did successfully turn away a number of mages, though there were others they could not locate ahead of time or persuade to leave.

The raid on Grenoble is the latest Atlantean trap, using Madame Pierredure as a lure. Convincing reports have emerged of Madame's death eight and a half years ago, which had never been publicized because she took her own life. (It was well known during the rebellions of ten years ago that Atlantis had captured her children and grandchildren, then tortured and eventually killed them.)

But many of the traps, before the truth came out, had been quite effective. The death of the late Inquisitor and the rumored death of the Bane had been seen as an opening, a sign of weakness on the part of Atlantis. New underground resistance groups formed; older ones were roused out of dormancy. The Bane's apparent subsequent resurrection did not dampen their enthusiasm—the common thinking was that he could not go on resurrecting.

Now many of these resistance groups, old and new, have been decimated, their boldest and most enthusiastic members taken into Atlantean custody.

I tender my humble good wishes for Your Highness's health and well-being.

Your Highness' dutiful subject and servant,

Dalbert

Having spent her summer in near-complete isolation, Iolanthe had no idea that what she and the prince had accomplished the night of the Fourth of June would inspire so many others to organize against Atlantis, nor that Atlantis had already swiftly and ruthlessly responded to quell these new ambitions.

Her heart ached with a dismay that had nothing to do with her own dismissal from the narrow path of destiny, but for the crushed hopes of all those who had believed that the first light of dawn was at last upon them.

She set down the message from Dalbert on the worktable. Already on the table was a copy of *The Delamer Observer*, made of a fine yet hardy silk, which could be folded up and carried around in the pocket. The newspaper was open to the very last page, thick with three-line advertisements for unicorn colts, beauty tonics, and cloaks that promised to make one almost impossible to see at night.

What had the prince been looking for?

Then she saw it, buried near a corner, an advertisement for *Large Bird Sightings. Curious and unusual birds, last seen in Tangier, Grenoble, and Tashkent.*

As she read, the text changed to *last seen in Grenoble, Tashkent, and St. Petersburg.*

With the exception of Grenoble, all the other nonmage cities had sizable Exile populations. Atlantis was far from finished with its crackdown.

She entered the reading room with a heavy heart and stood

before the help desk, still distracted.

Perhaps it was good and right that Wintervale came along. If the vortex that sank the *Sea Wolf* was any indication, his powers put hers to shame. And one needed power of that magnitude to pit oneself against Atlantis.

The sight came back to her again, the ship caught like a leaf in an eddy, powerless to escape. "A maelstrom that dines on ships," she murmured.

A book appeared on the shelf behind the help desk, which must have thought she wanted something on the subject. She pulled it out and absently flipped a few pages.

It was a travelogue written by a mage who sailed with a group of friends from the Domain to Atlantis, to witness the demolition of a floating hotel that had been condemned.

On the way into the Bay of Lucidias, we passed near the Atlantean maelstrom, a sight at once terrifying and awe-inspiring. In diameter it was nearly ten miles across, the dark waters churning ceaselessly around a funnel-like center. Overhead circled chariots and riders on pegasi—this phenomenon is as novel and jaw-dropping for Atlanteans as it is for the tourists. And though much of the country is dirt poor, the elites still possess enough beast-power to make the fifty-mile trip from the coast.

No one knows how the vortex came to be. One day it was not there, the next it was. My friends declare it as remarkable a sight as the shifting peaks of the Labyrinthine Mountains, and I must agree.

She looked at the front of the book. It was published in YD 853, almost a hundred and eighty years ago. She knew that the stylized whirlpool that was the Atlantean symbol represented a real maelstrom not far from the island, but she did not know that the maelstrom hadn't always been there.

Interesting, but she had come with a different purpose in mind. She put the book back. "Show me everything with this sentence inside: *Oysters give pearls, but only if you are armed with a knife and willing to use it.*"

The travelogue disappeared, to be replaced by hundreds of editions of Argonin's plays.

She modified her command. "Everything that is not a play."

Still too many books left. "Take away the textbooks and the books of quotation."

Three books remained. First, perhaps unsurprisingly, was Master Haywood's dissertation. The line was on the final page, with no context or explanations.

The next was the annual compilation of *The Delamer Observer* for YD 1007, six years before Iolanthe was born. The article that contained the quote had for its subject the fancy-dress ball held to celebrate the tricentennial of Argonin's birth—and to mark the start of a year of revival of his plays, major and minor.

Most guests came dressed as better-known Argonin characters. A fair number arrived as Argonin themselves—it is always a surprise to some that Argonin was not one, but two writers, a husband-and-wife team.

And one young lady, who did not want us to use her name or image, as
she was a minor in attendance without permission, rather scandalized in
an oyster costume that opened to reveal a large, luminous pearl; together
with her friend, who carried a raffish cutlass, they formed a visualization
of her favorite Argonin line, "Oysters give pearls, but only if you are
armed with a knife and willing to use it."

The last was a feature in the official publication of the Domain's
premier school for the training of military officers. Five cadets were
featured as the year's most promising graduates.

And the Argonin line was given as the favorite quote of a cadet by
the name of Penelope Rainstone.

Iolanthe's heart thumped. Who was Penelope Rainstone?

Her question was easily answered by the resources in the reading
room: Penelope Rainstone was the regent's chief security adviser,
specializing in external threats to the Domain.

Iolanthe went back to the original article, which painted a glowing portrait of the young Commander Rainstone's loyalty, brilliance,
and perseverance. It would seem she had the makings of a perfect
soldier, but then in the interview section, when she was asked
whether she would ever break rules, she said, *I enjoy order and orderli-*
ness as much as the next soldier. But we must remember, rules and regulations
are often made for peacetime and typical conditions, whereas we, the future
officers of the Domain's security forces, are being trained for war and chaos. In

extraordinary circumstances, extraordinary decisions must be made.

In other words, should the need arise, she would not hesitate to break every rule in the book.

Iolanthe's hands clutched the edge of the table. But there was nothing to do but ask the help desk the next logical question. "Show me everything you have of Horatio Haywood and Penelope Rainstone together."

And there they were, in a special supplementary section to *The Delamer Observer*, posing together at a reception held at the Citadel, for the year's top upper academy graduates from across the Domain.

The caption read,

Horatio Haywood, 18, of the Trident and Hippocampus School on Sirenhaven, Siren Isles, and Penelope Rainstone, 19, of the Commonweal Academy of Delamer. They are headed to the Conservatory of Magical Arts and Sciences and the Titus the Great Center of Martial Learning, respectively. Though Mr. Haywood and Miss Rainstone met only at the reception, they could not heap enough compliments on each other.

The young man and the young woman in the picture were turned toward each other, their faces glowing with pleasure.

Was this it? Was Commander Penelope Rainstone the memory keeper?

Was she Iolanthe's mother?

CHAPTER ✦ 19

The Sahara Desert

THE ROAR CAME AGAIN.

Fairfax dove for the satchel. Titus grabbed his tunic and yanked his wand from his boot.

She made a pushing motion with her hand. A noise almost as terrifying as a dragon's roar rumbled through the tent—she was causing an avalanche, meant to startle and distract the sand wyvern outside.

"Stay here," Titus ordered as he put on the tunic.

He vaulted out—and was immediately buried under a landslide of sand. He vaulted again, toward the top of the high dune, just as a sand wyvern, almost exactly the same color as the Sahara, took to the sky screeching, its wings beating hard.

He knew that sand wyverns were bigger than normal wyverns, but this one was at least three times the size he had anticipated, its wingspan the dimensions of a small manor, and carried two riders, instead of the usual one.

The riders, in Atlantean uniforms, tried to rein in the sand wyvern and point its nose in Fairfax's general direction again. Titus launched a succession of shield-punching spells at the riders, followed by a stunning spell.

One rider slumped over. The sand wyvern turned and blasted a stream of fire toward Titus. He tossed up a shield and aimed an attack at the beast's belly. Wyverns—ordinary wyverns at least—had a soft underbelly, the reason they could be caught and tamed by skilled mages.

But the sand wyvern did not even react as Titus's destabilizing spell hit it squarely in the abdomen, except to lunge at him, one enormous claw extended.

Hoping to draw the sand wyvern away from Fairfax, he vaulted toward the top of the next dune—he had set up camp in the narrow valley between two waves of towering dunes that ran close and parallel to each other, hoping for better protection from the heat of the sun during the day. Blind vaulting being what it was, he ended up halfway up the sand slope he had aimed for, instead of at the top, with the sand wyvern already on his heels. Looking down the valley toward the point in the distance where the dunes appeared, he vaulted again.

This time, he rematerialized at least a quarter mile away. The sand wyvern wheeled about and shot toward him. Then in midair it jerked—convulsed, almost—and with a huge roar, turned back toward Fairfax, even though Titus prodded it with several thorn spells.

He swore and vaulted back to the tent—only to find himself completely entombed in sand. Not only was Fairfax gone, the tent, too, was gone. Swearing again, he took himself to a high spot.

Fairfax stood in the valley between the dunes, completely dwarfed by the sand wyvern, no more than twenty feet from her. Her arms were raised, as if she were signaling the beast to stop. And the beast seemed to be cooperating in a most civilized manner, hovering, the tip of its tail almost touching the ground.

Two seconds passed before Titus understood exactly what he was seeing. The sand wyvern was trying to advance, inch by inch, against the headwind Fairfax had created, which sent sand billowing in its path. She shouted. The sand wyvern, with its hundred-foot wingspan, was actually blown back a few yards.

Titus aimed more attacks at the remaining rider on the sand wyvern. But the rider crouched low behind the dragon's right wing, shielded from attacks.

Titus vaulted several times, trying to find a good angle—he hoped the sand wyvern was not accustomed to working so hard for its supper and would gladly leave the uncooperative elemental mage for easier prey if only he could render the rider comatose.

Finally, he found a suitable spot that gave him a relatively unimpeded view. He raised his arm. But what was he hearing? Mixed in with the howling of the headwind, the sand being carried away like sediments of a river, and the beating of the sand wyvern's wings, was there something else?

He vaulted away just as a shock of heat reached his skin.

A squadron of albino wyverns had arrived. He vaulted back to Fairfax. It would still be far too risky for her to vault, but he did not know how else to get her out of this.

He threw up a shield over her, barely in time for a combined torrent of fire from the wyverns. She held out a hand toward the wyverns, redirecting their fire toward one another, forcing them to break formation and disperse.

But with this disruption in her concentration, the air current she had been using to hold back the sand wyvern became less intense. The sand wyvern, still beating its wings mightily, shot past them.

He called for another shield, the strongest one he knew. "If you burrow, the sand wyvern will burrow faster than you. And even if you hold all the wyverns at bay, it would only give time for more reinforcements to arrive."

And should the riders manage to delineate a temporary no-vaulting zone—one with a ten-foot diameter, doable in fifteen minutes, which would imprison both of them—then even he would not be able to leave.

The only choice left was for him to vault her, a potentially fatal decision that he did not wish to make for her. He took her hand. "Do you want to come with me?"

Her fingertips trembled against his. "What are my chances of survival?"

"Ten percent. At best."

"I don't want to die," she murmured. "Or be taken. Are there no other choices?"

His voice shook. "Summon a cyclone. Blow them all away."

"If only I could." She sucked in a breath. "Wait a minute, what had my admirer said? *The day we met, lightning struck.* Do you suppose he could have meant it literally?"

That was not possible. "Listen, Fairfax—"

Almost casually, she lifted her free hand toward the zenith of the cloudless sky. Her hand clenched into a fist. And down the lightning came.

He opened his mouth, to gasp or scream he could not tell. But no sounds emerged. He only stared, his eyes watering, as the brilliant comet of electricity hurtled earthward.

As it neared ground, the lightning split into half a dozen offshoots. Each offshoot lashed onto a wyvern. Each wyvern twitched and fell, hitting the desert with thuds that rattled Titus's skeleton.

Blinking, he turned toward her. She looked as flabbergasted as he felt.

"Fortune shield me," she murmured. "Is this why Atlantis wants me?"

The mention of Atlantis snapped him out of his daze: the lightning would act as a beacon to any and all nearby pursuers. He broke into a run, pulling her with him. "Hurry. Armored chariots will be here any minute."

The sand wyvern was the only one with a double saddle. He unstrapped and shoved aside the unconscious but still breathing riders, while she searched for tracers—Atlantean steeds usually wore several as part of their tack.

When she had discarded a handful of small disks, he helped her up into the saddle in front of him. Already in the distance he could make out a trio of armored chariots approaching.

She pointed her wand at the sand wyvern. *"Revivisce omnino."*

The beast jerked and wobbled to its feet. Titus flicked the reins. The sand wyvern spread its wings and lurched into a rather drunken flight. A wyvern in peak condition might hold its own with armored chariots for a short sprint, but this one was not in peak condition and they had a long way to go.

He turned the sand wyvern east. "You wanted to head east, if I remember correctly."

"As far from Atlantis as possible." She looked north, at the sight of approaching armored chariots. "Should I assume those are built to withstand lightning strikes?"

"Yes, you should."

She sighed. "Does no one ever think about making things easier for me?" She pointed to the ground below. "Have the wyvern fly between the dunes."

He steered the sand wyvern lower. The pursuing armored chariots followed them into the valley, closing in all the while.

"Even closer to the ground," she said.

He was beginning to have an idea what she planned to do. He looked over his shoulder. The armored chariots were a quarter mile behind and gaining; they too flew close to the ground.

"Come," murmured Fairfax, peering around him. "Come a little nearer."

"You might be the scariest girl I have ever met," he told her.

"Let's not be dramatic," she said drily. "I'm the only girl you can remember ever meeting."

Then she bared her teeth and pointed her wand. The dunes rose, like two huge waves cresting, and came crashing down onto the armored chariots, burying them beneath a literal mountain of sand.

He urged the wyvern to fly higher, banking once more toward the east. "If there is a scary girl competition, I would put my last coin on you."

She only laughed softly and laid her head against his shoulder, asleep again within minutes.

CHAPTER · 20

England

It is murky—dusk or dawn I cannot tell. From the back, I see two men—or nearly grown boys—walking, one supporting the other. They move stealthily, constantly looking in all directions.

When they finally stop and crouch down behind a boulder, I see the place they are approaching. A palatial fort, or a fortress-like palace, set atop a rocky hill that dominates the center of a wide valley surrounded by toothlike peaks.

Almost all the peaks have guard towers on them, their narrow windows glowing like the slitted eyes of nocturnal beasts. The floor of the valley is brightly lit, revealing rings of defenses.

I had written the above in the morning, harried because I was about to be late for a meeting with the high council that Father wished me to attend. All throughout the day I would remember the vision and wonder what in the world I was looking at.

Just now I visited Father in his classroom. He is so difficult in the present, but the old him, the "record and likeness" he had left behind in the teaching cantos of the Crucible—I adore that young man. And it breaks my heart to realize that I consider someone who no longer exists not just a dear friend, but the only person who understands the life I live now and all the responsibilities I will face.

How I fear that I will turn out to be like Father someday, hard and grim, full of anger and recrimination. Being reminded of how charming and exuberant he had once been only deepens that fear.

But I digress. Young Gaius told me that without a doubt I had seen the Commander's Palace, the Bane's retreat in the hinterlands of Atlantis.

The young men I saw in the vision are either the bravest or the stupidest mages alive.

After the revelation at tea, what Titus wanted to see was something about Kashkari. But the diary chose once again to confirm that Titus would go to Atlantis with only one other person, someone who needed help walking.

He closed the diary. Across the table, Fairfax was just sitting up, coming out of the Crucible.

"Do you know anyone named Penelope Rainstone?" she asked, with a strange flatness to her voice.

"She is the regent's chief security adviser."

"What kind of person is she?"

"Extremely capable. Seems devoted to the crown. No evidence of any extracurricular dealings with Atlantis. Why are you interested in her?"

She did not answer, but only looked unsettled.

Could it be? "Did you come across her name while you were searching for clues to the memory keeper's identity?"

For that was how he would find his way to Horatio Haywood, by first unmasking the identity of the memory keeper.

She got off the stool and shrugged into the uniform jacket she had set aside on the worktable. "The Argonin line is her favorite quote. And she and Master Haywood had met many years ago, during a reception at the Citadel, before they even started their university studies. But nothing conclusive."

He did not know what he had expected, but this was a shock. Commander Rainstone?

"I'm headed back," said Fairfax.

The house was locked down before supper. After that, to go back in, one either had to climb through a window or vault. And any time one vaulted, there was a chance of being seen. For him it did not matter. For her, everything mattered. Even climbing in through a window, if there were witnesses, could arouse Mrs. Hancock's suspicion.

She had always been scrupulous before. She ought to remember that even though he could not take her on his mission, she was still the most hunted mage on Earth.

But he did not have the heart to lecture her, so he only said, "Let me go first and make sure the coast is clear."

After Titus had seen Fairfax safely back, he looked into Wintervale's room for Kashkari. But he only came across Cooper and Sutherland, already on their way out. Wintervale yawned hugely, his eyes closing.

Kashkari was in his own room. "Have a seat, prince," he said as Titus entered. "The sound circle has already been set, by the way."

Titus got to the point. "Who are you?"

"I am no one important, but you might have heard of my late uncle. His name was Akhilesh Parimu."

Titus stared at Kashkari—the name meant nothing to him. Then it suddenly did. "Akhilesh Parimu, the elemental mage born on the night of the great meteor storm in 1833, the one who reawakened a dead volcano?"

Kashkari nodded. "Then you would also know what happened to him."

"His family killed him rather than let Atlantis have him."

"He begged them to kill him, rather than be taken—or that has always been the version told to me," said Kashkari. "In any case, in retaliation, Atlantis killed everyone else in his entire family, except my mother, who was very young at the time and had been sent away to stay with a friend as soon as Akhilesh's powers manifested themselves.

"The friend, the woman I've always known as my grandmother,

convinced her husband that they must take my mother and flee to a nonmage realm, so they did, leaving their island in the Arabian Sea to settle on the subcontinent, in Hyderabad.

"My mother grew up knowing she was a mage refugee, but she didn't know anything about the history of her biological family. A spate of uprisings in the subcontinent realms brought an influx of mage refugees to Hyderabad. Some of them wanted to form a coherent new community; others simply wished to disappear into the crowd. She married a young man of the latter group. He became a lawyer, they had two children, and they lived a life that on the outside was scarcely distinguishable from those of the nonmages all around them.

"And then she became pregnant again and I was born during the great meteor storm of 1866. This frightened my grandparents, who remembered what had happened the previous time a child of my mother's bloodline was born during a meteor storm. They finally told my mother the truth about her brother and her parents, and even though elemental powers rarely run in families, together they watched me anxiously.

"My power, it turned out, was not in elements, but in prophetic dreams. Did Fairfax tell you?"

Titus debated whether to involve Fairfax in the conversation. "He finds your ability quite novel."

"When my family realized that I was no elemental mage, they relaxed enough to allow me to make my own decision as to whether I wished to come to England for schooling. We of Eastern heritage do not view visions of the future as something that must be accepted, so I leaned toward staying with my family, until I had a new dream that tipped my decision.

"The dream was only a fragment, of a number of people in a room—your room, in fact—and one of them saying to me, 'By staying close to Wintervale, you saved him.'"

This was not what Titus had expected to hear. For some reason, because his knowledge of Kashkari's prophetic dreams had first come from Fairfax, and because the Oracle had told her that Kashkari was the one from whom she should seek aid, he had come to anticipate that anything else Kashkari would say to him would also revolve around Fairfax.

But of course he should have known better. From the moment Kashkari began his explanation, even though he had yet to specifically mention it, every word he had uttered had centered on one thing: the great elemental mage not of his uncle's time, but of their own.

And despite everything Titus fiercely wished for, that mage was Wintervale, and not Fairfax. "So you came to save Wintervale," he said, careful to keep his disappointment out of his voice.

"I knew who Baron Wintervale was—the January Uprising was so successful for a time that his name became synonymous with hope in all the mage realms. My family could not stop talking about all his new victories—we didn't learn until later that he had

Baroness Sorren as his strategist; we thought it was all him, single-handedly outwitting and overpowering Atlantis. And I remember my grandparents whispering to each other about the possibility of finally going home again, to be Exiles no more.

"All that hope came crashing down when the January Uprising was crushed. And by the time I started having that particular dream, Baron Wintervale was already dead. But I thought to myself, what if this means I have some greater role to play than I had imagined? What if I am meant to rescue Baron Wintervale's son from some terrible danger and help him to rekindle his father's dream?"

"And to think I once thought your ambition was to help India achieve independence from Britain."

"No, my ambition has always been the overthrow of the Bane," Kashkari said easily, as if it were the most natural thing in the world. "Justice for my uncle and his entire family. Justice for all the other families that had been sacrificed in the Bane's quest for ever more power."

"And you think Wintervale is the key to all that?"

"I don't know one way or the other. Just as I can't say my lingering about Wintervale all these years has had any effect."

Titus had noticed how closely Kashkari stuck to Wintervale in recent weeks. But come to think of it, the two had been nearly inseparable for years.

"Have you told Wintervale?"

Kashkari shook his head. "You know how he is. Either he has to become much more discreet or the situation has to become much more dire, before I'd risk telling him the whole truth."

"Why are you telling me, then?"

"I need some advice."

Titus felt a strange premonition. "Go on."

"I recently had the dream again and this time I finally saw the face of the speaker, the one who said, 'By staying close to Wintervale, you saved him.'"

"Who is it?"

"Mrs. Hancock."

"What?" Mrs. Hancock, special envoy of Atlantis's Department of Overseas Administration?

"I have been in her parlor. I have seen the maelstrom symbol on her drawer pulls," said Kashkari. "I know she is an agent of Atlantis. But Atlantis has many agents, and not all of them are loyal to the Bane."

"I have seen *nothing* from Mrs. Hancock that would suggest she is not extremely loyal to the Bane."

Kashkari's face fell. "I'd hoped that you knew something about her that I don't. That perhaps she is sympathetic to our cause."

"Your cause, not ours," Titus reminded him, pointedly.

"But Amara told me that Atlantis considers you an adversary. She said Atlantis also believes that you are harboring an elemental mage as powerful as my uncle had been."

Amara must be the one who had crashed the party at the Citadel, the one allegedly engaged to Kashkari's brother.

Titus made his tone dismissive. "A misunderstanding that got out of hand. When the elemental mage brought down a bolt of lightning, I got on my peryton and went for a look. Agents of Atlantis reached the spot with me still circling overhead and they have hounded me ever since."

"I see," said Kashkari carefully.

"But you need not worry that anything you say here will find its way to the wrong ears. I might not have the same ambition as you, but I have no love for Atlantis and will not stand in your way."

Titus was about to head for the door when he remembered something. "Mind telling me why you were late for school? Knowing what I do now, I imagine you were not stuck on a nonmage ship in the Indian Ocean."

"No, I was in Africa at my brother's engagement—his fiancée's family moved to the Kalahari Realm several generations ago and even in Exile they did not relocate far from the Kalahari."

"So the woman really is your future sister-in-law?"

"I'm afraid so." Kashkari's gaze wandered briefly to the photograph from the engagement fête. "In any case, there we were, talking. Amara related what she'd thought of as heartening news, that Madame Pierredure had emerged to distribute armament and know-how to mages in several realms who were secretly planning attacks on Atlantean installations."

"When in fact she committed suicide years ago."

"In our home, no less—she and my grandmother had been friends at school and she had shown up at our door after the rebellions had failed. We told Amara everything. The next few days were a blur—that was what delayed my return to Britain."

Titus nodded. "And is there a particular reason you chose to tell Fairfax about your prophetic dreams?"

"Fairfax is an odd case. I was hoping you'd be able to tell me more, since it was always understood that he was your friend. But while I know he had never been here before the beginning of last Half, what I cannot decide is whether you put him here, or whether Atlantis put him here and you must do your best to tolerate him."

Titus stared at Kashkari. He worried about many things and concocted endless possible scenarios to defend against, but it had never occurred to him that anyone would see Fairfax as a possible agent of Atlantis. "Why do you think Atlantis put him here?"

"Because for two people who are supposed to be friends, sometimes you certainly seem as if you can't stand each other."

Sometimes Titus forgot the great falling-out between himself and Fairfax at the beginning of Summer Half. The divide between them had seemed an abyss—completely unbridgeable. Which they nevertheless managed to bridge.

Did this mean there was hope for them this time as well?

"Have you mentioned your suspicions about Fairfax to anyone, anyone at all?"

"No. However he arrived at our midst, he has been nothing but helpful all around."

Inner beauty. That was what the boys had responded to in Fairfax from the beginning, her kindness, her comfortable company, her easy acceptance of them as they were. "I would go on saying nothing of Fairfax."

"I understand. And Mrs. Hancock?"

Mrs. Hancock was a very different problem. Titus had no intention of ever trusting anyone with the maelstrom symbol on her drawer pulls. "Let me ask around."

They bade each other good night and Titus walked to the door. As he was about to let himself out, however, Kashkari spoke again. "Your Highness."

Titus did not turn around. "What is it?"

"You may say nothing of what you believe, Your Highness, but remember my powers," said Kashkari, his voice quiet and cool. "I have seen who you are, and that is the only reason I have risked my life and the lives of all those I love by telling you the truth. Someday I hope you will return that trust."

CHAPTER · 21

The Sahara Desert

HALF AN HOUR HAD PASSED since Fairfax brought down lightning and buried the armored chariots, half an hour untroubled by minions of Atlantis. The sun beat down, white and relentless; the sand rippled, like the surface of a wind-driven sea. The sand wyvern, a hardy creature, had largely recovered from the electric shock it had received, and flew steadily at speeds in excess of eighty miles a hour. But Titus did not dare let his guard down and kept scanning different parts of the sky with far-seeing spells. Once he and Fairfax had been found, it became much easier for Atlantis to establish a new search range. Its forces no longer needed to comb every inch of sand in every direction from the original blood circle, but could concentrate on a sharply reduced area.

Sure enough, before another five minutes went by, he spotted a trio of albino wyverns. They were several miles behind, but they were faster—smaller, sleeker creatures were often swifter in flight.

Besides, the trouble was not in those three wyverns, but in all the others that were sure to come, now that he and Fairfax had been spotted again.

After studying the riders more closely, however, he changed his mind about their not being his biggest concern. The riders had released a net behind them, which resembled an impractical-looking hood worn on an invisible head.

A spell accelerator: they were about to deploy distance spell-casting.

In distance spell-casting, the party in pursuit was at a disadvantage, as the target kept moving away, which meant a spell had to travel farther. While a certain amount of distance was necessary for the strength of the spell to build—three miles was generally considered the optimum distance—beyond that the spell began to weaken again.

But a spell accelerator boosted both the power and endurance of the spell, which portended trouble for two fleeing fugitives.

Titus pulled out his wand—the Atlanteans were not the only ones familiar with distance spell-casting. He focused, steadied, and locked his own aim, spells leaving his lips one after another.

He could see what they were doing and they were no doubt aware of his action. But neither party dodged, each determined to deploy as many spells as possible, in case most of them, just a hairsbreadth off in aim, would fizzle into nothing somewhere high in the atmosphere, or against the surface of the desert below.

At the last possible moment, Titus sent the sand wyvern into a near vertical dive.

Behind him, the trio of albino wyverns, who had been flying in close formation, responded to the slumping weight of their riders and veered off in different directions.

The sand wyvern pulled out of the dive and began gaining altitude again.

"What's the turbulence?" Fairfax mumbled, her eyes closed.

"We dodged some distance spell-casting."

"My hero. But can't a girl sleep in peace around here?" There was a hint of a sly grin at the corner of her mouth.

He kissed the top of her head. "Of course. I will personally guarantee a ride as smooth as that of a square-mile flying carpet."

But the sand wyvern did not want to cooperate. The moment a tiny oasis appeared on the horizon, it headed straight for the grove of date palms. And Titus, despite his best effort, could not dislodge it from its course.

He could only aim a spate of pacification spells at the train of camels standing nose-to-tail just beyond the palm trees.

The camels masticated and stared placidly at the sand wyvern, as the palms swayed in the current generated by its massive wings. The humans, however, possessed no such equanimity. Of the four bearded, sun-browned men, one fainted outright, two reached for their rifles, and one for his Koran.

Titus dismounted and led the tall-as-a-two-story-house beast to the puddle at the center of the oasis.

"*Assalamu alaykum*," he said to the three men who were still conscious.

Peace be upon you.

The older man with the Koran opened and closed his mouth several times, but no words came out.

A young man in a dusty-red keffiyeh rasped something, but as Titus's grasp of Arabic was restricted to a few phrases of courtesy, he did not bother to respond.

Another young man in a brown turban cocked his firearm, but the old man put a hand on his arm. The wyvern drank and drank and drank. When it was done, Titus persuaded it to pull down a date palm branch, so he could cut off a large cluster of dates.

With another "*Assalamu alaykum*" to the caravanists, still agape, he urged the sand wyvern to take to the sky again.

After another hour or so, Titus set down the sand wyvern about a mile away from a low rocky hill. The hill looked barren, but any shade in the desert, anywhere water could condense and collect, played host to life. He sent out the two lengths of hunting rope still in his possession to find the sand wyvern a good supper and crouched down to give Fairfax some water.

She drank with her eyes closed. "Did I fall asleep *again*?"

"With panacea, even when you stop sleeping all the time, you will still sleep a great deal. Besides, you exerted yourself when Atlantis found us."

Which could impede her recovery. Ideally it should be nothing but rest for her, until her sleep pattern returned to normal.

"Did more dangerous things happen after the distance spell-casting?"

"Not to us, but there are some caravanists who will have stories to tell their grandchildren. They will probably weave in elaborate details about the sand wyvern eating half of their camels, while the demonic, horned rider laughed."

She tittered. "That *does* sound like you."

"I am very proud of my forked tail, but I will deny the existence of horns to my last breath."

Now she half opened her eyes. "All I see is a halo."

"Your compliment made my tail fall off. Now look what you have done."

She laughed again, softly. "So did the sand wyvern get enough water?"

"I think so. And that was pure greed on the sand wyvern's part—they can go ten days without."

"It'd be nice if we could, though I'm not sure I want my skin to look like that." The sand wyvern was very nearly invisible when set against the desert floor, its exterior resembling exactly a pile of small boulders half-buried in sand.

"I hate to tell you this, but that is how our skin already looks."

She closed her eyes again. "Your looks are no doubt suffering. *My* beauty, however, is as indestructible as the Angels' wings."

"Well," he said, "you do look very nice . . ."

Her eyelashes fluttered.

". . . ly shriveled."

Her lips curved. "May I remind you that you are speaking to someone capable of smiting you with a thunderbolt?"

"Is there any point to flirting with a girl who is not capable of that?"

"So this is your idea of flirting?"

He cradled her hand in one of his to check her pulse. "Whatever I call it, your heart is beating fast."

"Are you sure that is not a residual effect of the panacea?"

He rubbed his thumb over her wrist. Her skin was as soft as the first summer breeze. "I am absolutely certain."

Her breaths quickened. Her lips part slightly. And suddenly his own heart thumped, blood rushing in his ears.

The next moment he was knocked flat by a returning hunting rope, wrapped around a still-writhing snake.

She laughed and laughed as he wrestled with the hunting rope, trying to loosen it without getting bitten by the snake, while the hungry sand wyvern growled with impatience.

With the sand wyvern at last enjoying its afternoon snack, he returned to her side. She was already almost asleep again.

"Well," he said, "at least this time we were not interrupted by a sand wyvern."

"No," she replied, her voice barely audible. "I thought we might create some sparks together. But now I know nothing we do will ever rival the passionate embrace between a hunting rope and a snake."

She fell asleep with a smirk on her face. He looked at her a long time, smiling.

CHAPTER · 22

England

WINTERVALE'S BALANCE AND MOBILITY REFUSED to improve. A week after he woke up from his long sleep, he still could not stand upright on his own, let alone slide down the banister with a thump and a triumphant whoop, as he used to do.

To walk to and from classes, to have his meal in the dining room, even to go to the lavatory, someone else had to accompany him. That someone was almost always Kashkari, who had taken to sitting in Wintervale's room, so the latter did not need to shout at the top of his lungs if he needed a biscuit from his cabinet or felt like opening his window for a breath of fresh air.

But that was not the only thing different about Wintervale.

He had always been more open with Titus than with the other boys, more frank about the frustrations of his life: his fragile mother, his homesickness for the Domain, and, more obliquely, his fear that he would not live up to the great Wintervale name.

Glimpses of an inner life. Fleeting glimpses, as Wintervale was determined to enjoy himself to the maximum and quite adept—or so Titus suspected—at burying any emotional turmoil beneath a new round of fun.

The new Wintervale still maintained that outward appearance of bubbly conviviality. But now, when they were alone—infrequently since Kashkari was his near-constant companion—Titus found him to be quieter and more inquisitive.

His main anxiety was for his mother and Titus was happy to tell him the truth: there was no news on Lady Wintervale. Wintervale also wanted to know what had happened to all the other mages entrapped by Atlantis that night in Grenoble; on that Titus also let him have the truth, which was that Titus did not really know.

It was when Wintervale asked about the state of the resistance as a whole that Titus fudged his answers. He did not want Wintervale demoralized by the heavy blow Atlantis had dealt the resistance, nor did he want to give the impression that he was personally interested in the developments taking place.

It was six days after Wintervale woke up that he spoke of the future for the first time, two simple, declarative sentences. "I am going to find the resistance. And I am going to join it."

"You cannot walk on your own."

The problem baffled Titus. Wintervale could move his toes. His lower limbs most certain had feelings—heat, cold, touch, he felt them all. With support, he shuffled along, effectively enough to reach where he needed to go. But without the strength of another to make up for his own lack of balance, even if he stood with his back against a wall, after a minute or so he would start tipping to one side and not be able to right himself.

They told everyone that Wintervale had badly strained a muscle, keeping the truth hidden as otherwise Mrs. Dawlish would insist on additional medical attention, and Wintervale did not want to be poked and prodded.

"I don't need to walk to use my elemental powers," said Wintervale. "They can put me on a wyvern."

"You have never been on a wyvern."

"I can learn, after I find the rebellion. You are sure you don't have any contacts?"

"I am sure." At least on this front Titus did not need to lie. His mother had died for her involvement with the rebels; he had no plans to repeat that mistake. "Good luck locating the resistance without getting caught by Atlantis."

The look on Wintervale's face was not so much disappointment as despair—he had survived being pursued by Atlantis, he had discovered a rare and marvelous ability in himself, and yet he remained stuck at this nonmage school, with no way of finding his mother or contributing to the resistance.

Kashkari came into the room then, Cooper and Sutherland in tow. Titus slipped out, but Wintervale's distress stayed with him.

By nature and by necessity, he prepared incessantly for the

future. After discovering that all along his mother had meant Wintervale, however, he could not think of the next week, or even the next day without some part of himself recoiling—without Fairfax, what future was there?

But he could not allow that dangerous self-indulgence to continue. His personal feelings did not matter—they never had. Only the task was paramount.

What he needed most, obviously, was for Wintervale to recover his balance and mobility. It was impossible for him to drag Wintervale in his current condition across the breadth of Atlantis to the Commander's Palace in the uplands—or at least extremely inadvisable.

At some point he would have to tell Wintervale everything—or at minimum admit to Wintervale that he, too, was willing to take on Atlantis. But with Wintervale's history of indiscretion, Titus planned to wait until he absolutely must.

What he could do in the meanwhile, both to prepare Wintervale and bolster the latter's morale, was to take him into the Crucible. Atlantis already knew about the Crucible. So even if Wintervale inadvertently blabbered about it, he would not alert Atlantis to anything new.

Before he dared show the Crucible to Wintervale, however, he must purge all traces of Fairfax from the book.

He sat down in the laboratory and studied her images for a long time, in the illustrations of "The Oracle of Still Waters" and

"Sleeping Beauty." Without those illustrations, after she left the school, he might never be able to see her again.

He undid the changes he had made and returned the illustrations to their original state.

As he was about to close the Crucible, he remembered to check "Battle for Black Bastion," Helgira's story. And there it was, Fairfax's face. He had added her image to the other two stories, but not this one. A quick scan of the log of modifications that the Crucible kept informed him that the image was altered twenty years ago.

Twenty years ago this copy of the Crucible belonged to his mother.

Do not, he told himself. What did it matter now why Princess Ariadne had made the change?

But he reached for the diary and opened it.

5 February, YD 1011

Many times I see a place in my visions and I have no idea of the location. Not this time. This time I immediately recognize the hulking shape of the Black Bastion, one of the most difficult locales in the Crucible.

It is night, but the fortress is lit with torches. And near the very top of the bastion, upon a balcony that during the day would have a magnificent view, stands a young woman in a white dress, her long, black hair whipping in the wind.

Is this Helgira?

Father had wanted me to practice getting into the inner chambers at the Black Bastion in order to use Helgira's prayer alcove as a portal. To that end I had once dressed up as a serving maid delivering a flagon of wine, but I had been recognized as an imposter almost immediately and had barely the time to shout "And they lived happily ever after" to avoid being hacked to pieces.

When the vision had left me, I found my copy of the Crucible and turned to Helgira's story. The illustration shows a woman in her thirties, still handsome but scarred and battle-hardened, nothing like the courtly beauty I had seen on the balcony.

Who is she, then?

3 September, YD 1011

It is Helgira.

The young woman with the white dress and the whipping long hair raises her hands and down plunges the most awe-inspiring bolt of lightning I have ever witnessed, the energy of an entire turbulent sky focused into a singular beam of power.

Helgira the lightning wielder. There has never been any other.

So this is what she looks like.

19 September, YD 1011

I have changed Helgira's face in my own copy of the Crucible, the monastery's copy, and the Citadel's copy—I hope Father would not mind, as he considered the Citadel's copy his personal copy.

But now that I have done that, I begin to wonder why I should have seen this vision at all. The deeds of a folkloric character who only exists in fiction—and in the Crucible—are not something that one ought to see in a vision about the future, are they?

But his mother had indeed seen the future. That had been Fairfax standing on Helgira's balcony, calling down the bolt of lightning that would strike the Bane dead. Dead temporarily, at least.

Because Princess Ariadne had altered Helgira's image inside the Crucible, Fairfax had been able to move about Black Bastion freely. And when the Atlanteans had demanded answers about the girl who brought down lightning, Titus had been able to shrug and tell them to learn something about the Domain's folklore.

Fairfax had been writ large across his life.

Why then could she not remain the One?

The lake parted.

It was an inland sea, actually, so large that the far shores were below the horizon. At its bottom, a group of schoolchildren had been trapped inside an ever-shrinking air bubble.

Fairfax had spent a good bit of time in this tale, trying to rescue the schoolchildren. She had never completely succeeded. But now, with Wintervale at the task, the deep waters of the lake parted to reveal a muddy, mile-long path to the air bubble.

Titus shook his head slowly. What could one do but marvel at power of this magnitude?

He took Wintervale to a different story, "The Locust Autumn." Wintervale took a look at the locust swarm approaching the field of a poor farmer, and, with a wolfish grin, raised his hands. He summoned such a cyclone, the entire swarm was blown away without a trace.

In yet another story, he lifted fifty-ton boulders as if they were no heavier than tennis balls and easily constructed a high wall around a town about to be trampled by giants. From the top of the wall, the townspeople attacked the vulnerable soft spots on top of the giants' unprotected heads, leading to a rousing victory.

"This is the best feeling I have ever had, in my entire life!" Wintervale shouted at Titus, as giants fell like dominoes, making the rampart beneath their feet thump.

Titus ought to be happy: he had read *The Lives and Deeds of Great Elemental Mages* time and again and Wintervale was most assuredly measuring up. He ought to be relieved, too, that he had made the right choice: other than his inability to command lightning, Wintervale's powers were in every way superior to Fairfax's.

Yet Titus felt . . . uneasy: he had never known what it was like to achieve one's goal in one giant leap, rather than through years of strenuous toil. He shook his head and reminded himself that he had better enjoy the moment, because the harder part was to come.

Always.

Wintervale's excitement remained unabated as they exited the Crucible. "I can't even tell you how ready I am to take on a squadron of armored chariots and greet them with these huge boulders."

"Which you can only do when there are such boulders lying about."

"Or I can yank them off the bones of the earth," Wintervale enthused. "Imagine if my father had someone like me during the January Uprising."

The outcome would have been different, Titus had to admit, at least for some battles. The Crucible in hand, he rose from Wintervale's cot, on which they had been sitting shoulder-to-shoulder. It had been a calculated risk to bring the Crucible to school, but Wintervale had never vaulted well and Titus was not ready to divulge the location of the new entrance to the laboratory.

"Mind taking me to the privy before you go?" asked Wintervale.

Wintervale's elemental powers had exploded in amplitude, but his bladder seemed to have shrunk in size, at least when Titus was around. "Come on, then."

Wintervale sprang up, not in the direction of Titus's outstretched hand, but toward the window—and nearly took a header for his trouble. Titus barely kept him from hitting a corner of his shelves. "Careful!"

Wintervale stood with his forehead pressed against the window pane. "For a moment—for a moment I thought it was my mother."

But all Titus saw as he looked out, besides a hawker he had never seen before this Half, was the usual street outside Mrs. Dawlish's house.

When Iolanthe arrived at the laboratory, after lights-out, the prince was already there. Or rather, he was in the Crucible, his hand over the book, his head resting on the table.

Even seemingly asleep, he looked tense and worried. Her heart clenched—she wished she could still help him.

Then why don't you? asked another part of her. *Even if you are not the great heroine you imagined yourself to be, there is still so much to do.*

But he doesn't want my help.

He only said you are not the One. When did he say he no longer needed your help?

Next to the Crucible on the table was a pastry box with a note underneath. She pulled out the note to read.

> *Dalbert told me Mrs. Hinderstone's shop also sells Frankish pastry, which are very popular with the patrons. These are from Paris. I hope you like them.*

"These" were two cream puffs, a tiny fruit tart, and a mille-feuille, which consisted of alternating layers of smooth pastry cream and buttery puff pastry.

She almost pushed the box away from herself, afraid its contents would only ever taste of heartache and rejection. But somehow a piece of the fruit tart found its way into her mouth. It was delicious beyond belief—and all she could think of was the care he had always taken with her.

She laid her hand over his and kept it there for several minutes, before she started the password and the countersign to enter the Crucible.

In the reading room, Titus sat with his forehead on the cabinet-size book before him, his eyes bleary.

"Are you all right?" came Fairfax's voice.

He straightened. "I hate to sound like a broken clock but it is not safe for you to leave Mrs. Dawlish's after lights-out."

"I know."

She looked at him oddly. He could not decide whether she was displeased with him—or completely the opposite.

"You are not sleeping enough," she said.

"I do not sleep well, in any case. But I was not sleepy, just over-whelmed with information."

"What information?"

"I need Wintervale to be able to walk on his own power before we can set out for Atlantis. But before that, I have to find out what exactly is the matter with him." He tapped the tome on the table. "This is the most comprehensive reference on how to interpret the Kno-it-all gauge's readings. Some combinations immediately narrow the choice down to one or two likely diagnoses. But gross motor impairment and mental instability open up endless possibilities—anything from the onset of a new phobia to an irreparable splintering of the psyche."

"What?"

He shook his head. "The splintering of the psyche case dates to almost fifteen centuries ago, back when mages were still debating whether cancer was divine punishment for illicit misdeeds. I am not going to pay any mind to that."

"Then what are you worried about?"

"Earlier today, he almost fell over getting to the window, because he thought he saw his mother outside. Yet from where he was sitting, he would have seen nothing but the sky—and maybe a bit of roof on the opposite side of the street."

"Did you think he was hallucinating?"

"No, I did not. He was very much lucid. But the incident made me remember that when I used the Kno-it-all gauge on Wintervale, he was still under the effect of the panacea, sleeping all the time. At the time I had thought the gauge gave a reading of impairment on gross motor skills because he could not move without being carried—that the gauge had been fooled by the panacea, if you will."

"And you hoped that the reading of mental instability had also been influenced by panacea," she said, "because it isn't normal for someone to sleep all the time."

"Except the gauge turned out to be quite correct on his trouble moving around."

He half wondered whether she would again blast him for his lack of commitment to Wintervale, but she only said, quietly, "Nothing has ever been easy for you, has it?"

Something in her tone caught his attention: the absence of anger. Ever since the day of the maelstrom, no matter how politely she spoke, he had always heard, loud and clear, the fury underneath.

But not this moment. This moment she was just his friend.

"No, you are wrong," he said. "I have been immensely fortunate, especially in my friends."

In you.

She gazed at him for a long moment, then she reached into her jacket and took out a small envelope. "Take this. A birthday present."

It was his seventeenth birthday, a day that he had meant to let pass unremarked, but it thrilled him that she remembered. When he opened the envelope, however, he saw that it contained the vertices of the quasi-vaulter.

"No," he said in shock. "No, I cannot. They are to keep you safe."

She came around the desk and pushed the envelope into his pocket. "I'm safe enough. You need to take care of yourself."

After he had seen her safely back to her room, Titus lay in bed for a long time, the envelope upon his sternum, thinking about how immensely fortunate he was in his friends.

In her.

CHAPTER 23

The Sahara Desert

IT TOOK THE TWO HUNTING ropes several trips each to satisfy the sand wyvern's appetite. While the beast dined, Titus looked it over, as a rider's courtesy, to make sure that the steed did not have any injuries or discomforts.

He almost did not see the slight discoloration on the wyvern's spine ridge. A sensation of chill at the back of his neck made him look again: a tracer that had been made the exact same color as the wyvern, except it had faded slightly from exposure to the elements.

Almost numbly, he checked the rest of the oddly shaped ridge bumps. Two more tracers. How many more that he had not found?

He destroyed all the tracers and glanced up. Nothing loomed in the sky yet. The group he had dispatched with distance spells earlier had probably come across them by luck; the kind of tracers that had been put on the sand wyvern took some trial and error to track down.

Indecision paralyzed him: half of him wanted to leap atop the wyvern and take flight; the other half recognized that there was no point in going anywhere unless he cleared the steed of all the tracers.

He searched, inspecting every square inch of the creature's scaly exterior and its entire wingspread. He found a tracer attached to a talon, another one at the tip of a wing bone.

Was that all?

It was turning dark, but there was no mistaking the storm cloud that fanned out from the horizon, which was no storm cloud at all, but hundreds of wyverns flying in close formation.

Fortune shield him, for nothing else would.

Instead of destroying the last batch of tracers, he threw them down. He took his seat on the saddle behind Fairfax, already strapped in and fast asleep, and urged the sand wyvern to take flight, but as close to the ground as possible without the tips of its wings striking the surface.

When he had gone perhaps a mile, he landed the wyvern, made it lie down, and performed a hypnosis spell. The wyvern snorted a couple of times and closed its eyes. He lifted Fairfax out of the saddle, removed the saddle from the wyvern's back, and hid it under one of the wyvern's wings. Next he set a sound circle and a tensile shield beyond, so that the wyvern's presence could not be detected by either its smell or its snore-like breathing.

Fairfax and himself he hid under the wyvern's other wing. He should distance them from the wyvern, but if the beast proved to be still tracked, they were doomed in any case, as he could not dig them into the dunes and the camouflage tent was not something he dared rely on when a bright light might be shined squarely upon it.

With a noise like thousands of banners streaming in a gale, their pursuers arrived. He held his breath and lifted the sand wyvern's wing just enough for a peek. Wyverns and armored chariots darkened the already shadowy sky. Some circled overhead, some swooped in crisscross patterns, and others headed straight toward the spot where he had dropped the tracers.

The scale of the hunt took his breath away.

A wyvern landed two hundred feet away. He took Fairfax's hand. It did not make him any less afraid to have her hand in his, but it made the misery of being fearful more bearable.

Another wyvern landed, even closer.

A commotion went through the Atlanteans. Shouts rose. "The base is being attacked!" "We must head back!" "We must protect the Lord High Commander!"

The Lord High Commander. Fairfax whimpered—Titus was crushing her hand in his. He forced his fingers to unclench. The *Bane* was in the Sahara?

"We will go nowhere!" countered a gruff, authoritative voice. "Our order came directly from the Lord High Commander and that order is to apprehend those two fugitives."

Something streaked through the air. It was followed by a piercing scream, as if a rider had been gored in the stomach.

More projectiles, a forest of long, thin objects, hurtled toward the Atlanteans. For a moment Titus thought he was looking at hundreds of hunting ropes. But no, they were spears, bewitched to chase and impale enemies.

He was speechless—it must have been a millennium, at least, since bewitched spears were the most advanced weaponry in a mage battle.

But the advantage to raining down antique armaments was that few modern soldiers had been trained to deal with them. The spears sought out riders, instead of wyverns, the hide and scales of which were too tough for them to penetrate. The riders ordered their wyverns to bat at the spears with their wings, but a spear that had been knocked down to the ground simply sprang back up again and went after the nearest rider.

Some wyverns breathed on the spears, but wyvern fires were not hot enough to melt the spears, only hot enough to heat them to a glowing red, making them even more dangerous.

"Fly!" rose a clear, sharp voice above the chaos and the confusion. Titus recognized it as the brigadier's, from the first day of Atlantis's hunt. "The bewitchment on these spears cannot last more than a few miles in distance. We can outrun them!"

The din grew more distant as the Atlanteans followed the brigadier's advice. Titus listened tensely. It could be a feint, to make him come out of hiding. But he did not have many choices. To flee was dangerous; to remain in place, equally so.

He murmured a quick prayer before he got to his feet and set the saddle on the sand wyvern's back again. Lifting Fairfax in his arms, he carried her to the saddle and strapped her back in.

"Come on, old girl. If we are lucky, we could see the Nile before sunrise."

If not, they might see the Bane instead.

CHAPTER · 24

England

"IS WINTERVALE ANY BETTER?"

The question came from West, at the end of practice, as Iolanthe put on a wool coat over her kit. In the last few days, the weather had turned chilly, almost harsh. The twenty-two had practiced in a light misting of rain, with the spectators rubbing their hands and leaping in place to keep warm.

"Same as before, more or less," said Iolanthe, buttoning her coat.

"How is he taking it, not being able to get about on his own?"

"With commendable stoicism, I must say."

She had heard about his ease at wielding his power from the prince, who had accompanied him into the Crucible. Which was likely the reason that an otherwise active, almost restless Wintervale had been able to handle his loss of mobility with such grace. What did victories and losses on the cricket pitch matter anymore, when the boy who had always feared a life of mediocrity now had the opportunity to be a hero for the ages?

"I'll call on him in a few days," said West. "Don't want Wintervale to think he stopped mattering when he stopped being one of the twenty-two."

West had shaved off the mustache he wore at the beginning of the Half. Without facial hair he looked quite different. And it struck her for the first time that he resembled the prince somewhat—not like brothers, but they could pass for cousins.

"I'm sure Wintervale will be thrilled at your visit." Or at least the old Wintervale would have been.

Iolanthe gathered up her equipment and started for Mrs. Dawlish's, Cooper and Kashkari beside her. After a minute or so, it occurred to her that Kashkari was walking with a slight limp.

"What's the matter with your leg?" she asked.

"You wouldn't believe it if I told you."

"I would," Cooper said eagerly, as he wrapped a muffler around his neck. "My brothers always tell me I'll believe anything."

Iolanthe shook her head in fond exasperation. "At least you *don't* want to be a lawyer—there's something to be said for self-knowledge."

"Well, here's the story," said Kashkari. "Wintervale and I stopped by the library yesterday—since he has to spend so much time off his feet, he wanted something to read. So there I was, browsing, and this enormous book fell off the opposite shelf and hit me on the back of the calf."

Books didn't just fall off shelves, though they could be made to, easily enough. At Iolanthe's old school in Delamer, there had been a prominent notice in the library: *No summoning spells allowed. Violators will report directly to the headmaster's office.*

"Did someone push it off on the other side?" asked Cooper.

"Nobody was on the other side. I was lucky I'd moved just then, or it could have fallen on my head." Kashkari glanced at them. "Will you two disbelieve me now?"

"I don't remember you limping yesterday," said Iolanthe. Kashkari had supported Wintervale both going into and coming out of supper, last evening.

"I feel it more today. And the practice has made everything worse."

"You don't think the book fractured a bone, do you?"

"No, but it certainly left a big bruise."

"Sometimes poltergeists do that," said Cooper in all seriousness. "I haven't heard about the library being haunted, but this is an old school. There must be disgruntled ghosts of old boys roaming about."

A fierce wind blew. Iolanthe pressed down on her cap to prevent it from being carried away.

"Maybe Mrs. Dawlish has something for it. You know, old ladies and their aching muscles," Cooper continued.

"I might ask her," said Kashkari, not sounding overly enthused about being physicked by Mrs. Dawlish. "If this gets much worse, I won't be able to haul Wintervale to his classes."

Cooper, always looking to be of use, leaped at the opportunity. "I'll do it. You've already done so much."

"Thank you," said Kashkari. Then, after a beat, "I'm afraid Wintervale finds my company rather stale, these days. A change for him might be welcome."

Wintervale used to be quite indiscriminate: he spent a great deal of time with Kashkari, but he was equally happy to pass time with other boys from Mrs. Dawlish's house. Now, he seemed to crave only Titus's company.

It was perfectly understandable—only with Titus he could be himself. All the same, Iolanthe felt bad for Kashkari.

"That can't be true," said Cooper. "I think Wintervale is downright grateful that you are always there to help him. Goodness knows I'd be."

Kashkari sighed. "I hope—"

Something caught Iolanthe's senses, an impression of objects crashing toward her. She swung her cricket bat—and felt the impact of the hit deep in her shoulder.

Cooper yowled, amid a racket of thuds and cracks.

Roof tiles—from Mrs. Dawlish's house, as they were almost about to enter her door.

Iolanthe had struck one tile and sent it in several pieces to the middle of the street. Kashkari looked shaken, but unhurt. Cooper, however, had been hit by another tile and was bleeding a little from the side of his head.

Iolanthe glanced at the roof—no one was up there. Across the street, the rather suspicious hawker who had been loitering about of late also wasn't there. She broke into a run and circled the house, but there was no one on the other side of the roof ridge, nor anyone either clambering back into windows or flat-out running away.

When she came back to the curb outside the front door, Kashkari was holding a handkerchief against Cooper's skull. "Do you feel faint? Or nauseous? Or anything out of the ordinary?"

Cooper stared in fascination at a smear of bright red on his hand. "Well, my ears are ringing a little, but I think I'm fine." He grinned. "I'll have a story to tell at supper."

Kashkari shook his head. "Come on. Let's get you to a dispensary first."

After Cooper's wound had been cleaned and bandaged, Iolanthe bought him a paper cone of roasted chestnuts from a street hawker. Back at Mrs. Dawlish's, they settled him into his room with a pot of tea and a sandwich. Sutherland, Rogers, and a few other boys crowded into his room.

Cooper recounted his freak accident with great relish.

Sutherland, however, frowned. "You don't suppose Trumper and Hogg are behind this, do you?"

Iolanthe shook her head. Trumper and Hogg, two pupils who had made a great deal of trouble for Mrs. Dawlish's boys the previous Half and had been humiliated in turn, were no longer at the school. And even if they had come back to Eton specifically to seek vengeance, they lacked the competence to organize a remote precision strike, for there had been no one on the roof.

Such an attack, however, would be all too easy for a mage.

But against whom? Iolanthe, who was still the most wanted mage in the world, or Kashkari, who, at least according to what he had told the prince, was an implacable foe of the Bane?

More boys came to see Cooper. Iolanthe and Kashkari yielded their places and went out into the corridor.

"Thank you," said Kashkari.

"It was nothing."

"I might have been hit by that roof tile, if you hadn't reacted so fast."

"Or maybe I would have been."

"Maybe," said Kashkari, not sounding terribly convinced. "I'd better go check on Wintervale."

And she, decided Iolanthe, had better go speak with the prince.

The prince was not in his room. He was also not in the laboratory. The laboratory's other entrance was via a lighthouse on Cape Wrath, Scotland. She put on the lighthouse keeper's mackintosh and went out despite the howling wind and the driving rain—sometimes the prince liked to walk on the headland, when he had been reading for too long.

There was no sign of a single soul out and about. Puzzled, she returned to Mrs. Dawlish's. From there, she walked to High Street, wondering whether he had gone to buy some foodstuff—he usually didn't, preferring to vault to London for his supply, going to a different shop each time, so he could be sure his cakes and tins hadn't been tampered with.

An enemy of the Bane had many worries.

She bought a hot cross bun for herself at the baker's and had just stepped out of the door of the shop when someone took her by the arm.

Lady Wintervale, pale, drawn, and just short of skeletal.

Iolanthe almost dropped the bun in her hand. It was a long moment before she could raise her bowler hat an inch. "Afternoon, my lady."

Without a word in reply, Lady Wintervale led Iolanthe into an alley and vaulted. They rematerialized in a room with ivory silk wallpaper, an enormous fireplace, and a gilded ceiling. A large window looked out onto—

Iolanthe took a few steps closer. It was the Thames River, and Eton College on the other side. "Are we in the English queen's home?"

"We are." Lady Wintervale pulled off her gloves and tossed them aside. "Such a hovel."

The interior of Windsor Castle was stodgy, to be sure, but it felt respectable enough. Then again, the Wintervale estate, before its destruction at the end of the January Uprising, was supposed to have rivaled the Citadel in magnificence. "Do the staff know you are here?"

"They do. They think I am one of the queen's German relatives."

Lady Wintervale sat down in a daffodil-yellow stuffed chair. "Now tell me, how is Lee?"

Wintervale's given name was Leander, but no one ever called him that—or any variants of it. "He can't walk by himself, but otherwise he seems fine. He asks about you a lot."

"What does he ask about me?"

"I . . . He never does it in front of me, so I can only relate what I have heard from His Highness. The prince says Wintervale is always anxious for your news. And His Highness has been glad not to have your news, so he doesn't have to lie to Wintervale."

Lady Wintervale placed two fingers against her temple. "And why can't Lee walk by himself?"

"We don't know. Would you like me to have the prince bring him here to meet you?"

Lady Wintervale's head snapped up. "No. *No*. That would be far too dangerous. Absolutely not. And say nothing to Lee of my presence, you understand? *Not a word*."

The woman always made Iolanthe nervous. "Yes, my lady, I understand. Wintervale is not to know you are here."

"Good. You may go," said Lady Wintervale, closing her eyes as if she had been exhausted by the conversation. "If you learn anything I should know, come back to this room and say *Toujours fier*."

This time the prince was in the laboratory.

"Where were you?" Iolanthe could barely contain herself. "I

have been looking for you all over."

"I was in Paris."

Paris again. "What were you doing there?"

"Buying things for you, obviously." He pointed at a bag of pastries sitting on the worktable.

She didn't think he had hopped across the Channel just for the baked goods, but that was a topic for another time. "I just spoke to Lady Wintervale."

His expression changed instantly. "How did she escape? Or was she let go?"

Iolanthe's heart dropped half a foot. "I didn't ask."

Part of her was always petrified with fear at being face-to-face with Lady Wintervale, since Lady Wintervale had very nearly suffocated Iolanthe to death when she first came to England. "I was in shock. She vaulted me to Windsor Castle, asked me a few questions about Wintervale, told me not to mention anything of her presence to him, and dismissed me."

And she had been all too glad to be let go.

"Tell me everything again," asked Titus. "More slowly this time. Give me all the details."

She did, as he listened carefully. Then she asked, "Why do you suppose Lady Wintervale came to me, instead of you?"

"She knows I am watched, now more than ever."

The hawker who always loitered before Mrs. Dawlish's house, the person who might or might not be hiding in the copse of trees behind—they were but the tip of the iceberg. Some days, when Iolanthe walked to school with the other boys, she could feel the surveillance the entire length of the way.

"And what were you doing on High Street?" asked the prince. "It is not your turn to provide for tea."

Mrs. Dawlish supplied three meals a day, but the boys were responsible for their own tea, which was in essence a fourth meal. The prince, Wintervale, Kashkari, and Iolanthe took turns buying a week's worth of teastuff for the four of them.

Iolanthe started. "I completely forgot why I was there in the first place. The tiles."

She related the incident of the roof tiles, and of the book that fell off a shelf and struck Kashkari. "Too many falling items to be a coincidence. Kashkari thinks they were all for him, the book and the tiles."

Titus's face was grave. "Far too many, especially roof tiles. Before I was sent here, mages from the Domain came and improved the house from top to bottom. Have you ever noticed clogged drains, creaking steps, or bad flues in this house?"

She had to think about it. "No."

When things went smoothly, they did so unnoticed.

"And there would not be, not while I remain here, and perhaps not even for years afterward. So it is quite impossible for roof tiles to have blown off. Those roof tiles should have stayed in place even if a tornado took a running leap at Mrs. Dawlish's house."

He opened the bag of pastries, handed her an éclair, and took one for himself. "Anything else I need to know about?"

Something nagged at the back of her mind. It took her a few seconds to realize what it concerned. "West, the cricketer. He seems more interested in you than he has reason to be."

Titus's brow knitted. "I am not sure I remember what he looks like. I will come and see at your next practice."

They spent a few minutes in silence, eating. It felt comfortable, almost.

When he was done with his éclair, he looked at her, as if he had come to a decision. "About Lady Wintervale, I actually think it is good news. She knows about you, so if she is not being interrogated by Atlantis, all the better for you. As for West, I do not know enough to fear. But the flying tiles are a different matter altogether.

"They were probably not meant for you—Atlantis wants you whole, not maimed. But anything striking so close to you worries me. Whether the mischief-doer wants to harm Kashkari because he is part of the resistance or because he guards the path to Wintervale, the point is, someone knows something."

He exhaled. "You should leave. Soon."

Her heart slowed; perhaps it stopped altogether. "You want me to go?"

"The more I think about the roof tiles, the more it disturbs me. We might all have to go, before too long. Once we part ways, however, I will not be able to help you find your guardian, and I want to—or at least get you close enough."

Once we part ways.

Something almost choked her—like anger, but not quite. Opposition. She had been resigned to her eventual departure from the school, from his life. But now that he had spoken these very words, that resignation had evaporated like morning mist.

She did not want to go.

She never did.

A quarter of an hour later, Iolanthe was the first person to walk into Wintervale's room for tea.

Before Wintervale became the One, she and he had rarely spent any time alone—they had always interacted as members of a group. Afterward, she saw no reason for that to change. All the better to keep the buffer of someone else's, or lots of someone elses', presence between them. Easier for her to act as if nothing had changed, just another cocky young man who happened to be a bit too big for his britches.

She walked to the fire burning in his grate and held out her hand toward the warmth. "Getting cold."

"I heard you swatted a flying roof tile today," said Wintervale from his cot.

Iolanthe shrugged. "Gaining West's admiration on the pitch. Saving my mate's life on the way home. Just another day in the extraordinary life of Archer Fairfax."

The old Wintervale would have guffawed, and then moaned for the rest of the day that he had missed such a terrific sight. But the new Wintervale only smiled—and only a half smile at that.

It occurred to Iolanthe that he looked tired, as tired as the prince sometimes looked, a weariness beyond what could be cleared up by a good long night of sleep.

The stab of guilt was sharp. More than anything else, she had envied him. His power. His destiny. His now unbreakable claim on Titus. When she, of all people, should understand what a terrifying ordeal it must have been. And to lose his mobility on top of it.

And his mother too, or at least he so believed.

"Is it getting to you, not being able to move around?"

He sighed. "So many plans, so many visions of greatness, and I can't even take a piss by myself."

"Have you improved at all since you stopped sleeping all the time?"

"Sometimes I think I have. Sometimes I am sure I have. And then, the next time I get up, it's the same thing all over again."

"Well, you can't give up," she said softly. "Those plans and visions of greatness don't realize themselves, you know."

This less robust, more serious Wintervale nodded. "You are right, Fairfax. And that may be exactly what I need to hear right now."

Sane, so sane. Drained, perhaps, but unquestionably sound and sober. And now, with proof that his mother was nearby, they knew for certain he had never hallucinated, but had actually seen Lady

Wintervale, who had probably been on top of a roof on the opposite side of the street, to get a better look into his room.

So why then was the Kno-it-all gauge so correct about his gross motor skills, but so wrong about his mental state?

The junior boys bustled in with platters of fried eggs and grilled sausages. Kashkari entered in their wake, looking calm if a bit grim. And conversation moved on to things that, essentially, mattered to nobody.

CHAPTER · 25

The Sahara Desert

THE GIRL WOKE UP TO a star-studded sky and the sound of air rushing over her ears.

She was moving, strapped into the saddle on the back of a large flying steed. Someone held her from behind with one arm.

"A star just fell," said Titus.

She leaned her head on his shoulder. "You saw a meteor?"

"I am beginning to think that perhaps your admirer was not being hyperbolic, but literal, in what he wrote: you could have been born during a meteor shower and you could have made lightning strike on the day you and he met."

"So he is pardoned for his heinous literary offenses because he was being truthful?"

"The parts having to do with elemental magic, maybe. But it is still the height of unmanliness to mewl 'you are my hope, my prayer, my destiny.'"

"May I remind you that is the only way to properly address a girl who wields lightning? Anything less reverent and, poof, one's hair is on fire and one's brain scrambled."

"All right, my hope—but I am not saying the rest of it—I have something you need to feel."

She feigned the sound of outrage. "But we barely know each other, sir!"

He laughed softly. "But you must hold it in your hand and feel it change," he urged, in her ear. "I insist. I can wait no longer."

She knew they were on a serious subject, but the flutter of his breath on her skin, the low drawl of his words—heat raced along all her nerve endings. "Will I like it?"

"Well, I do have to apologize for its size. It is rather small." And with that, he pressed something rather small into her hand.

It was a pendant on a chain, and while the chain was cool, the pendant was warm.

"Remember the first day, you asked me what was so cold under my clothes? It was this."

Then it had been icy; now it was not cold anymore. It must be half of a pair of heat tracers: a heat tracer's temperature increased as distance to its mate decreased. The mate of this particular tracer had been quite far away earlier. But now whoever carried the other half of the pair was much, much closer.

"Before too long, we should land and put the pendant some distance away," Titus continued, "so we can conceal ourselves and see who is coming before they see us."

"How much time before this mage catches up with us?" That idea would work better during daylight hours.

"Depends on our relative speed. Just keep an eye on it."

She nodded and put it back into the bag.

"There is something else you should probably know," he said.

She couldn't quite decide from his tone whether he was making a silly subject sound serious or making light of a grave one. "Will we be talking about dimensions again?"

"Yes, the eye-poppingly enormous size of my—well, if I must be specific, our—trouble: the Bane is here in the Sahara."

She shivered. "For us?"

"For now I would assume so, until I learn otherwise."

"And how did you learn about it to start with?"

He gave a brief account of the additional tracers he had found on the wyvern, which had led Atlantean forces to close in on them, before those battalions were themselves attacked.

"Bewitched spears?" Her jaw dropped. "Which century are we living in?"

"It was like watching a reenactment of a historic battle, no doubt about that."

"What kind of mages carry hundreds of bewitched spears with them?"

"The kind who does not want Atlantis to find out who they are."

"And they are helping us?"

"Accidentally, I would imagine. They are probably causing Atlantis trouble because that is what they live for."

She nodded slowly, digesting everything he had told her. "And this is the same sand wyvern as earlier?"

"Yes."

"You are sure you have rid it of all Atlantean tracers?"

"Hard to tell. But we have not had trouble in the past hour and—"

He looked at his watch and swore.

"What's the matter?"

"According to the compass built into my watch, we are flying in the wrong direction. I had set a course with a racing funnel for southeast, but now we are headed almost due north."

A racing funnel was a spell used to keep a wyvern on the straightest possible path during a speed trial. A wyvern in a racing funnel had no reason to deviate from its set course.

He murmured, resetting the racing tunnel. But instead the wyvern turned due north, then gradually, north-northwest.

"Is it taking us to the coast of the Mediterranean?"

His arm tightened around her middle. "No, I think it is taking us in the direction of the Atlantean base."

"What?"

"Homing elixir."

For cavalry, and even for large private stables, the practice was fairly common. Beasts raised in those establishments were fed small amounts of elixir that kept them docile and happy. Those elixirs, when formulated specifically for the establishment, also served to prevent lost or stolen beasts from straying too far, because going more than twenty-four hours without will make them automatically turn toward home.

"But I thought this wyvern didn't come from around here. I thought it had to be transported in from central Asia. Besides, we haven't had it for twenty-four hours yet. Twelve hours barely."

"The Atlanteans may have left an aerosolized trail of its particular homing elixir, to lead it—and us—in the direction of the nearest base."

"We have to get off, then. Take it down!"

He swore again. "It is refusing to follow directions—and we are half a mile up."

She swallowed. "Can you blind vault us to the ground?"

"It is still too soon for you to vault. I cannot take that chance."

She used a far-seeing spell. "But there are armored chariots ahead!"

"I can see that! And I do not want to hear you get all martyrish and tell me to vault off alone—I have not dragged you this far to hand you to Atlantis."

She could scarcely breathe. "Then what do we do?"

"We will jump."

"What?"

He was already unbuckling her harness.

"If you can produce enough of an air current to hold a hard-flying sand wyvern in place, then you can produce one to break our fall."

He came to his feet and pulled her to hers. She was barely able to stand with the force of the wind rushing past.

"What if I don't produce that air current?"

"You will." He took her hand in his, his tone brooking no dissent. "Now on the count of three. One. Two. Three."

They fell, accelerating toward the ground at thirty-two feet per second squared.

The free fall seemed to push Titus's heart and lungs upward, compressing them into half their size against the top of his ribcage. The air roaring past made his eyes water, but he dared not close them.

Where was the air current that would save them?

"Do something!" he shouted.

"Shut up! I'm trying!"

They bumped into little pockets of air that did nothing to decelerate their plunge, but made them flip and tumble. The starry night and the dark desert chased across his vision as he spun in every which direction.

The ground rose toward them at terrifying speeds. They screamed.

And kept on screaming.

CHAPTER 26

England

AT HER DESK IN THE reading room, Iolanthe stared at the image of a young Commander Rainstone, looking dashing as a pirate wench, a cutlass in hand. The picture was from a different article Iolanthe had found about the Argonin tricentennial fancy-dress ball, evidence that Commander Rainstone had indeed been part of the duo that attended as the visualization the Argonin quote *Oysters give pearls, but only if you are armed with a knife and willing to use it.*

It was easier to dig up information about Commander Rainstone's youth than to find out about her in the present. The current her made no news and stirred no controversies. She never married or had children—at least none on record. And she lived a simple life outside of her work, preferring quiet evenings spent at home to the glamorous social life of the Citadel.

That she lived alone could be a result of her already having a secret life. That secret life was also made easier by the fact that she had no family. And the signs had always pointed to the memory keeper being well-placed in life and close to the center of power, which certainly could be said about Commander Rainstone.

"Show me everything that has Penelope Rainstone and either Baron or Lady Wintervale," Iolanthe asked the help desk.

On the day she had revealed her powers, Master Haywood had put her into a portal trunk. She had been transported to its twin, located in the attic of the Wintervales' residence in Exile, in a fashionable part of London. Which meant there must be some connection between Commander Rainstone and the Wintervales.

And which was confirmed by an image of Commander Rainstone standing next to Baron Wintervale, who had been the one to give her the distinguished graduate award she had received at the end of her studies at the Titus the Great Center of Martial Learning.

Iolanthe rubbed her temples. All the pieces she found were useful, of course. But none of them took her anyplace definite.

"No progress?" said the prince from across the table. He had been helping her with her search for the past hour, once he returned from his mysterious purpose in France.

She blew out a breath. "It's so hard to find . . ." She trailed off. The light of excitement on his face—*he* had unearthed something useful. "What do you have?"

"The second time my mother saw a vision about me, standing on the balcony, she mentioned someone named Eirene, who lost her trust by reading her diary without her permission."

Iolanthe had a very vague recollection of it. She had not read those visions under optimal conditions.

"I just asked the help desk for anything that mentioned both Commander Rainstone and Eirene," Titus went on. "And this is what I found."

"This" was a different interview young Penelope Rainstone gave, also around the time of her being named an outstanding graduate from the officers' school, but to the student newspaper of her old academy, located in a less affluent area of Delamer.

Titus pointed at a specific paragraph.

Q: Do you have a nickname?
A: Some of my friends call me Eirene, for fun. Eirene is the goddess of peace, but I study the art of war.

Iolanthe's fingertips prickled. What she did remember from reading Princess Ariadne's visions was that the first time it had been seen on the day of the prince's birth, and the second time, in the hours immediately preceding Iolanthe's birth.

"Do you remember what your mother was doing the second time she saw the vision?"

"Yes," said Titus. "She was at someone's confinement."

At Eirene's confinement. And Eirene had read her diary, a vision which probably made no sense to Princess Ariadne, but which Eirene had recognized as being about herself and her child, and which had led her to go to such extremes to ensure that her child would not be found by Atlantis.

And Eirene was Commander Rainstone.

"I checked," said Titus. "At that time Penelope Rainstone had been on my mother's personal staff, but within weeks was reassigned to the Citadel's general staff: she had lost my mother's trust."

It felt strangely disheartening to hear this of Commander Rainstone. Iolanthe supposed it was because she still couldn't quite connect Commander Rainstone to the faithless memory keeper.

"Commander Rainstone has no children. She would have had to disguise an entire pregnancy. And if she passed off her own child as Iolanthe Seabourne, what would she have done with the Seabournes' baby, the real Iolanthe Seabourne?"

"It has been done before, a woman hiding a pregnancy from everyone. And she could have found foster parents for the baby."

The real Iolanthe Seabourne had been born at the Royal Hesperia Hospital, near the end of September. Her birth had been two and a half months premature. For weeks she remained at the hospital, her anxious parents visiting every day and staying as long as they could.

At the end of one particular visit, driving home in a borrowed chariot, they had collided in midair with a much larger vehicle full of drunken tourists. According to Master Haywood, both Jason and Delphine Seabourne had died instantly.

On the fateful night of the meteor storm, the real Iolanthe

Seabourne had been six weeks old, but would have easily passed for a newborn. And a switch had taken place. She had gone . . . somewhere. And Commander Rainstone's baby had been brought up by Master Haywood as Iolanthe Seabourne.

Titus was before the help desk again.

"What are you getting?"

"Records from the Royal Hesperia Hospital around that time." He scanned various volumes. "Nothing about a Rainstone giving birth. Someone, however, did pay for the hospital's best maternity suite and request complete anonymity. That expectant mother did not even use the hospital's staff. But listen to this, half an hour after the baby was born, it was taken to the nursery, and not brought back to the mother until several hours later, at dawn."

When it was brought back, it was no longer the same baby.

"And your guardian visited the hospital at the same time."

Titus pushed a thick book of visitors' logs at Iolanthe. She flipped through it, the sound of pages turning unnaturally loud in her ears.

Master Haywood had first visited the hospital's nursery in September, shortly after the real Iolanthe Seabourne was born. In subsequent days he came frequently, his reason for visit always "To take the parents' place so they may have some rest." After the Seabournes died, he still came several times a week, to "Look in on my friends' orphaned daughter."

At which point did he begin to conspire with Penelope Rainstone to plan a switch? Penelope Rainstone, who had learned what would happen to her own child because she snooped inside Princess Ariadne's diary of visions? Had he mentioned in passing that there was an orphan girl at the hospital, one who was about to be entrusted to the care of an elderly relative who had never seen her before? Did the inspiration grow from there?

The last time Master Haywood visited the hospital was on the night of the meteor storm. He had signed in at seven o'clock in the evening and signed out an hour later. Next to the entry, however, there was a note from the hospital's administrative staff: he had been found by security at half past three in the morning and escorted from the premises.

But he would have had enough time for the switch.

"I want to speak to Lady Wintervale," Iolanthe said.

When she had arrived in the attic of the Wintervale house in London, Lady Wintervale had nearly killed her. Not because she thought Iolanthe an intruder, but because she held Iolanthe responsible for someone's loss of honor.

Iolanthe had escaped convinced that Lady Wintervale was completely mad. But now that she knew Lady Wintervale was mostly lucid and only occasionally unstable, she saw Lady Wintervale's words in a different light.

"It is not a bad idea—she could know more than we think," said Titus. "I will come with you."

Five minutes later, they were inside the sitting room at Windsor Castle where Lady Wintervale had first brought Iolanthe. "*Toujours fier*," said Iolanthe.

They did not have to wait long before the door of the sitting room opened and in came Lady Wintervale. At the sight of the prince, she bowed.

"My lady, have a seat," said Titus.

"Thank you, Your Highness. Shall I ring for tea?"

"No, that would not be necessary. We would be glad if you could answer a few questions for my friend."

"Of course, Your Highness," said Lady Wintervale.

"Can you tell me, my lady," said Iolanthe, "why I was translocated to your house, when I left the Domain?"

"You are my late husband's illegitimate daughter," Lady Wintervale said calmly, "and he had promised to protect and look after you, should the need arise."

A gong went off in Iolanthe's head. Titus looked almost as flabbergasted.

Her lips opened and closed several times before she managed to make a sound. "I am *Baron Wintervale's* child?"

"Yes."

On his deathbed he asked me to swear a blood oath that I would protect you as I would my own child, Lady Wintervale had once told her. She should have guessed then. For who else would a man ask this, if not his flesh and blood?

"And—" Iolanthe's voice seemed to echo in her own head. "And you know who my mother is, too?"

"Of course. But I do not speak that woman's name."

"So . . . they had an affair?"

Iolanthe could have kicked herself, as soon as the question left her lips. Of course they'd had an affair.

"Yes, an affair of long standing. It continued even into his Exile— they used to rendezvous at Claridges', in London."

"Is she also an Exile?" That would mean the memory keeper was someone other than Commander Rainstone.

"No, she was never an Exile—she was too clever to be mixed up in the rebellion. When Atlantis restricted all the instantaneous modes of travel, she managed to have some loopholes made just for herself. So it was not difficult for her to slip away for an afternoon and meet him."

For you he gave up his honor, Lady Wintervale had once said to Iolanthe. *For you he destroyed us all.* "Was that why you said I caused him to lose his honor?"

Lady Wintervale raised her chin a fraction of an inch. And suddenly she was no longer the frail-looking Exile, but a mage of great dignity and power. "I married my husband knowing full well that he was never going to be faithful to one woman. But at that time I believed him to have the markings of greatness and I was proud to be his wife.

"But alas, I was deceived. At the end of the January Uprising, when the outcome became clear, Baroness Sorren had the courage of her conviction to face execution, but he could not bear the thought of losing his life.

"He needed to live, he convinced himself, because you, his daughter, would someday be the greatest elemental mage on Earth, and must be protected from the forces of Atlantis—though why Atlantis would be after you I never fully understood. He had awakened from a nightmare, you see, screaming in fright of the judgment of the Angels. The story spilled from his lips. But after a while I became incapable of hearing properly, because it dawned on me what he was telling me: he had given my cousin to Atlantis in exchange for his own life."

Titus rose to his feet, his face deathly pale. Understanding hit Iolanthe like a mallet to the temple: the cousin Lady Wintervale was talking about was none other than Princess Ariadne, Titus's mother. And Baron Wintervale, the hero of the rebellion, had been the one who betrayed her.

"Why did you never tell me?" His voice was hoarse.

"For Leander's sake, I kept it a secret. I never wanted Lee to know that his father had been such a faithless coward." She smiled a little, a strange, hollow smile. "But fear not, Your Highness. I avenged your mother."

He shook his head. "Atlantis put the execution curse on him."

"No, Your Highness, it was me. I could not suffer him to live after that. He did not try to stop me, but asked that I swear a blood oath to look after his daughter as if she were my own flesh and blood. I did no such thing; I only finished him."

Lady Wintervale clenched and unclenched her hands. "Murder, it changes a person. I used to be calm, unflappable, even. But after that, sometimes I . . . I . . ." Stiffly, she rose from her chair. "I hope I have answered all the questions to your satisfaction, sire."

Titus's jaw moved. "Thank you, my lady. Is there any message you would like us to take back to your son? He would be much relieved to know you are safe and well."

"No." Her answer was adamant. "He must not know that I am here."

"But he has become more tight-lipped. Would you not agree, prince?" said Iolanthe. "I hardly think that—"

"Young lady, you will allow me to know best what to do in this situation," Lady Wintervale cut her off. She bowed again to Titus. "Your Highness."

After the door closed behind Lady Wintervale, neither Titus nor Iolanthe said anything for a minute. And then, at almost the exact moment, they turned to each other and came together in a tight embrace. Iolanthe wasn't sure whether he was comforting her, or vice versa. Most likely both.

"Are you all right?" she asked.

"I am fine," he answered, dropping his head into the crook of her shoulder. "Strange, is it not? I have always wanted to avenge my mother. But now that she has already been avenged, I wish it had not been at the cost of a father for Wintervale—and a father for you."

"And Lady Wintervale's peace of mind, forever destroyed." She sighed. "I don't think I can ever see Baron Wintervale as my father."

"It might be easier after your suppressed memories resurface," he reminded her.

She was silent for a minute. "Does it bother you, that my father is responsible for your mother's death?"

He shook his head. "I am the grandson of a man who murdered his daughter—far be it for me to judge anyone on their bloodline. Besides . . ." His voice trailed off.

"What were you going to say?" She ran her fingers through his hair.

He took a deep breath. "That it has long been my suspicion that my father is Sihar."

She went still. "Are you sure?"

"One hundred percent sure, no. And yet all sorts of gossip sleuths and investigative reporters, with all the resources at their disposal and promises of great reward—everyone wanted to know the identity of the man who had fathered the next heir to the throne—came up empty in their quests.

"This tells me that my grandfather was involved in some way. The House of Elberon is nothing of what it once was, but within the Domain, it is still a force to be reckoned with. And if my grandfather wanted to silence witnesses, he had his means.

"The citizenry of the Domain enjoy trotting out the number and relatively unmolested existence of the Sihar as a sign of their enlightened attitudes. But the truth is that the Sihar are pariahs in the Domain, just as they are elsewhere. And my grandfather would never have allowed even a breath of insinuation that his daughter and heir might have taken up with a Sihar."

Iolanthe's schoolbooks had strenuously emphasized that blood magic, which the Sihar specialized in, was not sacrificial magic—and that the Sihar had been unfairly ostracized throughout history, an easy scapegoat whenever things went wrong and mages wished to point fingers as to who had incurred the wrath of the Angels.

Despite the official insistence, the Sihar were still the Others. Refugees from the Frankish realms, the Subcontinental realms, and the sub-Saharan realms had all become assimilated—she'd gone to school and made friends with their children. But the Sihars, although she'd stopped to listen to Sihar street musicians, bought cream cakes from Sihar bakeries, and once, when she still lived in Delamer, watched a Sihar midsummer procession down Palace Avenue, a celebration that marked their new year and high holiday, she had never visited the home of a Sihar, never met a Sihar at school, and never known Master Haywood to have any Sihar colleagues—at least, no one who admitted it.

Until the Master of the Domain.

She cupped his face. "You are still you. Nothing has changed."

He gazed at her a moment. "The same goes for you, remember

that. For me, you are—and always will be—everything worth living for."

And for me, you are—and always will be—everything worth fighting for.

She did not say the words, she only pulled him close and kissed him.

Wintervale was on his cot, as usual, propped up on a pile of pillows. He smiled slightly as Iolanthe walked in. "Fairfax, old chap, come to see the patient? Where is His Highness?"

"Probably in the baths, scrubbing his princely hide." Or, more likely, in Paris, on his mysterious business, which Iolanthe suspected had something to do with Wintervale's condition. Paris hosted one of the largest Exile communities in the world, with a mage population bigger than that of some smaller realms. And she had heard good things about the reputation of its mage physicians. "How are you?"

Wintervale shrugged. "Could be worse, I suppose, but I wouldn't wish this on anyone."

He had several books next to him on the cot and the sight of them rather saddened her: Wintervale preferred vigorous activities to those that required him to sit still for long periods of time.

"Are the books any good?"

He shrugged again. "They help time pass."

He had become paler, from being indoors so much. And pudgier—that big, athletic build beginning to lose its muscularity from the lack of exercise, or even movement.

"If I were a better card player I'd play with you—except I don't think you care that much for cards either."

"No, never saw the point of them," he said, tapping his fingers on the top of a thick, red-leather-bound book.

She studied his face. Did he look anything like her? If his mother was correct, then he was her half-brother. But try as she did, she could not see any of her own features in him.

A drop of blood from Wintervale, that was what she needed. A drop of blood from him, a drop of blood from her, and Titus would be able to let her know whether she and Wintervale were truly related.

But one couldn't simply go up to a mage and ask for a drop of blood. The stigma of blood magic ran deep and most mages guarded their blood as they would their lives.

"You think you can ask Titus to walk me down to supper tonight?" Wintervale asked.

The plaintiveness in his voice made her feel guilty: if it weren't for her, Wintervale would most likely have Titus's complete and undivided attention.

"If I see him before supper, I'll let him know."

"I wonder why Titus is so busy all the time," muttered Wintervale.

No, she thought. She could not see him as a brother. At least, not yet. Perhaps someday, if they were able to work together toward the same goal . . .

The door opened and in walked Kashkari. "Fairfax," he said, a little surprised. "Are you walking Wintervale down to supper?"

"I would if he wants me to. But I think Wintervale has his heart set on the prince—as any right-thinking man would," she said, slipping past Kashkari. "Off I go to find your prince for you, Wintervale."

In the middle of the night, Titus bolted upright in his bed.

He had been in a state of half dreaming, but now he could not remember what had caused him to jerk awake. He got up to drink some water, and, glass in hand, peered out from behind the curtain.

For the first time, he saw the watchers Fairfax had suspected of being there—three men, dressed in nonmage clothes and standing close together, their attention fixed on Mrs. Dawlish's house.

As he turned away from the window, the idea that had yanked him out of his uneasy sleep returned: it had to do with his mother's vision of Baron Wintervale's death.

And *her misinterpretation of it.*

Most of the time Princess Ariadne did not offer her own view on the significance of her visions, trusting that a long enough, detailed enough vision was its own best explanation. But with the vision of Baron Wintervale's death she had immediately construed the execution curse to have been ordered by Atlantis, never suspecting that his grieving wife, a skilled and powerful mage in her own right, could be his killer.

And if Princess Ariadne was wrong once, who was to say she

could not have made another mistake somewhere else, in a vision that had far greater impact on Titus's life?

Iolanthe had wanted to go to Claridge's the day they met with Lady Wintervale, to see whether the memory keeper was still making use of it. Titus persuaded her to wait until he had Dalbert check Commander Rainstone's schedule, so that they could choose a time during which Commander Rainstone would be otherwise occupied.

That opportunity came a few days later: Commander Rainstone was expected to be handing out awards at her alma mater all afternoon, and Titus and Iolanthe had a short day at school and no cricket practice requiring her attendance.

Claridge's, a large hotel located in the Mayfair area of London, brimmed with respectability and Englishness. While the prince did his reconnaisance inside the hotel—he was still reluctant to let her be seen anywhere except school—Iolanthe waited at a newsagent's stand around the corner, pretending to browse the selection.

The day was cold and overcast. The grayish leaves that still remained on the trees shook and shivered. A trio of street musicians on the opposite side of the intersection played an incongruously cheerful tune on their fiddles. Pedestrians, dressed almost invariably in coats of black or brown, rushed to and fro, paying little attention to the playbills that two boys were pasting onto a lamppost or the sandwich-board man advertising Mrs. Johansson's Miraculous Slimming Tonic.

Presently the prince appeared at her elbow. "I found a suite from which I cannot proceed beyond the anteroom."

The soles of her feet tingled. She paid the newsagent for a map of London and stuffed it into her coat pocket. "Let's go, then."

"Let me go first to make sure it is safe," he said, after they were out of the newsagent's hearing.

"I want to come with you." The memory keeper had gone through a great deal of trouble to keep her out of Atlantis's reach, so she should not be in danger from that quarter. And in any case, if Dalbert was correct, Commander Rainstone would be busy all afternoon. "Your safety is at least as important as mine—I'm not sure Wintervale can last five minutes on Atlantis without you."

"All right," he relented. "But do not let your guard down."

From an empty alley nearby, he vaulted her to the anteroom of the hotel suite. The small space was covered with crimson wallpaper—Iolanthe remembered somebody, probably Cooper, telling her that there was no point making interior walls in London anything except dark colored; the quality of the air was such that one was guaranteed to have dark-colored walls in a few years, no matter what.

The prince set to work, unwinding the anti-intrusion spells. She didn't know enough of the techniques to help him, so she kept herself in a corner, out of his way, and tried to breathe slowly and evenly. To not grow too excited, or let her hopes get away from—

Footsteps approached from the other side of the door.

Titus leaped back and immediately began putting up shields.

Iolanthe had his spare wand out, pointed at the door, fear and a sensation of giddiness taking turns accelerating her pulse.

The footsteps stopped. The door handle turned and slowly the door opened a crack, revealing the familiar face of Master Haywood.

Master Haywood's hair had been cut short, and he sported a funny-looking mustache, but there could be no doubt it was him.

It was him.

And then Iolanthe could hardly see him for the tears in her eyes. She launched herself at him. "Forgive me! Forgive me for taking so long to find you."

He banded his arms tightly about her. "Iola. Fortune shield me, it *is* you. I thought I would never see you again," he said, sounding dazed.

Tears rolled down her cheeks. Baron Wintervale might have provided the biological beginning to her existence, but Master Haywood was her true father, the one who sat by her bedside when she was ill, checked her homework, and took her to Mrs. Hinderstone's on summer days for pinemelon ice and then to the zoo to look at the dragons and the unicorns.

"I'm so glad you are safe," he said hoarsely. "So very, very glad."

Only then did he look up and notice that she had not come alone. He let go of her and bowed hastily to the Master of the Domain. "Your Highness."

"Master Haywood," Titus acknowledged him. "With your

permission, I should like to search the premises for translocators."

"Of course, sire. Shall I ring for some tea, sire?"

"No, no need. You may be at your ease."

Titus moved off to the interior of the suite. Master Haywood gaped at him for a second longer, and then turned to Iolanthe and drew her into the sitting room. "So all along you have been at that nonmage school they took me to, the prince's school?"

"Yes, yes, and I'll tell you everything," Iolanthe said. "But first tell me, how did you disappear from the Citadel that night?"

"I wish I had a better idea of what had happened. All evening long Atlantean guards around me kept whispering to one another about the Lord High Commander. It made me quite afraid, thinking the Bane himself might interrogate me.

"I was at the Citadel for almost an hour before I was marched into the library. My knees knocked. I could barely feel the floor beneath my feet. The next thing I knew, I was inside this hotel suite, with a note on the table that instructed me to never leave the perimeters, if I wanted to stay out of the Inquisitory. And this is where I have been ever since."

"Have you really not stepped out once?"

The sitting room, with the same crimson-colored walls, was of a decent size. And the bedroom, which she could see through its open door, likewise. But still, to not leave this limited space for four entire months . . .

"Compared to the Inquisitory, this is heaven. Plenty of room to stretch my legs, no one to question me, and all the nonmage books and newspapers I can ask for to be delivered. Except for a lack of your news, I really can't complain."

Her heart constricted as she remembered his tiny cell at the Inquisitory. "But can you leave this hotel if you wanted to?"

Master Haywood blanched. "I . . . I don't want to. It is too dangerous out there. I'm much better off here, inside."

"But if you walked out of here, then no one will know where you are. You will be completely anonymous and that will protect you better than any anti-intrusion spells."

"No, no. It's unthinkable." Master Haywood clenched the back of a chair. "It was because I destroyed that batch of light elixir that you called down lightning—and now you will never be safe. By staying here at least I will cause you no more trouble."

His adamancy baffled Iolanthe. Was it yet another symptom of the harm the memory spells had caused?

"By the sound of it, Fairfax, I would say your guardian has been placed inside a fear circle," said the prince, coming out from the bedroom.

"What is that?" Iolanthe had never heard of such a thing.

"An old spell from when wars were more intimate affairs. If you can set a fear circle around your enemies, you can practically starve them to death within."

Iolanthe glanced at Master Haywood, who was trying to absorb the news that what he feared most was fear itself.

She turned back to the prince. "Did you find any portals?"

"There are two armoires and a bathtub; I set alerts for—"

His expression changed. Taking Iolanthe by the arm, he concealed them both behind the heavy blue curtains.

Iolanthe peeked out. Master Haywood was just turning toward the open bedroom door. The edge of what looked to be a brown cloak appeared for a moment near the floor—on the other side of the wall, someone was hiding, waiting to reconnoiter the situation in the sitting room.

The prince quietly opened the French window that led out to the narrow balcony. Iolanthe held the air still so the curtains would not flutter with the draft coming in. He disappeared from the balcony. A few seconds later, he rematerialized, looking slightly dazed.

"She is here," said the prince. "I put her under a time freeze from outside the window of the bedroom—but I could not get in that way because it still has anti-intrusion spells."

"You mean Commander Rainstone?" Iolanthe's voice sounded like a squeak.

"Go and see. She cannot harm anyone now."

A time freeze lasted at most three minutes. Iolanthe took a deep breath and entered the bedroom—and almost fell backward in shock as she stared into the beautiful face of Lady Callista.

CHAPTER ·27

The Sahara Desert

STARS WHEELED ACROSS TITUS'S VISION, bright, cold streaks. Fairfax's hand threatened to slip from his. He instinctively tightened his grip, even as he tumbled head over heels.

The next moment he realized that he was no longer falling as fast. He had thought that should she succeed, they were sure to suffer injuries, slamming into a powerful current of air blasting in the exact opposite direction of their acceleration. But she had summoned multiple streams of air, so he felt harnessed—cuddled almost—and at just enough velocity to slow them down instead of making them come to a dead stop.

As the ground rose to meet them, they decelerated steadily, and then more sharply as the distance to impact decreased. When he fell face-first onto cold, hard sand, it was as if he had jumped from a height of ten feet, instead of nearly three thousand feet.

Pushing up to his knees, he began to laugh. Oh, it was the most marvelous feeling to be alive. "You did it. Fortune shield us, you actually did it."

She was also on her knees, clutching her chest. "My heart is going to explode. It is going to burst open from my chest and spray blood over a ten-mile radius."

"We are fine. We are *fine*. You were magnificent."

"Magnificent, my behind. You were not responsible for saving us while in free fall, you frigging idiot. Toward the end we must have been nose-diving at more than two hundred miles an hour. How do you expect someone to just counter that with mere air? What sort of stupidly blithe assumption was that? If I didn't die of fright, I would have died of shame of failure!"

Her irateness only seemed to build as she inveighed against him. "It was the rashest, dumbest, most arrantly thoughtless, most—"

Words failed her. But her fist did not: it connected with his solar plexus and knocked him flat.

Right. One should never anger an elemental mage, who would have been specifically taught violence as an emotional outlet from an early age.

But he only laughed again, giddy to be safe. His mirth infuriated her further. She leaped on top of him, seized him by his collar, and raised her fist.

He yanked her down and kissed her instead. A shudder went through her.

He raised her face and repeated himself. "You were magnificent."

She panted as if she had run a footrace. Her finger traced over his lower lip. Her other hand clutched his upper arm. His heartbeat, already unsteady, turned completely erratic.

He plunged his hands into her hair, pulled her close, and kissed her again.

"And the armored chariots will be here in three, two, one . . ." she murmured, her breaths more ragged than ever.

The armored chariots did not come on schedule.

"Well," she said, "this is vexing. Just when I thought my kisses had the power to alert Atlantis to my presence anywhere in the world."

"I am now willing to write very bad verses for you. Does that not testify to the power of your kisses?"

"How bad?"

"Ecstasy will be forced to rhyme with destiny."

She laughed and rose to her feet. "That is, I must admit, satisfyingly atrocious. Have it framed before you present it to me."

He took the hand she offered him and got up also. "Framed? I will have it chiseled into a fifty-ton slab that even you would have trouble moving."

"Hmm, I might have to build a house on that and call it the Maison de Doggerel."

Hand in hand, shoulder to shoulder, they scanned the sky.

"And there they come," he said. "Would you believe it, they brought back our sand wyvern to sniff us out, in case we hide underground or inside dunes."

Not the best idea in any case. If she fell asleep again, they would be stuck inside bedrock. Or worse, buried under a mountain of sand. "Do you think the Bane is with them?"

"I certainly hope n—"

A movement at the periphery of his vision made him turn to the west; she mirrored his motion almost in unison. Someone was hurtling toward them on a flying carpet.

They had their wands at the ready.

The flying carpet came to a sudden and complete stop. "Can you not see what is coming?" cried the rider. "Why are you two just standing there? Get moving!"

Titus and Fairfax glanced at each other. They could not see him very well in the dark, but his voice was that of a young man.

"We have no steed and she cannot be vaulted," said Titus.

The rider seemed flabbergasted. "What happened to the carpet I gave you?"

He leaped off his own carpet and came toward them. "Can you give me a spark or two, Fairfax?"

She was so stunned by his calling of her name she almost did not do what he asked. But she recovered in time to produce the faintest flicker of fire, which lit a slim, handsome young man of about their age in the robe and keffiyeh of the Bedouin tribes.

In one swift, violent motion, he ripped off the outside of the satchel that she carried across her person, making her gasp.

The outside of the satchel was in fact not a part of the satchel, but a shell with pockets. And the shell was a larger piece of fabric that had been folded thinly and tightly so as to fit around the body of the bag without gaps or bulges.

With a vigorous shake of the rider's wrists, the shell unfurled entirely. And with a murmured password, it rose off the ground, a flying carpet ready for use.

Titus and Fairfax exchanged another look, stupefied.

"Hurry up!" the rider shouted again, physically pushing them toward the flying carpet. "What is wrong with the two of you? Let's go!"

CHAPTER · 28

England

"I DON'T UNDERSTAND," IOLANTHE SAID, dumbfounded. "What is *she* doing here?"

Was *Lady Callista* the memory keeper?

"Quick," said the prince. "I need everyone's help for a containment dome."

A containment dome did not protect the mage inside against forces outside, but the other way around: it was to shield those outside from the one inside.

They barely finished the dome before the time-freeze spell wore away. Lady Callista blinked, finding herself suddenly surrounded.

"I guess my secret is out," she said, seemingly unconcerned, but her fingers clutched tightly around a jeweled wand not unlike the one that belonged to Iolanthe.

Lady Callista had been the one giving birth on the night of the meteor storm. Lady Callista had been the one conducting an affair with Baron Wintervale. Lady Callista, the last one to walk into the library at the Citadel before Master Haywood, had been the one to distribute the vertices of a quasi-vaulter that whisked him away.

"It can't be you," Iolanthe heard herself say. "You've been working against us all along."

"If you refer to the instance on the day you brought down lightning, when I set a tracer on the prince's sleeve, that was done purely at Atlantis's behest. I had no idea that I would lead them to you, until I myself arrived on the scene and saw agents of Atlantis working to undo the anti-intrusion spells His Highness had put in place."

"You were there?"

"Of course—I had made your wand into a tracer. I should have scooped you up that day and been done with all this nonsense a long time ago."

But she hadn't been able to. Titus and Iolanthe had escaped into the laboratory. Ever since then, Iolanthe's wand had been stored in the laboratory, a folded space that could not be located—and so Lady Callista had lost track of Iolanthe.

"I do not believe you," said Titus. "You gave me truth serum at your spring gala, just before my Inquisition. What could you possibly have hoped to achieve? For the Inquisitor to learn of your daughter's whereabouts even sooner?"

"For that you have only yourself to blame, Your Highness," Lady Callista shot back. "Yes, I made Aramia administer the truth serum to you—the Inquisitor had told me in no uncertain terms to see that accomplished. But what the Inquisitor didn't know was that I had substituted a different type of truth serum, a slow-acting one."

Titus narrowed his eyes.

"You were to have your interview with the Inquisitor as soon as she arrived," Lady Callista went on. "She would see the drink in your hand and know that you'd been dosed. But the serum would have no effect on you for almost an hour, by which time you would be done with her and no worse off than when you'd begun. Then I could ask you questions just as the truth serum began acting, and find out my daughter's whereabouts.

"But you didn't have your chat with her at the Citadel. Instead, over everyone's objections you went to the Inquisitory. And didn't begin your Inquisition until after the truth serum had taken effect."

Something still didn't make sense for Iolanthe. "You were there at our school on the Fourth of June. The Inquisitor could have hauled me away. You just sat there. You did nothing."

"What could I have done? I was there, as you said. I had to suppress all my memories to not give myself away. And I risked everything to get him out of the Citadel that night, didn't I?"

Lady Callista pointed to Master Haywood, who looked completely stunned by the goings-on.

"Only because you yourself were in danger of being unmasked," Iolanthe shot back, growing angrier with each word. "You were afraid that if the Inquisitor could really see past the memory spells, your own position would be in jeopardy. If you cared about him at all you would not have escrowed his memory in such a way as to never allow him access."

Lady Callista's features hardened. "Difficult decisions must be made sometimes. You are too young and you don't know men. When they want you they will say and do just about anything, but you can't expect constancy on their part. How could I trust that if I let him remember, he would still continue to keep my secret, or to keep you safe?"

Iolanthe's fingers clenched into a fist. "Is that how you treat people who love you, who give up everything for the love of you?"

"Yes. Because he"—Lady Callista again jabbed a finger in Master Haywood's direction—"does not love me. He loves a figment of his own imagination. The real me uses people, discards them, and has absolutely no regrets. Does he love that?"

Iolanthe was speechless.

"And you, you little ingrate." Lady Callista was only becoming more vehement. "Do you have any idea how difficult it was, how frightful, to figure out how to do everything my future self was telling Haywood we needed to do?"

A clanking sound. The prince opened his hand and his wand, which had fallen to the floor, returned to his palm. Iolanthe stared at him: he was no more likely to drop his wand than he was to lose his mother's diary.

"And for what?" Lady Callista went on. "Never have I had a single thank you from you. All you ever do is whine about how I am not helping your precious Master Haywood."

There was no arguing with self-justification of such magnitude and Iolanthe did not bother to try. "Break the fear circle. You let him go, we will let you go. It's a fair enough trade."

"Absolutely not. I will not have you running about and causing me more trouble. You will come with me. You will lie low. And you will not be heard from again until either the world ends or I go to the Angels."

The prince tapped Master Haywood on the arm and whispered in his ear. Master Haywood looked irresolute. But Titus spoke again. And Master Haywood nodded at last.

He came before Lady Callista and began to chant a long series of spells.

"How dare you?" shouted Lady Callista.

She fired various spells to stun and silence him, but the containment dome rendered them ineffectual.

"How dare you!" she shouted again.

But Master Haywood went on doggedly with his spells. And when he fell silent, Lady Callista dropped to the floor, unconscious.

Titus put her under another time freeze before he undid the containment dome. Lifting her from underneath her arms, he began dragging her toward the front door.

"What did you do to her?" Iolanthe asked Master Haywood.

"The prince asked me to put away all her memories having to do with you. When she comes to, she will know how to return to the Citadel. But she will not think to come back and pursue you."

"Not that she would, in any case," said Titus. "All her memories having to do with the two of you have probably been suppressed for a while, since Atlantis has been interrogating her day in and day out."

Iolanthe shook her head a little. "Then how did she know to come here?"

"You can make special provisions. For me, my memory of reading the vision of my death will return in full force when I step onto Atlantis itself." He propped Lady Callista up against the door and placed her hand on the handle.

"What are you doing now?" Iolanthe asked.

"I need her hand on the door to break the fear circle. Thank goodness she did not set a blood circle—that would not be so easy to break. But then again, the authorship of a blood circle can be verified, so she probably would not take that kind of a chance unless she felt she had no other choice."

He murmured the necessary incantations. Iolanthe watched him carefully, wondering what exactly Lady Callista had said earlier to cause him to drop his wand. He looked a little grim, but other than that, he seemed normal enough.

When he was done, he and Master Haywood together carried Lady Callista to the chaise longue in the sitting room.

"Master Haywood," Iolanthe said. "Is there any chance you might have changed your mind about leaving this place?"

Master Haywood began to shake his head, but then he stopped. A smile slowly broke out on his face. "Now that you asked again, Iola, I do believe I have had quite enough of this place."

Lady Callista remained unconscious after the time freeze expired.

"Not to worry," said Titus. "As memory spells take effect, it is not uncommon for a mage to remain unconscious for up to an hour."

Master Haywood sighed. "Alas, I had thought her so very charming."

"We need to check you for any tracers that might be on your person," Titus said to Master Haywood.

As they searched, Iolanthe asked, "How did you meet Lady Callista, Master Haywood?"

"Through my friend Eirene. You might know her as Commander Rainstone, the regent's chief security adviser, Your Highness," said Master Haywood, with a deferential half bow toward the prince.

Strange how she knew both men so well, yet they were essentially strangers to each other. And Master Haywood, at least, seemed determined to observe every etiquette.

"I do know her in that capacity. Please go on," said Titus.

"I met Eirene—Commander Rainstone—for coffee and she told me that she was meeting her friend Lady Callista at Eugenides Constantinos's bookshop afterward and asked if I'd like to come along. I said I did, so that was how it happened."

Iolanthe removed Master Haywood's shoes and socks to make

sure they were free of tracers. "And what was Lady Callista doing at the bookshop? She does not strike me as someone with a keen interest in books."

"She said she was there to buy a book that a friend of hers had defaced. Her company was such a pleasure, I volunteered to buy the book for her."

"*The Complete Potion.*"

"Yes, how did you guess?"

Iolanthe bit the inside of her cheek. "You always hauled that book everywhere with us, even though you said it was a terrible book."

"Yes, sentimental value. She was beautiful, but I was struck by the vividness of her presence. I always thought it was a shame that I never saw her again, though I had every intention of doing so." Master Haywood fell silent as he realized that he was speaking from incomplete memories. "Perhaps it would have been better if I really never saw her again."

"Speaking for myself, this is the most charming I have ever seen her," said Titus. "At least she was truthful, for once. My guess is there is still truth serum remaining in her system from her latest interrogation."

Once they were satisfied that Master Haywood did not have any tracers on his person, and that they themselves had not picked up any either, Iolanthe suddenly realized she had not planned for where to take him.

"Should we put you up at a different hotel for now, until we find a more permanent lodging?" she asked.

"I have a place that I would gladly put at your disposal," said Titus to Master Haywood. "If you do not mind that it is on the other side of the English Channel."

On the other side of the English Channel?

Paris.

Autumn in Paris bore little resemblance to its counterpart in London. The air was cool but crisp, the sky blue, and the tall, clear windows up and down the quiet boulevard ablaze with the light of the lowering sun. The apartment the prince had chosen had spacious rooms, high ceilings painted a soft gold, and enormous paintings of nonmages dressed in clothes from a different era, frolicking in a nostalgia-tinged countryside.

Iolanthe, even with her headache from having been vaulted nearly a hundred fifty miles—though split into three segments—was enchanted. "It's a lovely place."

Titus gave her another dose of vaulting aid. "The concierge below is under the impression that there are several people in the family—an uncle, and a niece and a nephew who are twins. So she will not be surprised to see either a young man or a young woman come by—or an older man."

He opened a drawer and pulled out cases of calling cards for Mr.

Rupert Franklin, Mr. Arthur Franklin, and Miss Adelia Franklin. "The bakery around the corner is quite good. The brasserie likewise. Three times a week there is a market on the square down the road. And the Franklin family has an account with the Banque de Paris that should last you years."

"So this is what you have been doing in Paris," Iolanthe said softly, more than a little bowled over by everything he had done.

"Part of it."

"Part of it? What was the other part, then?"

He led them down a corridor toward another room. It had been set up with a large desk at the center, and shelves on the walls. Iolanthe recognized some of the equipment on the desk as having come from the laboratory.

"Once I realized that your memories might not resurface again, I wanted to protect you against damages brought on by permanent suppression. Which meant I had to find a way to bring back your memories.

"I decided to duplicate the kind of protection that had been placed on me. If someone tampers with my memory, and someone who meets the contact-requisite threshold still could, my memory will recover within weeks, if not days. But some of the ingredients required for the potion base do not travel well—they must be used very fresh, and they lose their effectiveness if they are vaulted.

"So I needed to set up a temporary laboratory here in Paris—it is the nearest city with a master mage botanist who can supply my needs. And while I looked for a suitable location, I decided that I might as well make it a place where the two of you can live together comfortably, after you are reunited."

Master Haywood bowed deeply. Iolanthe did nothing—she didn't know what to do.

Titus waved them toward the desk. "Anyway, I did not tell you earlier because I did not have the potion base ready yet and I did not want you to think I was making it easier for you to leave Eton. I mean—" He shrugged. "You know what I mean."

He brought out two glasses and poured them each half-full from a pitcher that he said contained seawater. "It needs water from the first ocean in which you had set foot—which I assume is the Atlantic for the two of you. And then you must add three drops of your own blood, and three drops of voluntarily given blood from someone who loves you. Would you mind giving us some fire, Miss Seabourne?"

She called forth a small sphere of flame.

The prince opened his pocketknife, passed the blade through the fire, and handed it to Iolanthe. She let fall three drops of blood into each glass, passed the knife through the fire again, and gave it to Master Haywood.

When Master Haywood had squeezed three drops of his blood into one glass and was about to do the same for the second glass, the prince stopped him. "I would like to have the honor for Miss Seabourne's potion."

Blood from someone who loves you.

Master Haywood glanced at Iolanthe, not so much shocked as thoughtful.

Now Titus brought out a vial of gray powder, divided it between the glasses, and stirred until the potion turned bright and golden.

It tasted of sunlight and chamomile tea.

Master Haywood again bowed deeply to Titus, who took him to yet another room and showed him where a supply of cash was kept. "This should last you until you can go to the bank. You also have credit at most of the nearby shops, if you would care to use that."

He turned to Iolanthe. "Almost time for another blasted Absence at school. We had better head back."

"Head count," Iolanthe explained to Master Haywood. "They are always counting the boys."

"But I haven't heard your story yet," Master Haywood protested.

"Another day," she said, hugging him. "I will come and see you as often as I can."

Back in her room at Mrs. Dawlish's, Titus turned to her and said, "These are for you."

"These" were calling cards for A. G. Fairfax, of Low Creek Ranch, Wyoming Territory.

"Before you leave Mrs. Dawlish's, give these cards to your friends. When they write to this address, the letters will go to the safe house.

And the letters you send out from the safe house will reach them as if having come all the way from the American West."

"Thank you." More words wouldn't express her feelings better.

"No need," he answered softly. "It is a compulsion on my part to give you everything, while I still can."

CHAPTER ·29

The Sahara Desert

THE NEWCOMER WAS UNBELIEVABLY FAST on his carpet. Titus had to put in real effort to not fall more than a body length behind.

And whereas Titus set his carpet on an approximately ten-degree angle, with the front of the carpet rolled underneath, the newcomer's carpet was tilted at an incline of at least thirty degrees, with two creases in the body so that in profile it looked like an elongated, backward Z.

A dragon could keep its own course, but a carpet usually relied on the distribution of the rider's weight for directions. A new rider, while learning, could accidently set the carpet into a tailspin by doing nothing more than trying to look over a shoulder. This young man, however, casually turned around, one hand holding the carpet to its course, the other raised in spell-casting.

Distance spell-casting—as the nearest pursuers were still miles behind—and with amazing accuracy. The boy was a sniper to behold.

Titus turned to Fairfax, who was still gaping at the newcomer, and said, "Is there any chance *he* is your admirer?"

At his question, she squinted. "Probably not. Since he already came off his carpet to get us onto ours, he could have easily given me a kiss. But he just shoved me onto the carpet like a sack of potatoes."

"But what if he is?"

"Hmm." Her tone turned teasing. "Are you asking me to make a choice right now between the two of you?"

"Now you will choose me, of course. But what about after you remember?" The question made him more nervous than he cared to admit.

"Can't you do something about the armored chariots, Fairfax?" shouted the subject of their discussion. "They are closing in fast."

"All right!" she shouted back. "I'll try."

Then, into Titus's ear, "I don't think he even knows—or cares—that I'm a girl."

Titus had to agree with her on that account—and he was glad for it.

"Hold the carpet steady," she told him, and turned halfway around.

After a minute or so, she lay back down. "I can't destabilize the armored chariots. Let me try something else. Hold on tight!"

The last few words were shouted for the other boy to hear. A second later, a tailwind very nearly blew Titus off the carpet altogether. Both the carpets accelerated as if they had been set on rockets. And behind them, barely visible in the dark of the night, sand rose like a curtain, obscuring them from the view of the Atlanteans.

The other boy signaled for them to descend. "My carpet has almost reached the limits of its range."

Once a carpet neared the limits of its flight range, it had to be set down, or it would drop out of the sky like a rock. And once on the ground, it needed some time before it could take to the air again.

"Would you like some water?" asked Fairfax. The sphere of water she had summoned shimmered just barely under the starlight.

The boy held out a canteen. "Yes, I would, thank you."

"Some food or a heat sheet?" asked Titus, placing his arm around Fairfax's shoulder.

If the boy was her admirer, then he ought to either come forward to contest her affections or relinquish them forever.

The boy looked at them a moment, with neither dismay nor jealousy, but something rather like wonder. "No, thank you. These clothes are meant for the desert and water is all I need."

A small silence fell. Titus was just about to tell the boy that they had no idea who he was when he spoke again.

"The pendant was so cold at the beginning I had to put it away from my person. And since I wasn't looking for you specifically, but just traveling to meet my brother, I didn't make it a point to check. Imagine my surprise when I came across it about noon and it was almost lukewarm.

"I had a two-way notebook on me so I contacted my brother and—his fiancée. They wrote back immediately saying phoenix beacons had been seen in the desert a few nights before, and their scouts were already on the lookout for you. Lo and behold, a few hours later you walked into an oasis leading a sand wyvern."

Titus's jaw dropped. "Those caravanists, they were mages?"

"They most certainly were."

"But one fainted and two reached for their rifles when they saw the sand wyvern."

"It's a good policy for at least one member of the group to pretend to fall unconscious at a mage sighting. And I always think the rifles are a touch of genius—any time you see someone holding a firearm, your instinct is to dismiss that person as a nonmage."

"I must remember that," murmured Fairfax.

"And not only were the caravanists mages, the oasis itself is a translocator," said the boy with obvious pride. "We have built three like it. Atlantis does not pay much attention to nonmages and their camels huddled around a piddly hole in the ground. It allows for our scouts to move quite freely around the desert.

"Anyway, the scouts recognized you and Fairfax. They reported back. The choice was made to take any measure necessary to keep you out of Atlantis's hands. That was why, when they saw a large contingent of beasts and armored chariots leaving the base, they decided to attack the base to force the Atlanteans to return and defend their installation."

"Why did your friends decide to use bewitched spears?" asked Fairfax.

"What?"

Fairfax turned to Titus. "I thought you said those who helped us used bewitched spears."

"We have had to use quite a few unorthodox methods, but not bewitched spears," said the boy. "We are not that desperate yet."

"The Atlanteans who were literally on top of us were not going to head back to the base to help. They had their orders to hunt us down and they were going to obey those orders until they heard otherwise," Titus told the boy. "I do not know what would have happened if that thicket of bewitched spears had not arrived in time to force them to leave."

"That's strange. I don't know of any rebel groups that use antique weaponry. Is there anything else you can tell me about them, prince?"

Fairfax was just about to refill the boy's canteen again. The stream of water she aimed at it missed altogether, landing with a splat in the sand.

Titus too felt as if the ground had shifted underneath his feet. "Did you call me prince?"

The boy sounded taken aback. "My apologies, Your Highness. At school we did not closely observe protocol. But I will be sure to accord you all the respect due the Master of the Domain."

The Master of the Domain.

He gripped Fairfax's arm, not sure whether he could even understand those words.

Or whether he wanted to.

The boy scanned the sky. "Night patrol from the base—excellent. I can hitch a ride with them and we don't have to wait until my carpet is ready again."

"You are sure we can trust them?" asked Fairfax.

He folded his carpet, then rolled it into a tight tube and fitted it into a slender bag that he strapped diagonally across his back. "They are Amara's cousins, so yes, I'm quite certain they are not Atlanteans masquerading as rebels."

When the rebels landed, the boy presented the two women as Ishana and Shulini. When it came time to give Fairfax's name, he asked her, "Should I introduce you as Fairfax, or by your real name?"

Fairfax hesitated. "My real name."

She sounded almost afraid. Titus *felt* afraid. Would learning her true identity be as unhappy an experience for her as learning his had been for him?

"Iolanthe Seabourne," said the boy.

Iolanthe Seabourne—a name of both structure and strength, yet one that brought no recognition, from either of them. She took his hand. She was relieved, he could tell. But mixed in her relief was perhaps also a slight disappointment that she remained unclear on who she was.

"Pleased to meet you," said Titus to Ishana and Shulini.

The women inclined their heads respectfully. "A pleasure to meet Your Highness again," said Ishana. And then to Fairfax. "We saw you earlier too, but you were asleep on the back of the sand wyvern."

Titus's eyes widened. "You were at the oasis?"

They laughed softly. "We were the ones who grabbed the rifles, sir. It's much less suspicious for us to go around as nonmage men," said Shulini.

Fifteen seconds later, they were airborne. The carpet that carried Shulini, Ishana, and the boy was, if possible, even faster than the boy's had been. But this time, Titus did not mind. He deliberately fell a few lengths behind. Fairfax held his hand and said nothing.

Miles passed. The desert night air cut hard against the exposed skin of his face, but he was almost glad of the numbing pain, for the distraction it offered.

"I do not want to be the Master of the Domain," he said, after a long time. The Master of the Domain was not someone to be envied at the best of times. The Master of the Domain as a fugitive from Atlantis was an untenable position. "Is it possible for me to arrange to become his stable boy instead?"

"You should try," she said, her fingers tightening over his. "I really like stable boys, especially when they smell like the muck they have been shoveling all day."

He was halfway between laughter and tears. "I cannot think of anything I want to do less than being responsible for an entire realm."

"Well, if you take care of the Domain half as well as you have looked after me, both you and the Domain will be all right."

"You think so?"

"Yes, I do. Not to mention, now you know of at least one girl who would kiss you even if you weren't a prince—isn't that what all princes are trying to find?"

"This has been such a terrible shock," he said slowly. "I will need kisses by the dozen to help me deal with it."

"I was going to hoard my kisses until I see that fifty-ton slab chiseled with unspeakably bad verses. But extraordinary circumstances call for extraordinary measures, so you may have one kiss now."

He managed, just barely, not to send the carpet into a tailspin.

"Better?"

"One more, and I might be able to carry on."

But one more was not in the cards. Up ahead, Ishana shouted, "Your Highness, the base is near. We must start our descent now. Please follow closely."

CHAPTER · 30

England

"WHAT'S THE MATTER?" CAME FAIRFAX'S voice.

Titus started—he had not even noticed she had arrived in the laboratory. "I see you are still determined to not listen to me about not venturing abroad after lights-out."

She sat down across from him at the worktable. "I never listen to you when I know enough to make up my own mind."

Her tone was light, but the truth of her words struck him hard: she relied on her own judgment. He, on the other hand, was accustomed to running his life according to directions his mother had left behind. Which was all well and good when he did not question those directions. But when he did, it plunged him into a state of paralysis.

"Is it something Lady Callista said?" asked Fairfax.

She had been shocked to see Lady Callista revealed as the memory keeper, but she had not seemed particularly affected afterward, probably because she had always disliked the memory keeper—and probably because all her personal memories of Lady Callista as her mother were still inaccessible.

"There was something she shouted when she was accusing you of being ungrateful," answered Titus. "I have not been able to get it out of my head."

Do you have any idea how difficult it was, how frightful, to figure out how to do everything my future self was telling him we needed to do?

He repeated those words aloud to Fairfax. "Notice anything?"

"Yes, I do," she said slowly. "We have always assumed that the memory keeper had been working *against* a vision of the future, which was why everything eventually went wrong. But it was the other way around: Lady Callista had done everything in her power to make a vision come true."

"There is that. And there is the fact that the vision she had let dominate her life was not a vision of action, but one of speech: in that vision, her future self was *telling* your future guardian what they needed to do."

Fairfax frowned. "I'm not sure I understand."

"There has never been agreement on what mages ought to do when they have foreknowledge of events that have yet to transpire. Some feel that as long as one is not trying to prevent that future, nothing more needs to be done. Some feel the opposite: the future had been revealed for those in the present to work toward.

"You mentioned the paradox of created reality some time ago: a future that probably would not have come true, if it had not been revealed and then assiduously brought to pass. Obviously I do not mind a little created reality. But even among mages who believe one should work toward a revealed future, there are huge differences of opinion on just how much should be done.

"For example, my mother saw herself writing *There is no light elixir, however tainted, that cannot be revived by a thunderbolt* in the margins of a copy of *The Complete Potion*. There is not much argument there— she should definitely do it when she finds herself in the foreseen situation.

"But what if she had seen herself *telling* someone that is what she had done? Should she still write about light elixirs and thunderbolts in the potions manual?"

Fairfax blinked. "This could get complicated. Strictly speaking, to fulfill the prophecy she only needs to say the words, no need to actually do the writing."

"It gets more complicated still. What if she had seen herself telling someone that she *plans* to write these words inside a copy of *The Complete Potion*?"

"And you are saying that is the equivalent of the vision Lady Callista worked from, a vision of a plan being spoken aloud."

He nodded. Just as seers came in vastly different calibers, so did visions. "A vision of someone discussing her plans is far less significant than a vision of actual events. But it is not anything to do with Lady Callista that I am worried about . . ." He almost could not speak the next few words. "It is my mother's vision that is giving me pause."

She rose from her seat. "What?"

"My mother's visions almost always concerned events. My coronation was an event. The Inquisitor's death, an event. She herself writing the words that would one day inspire you to bring down a bolt of lightning, a series of actions that constituted an event." He set his hands on top of the diary, which for so long had been his life raft in a sea of uncertainties. "But now I realize that some of my mother's most important assumptions rest not on a vision of action, but one of speech."

This then is most likely what Titus is witnessing, the manifestation of the great elemental mage who would be, as he would say in a different vision, his partner for the task.

As he would say.

"Can you ask the diary to show you that vision, so you will know one way or the other?"

"I can, but I am afraid to." He looked up at her. "Have I told you that she foresaw Baron Wintervale's death? But she misinterpreted what she saw to mean that Atlantis had been responsible for the execution curse. She was a flawless seer, but she was not infallible in the interpretations of her visions."

Yet the directions for his entire life had been set down on the strength of those interpretations.

She rounded the table and came to stand next to him, her hand on his shoulder.

He put his hand over hers. "Am I a coward?"

"Because you are afraid? No. Only fools are never afraid."

He stared at the gilt edge of the diary's pages. "What if everything changes?"

"Sometimes it does."

"I hate changes like that."

"I know," she said gently. "So do I."

He inhaled deeply and opened the diary, silently asking to be shown the vision in which he spoke of the great elemental mage who would be his partner for the task.

24 April 1021

Only a few days before Princess Ariadne's death.

It is Titus—or at least I think it is Titus, perhaps ten years or so older than he is now, a boy of sixteen or seventeen, lean and handsome. Next to him is another boy, about the same age, good-looking, but in a way that was almost too pretty for a young man. They seem to be standing on the bank of a lake or a river, tossing pebbles, but I do not recognize the place as any I have ever visited.

"I am going to bring down the Bane," Titus says.

I had to step away from my desk for a moment to collect myself. So this is what all the other visions had been leading up to. For the thousandth time, I wish I had never been cursed with this "gift."

"Why?" asks the other boy, sounding as afraid and flabbergasted as I feel.

"Because that is what I am meant to do," Titus replies, with an adamantine certainty.

He snapped the diary shut. It *was* the conversation he and Fairfax had on the bank of the Thames, when he had told her about their destiny.

"Remember, this does not diminish your mother's power as a seer," Fairfax said urgently.

No, but it cast doubt on her interpretation of everything. Princess Ariadne wrote that there was to be one partner for Titus because the future Titus had said so. But the future Titus had said so because Princess Ariadne had written so. It was a complete and vicious paradox.

"Fortune shield me, what does this mean?" he heard himself mumble. "Is there a Chosen One or not?"

It had been the most gut-wrenching thing to do to tell Fairfax that she was not part of his destiny, but he had done it without hesitation because, as he told her, one did not argue with the force of destiny. Now, however, the force of destiny was proving itself to be nothing more than a wobbly conundrum.

"Does it matter?" she asked.

"How can it not matter? If there is no Chosen One, then what am I, the one whose task is to train and guide the Chosen One, supposed to do?"

She turned his chair around so that he faced her. "Listen to me. Forget how she interpreted everything—visions are and have always been squirrelly things. Look instead at what her visions have led you to accomplish: you saved me twice *and* you brought down the Inquisitor, the Bane's most capable lieutenant.

"You mother died because Atlantis wanted her dead. You were always going to be an implacable enemy of Atlantis. You were always going to do your best to upend the Bane's reign. The only difference was that Princess Ariadne made sure that you were ready far sooner than you would otherwise have been.

"Wintervale doesn't need to be the One to take up his wand against Atlantis—he wants to be part of something greater than himself. I don't need to be the One either—if I can make a difference, then I am willing do to my utmost. But we do need you—you are better prepared to bring down the Bane than any other mage on Earth. So don't tell me that you don't know what you ought to do anymore. Your role hasn't changed at all. Dust yourself off and get back to it."

He looked into her eyes and felt some of his despair drain away. "So you do not think everything I have done is in vain?"

"No, I don't think anything you've ever done has been in vain. It will all come to fruition someday. And furthermore, I'm convinced you will live to see that day."

He took her hands in his. "When the time comes, will you come to Atlantis with Wintervale and me?"

"I will." She kissed him on his hair. "Now go get some sleep. The road is long yet."

"I can't believe it," said Cooper, looking at the calling card. "Low Creek Ranch, Wyoming Territory. Are you really leaving us?"

Iolanthe walked to Cooper's window. "Won't be too long now. And I'll really miss this easy life."

Cooper came to stand next to her. "You know what? Maybe someday I'll run away and join you in Wyoming Territory. At least I won't have to be a lawyer, if I'm herding cattle."

"Good luck finding me. I'll bet this godforsaken ranch is three hundred roadless miles away from the nearest railway station. You'll be better off applying to the prince to become his secretary."

"You know what I would like? I would like to see my future, so I can stop worrying about it."

Iolanthe snorted and shook her head.

"Oh, look, there's West. I think he is coming to Mrs. Dawlish's." Cooper opened the window, his dreaded future as an unwilling lawyer momentarily forgotten. "West, are you coming inside? Have you seen where I got brained by a flying tile?"

He no longer needed to wear his bandage, but he still enjoyed showing off the scab.

"Yes, I am coming inside," said West, already dressed in his cricket kit. "Thought I'd have a look at Wintervale, but I'll gladly inspect your war wounds too, Cooper."

"You have to first go to Mrs. Hancock's office to sign a visitor's register. She is determined to keep unwholesome influences out of this house," Iolanthe told him.

"Then what are you doing inside?" West retorted good-naturedly.

"Obviously her vigilance is no match for my cunning."

A visit from the future captain of the cricket team turned out to be a far bigger deal than Iolanthe had imagined. Mrs. Hancock herself accompanied West up the stairs, looking as flustered as a young girl at her first ball. Wintervale, whom Iolanthe had thought to be beyond such things as cricket and school teams, after a moment of surprise broke out in a grin of such delight that Iolanthe would have thought he'd already defeated the Bane.

Other senior boys lined Wintervale's wall, while junior boys piled outside his door.

Iolanthe had to push her way out when she realized she still hadn't changed for cricket practice. She looked into Titus's room—this would be a good opportunity for him to see West up close and perhaps find out why West was interested in him.

But Titus was not there.

From the laboratory, Titus returned to his room to grab an overcoat. He had told Fairfax that he would come and take West's measures at the cricket practice, and he intended to be warm and comfortable while fulfilling his promise—or at least as warm and comfortable as possible, on yet another dreary, chilly day.

As he buttoned his overcoat, he poked his head into Wintervale's room, to see how the latter was getting on. Wintervale's room was empty. But a quick look out of Wintervale's window showed Wintervale and Cooper not far down the street, moving in the direction of the playing fields.

He left the house and caught up with them.

"Come to watch the cricket practice with us, prince?" said Wintervale.

"That is my intention."

"Excellent," said Wintervale. "Then you can be my crutch. Sorry, Cooper, but His Highness is a better height for me."

Cooper yielded his place and gave a full recital on how grandly West's visit to Wintervale had gone off. And Titus was stuck listening to the detail-laden account, as Wintervale proceeded at the pace of a sleepy snail. It took them a ridiculous amount of time to arrive at the playing fields, where half of the boys from Mrs. Dawlish's house—plus Mrs. Hancock—were on hand as spectators.

Crouched behind Fairfax, keeping wicket, was a boy whose face was instantly familiar.

West.

Even if one had very little interest in the school's sporting elite, one still ended up knowing who they were. But that was not the reason for the recognition that reverberated in Titus, producing ripples of what he could only label as fear.

Fairfax struck the ball and took two runs, returning to her original position. West left his spot, approached her, and spoke to her briefly.

As he took his place again, he glanced in Titus's direction, studying him, almost, before returning his attention to the game.

Titus felt as if he had fallen through thin ice.

When he had had his brief glimpse of the Bane on the night of the Fourth of June, he remembered thinking the Bane looked vaguely familiar. Now he knew why. There was an eerie resemblance between West and the Bane.

They were at least thirty years apart in age, and the Bane had sported a perfectly groomed beard. But there could be no doubt about it, their features were of a remarkable similarity.

If the Bane could resurrect, who was to say he would not be able to look a few decades younger? And come to Eton to hunt for Fairfax himself, where his lieutenants had failed?

Fairfax scored another two runs and was once again talking to West—to the Bane himself, possibly. Titus had to sit down for a minute so he could try for a measure of calm.

What if West simply reached out and grabbed Fairfax? How fast could she react? How fast could Titus react? And how fast could he make Wintervale, also seated on the ground and avidly enjoying the game, by the expression on his face, understand that he was to unleash all the power at his disposal to keep Fairfax away from harm?

Yes, he was willing to expose Wintervale's elemental powers for her. Yes, he was even willing to risk Wintervale's life for her. He ought to be ashamed, but he did not care.

The match, however, went on quietly, placidly. As the sun touched the western horizon, West signaled that they would disperse for the day. And Fairfax walked off with no idea that for two hours straight she had been within touching distance of the Lord High Commander of the Great Realm of New Atlantis.

The prince was capable of enormous sangfroid—sitting with apparent nonchalance atop the back of a chair at his own Inquisition, holding completely still and acting bored when he must have believed that Iolanthe was on the cusp of being hauled away—but for the duration of the practice he sat down and stood up at least three times.

It was the equivalent of someone like Cooper running down the street, screaming and tearing off his clothes.

He did not approach her immediately after the end of practice. In fact, he was nowhere to be seen.

"So His Highness does come to watch a practice from time to time," said West to Iolanthe as he gathered up his things.

"His Highness, as always, does as he pleases."

Wintervale was disappointed that Titus had slipped away without a word to anyone. Kashkari offered himself as Wintervale's crutch on the way back, an offer Wintervale accepted with tepid gratitude.

Normally, when Iolanthe found herself sharing a sidewalk with Wintervale, she would slow down enough to walk beside him. But today she needed to speak to Titus to find out what had unsettled him so.

Using her thirst as an excuse, she passed Kashkari and Wintervale, striding so fast that poor Cooper could barely keep up.

At Titus's door, before she could knock, a hand settled on her shoulder. She jumped. But it was only Titus.

"I have been behind you all this time," he said quietly.

He ushered her inside. And once the door was closed, he set a sound circle and applied the sort of anti-intrusion spells that would kill a charging rhinoceros, making Iolanthe's brows rise almost to her hairline.

Clutching her to him, he kissed her cheek, her ear, and her lips. "Take a dose of vaulting aid. I am taking you to Paris right now. No need to pack anything. Whatever you need you can buy new there."

"What?" she cried. "What is going on? You are shaking like a leaf in the wind."

An exaggeration on her part, but his fingertips did tremble.

"West could be the Bane."

She stared at him. "You are not making any sense. Did you say that West could be the *Bane*?"

"I saw the Bane up close, remember? Believe me when I tell you that West resembles the Bane almost exactly, if you subtract the effects of aging."

"But West didn't come out of nowhere. He's been at Eton for as long as you have. You can't expect me to believe that for four years the Bane has been walking among the students of a nonmage school."

"I do not know how to account for that. All I know is that you cannot stay here a moment longer."

"But I stood next to him for two hours and nothing happened to me."

"Yet. Anything could happen any minute."

That she didn't doubt, though she remained unconvinced that he was right about West. "I'm not opposed to erring on the side of caution. But for me to disappear without a word to anyone, leaving all my belongings behind—it would appear suspicious, wouldn't it?"

He frowned but didn't reply.

"Besides, if it has become too dangerous for me to remain at school, then it is also too dangerous for you and Wintervale. And probably Kashkari too."

He rubbed his temples. "What do you suggest we do?"

"We should speak to Kashkari and Wintervale both."

"No, not Wintervale, not yet."

"Don't you think you are being overcautious?"

"No more than his mother is."

Iolanthe couldn't argue with that. "All right, then. We talk to Kashkari. He excels at keeping secrets. And a quid says he already has plans for leaving school in a hurry, in case of emergency."

Kashkari, however, was nowhere to be found. He didn't even

show up at supper—it was Sutherland who helped Wintervale down to the dining room.

"Where's Kashkari?" Iolanthe asked Sutherland.

"He is fasting. And there are some rituals he must follow while he's fasting. He has permission to stay in his room tonight."

Iolanthe exchanged a look with Titus. Kashkari's native realm was not one that fell under the banners of the Angelic Host. But still, rare was the mage belief that looked to fasting as a means of becoming closer to the divine.

Mrs. Hancock also did not come to supper, which caused a bigger stir than Kashkari's absence—Mrs. Hancock was never not at supper.

"I know it is unusual, but Mrs. Hancock is feeling a bit under the weather this evening," explained Mrs. Dawlish.

Iolanthe had not been particularly nervous earlier, when Titus had been nearly undone by his belief that West was the Bane. But the unexpected and simultaneous absence of the two mages made her tense. She spoke little, and listened with only half an ear to Cooper.

After supper, as he often did, Cooper walked back with Iolanthe to her room, for a bit of help on his schoolwork. He opened a notebook and flipped through the pages. "Ah, here it is. Is this the word that means swift in Greek?"

Iolanthe took a look. "*Okeia*? Yes."

"But when has Aphrodite ever been described as swift?"

It took Iolanthe two seconds to understand what he was talking about—most of her attention was on the footsteps in the corridor, listening for Titus's return. He had gone to look for Kashkari again and she was beginning to worry about the latter.

"Wait a minute. Let me look at my notes." She opened one of her own notebooks. "I think you copied it wrong. The word is actually *okeanis*, from the ocean, which Aphrodite is."

The two looked similar enough in Greek that it was an understandable mistake.

"Ah, that's much better." Cooper closed his notebook. "Are you sure you have to go to the Wyoming Territory?"

"Unfortunately, yes. And sooner rather than later, I'm afraid."

The prince walked in then. He took one look at Cooper and said, "Leave us."

As always, Cooper was delighted to be sent packing by His Highness, who looked at the door a moment after it had closed. "Someday I might actually miss that idiot."

"Did you find Kashkari?"

"No. I could n—"

There came knocks—not at her door, but the prince's—followed by, "Are you there, prince?"

Kashkari.

Titus was instantly at the door. "Yes?"

"A word with you, Your Highness."

"Come in here."

Kashkari entered Iolanthe's room. Titus closed the door.

"My apologies to Fairfax," said Kashkari, glancing at Titus. "But may I speak to you in private?"

"I am His Highness's personal bodyguard," said Iolanthe. From the moment she knew that Kashkari had long realized there was something not quite right about Archer Fairfax, she had been thinking of what to tell him that would explain everything but still keep her secret intact. "There are others at this house and around this school dedicated to his protection, but it was decided earlier this year, due to increased danger to His Highness, that I would step into the identity that had been created long ago, in case someone was needed to defend him from even closer quarters."

"I see," said Kashkari slowly. "I see now."

Titus played along. "I would not be alive today, if it were not for Fairfax. Whatever you would like to say, you may say it before him. He already knows who you are and what your ambitions are, by the way."

Kashkari studied Iolanthe for a moment, took out a notebook from his pocket, and scribbled something inside. Barely a second later, Mrs. Hancock materialized in the room. Iolanthe was startled enough to take a step backward, bumping into the edge of her desk.

Titus stepped before Iolanthe. "What is the meaning of this, Kashkari?"

"Let me set a sound circle," answered Kashkari. When he was done, he turned to Mrs. Hancock. "Fairfax is His Highness's personal bodyguard. We may speak freely before him."

"Ah, that makes sense," said Mrs. Hancock. "I always thought there was something inexplicable about you, Fairfax."

"What are you doing, Kashkari," demanded Titus, "with the special envoy from Atlantis's Department of Overseas Administration?"

"I come tonight as who I truly am: a sworn enemy of the Bane," said Mrs. Hancock.

Titus snorted. "I have my doubts that this residence, which contains mostly nonmages who have never heard of Atlantis, except as ancient hearsay, could house that many sworn enemies of the Bane. It is statistically unlikely."

"But we are none of us here by chance," said Mrs. Hancock. "Kashkari saw his own future. Wintervale's mother sent him because of you, Your Highness. And you and I, Your Highness, are both here because of a man named Icarus Khalkedon."

Iolanthe had never heard that name before, but Titus apparently had. "The Bane's old seer, you mean?"

"The Bane's old oracle," answered Mrs. Hancock.

Titus and Iolanthe exchanged a look of astonishment. Seers were considered to possess a rare talent, but seers were receivers, limited by what the universe saw fit to reveal to them. Oracles, on the other hand, were able to answer specific questions. Most oracles in the mage world were inanimate objects, jealously guarded by devotees, and pilgrims could travel thousands of miles and still be denied a chance to ask their one burning question.

It was almost unheard of for a person to be an oracle.

"Where did the Bane find him?" Iolanthe asked.

"I don't know and neither did Icarus—though my guess was the Kalahari Realm. Mages from all over the world had settled there and intermarried. That sometimes produces a startling beauty in the children, different from anything else one is used to seeing."

Mrs. Hancock sighed. "I met him when I was honored with a summer apprenticeship at Royalis.[14] Nowadays the Bane rarely leaves the Commander's Palace in the uplands, but that summer he happened to stay in the capital. And of course, wherever the Bane was, Icarus was never far away.

"The Bane asked him one question a month. It took Icarus two weeks to recover from a question and the Bane usually let him have two more weeks of—normalcy, I suppose. Of not being so exhausted he could scarcely move an eyelid.

"On days he was strong enough to get up and walk around, he would come into the library, where I worked. We became friends— very good friends. And that was all we were allowed to become. He could not do more than speak to a girl, for it was believed fleshly contacts would tarnish his gift.

"Part of me wishes that our story is only that of a pair of star-crossed lovers—my life would have been simpler. But no, we both happened to be in the midst of a crisis of faith, concerning our devotion to the Bane. And in that sense, I was the best and worst possible friend he could have made—and vice versa.

"It rather horrified me to learn that the Bane did not ask

questions about the best direction for the realm, or the most quali-fied person to lead a given initiative. Instead, many of his questions ran along the lines of *Who will be my greatest threat in the next year?*

"But my dismay was only beginning. When Icarus was a child, he had often become unconscious at the end of an oracular session, and would have no recollection of either the question or the answer he gave. As he grew older and gained greater control over his gift, however, he began to be able to recall what took place during his sessions with the Bane.

"At night, on his bed, he would silently say those names that he had given as answers over the years. He repeated the string of names to me, those hard weights on his conscience. And when he came to one particular name, I—"

Mrs. Hancock closed her eyes momentarily. "I heard my sister's name. My sister was seventeen when she disappeared on a camping trip with her friends. She was seen getting into her tent at night, but in the morning she was not there. Her friends searched and searched. My parents and I—and everyone we ever knew, plus a great many mages we never knew—we combed the entire place top to bottom, but there was no trace of her. The area had been known to have giant serpents in the past and no one in the family could bear to mention it, but we had each become convinced that my beautiful sister had become some terrible beast's supper, for there could be no other explanations.

"But now her name came up. I asked Icarus if he remembered

the question. He did. The question was, *Who is the most potent elemental mage who has yet to attain adulthood?*

"My sister was an elemental mage. And my mother used to say that my sister was the most powerful elemental mage she had ever come across. She ought to know—she had been a headmistress for many years.

"Icarus and I stared at each other, stunned, paralyzed almost, by the possible implications of our discovery. But how could we know whether it was a coincidence, her name passing his lips followed by her disappearance a week later, or whether there had been sinister forces at work?

"The idea was Icarus's. He was near the end of his month and the Bane would soon be making use of him. But in two weeks, when he had recovered his strength, he wanted me to ask him a question: *The next time the Bane asks about the most potent elemental mage who has yet to attain adulthood, what would happen to that elemental mage?*

"We did as we planned. I asked the question, trembling all over, and he sank into a deep trance. After almost a quarter of an hour, he spoke in a deep, eerie voice: 'That elemental mage will be used in sacrificial magic.'"

Iolanthe felt as if she had been skewered through the chest. "But sacrificial magic—that is *taboo*."

"No," Kashkari muttered, as if to himself. "No. No. No."

"You already think the worst of the Bane," said Mrs. Hancock. "Can you imagine the force of the blow, upon two young people who had not yet become entirely disillusioned? It felt like an earthquake, the foundation of an entire life breaking apart.

"The next month I asked Icarus what the Bane would hope to achieve, the next time he performed sacrificial magic. *To prolong his life* was the answer we received. That made no sense. If the Bane were at the end of his life, perhaps one could understand the sordid desperation that drove him to sacrificial magic. But he was a man in his prime. So the next month we asked how old he would be on his next birthday. One hundred seventy-seven was the answer.

"I remember how nauseated I felt, how clammy. The very idea of it was repugnant and horrifying—that he had given himself this unnaturally long life by sacrificing young elemental mages like my sister.

"It was the last question I was able to ask Icarus, before he was whisked back to the Commander's Palace at the end of summer. But I had been offered a permanent position at the library and we made a pact to each find out as much as we could and meet again the next summer.

"When Icarus wasn't in oracular mode, people tended to regard him as something of an overgrown infant, because he was deliberately kept in a state of ignorance, allowed to read nature books and fairy tales, but not allowed any access to news, for fear knowledge of the actual world would pollute his answers. Icarus had always played to that. So during those ten months, he was able to use that perception—and the fact that he was one of the Bane's most prized possessions—to his advantage.

"And he found out that indeed, during the years of his tenure as the Bane's oracle, three elemental mages had had 'private audiences' with the Bane. The guards he had spoken to were lower-level security and were almost as ignorant as he—only much less curious. They simply assumed that after the audiences, the young elemental mages had been whisked back to the capital via some sort of expedited means, which was why no one had seen them again.

"He also found out about the lowest levels of the Commander's Palace. He had thought that the palace had three levels belowground, but it actually had five. Only the Bane himself, and occasionally one of his most trusted lieutenants, were allowed in the secret levels.

"I searched for information on the other names that Icarus had given to the Bane over the years, those who were the Bane's threats. Most were names I'd never heard of. Some I found in archives of overseas newspapers we had at the library, mages from various other realms who had been arrested shortly after their names had been given and who were often subsequently executed on charges of murder, corruption, or even gross indecencies.

"Ten months we had to accustom ourselves to the Bane's monstrosity. But still, when we finally met again and exchanged all that we had learned, neither of us could stop shaking. That was when Icarus told me that he could no longer live like this. That even last summer he had thought of taking his own life.

"I begged him to think no more of it. The idea that in the afterlife his beautiful soul would not be able to soar with the Angels—I could not bear it. But his mind was made up. It was the only way, he said. But before that we must still ask him a few questions.

"The question he wanted me to ask frightened me so much I almost could not speak it aloud. *How will the Bane be killed?* The answer: 'By venturing into the deepest level of the Commander's Palace and opening his crypt.'

"It was not a good answer for us. Besides his oracular powers, Icarus had no other training in any kind of magic. And I was a simple librarian far away in the capital. Icarus's despair almost threatened to tow both of us under, but I told him he must remain strong and appear normal, for I would ask a different question the next month.

"My question was, *How can I do my part to help kill the Bane?* It was the first time I had interjected myself into a question; tears of terror fell down my face even as I spoke. I remember his answer word for word. 'When the great comet will have come and gone, the Bane will walk into Mrs. Dawlish's house at Eton College.' "

"The great comet has already come and gone," said Kashkari, his voice unsteady.

Mage astronomers had first discovered the comet in August of the previous year. At its brightest, the comet almost rivaled the brilliance of the sun's corona, a beautiful, if also slightly ominous, portent that dominated the night sky and could even be seen during the day.

"I had to look up Eton College and Mrs. Dawlish's house. I found the former, but not the latter, and Icarus and I were both bewildered at why the Bane would deign to visit this impossibly insignificant nonmage school. Then we decided that it didn't matter. I would be there at Mrs. Dawlish's house at Eton College, ready and waiting, when the Bane walked in, whenever it would be.

"The Domain was still a wealthy realm with a relatively vigorous ruler and a centralized power structure—the Bane always saw it as a potential source of trouble. The crown princess of the Domain was expecting and the two most recent questions the Bane had asked of Icarus concerned the gender of the child and whether the child would someday take the throne. So we knew the future heir of the House of Elberon was most certainly on the Bane's mind.

"From time to time, he would ask Icarus what he should do as precautionary measures. Icarus was resolved that the next time he was asked the question, he would only pretend to sink into a trance—he had been so reliable for so long, the Bane no longer verified whether his trances were true trances—and tell the Bane that the heir of the House of Elberon should be sent to this nonmage school and I should be deployed as a special envoy of the Department of Overseas Administration to keep an eye on him.

"Icarus planned to go on as the Bane's oracle for another half year—so his words about Eton and me would not stand out. And then he would kill himself in such a way as to appear to have died of natural causes."

Mrs. Hancock exhaled slowly. "That was the last time I saw or spoke to him. He returned to the Commander's Palace three days later and by the next spring he was dead. His death aroused no suspicions—everybody had always assumed he wouldn't live long; those powers seemed simply too miraculous to go on existing.

"I requested a transfer to the Department of Overseas Administration. In time I was sent to reconnoiter Eton. Mrs. Dawlish had just started her own residence house for the boys. I applied for a position. She took someone else first, but the woman turned out to be unsuitable. I managed to get in a few weeks before His Highness came to the house.

"Now it was just a matter of waiting. The comet came last year. The nonmages were just as excited about it as the mages. Their newspaper reported sightings until February of this year. I thought I was ready but still, when Fairfax came that April, the first evening I was so nervous I could scarcely say grace before dinner."

Iolanthe was taken aback. "You thought I was the *Bane?*"

"I thought perhaps you were a scout. Then, this afternoon, West came."

Titus sent Iolanthe a what-did-I-tell-you look.

"I have seen the Bane quite a few times in my life. When West walked into my office to sign the visitor registry, I thought my knees—and my heart, too—would give out. It was exactly as Icarus had said, *When the great comet will have come and gone, the Bane will walk into Mrs. Dawlish's house at Eton College.*

"I watched him at cricket practice—to make sure I hadn't let some mistaken initial impression overwhelm my judgment. The more I stared at him, the more I was certain it had to be him. I decided that there was no point in waiting longer. I would proceed immediately.

"Imagine my surprise and dismay when I reached his house and found out that he had left only minutes ago—his father had sent for him because his mother was feeling poorly, according to the master of his house. I vaulted to all three of the nearest railway stations. He did not turn up anywhere. Not knowing what else to do, I stole into his room and searched through his possessions. The next thing I knew, Kashkari was in the room with me, a wand in his hand."

"If the prince told you what I told him," Kashkari said to Iolanthe, "then you already know that I came to Eton because of what some-one said about Wintervale in one of my dreams. But I did not learn, until very recently, that the person who spoke was Mrs. Hancock.

"The prince was convinced that Mrs. Hancock was a loyal agent of Atlantis. I hoped it would be otherwise, but I had no evidence. Then today, Mrs. Hancock came to watch cricket practice, which I thought was odd, since she almost never left the house—"

"I didn't want to not be here when the Bane walked in," said Mrs. Hancock.

"Then I saw her from my window, leaving again. I followed her, which led me to West's residence house. When she went inside West's room, I decided that I might as well confront her right there."

"Kashkari said, 'I am an enemy of the Bane. If you are too, say so now.' After I recovered from both my shock and fright, I demanded a truth pact.[15] With the truth pact in place, we proceeded rather swiftly. And when we dissolved the pact a quarter of an hour later, I recommended that we check school offices for West's record.

"His father is an Oxford University professor. Neither of us had been to Oxford so we couldn't vault. Kashkari volunteered his flying carpet. We gave some excuses, skipped supper, and flew to Oxford.

"The family was just sitting down to supper. We hid ourselves in the next room, but it was quite obvious Mrs. West was not in any kind of ill health. Then a girl asked whether her brother would be home for her birthday. And Professor West replied that he had received a letter from West today stating that indeed he would be home Saturday after next.

"Nothing made sense anymore. Why did West disappear? Did someone abduct him on false premises? And if he isn't the Bane, then what had Icarus meant, exactly, when he said the Bane would walk into Mrs. Dawlish's house?"

"I felt we ought to speak to you, prince," said Kashkari. "Mrs. Hancock agreed, because she had heard that your late mother was a seer. If Her Highness left any visions that can be of help to us, please let us know."

Iolanthe could have predicted to a word what Titus would say and he did not deviate from form.

"Before I help you, I will need a blood oath from the two of you that you are speaking the truth and do not seek to harm Fairfax or me in any sense, now or ever."

Kashkari nodded. Mrs. Hancock swallowed before she gave a

jerky nod. Titus called forth the green flame of veracity and administered the oath. "We will disperse for now and meet back here fifteen minutes after lights-out."

Fifteen minutes after lights-out, when Mrs. Hancock and Kashkari vaulted back into Fairfax's room, Titus laid the Crucible on the desk. "My mother's diary, which holds the record of all her visions, did not show me anything regarding either West or the Bane. But I can take you to see the Oracle of Still Waters."

The Oracle's garden was quite different from when Titus had last seen it, at the height of spring. That too had been at night, but it had been fragrant with the scent of blooming flowers and lively with the sound of amorous insects. Now the light of the lanterns shone upon bare branches and fallen leaves crunched underfoot.

"You can only ask a question that will help someone else," he told Kashkari and Mrs. Hancock.

"Can we each pose a question?" asked Kashkari.

"No. She will answer one question a week, if it is a good question. And you can only have one question answered by her in your lifetime. Although sometimes she might tell you a little extra, if she likes you."

"I'd like to ask a question," said Mrs. Hancock. She climbed up the steps and looked into the pool, but then turned back to the others. "I have no idea what to ask that would conform to the Oracle's requirements. Every night I think of the dead, all the dead—my sister, Icarus, and everyone else the Bane has murdered and tortured along the way. The need for justice has driven me all these years. I'm not sure I can honestly say that I am trying to help anyone living."

Before any of the mages present could say anything, the Oracle laughed softly in her silvery voice. "Gaia Archimedes, also known as Mrs. Hancock, welcome. I have not encountered a great deal of honesty like yours. At least you understand your motive is vengeance for the dead."

"Thank you, Oracle. But it does not help me with a question, does it?"

"What is it you seek to understand?"

"I want to know if Icarus was correct. If the Bane has come to Mrs. Dawlish's house. And how I can seize the opportunity to make a difference. I have devoted most of my adult life to the endeavor and I do not want to fail myself or the dead who are counting on me."

"I am sure there is at least one living soul who would benefit from it," said the Oracle kindly.

"I think the entire mage world would benefit from it. But I am at a loss to name one particular person."

"What about West?" asked Fairfax. "If we find out who is behind his abduction, that could help him."

Mrs. Hancock's face scrunched with agonized indecision. Titus understood her reluctance—if she only had one question, West seemed too peripheral a participant in these events to be featured in so central a role.

"Here is another option," he told Mrs. Hancock. "Ask the Oracle how you can help the one who needs your help the most."

This had been Fairfax's question last spring. He had thought then she had asked about her guardian; only later had she told him what her question had been.

Help me help the one who needs it the most.

And the answer she had been given had saved him.

Mrs. Hancock hesitated another minute. Finally, her jaw set, she said to the Oracle, "There has to be someone I can help in particular, even if I cannot name him or her. Tell me how I can help."

The water of the pond turned mirror bright. When the Oracle spoke again, it was as if the syllables issued from the very soil beneath their feet, gritty and resonant. "Destroy what remains of the Bane, if you wish to save the spares."

Mrs. Hancock looked back, incomprehension written all over her face.

Thank her, Titus mouthed.

Mrs. Hancock did so, her tone subdued.

The water hissed and steamed before quieting to that of a placid pool again. Wearily, the Oracle said, "Good-bye, Gaia Archimedes. And yes, you have seen it before."

✦ ✦

"What did the Oracle mean by 'you have seen it before'?" asked Iolanthe, after they came back into her room.

"This book, I think," answered Mrs. Hancock. "But of course I have seen it many times; the prince kept it in his room for years and I am required to check his room periodically, both as part of my duties in Mrs. Dawlish's house and as part of my role as Atlantis's eyes on him."

"What remains of the Bane," mused Kashkari. "What *remains* of the Bane. What is missing from the Bane?"

"His soul," Mrs. Hancock answered, not a question, but a statement. "A person who engages in sacrificial magic is said to have no soul left."

"The Bane doesn't seem to care too much about his soul, does he?" said Iolanthe.

"Or maybe he does. Maybe he began to care about his soul when it was already too late," said Titus. "Maybe that is why he is dead set on prolonging his life by any means possible, so he does not have to find out what happens after death to someone with no soul left."

Sometimes Iolanthe forgot that he had thought a great deal of life and death.

"And what do you suppose she meant by spares?" asked Mrs. Hancock. "And why would we want to save them?"

"I don't know why," said Kashkari, "but I am thinking of that book about Dr. Frankenstein—have any of you read it?"

Everyone else shook their heads. Iolanthe remembered that

Kashkari had the book with him the day Wintervale had spun the maelstrom.

"It's about this scientist who assembled a monster from spare human parts," Kashkari continued.

Iolanthe felt as if a cog in her brain suddenly engaged. "West is going to be cannibalized for parts?"

Titus stared at her. "You think 'spares' refers to *West*?"

"It makes sense, doesn't it? If you wanted spares, wouldn't you want spares that looked like you, instead of someone el . . ." She was struck by wonder and horror alike and had to grip the edge of the mantel before she could speak again. "Spares. *Spares*. Fortune shield me—do you think this is how he—how he—"

Titus looked equally overwhelmed. "Yes, it must be."

"Must be what?" asked Mrs. Hancock, her tone barely above a whisper.

"This must be how he resurrects."

Kashkari fell into a chair. "We have heard rumors, but I had never believed them."

"I have never even heard such rumors," Mrs. Hancock said dazedly. "Why have I never heard such rumors?"

"I imagine the Bane did his best to make sure his own people never heard of the rumors—anything remotely connected to sacrificial magic would undermine the legitimacy of his rule."

Iolanthe found her voice again. "That's why West was taken away. Not to cannibalize for parts, but to use as a whole." She turned to

Titus. "You remember what they said at the Citadel when the Bane resurrected last summer? They said he returned looking younger and more robust than before."

"Because he came back in a different, but similar-looking body," Titus concurred. "And that was how, even though they had blown out his brains in the Caucasus, he was still able to come back the next day, looking no worse for wear."

"Taking over another body entirely—it is a frightful power. Have you ever heard of another instance of it?" asked Mrs. Hancock, her voice weak.

Kashkari shook his head. "Only in stories."

"So it is not the first time West walked into Mrs. Dawlish's that we should worry about. It is the *next* time," said Iolanthe.

"What do you mean?" asked Mrs. Hancock.

"Next time we see him, it might very well be the Bane using West's body."

Silence fell.

"I wonder how long it takes the Bane to ready a body for use," murmured Kashkari.

"Something like that has to be contact requisite," said Iolanthe. "Seventy-two hours, at least."

"Let us assume the worst," said Titus. "Let us assume that he will be back tomorrow."

Mrs. Hancock made a sound like the whimper of a wounded animal. "What can we do? Do we attack him directly?"

Titus shook his head. "No use. We all know now that the Bane cannot be killed except in his own lair, where his original body is kept. Unless what I know of sacrificial magic is completely wrong, when he sacrifices another mage, the Bane must also sacrifice something of himself. That is why he always wants the most powerful elemental mage available—since he must sacrifice a part of himself no matter what, he would want to get as much out of each sacrifice as possible. And I would guess that what he gets from the sacrifice of a truly phenomenal elemental mage must be orders of magnitude greater than what he could achieve with a more ordinary one."

"How does the Bane know that for certain?" asked Kashkari. "My uncle was killed before the Bane could get to him. The girl who brought down lightning is still eluding his grasp, as far as anyone knows. Before them, there hadn't been any great elemental mages in centuries."

"There was one within the Bane's lifetime—there must have been, and in Atlantis itself, no less," Iolanthe said. "I recently came across an old travelogue. Some travelers en route to Atlantis, back when anyone could visit the realm, had described the great maelstrom of Atlantis, which had just come into being not long before. That is stupendous elemental magic, to create a whirlpool that still exists almost two centuries later. But I have never heard of such a mage. Anyone wants to bet that perhaps this poor elemental mage would have been the first the Bane sacrificed?"

"And perhaps when he had done so, he needed no more sacrifices for a long time, because it had been such a powerful sacrifice," said Kashkari. "And then, when the effect finally began to wane . . .'"

Titus nodded. "In any case, the Bane is here because he desperately needs the next great elemental mage—there are only so many body parts he can give up before there is nothing left of him. It is our task to make sure that he never nabs that elemental mage."

"But we don't even know where the lightning girl is."

"Not the lightning girl," said Titus. "Wintervale."

"What?" cried Kashkari and Mrs. Hancock in unison.

Titus briefly described his mother's vision, and then the fulfillment of that vision at Sutherland's uncle's house.

An almost beatific light came over Kashkari's face. "Finally! I have been wondering for years the exact purpose for which I am protecting Wintervale. We should take Wintervale and go. Right now."

"You can do it," said Titus, "but I cannot, unfortunately. I must give an account of my whereabouts every twenty-four hours. If I am missing for seventy-two hours then another warm body must be put on the throne. So I cannot leave until absolutely the last minute."

"Neither can I," said Mrs. Hancock, "without my overseers immediately knowing something is wrong."

"But I have been telling the boys that I am leaving for America," said Iolanthe. "No one would be that surprised by my departure. So if you need me to, I can take Wintervale to a safe house."

"I have a spare carpet you can use, if you don't want to travel by nonmage means," offered Kashkari. "It can carry four hundred pounds, cruise at one hundred twenty miles an hour, and go five hundred miles without touching ground."

"Wait a minute," said Mrs. Hancock. "Why is Wintervale not involved in any of our discussions?"

Kashkari glanced at Titus. "I'm not sure what the prince's reason is, but I'll tell you mine. Three weeks after we met, Wintervale showed me a trick. He cupped his palms together and when he opened them, there was a tiny flame suspended in midair. I wasn't the only one he showed the trick to—I'm sure half of the boys on this floor have seen it, at least everyone who plays cricket, that is.

"I had a bit of a crisis after that. I came eight thousand miles, leaving my family behind, to keep *this* boy safe? This boy who couldn't stop showing off to nonmages, because he needed approval and admiration that badly.

"Don't mistake me. I like Wintervale a great deal, but I don't think he has changed that much in all the years I've known him and I don't dare trust him with secrets that ought to remain secrets."

"So you plan to just grab Wintervale at the last possible second, without telling him anything ahead of time?" asked Mrs. Hancock, looking doubtful.

"His mother is here, but she does not want him to know that she is here," said Titus. "We should all exercise similar caution."

And his was the last word on the subject.

◆ ◆

After Mrs. Hancock and Kashkari left, Titus took Iolanthe into his arms.

She held him tightly. "Scared?"

"Petrified."

"Me, too," she admitted.

The revelations of the evening were a mad swirl in her head. She wanted to go to bed and forget for a while, but she was afraid that if she were to actually fall asleep, then she would be caught flatfooted if something were to happen in the middle of the night.

"And to think that Mrs. Hancock is the one responsible for your being educated outside the Domain, at this nonmage school," she went on. "It's true what they say, the threads of Fortune weave mysteriously."

"You were right about me—that my life was never going to be anything but thoroughly enmeshed with the Bane's." He exhaled. "But what if we fail?"

"We most likely will. You know this. As do I—and all the other mages who have ever taken up wands against Atlantis." She kissed him on his cheek. "So forget that and let's concentrate on what we need to do."

He nodded slowly. "You are right—again."

She put a kettle in the grate. They were not going to sleep much this night, so they might as well have some tea. "Last time Atlantis put a no-vaulting zone on the school. They could very well do the same thing again—and this time we wouldn't have Wintervale's wardrobe for a portal."

"But we do have a number of carpets—Kashkari has two and I have one, which together should be sufficient to ferry all of us. I have the Crucible, which can act as a portal in emergencies. Not to mention you have a quasi-vaulter."

"Give the vertices of the quasi-vaulter to Wintervale." They would need three days on his person before they could work on him. "He will be the most difficult to move for all of us—much better if he can use the quasi-vaulter."

He opened her cabinet and took out her tin of tea leaves. "I will do that. I am sure I can think of something to tell him without giving away everything."

Again this lack of confidence in Wintervale. "Is it possible your judgment is clouded by having known Wintervale for so long? I feel he has been far more sober and far less indiscreet after the maelstrom."

"It is quite possible that I am prejudiced against the old Wintervale and not the new one. But remember, no one is looking for Wintervale, but every agent of Atlantis is still seeking you."

He had said that to her several times, and she had always accepted it without questions. But now she wasn't so certain. "Are you sure that no one is looking for Wintervale? He sank an Atlantean vessel. Even if no one on board managed to send a distress signal, or survived to tell the tale, would Atlantis not investigate a whoesale disappearance of a ship?"

"Dalbert has an eye on the situation. He has heard nothing about the *Sea Wolf*."

Her conversation with Cooper earlier in the evening came to mind. Cooper had miscopied a word; what if Iolanthe had misread the name of the ship? After all, Greek had always given her fits.

"Maybe I was wrong about the name of the ship. Can you ask Dalbert if there is any news for a ship named *Ferocious*?"

Written in capital letters, ΛΑΒΡΑΞ—sea wolf—and ΛΑΒΡΟΣ—ferocious—would have been similar enough to cause confusion.

"I will do that tonight itself," he said.

"Have some tea before you go."

She added more fire to the grate, so the water would boil faster. Titus wrapped his arms around her from behind. She leaned back against him.

"Why do I have the sensation that the situation is about to spin out of control?"

"Probably because it is." He kissed her at the temple. "Part of me would like for you to be far away, beyond the danger and the madness. But the rest of me could not be more grateful that you will still be here, with me, when all hell breaks loose."

CHAPTER ♦ 31

The Sahara Desert

AN ESCARPMENT ROSE SHARPLY FROM the desert floor. It looked as if Titus and Iolanthe were headed directly at the cliff, when the carpet before them disappeared. Iolanthe clutched tight at the front of the carpet as it hurtled into a narrow fissure. The fissure twisted and turned—or at least she guessed that to be the case, for it was pitch dark, yet the carpet zigzagged at a breakneck pace.

"How are you steering? Can you see anything?"

"I am not steering," answered Titus. "The carpet knows the lay of the land."

All at once the fissure widened into a cavernous space, lit with a warm, bright light. Along the interior walls of this chamber, hundreds of smaller caves and niches had been carved into the rock, but Iolanthe could see no ladders or stairs to access them—until she remembered that, of course, everyone who lived in the rebel base probably had a carpet.

Half of the floor of the cavern was taken up with horticulture: leafy, green towers, placed so that they received maximum light and did not cast shadows on one another, rose to nearly the height of the ceiling. The other half was given over to the making and maintenance of flying carpets. And despite the lateness of the hour, at least a hundred mages were at work, harvesting fruits and vegetables, operating the looms that made new carpets, or repairing frayed-looking older carpets.

They landed on a large ledge twenty feet above the floor of the cavern. A breathtakingly beautiful young woman awaited them on the platform, clad in a simple, fawn-colored tunic with a pair of matching trousers.

She hugged the boy who had brought Titus and Iolanthe. "Good to see you safe. I'm afraid your brother isn't here. But don't worry, he is well—he was a member of the party that raided the Atlantean base and they cannot return for at least another five days, in case Atlantis is on their tails."

The boy turned to Titus and Iolanthe. "May I present Amara, commander of the base and my future sister-in-law."

Iolanthe caught something strangely bleak in the tone of his voice. She looked from him to Amara.

"Around here she is also known as Durga Devi—it's our tradition to take on a nom de guerre for times of war," continued the boy. "You might hear people refer to me as Vrischika, but feel free to go on calling me Kashkari."

So that was his name.

Titus nodded gravely at the young woman. "Pleased to meet you."

"We are honored by your presence, Your Highness. And yours, Miss Seabourne." Amara smiled, and Iolanthe was nearly blinded by her beauty. "Have you, Your Highness, at last brought Miss Seabourne into our safekeeping?"

"No," said Titus decisively. "We will intrude on your hospitality only briefly—Atlantis is too close for comfort. If you have a translocator on the premise, we would like to have use of it, especially if it would take us near or into a major nonmage city."

Iolanthe agreed completely. A crowded city made a much better hiding place for them. Cairo was her first choice. But even Khartoum, with its political instability, would do in a pinch.

"We have two translocators, but unfortunately neither has been functioning for the past three days."

Kashkari grew alarmed. "Are you sure Atlantis hasn't found you?"

A shadow crossed Amara's face. "We ask ourselves the same thing, but everything else has been normal."

"Do you have a fast, long-range carpet that we can borrow?" said Titus. "We must leave immediately—the Bane himself is in the Sahara."

This produced a ripple of shock in both Amara and Kashkari.

"Why didn't you say anything to me earlier?" Kashkari demanded.

"I've been meaning to tell you this," said Iolanthe. "We haven't the slightest idea who y—"

"Durga Devi!" Ishana came careening on a flying carpet, almost knocking into Iolanthe. "Durga Devi, the maintenance crew found a tracer on Oasis III."

"What?" Amara cried. "How is this possible? I thought you said you did *not* encounter anyone the entire time you were out."

"That's true. No one came to the oasis except His Highness and Miss Seabourne."

Titus swore. "The sand wyvern. We did not know then it still carried tracers. It is more than possible that one fell off when the sand wyvern brushed against the date palms."

Iolanthe gripped his arm. "Then Atlantis will believe we are here—and we are."

"Let's get some fresh carpets and I'll take you to Luxor," said Kashkari. "If we start now, we can be there before noon."

Ishana ferried them down to where the new carpets were stowed. Iolanthe didn't see anything that looked like a traditional carpet, thick and woolly. Instead, the carpets, hung up on steel rods, resembled picnic blankets, towels, and curtains—even capes.

Ishana stopped before a rack of carpets that had the look of bedsheets about them. "These are the best we have. They have a range of about a thousand miles and can cruise at one hundred fifty miles an hour with a cargo of up to five hundred pounds."

"I need carpets that cannot be recalled—in case the base is over-run," said Kashkari.

Ishana exhaled, clearly unnerved by the thought of something going so wrong. "Right. Then you better take these—eight hundred mile range, one hundred fifteen miles an hour, cargo weight two hundred pounds."

"Can you handle a carpet on your own?" Titus asked Iolanthe.

"I control air—I'll manage."

The rumble of drumroll filled the air, followed by a pleasant-sounding female voice. "All battle riders report to squadron leaders. Armored chariots sighted. Wyverns sighted. Lindworms sighted."

Lindworms were the largest flying dragons, not terribly fast, but brutal. Iolanthe had been under the impression they were impossible to domesticate, but apparently Atlantis liked to break new ground in animal husbandry.

A carpet streaked down and yanked to a stop behind them. It was Shulini, looking frantic. "Your Highness, Durga Devi asks that you come with me—and everyone else too. There is something she needs you all to see."

They followed her up to the ceiling of the cavern and hurtled into an opening, which led into a tunnel that wound upward. The air grew colder and colder and suddenly they were under the stars.

"Look! Look!" shouted Shulini.

Iolanthe could not discern anything out of the ordinary. Briefly she wondered if she should use a far-seeing spell, and then a movement near the edge of the sky caught her eye—a distortion of the air that made the stars beyond stretch and blinker. As she followed it, she realized that the distortion was like an enormous and somewhat uneven ring, going all around—and dropping rapidly toward the ground.

"Fortune shield me," said Titus, "a bell jar dome."

A bell jar dome was a siege weapon, almost as antique as bewitched spears. But once in place, it would be nearly impossible for those inside to breach.

"Hurry!" cried Kashkari. "We might still get Fairfax out."

As if it had heard him, the bell jar dome came down hard.

"Too late," Titus said, as if through clenched teeth.

A man's voice, golden and powerful, rang out. "The Lord High Commander of the Great Realm of New Atlantis seeks the fugitive Iolanthe Seabourne. Surrender her, and all the other lives will be spared."

Titus immediately had Iolanthe's hand in his. "No one will harm you."

She squeezed his hand. "And I'm not so easy to harm."

But all the same, she was frightened witless.

Ishana set down the carpet. They were on top of the massif that reared up from the desert floor. Standing on it, surveying the bell jar dome, was Amara.

"We seem to have a dilemma on our hands," she said calmly.

"No, not at all," countered Kashkari, when Iolanthe had expected

Titus to be the first to object. "We will not give her to the Bane, not even if the cost is ten times the lives of everyone in this base."

"Of course not," said Amara. "To let the Bane have her would be ruinous. But the truth is we are few and the force of Atlantis is great. We may not be able to prevent the Bane from taking her, even if we do our best."

Further surprising Iolanthe, Kashkari stepped before her. "No, you will not even think of it."

"We are at war, my friend. I must think of every eventuality."

"Then think it and dismiss it."

It dawned on Iolanthe at last that they were speaking of a way to make it impossible for the Bane to have her: by killing her themselves. Judging by the way Titus's hand tightened over hers, he also understood.

"I know what happened to your uncle, Mohandas," said Amara. "And while that was a tragedy, it prevented the Bane from becoming unimaginably strong."

Kashkari had his wand in hand. "And how did that help us? Unimaginably strong or not, the Bane is still in power all these years later."

"But if your uncle's family hadn't done what they did—"

"Then perhaps we would be living in a very different world. Help reached them soon after they killed my uncle—I see you did not know this, did you? Even my brother doesn't. If only everyone hadn't despaired prematurely, my uncle might have been able to grow into the fullness of his power and he might have made all the difference in the more crucial battles of ten years ago."

Kashkari took a deep breath. "Besides, I have already dreamed of the future: my friend will be approaching the Commander's Palace on her own power and of her own volition—to finish the Bane, not to be the next victim in his sacrificial rituals. That means she outwits the Bane this day and manages to keep not only her life but her freedom."

Iolanthe's jaw slackened. Her, nearing the Commander's Palace *voluntarily*? And why did Kashkari present a mere dream as if it had any significance?

But it certainly gave Amara pause. "You are sure that is what you dreamed?"

"Without a doubt. And believe me, our resistance against the Bane would be of little use if we cannot strike directly inside his lair."

"Very well then, Mohandas." Amara squeezed Kashkari's shoulder. "It's time for me to go down and muster the riders. Look after our guests for me."

Ishana and Shulini left with her, leaving Kashkari, Titus, and Iolanthe by themselves on top of the massif.

"Is it true, what you said about Fairfax? And about your uncle?" asked Titus, sounding doubtful.

"No, I made up everything."

"Oh," said Iolanthe. She hadn't believed Kashkari completely but he had sounded so impassioned, so certain of himself, that she had very much wanted what he had said to be true.

"At least you are safe for the moment." Kashkari laid a hand over his chest. "My heart hasn't pounded so hard since that business with Wintervale."

Iolanthe and Titus exchanged a glance.

"I'm more than a bit embarrassed to tell you," said Iolanthe, "but His Highness and I are under a memory spell and we remember nothing from before the desert."

"What!" Kashkari exclaimed. He looked from Iolanthe to Titus and back. "How do you not remember Wintervale?"

They both shrugged.

Kashkari gaped. "I don't believe this. Have you really forgotten *everything*?"

CHAPTER · 32

England

THE NEXT DAY WAS SUNDAY and morning service was mandatory for all the boys.

The chapel at Eton, though impressive-looking, had become too small for the student population. Usually the senior boys were given seats in the pews, and the junior boys had to stand in the aisles, at the back, and even spilling out the door of the sanctuary. Today Titus and Fairfax made sure they were standing at the very rear of the crowd, and when no one noticed, they slipped away.

Fairfax went to see Lady Wintervale—she thought the latter ought to know her son would not be at the school much longer. Titus returned to the laboratory to perform one last sweep for items that he might wish to put into the emergency bag.

He came across a pouch in an otherwise empty drawer—the remedies he had taken from the laboratory to give to Wintervale, when the latter's condition suddenly worsened, that day at Sutherland's uncle's house overlooking the North Sea. Unfortunately, every remedy Titus administered had made matters worse, the very last one sending Wintervale into convulsions that required a double dose of panacea to subdue.

Usually Titus never left remedies lying about. But when he came back to the laboratory that night, he had been in the depths of despair. Instead of putting the remedies back where they belonged, he had shoved the whole pouch aside so he would not have to look at it again.

But now that he and Fairfax had repaired their rift, there was no more reason for avoidance. He opened the drawer that held abdominal remedies and set the vials from the pouch back in their places, one after another. *Vertigo. Appendicitis. Bilious complaint. Infection-related emesis. Inflammation of the stomach lining.*

The last, *Foreign expulsion*, was the very one that had sent Wintervale into a seizure. Titus turned it around in his fingers, shaking his head at the mayhem it had caused.

He stilled. He had chosen the remedy because he had thought it would precipitate and expel harmful substances from the body, but that was the province of a remedy by the name of foreign extraction. Foreign expulsion, on the other hand, was meant for getting rid of parasites and such.

Or was it?

He pulled out a thick volume of pharmacological reference and looked up the remedy.

Foreign expulsion. An older remedy, now no longer common. Good for the purging of parasites. Can also be used to expel swallowed objects and objects stuck in various bodily orifices. May aid in the divestiture of intangible tenure.

What in the world was intangible tenure?

He wanted to look it up. But a quick pulse from his pocket watch reminded him that that morning service was almost finished. Kashkari would bring Wintervale back to Mrs. Dawlish's, and Titus was to give Wintervale the vertices of the quasi-vaulter to carry on his person, with a suitably dire report of the dangers rising all about them, without mentioning anything specific.

He made a mental note to look up intangible tenure later and left the laboratory.

"Things are moving so fast, we don't know what will happen in the next hour. Or even in the next minute," said Iolanthe, seated in the drawing room at Windsor Castle that Lady Wintervale had appropriated for her own use. "Likely we will have to take your son away from school—and likely soon—for his safety. I thought you might like to know that."

Lady Wintervale looked out the window toward Eton, just across the Thames River. Her voice had a faraway quality to it. "You mean, after this, I might not see him for a while, perhaps ever?"

"It's quite possible."

Iolanthe waited for Lady Wintervale to exert her parental right, something along the lines that if they were taking Wintervale out of school, then he might as well be under the protection of his mother. But Lady Wintervale only continued to stare out of the window.

"Would you like to see him before he leaves? We can make sure no one traces his physical movements to you. And I daresay he would not speak of your whereabouts to anyone. He has become more circumspect of late—certainly he has managed to keep the fact that he is now a great elemental mage to himself."

Lady Wintervale clenched her hand and again gave no reply.

Iolanthe was counting the hours until she and Titus had all the precautions in place, so she could have him vault her to Paris to see Master Haywood, who had to be anxious for her news. After that, there was no telling when they would meet again. Or if.

The distance Lady Wintervale insisted on keeping from her child made no sense at all.

"May I ask, ma'am, why you do not want to see your son?"

Lady Wintervale moved to a different window. Her jaw worked, but she remained silent. Against the deep vermilion drapes, she was pale as a wraith and almost as insubstantial.

Iolanthe's bafflement turned into uneasiness—for now she could feel the fear radiating from Lady Wintervale.

"Please, my lady, I beg of you. If there is something that matters, do not hold it back. There are lives at stake here, many lives."

"You think I do not know that?" Lady Wintervale snarled.

But nothing followed. After a fraught, interminable interval, Iolanthe had to accept that she would get nothing else out of Lady Wintervale. "Thank you for seeing me, ma'am. Long may Fortune walk with you."

As she rose, Lady Wintervale said, "Wait."

Iolanthe sat down again, tense with anticipation—and no small amount of dread.

Another minute passed before Lady Wintervale said, "I lost Lee on our last trip."

Iolanthe blinked. "I don't quite understand."

"Among the Exiles communities, we have built our own network of translocators. But since spring, Atlantis had actively interfered with the working of those translocators. By early September, when Lee and I set out, all the translocators the Exiles in London had depended on for years were out of service.

"We had a choice between using carpets or taking a steamer across the English Channel. Lee cares for neither. But nowadays there are excellent remedies for seasickness, so he decided on the steamer. Once I had seen him settled in his bunk—the remedy allowed him to sleep through the crossing—I went above to take in some fresh air, as I enjoy ocean travel.

"When the steamer docked in Calais, I went to wake him up. He was no longer in his bunk, and his suitcase too was gone. I thought we had missed each other, that he was now on the deck looking for me. But no, he was not on the deck either. And he was not on the pier, waiting. I enlisted the help of both the steamer's staff and the harbormaster's staff, but nobody could find him.

"I wrote frantically in my two-way notebook, but he did not answer. At last I went to the railway station, and there someone remembered a young man of his description, buying a ticket to Grenoble. I immediately started for Grenoble, asking at all the stations along the way. And when I reached Grenoble, I inquired at all the likely and unlikely lodging places, to no avail.

"Not knowing what else to do, I went back home. Only to receive a telegram, of all things, from Lee, from Grenoble, asking where I was. So I rushed back, and there he was, safe and sound. He said that when he couldn't find me on the steamer, he thought I must have been in a rush to catch the train, and so he'd dashed off to the railway station. But in Paris, where he was to change trains, he realized his mistake and went back to Calais, only to learn that I had indeed taken a train to Grenoble. So he started again for Grenoble, and probably reached the city just after I had left for home.

"I was terribly relieved to see him. The subsequent events you already know. We ended up on a ship in the North Sea, pursued by Atlantis. He didn't have his carpet with him—just as he didn't have his two-way notebook with him. So I had to put him on a lifeboat. I meant to go in the lifeboat with him, but we were under attack and I couldn't get away immediately. When I did, on my carpet, I was pursued all the way back to France. And I would have been caught, were it not for a tremendous fog that rolled in from the Channel.

"It took me several days to get back to England. If he had made it, he would have gone either home or to Eton. I didn't dare go home, so I tried Eton. And found Mrs. Dawlish's house guarded around the clock."

"It's the Atlanteans watching the prince," said Iolanthe.

"I thought so too. But then I remembered that Lee had been away from me for seventy-two hours on that trip."

Lady Wintervale looked at Iolanthe, as if Iolanthe should come to some meaningful deduction from what she had just said.

Iolanthe drew a blank. "I am not sure I grasp the significance of your words, ma'am."

"I am not sure I understand what I am saying either. I am not sure I want to." Lady Wintervale crossed the room to stand before the roaring fireplace, as if the drafts from the windows had chilled her. "But you are right. I should go and see Lee. It might be my last chance."

Iolanthe waited for her to say more, but Lady Wintervale only waved her hand. "Please leave me."

Iolanthe rushed into the laboratory. The conversation with Lady Wintervale had unsettled her deeply, and she needed to speak to Titus.

He was not there, but his typing ball was clacking away. When it stopped, she pulled out the message.

Your Most Serene Highness,

With regard to your query concerning the Atlantean naval ship the
Ferocious—ΛΑΒΡΟΣ *in the original Greek—a vessel belonging to*
the Atlantean Coastal Defense once bore the name. From what records
I can unearth, it was decommissioned three years ago and recently
scrapped.

Your faithful servant,
Dalbert

Iolanthe scanned the message again, and a third time, her confusion growing with each additional read. She had not heard anything about Atlantis being short on seaworthy crafts. Why was a decommissioned ship sent out when there were plenty of vessels in active service?

She sent back a message to Dalbert. *Can you confirm again that there is no Atlantean ship named* Sea Wolf?

Dalbert's response came promptly.

Your Most Serene Highness,

I can confirm that there is no Atlantean vessel, naval or civilian, by
the name of Sea Wolf *(or* ΛΑΒΡΑΞ, *to use the original Greek).*

Your faithful servant,

Dalbert

Something rattled in her memory. What had she read in that travelogue the first time?

She entered the reading room and ran to the help desk. The travelogue was in her hand in seconds. She flipped through the pages with suddenly clumsy fingers.

The tourists from nearly two centuries ago had sailed to Atlantis to see the demolition of a floating hotel that had been condemned. The method of condemnation had been none other than the dropping of the floating hotel into the maelstrom of Atlantis.

As spectacular as the destruction itself was, leaving Atlantis, we would come upon the not-so-pretty sight of the hotel's wreckage across our path, a current of rubbish. But at least, unlike a true maritime disaster, there would be no dead bodies carried alongside pieces of hull and deck.

A vein throbbed at her temple. When she had scanned the sea after the maelstrom had come and gone, she too, had seen wreckage, but not bodies.

If the ship that had tumbled into Wintervale's maelstrom had been decommissioned and empty, then there must have been collusion between some of the parties involved. It would mean somebody deliberately sent an old, useless vessel after Wintervale, so as not to waste personnel or ships in active service, because they knew at some point it was going to be destroyed.

Who could have known that the ship would be destroyed? Wintervale, according to both the prince and Kashkari, had been the feeblest of elemental mages, barely able to get a fire going in the grate. Who could have predicted, ahead of time, that he would singlehandedly put an Atlantean ship to ruin?

She bit her lips and reached for the emergency bag.

Nobody had returned from Sunday service yet—it was not that unusual for the sermon to run long. Titus stood inside Fairfax's room and looked around.

He had decorated the room years before she arrived, with a picture of the queen on the wall, postcards of ocean liners, and images that represented Bechuanaland, her supposed home. She had replaced the photograph of Queen Victoria with that of a society beauty and put up new curtains, but otherwise left the room more or less as it was.

His gaze fell on the photograph of her that did not look like her at all. She had passed around the photograph the day Sutherland issued his invitation for them all to go to his uncle's house, which seemed an impossibly long time ago.

She materialized next to him, the emergency bag strapped across her shoulders. Alarm pulsed through him.

"Why do you have the bag? What is the matter?"

"What do you think of my eyesight?" she asked, her tone tense.

That was not the question he had expected. "Perfectly good. Now tell me why you are already carrying the emergency bag."

She ignored his demand. "What do you think of my grasp of Greek?"

He could shout at the top of his lungs for her to answer his question first, but this was Fairfax, who never did anything without a good reason. He held himself back. "Not bad."

"Do you think it is likely that I have completely misread the name of the ship Wintervale sank?"

"But you just told me last night that you probably did misread it."

"I mistook it for a similar word—or so I thought. Is it possible that the actual name is nothing like what I thought it to be either time?"

"Anything is possible." He recalled the skimmer, whirling around on the outer rim of the maelstrom before being pulled under. "But if you were already paying attention, there is no reason you should have been that much mistaken."

She gripped his arm, hard. "If I am correct about the ship's name, then it must be either *Sea Wolf* or *Ferocious*. Dalbert had confirmed to you—and to me again today—that there is no Atlantean naval vessel called *Sea Wolf*. But there was one called *Ferocious*, and it had been decommissioned three years ago.

"I saw no bodies when I surveyed the sea that day. Wreckage but no bodies. Do you think it is possible that the ship had been empty?

That"—she swallowed—"it was all for show?"

He stared at her, beginning to feel as if he too had been caught in an enormous trap, with an undertow too strong to escape. "What do you *mean*?"

"I'm not sure what I mean, and I'm not sure I want to know." Her hand came up to her throat. "Fortune shield me, that's almost exactly what Lady Wintervale said."

"What? When?"

"When I visited Lady Wintervale just now, she told me that she and Wintervale had become separated on their way to Grenoble for more than seventy-two hours."

With the discussion of the Bane still fresh in his memory, a loud gong went off inside Titus's head: seventy-two hours was the threshold for the most powerful contact-requisite spells. "You have to be in direct physical contact with someone for that long in order to . . . to . . ."

A seventy-two-hour disappearance.

And when he returned, the boy who could barely light a candle with his elemental powers had become mighty enough to create a spectacular whirlpool.

Fortune shield him. "The remedy I gave Wintervale, the one that made him go into a seizure—do you know what 'intangible tenure' means?"

A choked sound issued from her throat. "I have heard of it before—Master Haywood had a colleague at the Conservatory who researched the occult. Isn't saying someone is under an intangible tenure just a wordier way of saying that person is possessed?"

Possessed.

"Fortune shield us all." Her voice was hoarse. "Did you give Wintervale an *exorcism* aid?"

Had he? "What happens if you give someone an exorcism aid by accident?"

"Nothing. That was how they used to tell whether someone is really possessed or just pretending. You slip an exorcism aid in their food and if they show no reaction, it's just an act. But if they start seizing—"

They gaped at each other in horror. That was exactly what had happened to Wintervale.

And then, in a panic, Titus had forced a king's ransom of panacea down Wintervale's gullet. The only goal of panacea was the stabilization of the entire system. It stopped the exorcism and it stopped any other battle Wintervale's body might have been pitching to rid itself of—of whatever had taken possession of him.

Titus remembered the nautical distress signal he received, alerting him to Wintervale's presence. He also remembered what Fairfax had said to him: *Had I been Lady Wintervale, I would have disabled the distress signal on the lifeboat. That was probably what allowed Atlantis to track him down.*

What if the distress signal had been deliberately *enabled*, to make sure that Titus saw everything?

They had already deduced that the Bane was capable of "driving" other bodies that looked like his. Who was to say he could not take command of one that did not resemble his original self?

"The mental instability the Kno-it-all gauge detected in Wintervale," he heard himself say, his voice almost flat. "What if it was exactly right?"

"And Wintervale's inability to walk unassisted—that must be because he looks nothing like the one driving his body," said Fairfax. "There is a reason that until now the Bane only used similar-looking bodies—the mind probably can't trick itself enough into fully controlling everything if the face looks that different."

"And the guards outside Mrs. Dawlish's house—they were not there at the beginning of the Half. They only came after Wintervale's maelstrom."

They had not been posted to watch Titus, as he had assumed, but most likely to ensure someone else's safety.

Fairfax pulled on her collar, as if it had become too tight. "I always did think it was miraculous that Atlantis let you return to school this Half. I wouldn't have."

Icarus Khalkedon had been correct. After the great comet had come and gone, the Bane had indeed walked into Mrs. Dawlish's house, and he had done so in Wintervale's body. And West had disappeared because he unfortunately resembled the Bane—and the Bane could always use yet another spare.

"What I still don't understand is what it is all for," Fairfax continued. "What is the Bane trying to accomplish by doing all this?"

Titus gripped her. "It is all for *you*, do you not see? He had failed to find you earlier, so all this trickery is to get into *my* mind, because if he could do that, all my secrets would be open to him. After what happened last time, there was no way he could put me under Inquisition again without first provoking a war—nor does he have anywhere near as powerful a mind mage at his disposal these days, after I killed the Inquisitor. And run-of-the-mill memory or mind-control spells do not work on me because the heirs of the House of Elberon are protected from birth against such shenanigans. His only way into my mind was via contact-requisite means."

She shook. "That's why he always wanted *you* to support him when he walked places. And that's why he attacked Kashkari with the book and the roof tiles, because Kashkari hindered his efforts at trying to accumulate enough hours of direct contact with *you*."

"But he does not have those hours yet. So I am still safe. And you are still safe. And—"

The door burst open. Titus nearly blasted a hole through the house before he realized it was only Kashkari.

"I know who you are," said Kashkari, to Fairfax.

She reeled, but recovered fast. "I already told you who I am. I am the prince's bodyguard."

Kashkari closed the door. "You are the girl who brought down lightning."

Titus stepped in front her, wand drawn. "If you—"

"Of course not. I was just in a state of shock and I had to confirm it."

"Did you just guess all of a sudden?" Titus demanded sharply. "And where is Wintervale? Is he here?"

"No, he is still milling about outside the chapel—Mrs. Hancock is watching over him. And I guessed because Roberts was passing around photographs taken several weeks ago."

"Who is Roberts and what photographs?" Titus demanded.

"Cricketer. Never made the eleven. Wanted to counterfeit photographic evidence for posterity that he was part of the school team. I was included in some of the photographs on the periphery and next to me was someone with"—Kashkari looked about the room and grabbed Fairfax's picture, the one that did not look anything like her—"this face. I didn't understand what I was seeing at first. I remember it was Fairfax sitting next to me that day. There was no reason for him to look so different—until I remembered the photograph in his room.

"Then I remembered that Atlantis has trouble finding the girl who brought down lightning because her image cannot be painted or otherwise captured. And that was also when I remembered that the day Fairfax first arrived at this school was the day the girl manifested her powers."

Fairfax gasped.

Titus instantly had his arm around her shoulders. "What is it?"

"Wintervale. Someone is going to pass those pictures to him, sooner or later."

"So?" said Kashkari.

"*Wintervale* is the Bane, or he has been since the day he came to Sutherland's uncle's house."

Kashkari shivered. "No. Please, no."

Mrs. Hancock materialized among them. Before anyone could demand why she wasn't watching Wintervale, she said, "Something is wrong with Wintervale. He was looking at these pictures then he suddenly started laughing—and wouldn't stop."

"Wintervale is the Bane. And I'm the one who brought down lightning. He has been trying to reach a contact-requisite threshold with the prince, so he can find out where I am," said Fairfax. "But those photographs he was looking at let him know that he has already found me, and I've been under his nose all along."

Mrs. Hancock stumbled back a step. "Now I finally understand." She turned to Kashkari. "By staying close to Wintervale, you saved *him*—His Highness, not Wintervale."

Kashkari gawked at her, thunderstruck.

"We must go," Titus said to Fairfax. "Right now."

She gripped the emergency bag already strapped to her shoulders. "Let's."

But they could not vault. The Bane must have come to the same conclusion Kashkari had. And if he had been at Eton this long, the no-vaulting zone must have been at the ready for almost as long, waiting for his command to be put into effect.

Kashkari rushed to the window. "You can't use a flying carpet either. There are armored chariots outside."

The armored chariots were high above, circling like a flock of birds. They would swoop down in an instant, should Titus and Iolanthe dare to make an escape on Kashkari's spare carpet. Not to mention, an armored chariot's top speed was much higher than the carpet's one hundred and twenty miles an hour.

"The quasi-vaulter, then," said Fairfax.

"We will save that until we have no other choice. For now we still have this." Titus set the Crucible on the table.

"You two had better leave this room," said Fairfax, to Kashkari and Mrs. Hancock. "You have not been compromised yet. The Bane does not know you are involved with us, so do what you can to keep yourselves safe."

"Will we meet again?" asked Kashkari.

Titus untwisted half of his pendant and gave it to Kashkari. "We can hope."

Kashkari and Mrs. Hancock left. Titus and Fairfax each laid a hand on the Crucible, hers over his.

Titus began the password.

"How far is Forbidden Island?" Iolanthe shouted, over the air rushing over the carpet at one hundred twenty miles an hour.

"Ninety miles," Titus shouted back.

Forty-five minutes, then.

They were a tight fit on the carpet, which was no more than three and a half feet wide and five feet long. At this speed there was only one way to ride: flat on one's stomach, hands tightly gripped onto the front of the carpet, a safety harness clipped over the torso.

Below, the ground rushed by. She recognized the Plain of Giants. And somewhere to the north, Briga's Chasm, made faintly visible by the vapor of miasma rising out of the depths of its deep ravine, a vapor that writhed and shifted, almost like a fog, under the sunlight.

There was also a portal at Briga's Chasm, but that one led to the copy of the Crucible that had been lost, and without knowing where that copy of the Crucible was, Titus had not been willing to take the risk. So they were headed for Forbidden Island, to access the copy of the Crucible in the monastery, which was still a safe place for the Master of the Domain, if he could get to it.

"Wish they had picked easier stories to use for portals," she said, knowing very well the point of selecting difficult locations was to decrease the likelihood one would be followed from one Crucible to another. "I can beat the Big Bad Wolf to a pulp on any given day."

"And I daresay the seven dwarfs are no match for my prowess," said Titus, turning carefully to look behind them.

"Anyone chasing us?"

"Not yet."

"I guess we can't ever go back to school again."

"No."

It was probably the last she'd see of the boys. She hoped Cooper would still remember her, when he was a portly, middle-aged lawyer, coming back to school each year on the Fourth of June to celebrate the memories of his youth.

And Master Haywood. She had one of her Wyoming Territory calling cards in her pocket—in case she couldn't go to Paris in person, she was going to send it to him, to let him know not to expect her for a while. She wondered if she could still post it somewhere, so that he would worry less.

She turned to Titus. "I hope Kashkari and Mrs.—"

The carpet spun wildly along its long axis, the world a stomach-churning kaleidoscope of earth and sky. She screamed. He swore and reached for a corner of the carpet. With a sudden yank the carpet stabilized—upside down.

But it hadn't stopped—it was still cruising at top speed upside down. Her view of the sky was obstructed, but when she tilted her head back, the ground below zoomed by, making her feel dizzy.

"On the count of three," shouted Titus, "kick your feet up and throw all your weight toward your head. One, two, three."

Their combined motion flipped the carpet over. They were no longer upside down, but the carpet had screeched to a stop, since they now faced the opposite direction.

And coming at them, in Wintervale's body, was the Bane, riding a carpet of his own.

Unfortunately, the Bane already knew how to get into the Crucible when it was in the middle of being used as a portal, and there was no one at school with the ability to stop him.

Titus and Iolanthe's carpet juddered to restart itself. They leaned their weight to one side. The carpet banked, turning.

A gust roared toward them and the carpet was blown end over end several times—they would have fallen off if it weren't for the safety harnesses holding them in place.

"Do not let the Bane play with us," shouted Titus.

She called for a bolt of lightning, aimed at the Bane. But the lightning only struck a shield, and the Bane passed under unharmed. She kept calling for more thunderbolts, which flashed and sizzled as if they were in the middle of a thunderstorm.

Skillfully, easily, the Bane wove between the currents of electricity, dodging Iolanthe's attacks.

And he was too fast. They would not reach Forbidden Island before he caught up with them.

She threw down several huge fireballs, setting the landscape beneath aflame.

"What are you doing?" Titus shouted.

"Making him have to come through smoke, at least. If only Wintervale suffered from asthma."

No sooner had she finished speaking than the carpet swerved north.

"Where are we going?" she asked, startled.

"Asthma," Titus said tightly. "Or perhaps something even better."

The season inside the Crucible almost always reflected that outside: there were no flowers on the trees of the orchard, which had also been picked clean of their fruits. In the distance rose a house shaped like a wicker beehive, small at the bottom, bulging out at the middle, and then tapering again toward the top.

Titus had brought Iolanthe here in the very early days of their acquaintance, before she could control air. In that house he had tried to force her, and she had almost drowned in honey.

Or rather, the sensations had been those of a near-drowning, but she had never been in real danger: the vast majority of the time they used the Crucible as a proving ground, and injuries—or even death—inside the Crucible had no bearing on the actual world outside.

But now they were using the Crucible as a portal, and all the rules changed: injuries caused actual harm and death was irreversible.

They flew low, between rows of neatly pruned apple trees. Iolanthe, a long branch in hand, overturned every skep they came across, releasing swarms of buzzing, agitated bees. Behind the carpet the bees billowed, kept together—and away from Titus and Iolanthe—by currents of air that trapped them like fish in a net.

The Bane was closing in. Iolanthe divided the bees into two groups and, forcing them close to the ground, dispatched them to the periphery of the orchard.

She sent another bolt of lightning the Bane's way. And, to further distract him, she ripped off smaller branches with high winds, set them on fire, and hurled them at him.

All the while she pushed the bees farther out of view.

The Bane waved away the flaming branches as if they were so many toothpicks. And he retaliated by uprooting entire trees in their path, forcing Titus to fly the carpet above the tree line, giving the Bane a clear line of sight.

"Just a little farther," Iolanthe implored under her breath.

Titus yelled and banked them sharply to the left. Something passed so close to Iolanthe's head that it lifted her hair. A fence plank, its triangular tip deadly at high speed.

One plank hurtled at them from behind, one from the right, one from the left, while a tree, clumps of dirt still falling off its roots, shot up in the air and came at them from the front.

With a scream Iolanthe called down another bolt of lightning, splitting the tree in two just in time for them to fly straight through, almost blinding herself in the process.

"Are the bees ready?" Titus demanded.

"Almost."

The ground itself swelled and almost knocked them from the flying carpet. A huge ball of fire appeared all around them. Iolanthe barely had time to punch a hole through the conflagration for them to fly through. Her own jacket caught on fire, but she put out the flames before they could hurt her.

It was now or never.

She looked back. Yes, she had managed to raise the swarm of bees to the height of the Bane's carpet. With the most powerful current she could generate, she sent them toward the Bane.

He laughed and fire rippled across the air surrounding him. Bees fell like raindrops. But among the entire swarm there was a smaller number that Iolanthe had protected. They punched through the fire and landed on his person.

The Bane stopped laughing. He gazed with something akin to incomprehension at his hand, upon which were not one, not two, but three bees. His hand swelled before Iolanthe's eyes.

He clutched at his throat. The carpet lost altitude, snagging in the branches of a tree before falling to the ground.

The mind that controlled Wintervale's body might be unimaginably powerful, but Wintervale's body had one great frailty: it was allergic to bee venom.

Titus landed the carpet and dug through the emergency bag. He had prepared antidotes for Wintervale, in case there were bee stings in the future. He pulled out a small case, which contained a few vials.

"No!" shouted someone. "Do not help him!"

Lady Wintervale.

She scrambled off a carpet of her own and set herself between Titus and Wintervale.

"We can't watch him die!" cried Iolanthe.

"Do you believe for an instant the Bane would leave him before then? No, as long as there is a chance that he can get you to believe that he is Leander Wintervale again, he will remain and it will be to the ruin of all."

On the ground Wintervale jerked and writhed. Iolanthe shook. She pressed her face into Titus's back. But she still heard Wintervale, gargling, like a mute trying to speak.

At last, silence.

"No, do not *assume* he is dead," cautioned Lady Wintervale. "Do you have any instruments?"

The prince found the Kno-it-all gauge. With a levitating spell he laid it on Wintervale's person. The tip of the gauge showed green.

They all three threw up shields at the same time, Titus for Iolanthe, Iolanthe for Titus, and Lady Wintervale for them both. Even so Titus stumbled backward, clutching his chest.

"I am all right," he said, already pointing his wand to set up another shield.

The Bane twitched again. His hand fell atop the gauge. The green slowly faded into a dark gray. The dark gray turned red.

Wintervale was dead.

Lady Wintervale had her son's hand in hers. Her lips trembled. "He had such a beautiful soul, my Lee. He worried that he would not be as great a man as his father, but he was always a far better man."

She looked about the orchard. "When we were small, Ariadne

sometimes brought me in here to play. I never thought this is where my son would meet his end."

Titus knelt down and kissed Wintervale on his forehead. "Good-bye, cousin. You saved us all."

He had tears in his eyes. Tears were already spilling down Iolanthe's cheeks. Wintervale, by being so open, trusting, and artless his entire life, had made his more cynical friends hang on to their secrets. And in doing so, they had preserved themselves from the Bane.

Wintervale's body disappeared. The Crucible keeps no dead.

"Do you want to come with us, ma'am?" Iolanthe asked Lady Wintervale.

Lady Wintervale shook her head. "No, I'm here only for my son. I will give a proper memorial and offer his ashes to the Angels. Long may his soul soar."

"Upon the wings of the Angels," Iolanthe and Titus said together.

"It almost kills me to say this," said Lady Wintervale, her own tears finally falling. "But . . . they lived happily ever after."

And she, too, exited from the Crucible.

Titus was the one to point out that Iolanthe's clothes were in tatters. She changed into a pair of tunics from the emergency bag and they took to the air again. More pursuers, on wyverns and pegasi, were close at hand—the Atlanteans must have raided the stables in a few stories.

"We will not make it to Forbidden Island in time," said Titus grimly.

Which left only Briga's Chasm.

They came down at the edge of Briga's Chasm, with the Atlanteans barely two hundred feet behind. The thick fog that filled the entire chasm writhed and flowed, obscuring everything beneath.

"Can we put on fog glasses and ride through that?" she asked as they ran toward the entrance of the tunnels that led to the bottom of the chasm.

He folded the carpet and attached it to the emergency bag, the way Kashkari had shown them. The carpet, which was actually a sheet of canvas with pockets, changed color to match that of the bag. "I tried it once. That is not fog and it is utterly impenetrable even with fog glasses."

She shuddered as she stepped on the strangely spongy ground in the tunnels. A sickly light filtered down from cracks in the rock ceiling above. All the surfaces looked damp. Slimy.

"Make sure you touch nothing," Titus said, pressing the vertices of the quasi-vaulter into her hand.

She had never used the locale for training, but she had read the story of Briga's Chasm long ago. Foul creatures lived in the tunnels, not so much guarding them as simply preying on anything or anyone that entered.

Someone screamed. They stopped for a moment and listened. Probably someone who did not know that one should never touch the walls of the tunnels, which secreted a corrosive substance.

Ahead, something slithered across the ground. It could have been a small snake—or a detachable limb of one of the foul pulp-wyrms, sent out to scout.

Another scream came from behind them.

"Idiots," Iolanthe muttered beneath her breath, acutely aware that injuries and deaths were all too real here. Some Atlantean families would be missing beloved sons and daughters on feast days this year.

None of them deserved it, to die for the megalomania of a twisted old man.

A pulpwyrm, with the diameter of a train and almost as long, shot past in a cross tunnel. Iolanthe gripped the prince's arm and tried to not heave.

"Something is coming behind us," he said.

But the way was still blocked by the slithering monster in front of them. And for all they knew, coming behind them was the exact same creature. They crept as close to the cross tunnel as they dared. Iolanthe didn't know which was worse, looking at the enormous hairy, wrinkly tube of flesh sliding past before them, or watching the head with six pairs of multifaceted, reflective eyes rapidly approaching from behind.

The mouth beneath the eyes opened. There were no teeth inside. Everything was terrifyingly, revoltingly soft—and dripping with what seemed to be bushels of black saliva.

Iolanthe stared, petrified.

The prince yanked her into the cross tunnel—the other creature, or perhaps the back end of this very one, had at last passed. But the one behind them, despite traveling at great speed, managed to turn in time into the same tunnel.

They ran, their boots sinking into the spongy ground.

Only to see another set of a dozen eyes coming at them.

This time there were no cross tunnels.

"Break a wall," Titus urged her. "You can do it."

She did it, though the sound of the wall crumbling was less that of stone cracking than the sickening snap of bone crunching. They raced through to an adjacent tunnel.

"Black Bastion feels like a luxury resort by comparison, don't you think?" she somehow managed to say as they ran.

"The occupants there are certainly much prettier, I will grant you that," he replied.

The tunnel led to a clearing of sorts.

He looked about. "I do not like this. All the tunnels lead up. There should be at least one leading down."

She swore: from each of the five tunnels that led into the clearing came one small slithering thing. "I hope this doesn't mean five big ones are following behind."

Her hope was dashed as five enormous, monstrous heads entered the clearing at almost the same time.

She dropped the vertices of the quasi-vaulter to the ground. "We are getting out of here. Now."

Titus did not object, but only took off the satchel on his back and strapped it on her. "In case we become separated."

Hands held, they stepped into the quasi-vaulter, just as the nearest creature shot a stream of black saliva at them.

CHAPTER ·33

The Sahara Desert

THE MOON HAD RISEN, AN enormous crescent low in the sky. The first group of rebel defenders took to the air, circling overhead, with a couple of small squadrons veering off to investigate the bell jar dome.

"So you don't remember me, either?" Kashkari asked as he accepted a nutrition cube from Titus. "All this time you've had no idea who I am?"

"Afraid so," said Iolanthe, refilling Kashkari's canteen.

She tried to keep fear at bay, but she wasn't sure whether she was succeeding. It was one thing to be hunted by Atlantis, quite another to know that even mages who should be her allies might have designs on her.

"Followers of Durga Devi," again came the resonant, golden voice, "give up Iolanthe Seabourne and you need suffer no casualties tonight."

She swallowed.

"Shut the hell up," Titus retorted, his tone almost casual. "The only time you will see her is with your cold, dead eyes."

"Thank you, Your Highness." She smiled at him, if a little weakly.

"For you, my destiny, nothing less."

Now she couldn't help grinning, remembering his earlier avowal to never call her "my destiny." Grateful for this bit of inside humor, she kissed him on his cheek. "It's almost better than bad verse."

He held her against him for a moment. "Nothing will happen to you, not as long as I can still wield a wand."

Kashkari's canteen was full. She capped it and returned it to him.

"So . . ." said Kashkari. "You don't remember anything else, but you remember each other?"

"No," Iolanthe replied, "but nothing builds camaraderie like running from—"

Her head felt strange, and not from the lateness of the hour. She jerked—bright streaks tore across the inside of her skull, like meteors crisscrossing the sky, burning, yet icy at the core.

She gritted her teeth and clutched her temples.

Titus had her by the shoulders. "Are you all right?"

She swayed. The next moment she was on her hands and knees, shaking.

"Should we take you below, Fairfax?" asked Kashkari urgently. "We have several good physicians."

She held up a hand. "I'm—I'm—"

She was beyond nauseated by the image flashing across her mind, that of a disgustingly large, wormlike creature, dripping black saliva, writhing toward her.

Lady Wintervale, tears falling down her hollow cheeks.

Wintervale, lying dead on the ground.

And then memories rushed back like water past a crumbling dam, in such torrents and deluges she was afraid they would overflow her cranium. But they seemed to fit back into her head just fine and already the discomfort was fading, leaving only a faint sensation of disorientation.

Titus was beside her, his arm around her middle. Kashkari had also crouched down, peering at her anxiously. She pushed herself up so that she was sitting on her heels and set her hand for a moment on Kashkari's sleeve. "I remember you."

Turning to Titus, she rested her palm on his cheek. "And I remember you. And I'm afraid that for you there is no escaping the shame of writing those overheated words on the strap of my bag—ever."

Relief crossed his face. And then, frustration. "But why do *I* not remember?"

"It will come back. The precautions that have been put into place for us ensure that we never have to suffer the effects of a memory spell for long—but the exact time will probably vary a little from person to person."

Ishana flew up and handed everyone a thin, flexible breathing mask. "Durga Devi wants you to have those, in case Atlantis puts something foul in the air."

Iolanthe strapped on her mask, which was much more comfortable than she had anticipated.

"So what happened to Wintervale?" asked Kashkari, adjusting his own mask.

"He is no more." He would have made a dedicated rebel and brought joy to all who fought alongside him—she blinked back tears. "I'm so sorry."

Kashkari passed his hand in front of his face. "I was afraid of that."

Iolanthe wiped the corners of her eyes. "Tell me what happened after we left. Is everyone at Mrs. Dawlish's all right?"

"I waited in the lavatory until the Bane went inside Fairfax's room," answered Kashkari. "Then I talked the other boys into a game of association football, senior boys against junior boys—I didn't want them to be in the house if it was going to collapse, or anything of the sort.

"We still all had to change before we could play—I was too nervous to remember that everyone was in their Sunday clothes. That was when Lady Wintervale came. I whispered in her ear that her son was the Bane and pointed her to your room. About a minute later, a team of Atlantean agents came up the stairs. Several of them took the Crucible and left immediately. The rest started carting everything out of both your rooms."

"In front of you?"

"In front of everyone. Cooper, bless him, immediately started blabbing about what the prince had said during our bonfire evening on the beach—that some treasonous bastards in Saxe-Limburg were looking to push him off the throne. And of course since you are known to be his closest associate among the boys, naturally your room also had to be sifted for evidence of the crimes with which they were going to charge the prince. And when they started to lug things out of Wintervale's room, Cooper made the further connection that Wintervale was actually from around the same parts as the prince and must therefore also be involved in those palace intrigues—which was exactly why his mother had suddenly come to Mrs. Dawlish's, because she knew danger was coming and wanted to warn him to flee."

"I cannot tell whether this Cooper is an idiot or a genius," said the prince.

"In either case, he was quite determined to travel to Saxe-Limburg someday to make sure that everyone is all right. I told him that even if you were in trouble, you would not be thrown into prison, but be put under house arrest, in a luxurious manor with gardens and a shooting park. I hope he believes me—or he would be in for a frustrating time, trying to find Saxe-Limburg."

"And how did you get away?" asked Iolanthe.

"I was going to wait a few days. But after your rooms—and Wintervale's—had been cleared out, a man came to Mrs. Dawlish's and said he was the prince's valet. He asked to speak with some of your friends. After he was gone, I found a piece of paper inside the pocket of my waistcoat. It could be a message for you, prince. I couldn't decipher it, but it made me nervous that he had singled me out.

"The Atlanteans had also looked into the other boys' rooms for suspicious items. They took a rug from my floor, a nonmage rug that doesn't fly any more than it speaks. But now I wondered whether this man had recognized that my curtain was actually a flying carpet—and whether some agent of Atlantis wouldn't realize the same thing.

"That night I bewitched all the seat cushions to fly out of the window of the common room, creating a distraction. While the Atlanteans were preoccupied with that, I slipped away and took the last train out." Kashkari took a piece of paper from his inner pocket and gave it to Titus. "And this is that message."

Titus called for a small sphere of light, scanned the message, and passed it to Iolanthe. "Have a look?"

The note read: *Lady Callista was interrogated under the effect of truth serum at a time coinciding with the resurfacing of certain memories. Apparently she has surrendered information crucial to the potential capture of the elemental mage who can control lightning.*

So Lady Callista had been caught after all.

It was possible her memory was protected, which meant Master Haywood's spell suppressing all her recollections of Iolanthe had only a temporary effect—and expired at an inconvenient time, in the middle of an interview with Atlantean investigators.

It was also possible that while Lady Callista was being questioned under truth serum, Iolanthe and Titus used the quasi-vaulter, the operation of which served as a special provision to trigger the return of Lady Callista's suppressed memories.

This implied Lady Callista had been the one to place the target of the quasi-vaulter in the Sahara Desert—and attach a memory spell to its activation: an Iolanthe who didn't know her own identity would be easier to deceive and control. The blood circle would have been a precautionary measure, so that Iolanthe did not wander off before Lady Callista could find her; as unflattering as her opinion of Lady Callista was, Iolanthe didn't think the latter actually meant to kill her.

An illumination much brighter than the blue mage light flickered on the message. Iolanthe raised her head to see a silver-white beacon expanding.

"Good!" said Kashkari. "Amara is calling back my brother and the others who raided the Atlantean base."

Iolanthe felt a leap of excitement. "And isn't that how you break a bell jar dome? By having allies approach from the outside?"

But the beacon dissipated as it touched the top of the dome.

Kashkari groaned. "It needs to rise much higher. Or they won't see it."

Titus gripped her hand. Even with the breathing mask, she could see that he was grimacing. She braced her weight against his just as he stumbled.

"I—I remember everything now," he said, leaning into her. "And I have made up my mind: Cooper is undoubtedly an idiot, but an invaluable one."

She grinned from ear to ear. "Should I ever see him again, I will tell him you said he was invaluable."

He laughed quietly and touched his forehead to hers. "You, and you alone."

She took his hands in hers. "Live forever."

They needed to say nothing more.

He raised his wand. A flame-colored beacon flared into existence, well above the bell jar dome.

"What is it?" Kashkari asked.

"The war phoenix," said Titus, "released when the Master of the Domain himself is under attack."

"Will it be any use?" asked Iolanthe. "We are thousands of miles from the Domain."

"True, but we are not without friends nearby. The first night we were in the desert, armored chariots were coming too close, so I released two phoenix beacons to distract them, without knowing exactly what I was doing. And one of the beacons was a war phoenix. When that happens, my exact location becomes known to the war council at home. Remember I told you that the second night there were riders on pegasi? Atlanteans forces do not make use of pegasi, but we do. And remember the bewitched spears? Guess who has that many bewitched spears?"

Iolanthe gasped. "Of course! You even said it was like watching a historical reenactment. Titus the Great Memorial Museum has thousands of them for that purpose."

"So we just have to hold out long enough for relief to get here. And then we will have you disappear into the crowds of a nonmage city until the danger is past."

"How long do you think it will be before relief gets here?"

"The sooner the better," said Kashkari, his voice tight. "Looking at what's coming, I'm not sure we can last long."

Two more groups of rebel defenders took to the air just then, obscuring Iolanthe's view of the sky. And then she saw it, entering the bell jar dome, a mountainous swarm of winged beasts, an ominous flamelike sheen to their scales in the light of the war phoenix.

"Fortune shield me," she murmured. "Is all of the wyvern battalion here?"

"The Bane is in the Sahara—where else would the wyvern battalion be?" said Titus, unfolding the carpet that had brought them to the rebel base. "Now, shall we?"

The wyverns hovered in midair, the beating of their wings like thousands of damp bedsheets being shaken out at once. Even without breathing fire, their presence brought a sulfurous odor to the air, one that was fortunately muted by the breathing mask.

The rebels' carpets also hovered. Iolanthe and Titus sat shoulder to shoulder on their carpet, her hand on his nape.

Titus tapped his wand twice against his palm. The seven diamond-inlaid crowns along the length of the wand began to glow. "Take this and give me yours."

"But that's Validus." She was flustered by his gesture: Validus had once belonged to Titus the Great. Not to mention, it was one of the last of the blade wands, a far more powerful amplifier of a mage's power than an ordinary wand.

"Yes, I know that—I also know which one of us can take on a greater number of wyverns." He pressed the priceless wand into her hand. "You will make better use of Validus."

"The Lord High Commander of the Great Realm of New Atlantis hails His Serene Highness, the Master of the Domain," the sonorous voice came again. "Atlantis and the Domain currently enjoy a peaceful and mutually beneficial association. Deliver Iolanthe Seabourne into the care of Atlantis and that friendship will continue."

"Do you not enjoy how it has been phrased?" Titus said softly.

"I would like to. But every time that voice speaks, I rather choke on fear."

Even the might of Validus in her hand was not sufficient to expel that fear.

"And I grow ever more incensed that anyone still thinks I am going to give you up." He murmured a spell. When he spoke again, his voice, though not raised in the least, carried for miles. "The

Master of the Domain will consider delivering a cubic mile of elephant excrement into the care of Atlantis, but nothing else. And he extends his warmest greetings to the Lord High Commander. Soon may the Lord High Commander depart for the Void, where he is long overdue."

Iolanthe was thunderstruck: Titus had just told the Bane to go to hell. Angry shouts erupted from the wyvern riders. The rebels, like Iolanthe, were overawed.

The sonorous voice was now both darker and scabbier. "The Master of the Domain is an impetuous child. But the Lord High Commander is willing to overlook the folly of youth for the greater good. Forfeit Iolanthe Seabourne and you may yet keep your throne."

"The Master of the Domain is no doubt the stupidest boy who ever lived," replied Titus. "But he prides himself on not being a vile old man who practices sacrificial magic, as the Lord High Commander does."

Iolanthe might have fallen off the carpet if she hadn't been strapped in. This time, the Atlanteans were stunned into silence; the rebels cried out in shock.

"Every word the prince says is true," rose Kashkari's voice. "I will vouch for it with my life."

What Iolanthe had come to think of as the voice of Atlantis spoke again, and it sounded like stones grinding together. "Atlantis is ever on the side of peace and friendship. But you have brought war upon yourself, Titus of Elberon."

Titus's hand came to rest on Iolanthe's. He was afraid—his fear pulsed inside her blood. But as she looked upon his profile, she was reminded of the day they met, that fateful conversation by the Thames River. She had thought him impossibly brave then, as if he had been born under the wings of the Angels—now she knew it to be so.

"I'm with you," she said softly. "Always."

His hand tightened on hers and he said to the Bane and all his minions, "So be it."

But he was not done yet. With his voice still audible for miles, he added, "Fortune favors the brave."

Another moment of utter silence. And then, Iolanthe found herself shouting at the top of her lungs, her voice nearly drowned by the bellow of all the rebels present, "And the brave make their own fortune!"

The rallying cry of the January Uprising, taken up again after all these years.

Tears fell unchecked down Iolanthe's cheeks. She pulled Titus to her and kissed him hard.

"Forgive me," he said, between kisses, "for being so wrong about everything this Half."

"There is nothing to forgive. And you weren't wrong about my not being the Chosen One, since there is no Chosen One."

"Still, when I think how close I came to losing you—"

"But you didn't. I'm here—and I love you. I have always loved you."

He kissed her again. "And I will love you until the end of the world."

With a roar a wyvern spewed a bright flame. A hundred more wyverns followed suit. Instantly the air turned hot and acrid. The wyverns swooped down upon the rebels, raining fire.

Iolanthe raised the wand that had once belonged to Titus the Great and summoned lightning, a white-hot flash that lit up the sky.

The war against Atlantis had begun at last.

✦ NOTES

1. (P. 10) THE DOMAIN is the common term for the United Principality of the Pillars of Hercules, so called because the two ends of its territory at the time of the unification, the Rock of Gibraltar and the Tower of Poseidon, a basalt column jutting out of the Atlantic, some thirty miles north of the northernmost tip of the Siren Isles, had been collectively known as the Pillars of Hercules.

—From *The Domain: A Guide to Its History and Customs*

2. (P. 19) IN REACTION to Atlantis's restrictions on travel channels, mages in realms under its dominion turned to older, less advanced modes of transportation that had been largely abandoned in favor of the speed and convenience of more modern means. Dry docks made a comeback in landlocked realms. Airframes were manufactured in large quantities in secret workshops. And flying carpets, in resurgence, reached a level of development that surpassed the glories of their former heyday.

—From *A Chronological Survey of the Last Great Rebellion*

3. (P. 27) A COMMON misconception concerning blood magic involves its original purpose—that it was first devised to force mages to act against their own will. The truth is far more complex: blood magic, since its inception, has been used to hold tribes and clans together and make sure that individual members did not harm the greater good of the group.

Does this mean that sometimes blood magic has been put to coercive uses? Undoubtedly. It is a double-edged sword, as is every branch of magic.

—From *The Art and Science of Magic: A Primer*

4. (P. 35) I STRONGLY advise caution to mages who intend to visit the Middle Ridges section of the Labyrinthine Mountains. The reasons are twofold. One, much of the section is a princely preserve not open to the public. Two, the entire region shifts and moves with no discernible pattern—a defensive tactic implemented centuries ago by Hesperia the Magnificent to protect her castle—making it difficult for even nearby inhabitants to act as guides.

Once, some twenty years ago, I managed to convince a local youth to take me for a quick excursion. The excursion turned into seven terrible days wandering in the wilderness. Had we not accidentally stumbled upon a way out, we'd have perished in those unforgiving mountains.

But how beautiful they were, the mountains, as pristine and vivid as the first day of the world.

—From *Labyrinthine Mountains: A Guide for Hikers*

5. (P. 74) LEVITATION SPELLS are some of the oldest achievements of subtle magic. Like all spells meant to imitate elemental magic, no levitation spell has ever come close to the glorious scale of the latter—only elemental mages can move enormous boulders at will. But whereas elemental magic shifts only earth and water, levitation spells have been adapted for a wide variety of purposes.

—From *The Art and Science of Magic: A Primer*

6. (P. 89) DRY DOCKS were once commonly to be found in landlocked mage realms—with a dry dock, one could launch a ship directly to sea, even if the nearest coast was a thousand miles away. But with the advent of more instantaneous transits that bypassed sea voyages altogether, dry docks became obsolete as a mode of transportation.

—From *Mage Travel throughout the Centuries*

7. (P. 102) BECAUSE BLOOD magic is so closely tied to the concepts of family and consanguinity, it is subject to the privilege of kinship. For example, a sister can modify certain spells woven by a brother, just as in real life she can persuade him to change his mind on something.

But if the object of a particular instance of blood magic is the brother's son, then the aunt's influence becomes limited: a father has a far greater claim on his own child.

—From *The Art and Science of Magic: A Primer*

8. (P. 107) AT VARIOUS points in the history of New Atlantis, its rulers had tried to install Classical Greek, the language, supposedly, of the mythical Old Atlantis, as the official language of the realm. The last king of Atlantis issued an edict that all official communication, both written and spoken, must be in Greek. The inefficiency and miscommunication caused by this policy played no small part in the fall of his house.

One of the legacies from these assorted bouts of Hellenization was that Atlantean ships, both those of the navy and those of the merchant marine, tended to bear Greek names. Around the time of the January Uprisings, vessels from actual Hellenistic realms had been known to repaint their names in the Latin alphabet, so as not to be taken for an Atlantean craft and sabotaged.

—From *A Chronological Survey of the Last Great Rebellion*

9. (P. 163) THE REGULATION of magic often lags behind the development of magic. Spells enthusiastically introduced to the mage world and just as eagerly embraced might very well be shunned a

generation or two later.

Such has been the case with memory magic, which has become frowned upon—and many of its cruder spells declared illegal—for its intrusiveness and the potential damage it inflicts.

These days memory magic is usually deployed by criminals who do not want their victims to remember by whom they have been robbed, and occasionally by licensed medical professionals to erase recollection of unspeakable trauma, but only after the sufferer of the trauma has gone through a substantial approval process.

—From *The Art and Science of Magic: A Primer*

10. (P. 187) THE QUASI-VAULTER had not been invented to circumvent no-vaulting zones, but to make mages who could not vault appear as if they possessed the ability. The four small lumps, called vertices, became activated when they were set on the ground in such a way as to mark the corners of a quadrilateral. A mage stepping inside this quadrilateral would be instantly whisked away to a preset target, and the vertices would disintegrate, leaving no traces behind.

When mages realized that quasi-vaulters could break through no-vaulting zones, they demanded that the inventor give up proprietary information so that new anti-vaulting spells could be formulated to disallow quasi-vaulters. The inventor, an eccentric old woman, pulled her products from the market rather than divulge her trade secrets, which she took with her to her pyre.

Needless to say, quasi-vaulters immediately became sought after on the black market—and only more so when Atlantis began building its Inquisitories in mage capitals around the world.

—From *A Chronological Survey of the Last Great Rebellion*

11. (P. 199) TODAY'S ANNOUNCEMENT that Princess Ariadne has named her firstborn Titus has caused a stir among palace watchers.

After the reign of Titus VI, one of the most reviled sovereigns in the history of the House of Elberon, the name Titus has dropped nearly entirely out of use among the population of the Domain. The House of Elberon has been hesitant to reclaim the name that had once been associated with several of its most illustrious members: the infant prince is the first boy born to the house to be called Titus in more than two hundred years.

—From "Reaction to Infant Prince's Name Mixed at Best," *The Delamer Observer*, 28 September, Year of the Domain 1014

12. (P. 199) IT SADDENS me greatly that Titus VI, one of the most principled and courageous mages who ever breathed, is casually referred to by the staff writers of *The Delamer Observer* as "reviled" in the article "Reaction to Infant Prince's Name Mixed at Best." It saddens me even more that *The Delamer Observer*'s general readership accepts that claim without any question.

Yes, we have all learned in school that Titus VI had to abdicate the throne in favor of his younger sister, after he used deadly force against his own subjects. But does no one outside the Sihar community remember the context of Titus VI's decisions?

Those had been some of the darkest days for the Sihar of the Domain: Sihar establishments in all the larger cities razed, Sihar children beaten in broad daylight, and perfectly law-abiding Sihar forced to flee their homes. Unruly mobs were converging on Lower Marin March, proudly proclaiming that they would not stop until they had pushed all the Sihar into the sea.

Titus VI ordered the mobs dispersed by any means necessary. There were 104 fatalities before the mobs finally disbanded, but the number of Sihar who would have perished, had Titus VI stood aside and done nothing, would have been in the untold tens of thousands.

And let it not be said that the name Titus has dropped out of use among the population of the Domain. We the Sihar make up 9 percent of the population of the Domain and we name many, many of our sons Titus, in remembrance and eternal gratitude.

—From "Letters to the Editor," *The Delamer Observer*,

30 September, Year of the Domain 1014

13. (P. 199) THE LARGEST Sihar population in the world lives in the Domain, concentrated mainly in Lower Marin March, although smaller communities are to be found in most sizable cities and towns.

The Sihar had historically been outcasts from the larger mage community for their practice of blood magic. Persecutions, especially in the realms on the Continent, reached a fever pitch during the reign of Hesperia the Magnificent. The oft-recounted story of their arrival in the Domain usually begins with the dramatic plea from the Grand Matriarch of the Sihar to Hesperia, that the latter, then a new mother, would sympathize with the matriarch's desperation and grant the Sihar a place of refuge.

Hesperia acceded to the matriarch's plea. The Sihar were offered special status as the princess's guests and given land in Lower Marin March for their use, the borders of the march secured by the princess's own guards for their protection.

The protection, however, also in effect segregated the Sihar from the rest of the Domain. It was not until two hundred years later that a princely decree by Titus V granted the Sihar the freedom of movement throughout the realm. Titus VI, during his reign, revoked the requirement that the Sihar must wear identifying marks while traveling outside Lower Marin March.

But still their status remained as guests and therefore subject to eviction at any time.

—From *An Ethnographic Review of the Domain*

14. (P. 343) IT IS often said that the construction of Royalis brought down the last king of Atlantis. That claim is only partly true. It was his father who began—and completed—the building of a new

palace, as famines raged outside the capital city of Lucidias.

So while the last king of Atlantis could not be faulted for erecting a large, lavish complex with so many of his subjects suffering, he could be amply blamed for deciding to tear down and rebuild half of Royalis because he disliked how it looked.

—From *Empire: The Rise of New Atlantis*

15. (P. 351) MAGES HAVE devised many different means of compelling or ascertaining the truth, many of which of questionable legality. The truth pact is one of the few methods considered to be above reproach, because it requires willing participants at the onset and metes out no punishment at the detection of lies: the halo that surrounds the parties to the pact dissolves the moment anyone becomes untruthful—no pain, no suffering, nothing but courtesy and civility all around.

—From *The Art and Science of Magic: A Primer*

◆ ACKNOWLEDGMENTS

Donna Bray, for the blessing she is as an editor.

Everyone at HarperCollins Childrens, for their kindness and helpfulness.

Kristin Nelson, for being my stalwart champion.

Colin Anderson, for the best cover art ever.

Erin Fitzsimmons, for the fantastic cover concept.

Dr. Margaret Toscano, for her generosity and friendship.

Justine Larbalestier, for her expert advice on cricket terminology.

Srinadh Madhavapeddi, for the names.

My family, for their unwavering support.

And if you are reading this, thank you. Thank you from the bottom of my heart.